T0265908

BY JOHN JACKSON MILLER

STAR WARS

Knight Errant
Lost Tribe of the Sith
Kenobi
A New Dawn
The Rise of the Empire (with James Luceno)
Canto Bight (with Saladin Ahmed, Rae Carson, and Mira Grant)
The Living Force

STAR TREK

Titan: Absent Enemies
The Next Generation: Takedown
Prey: Hell's Heart
Prey: The Jackal's Trick
Prey: The Hall of Heroes
Discovery: The Enterprise War
Discovery: Die Standing
Picard: Rogue Elements
Strange New Worlds: The High Country

STAR WARS

THE LIVING FORCE

THE
LIVING FORCE

JOHN JACKSON MILLER

RANDOM HOUSE
WORLDS

NEW YORK

Copyright © 2024 by Lucasfilm Ltd. & ® or ™ where indicated. All rights reserved.

Published in the United States by Random House Worlds, an imprint of Random House, a division of Penguin Random House LLC, New York.

RANDOM HOUSE is a registered trademark, and RANDOM HOUSE WORLDS and colophon are trademarks of Penguin Random House LLC.

Hardback ISBN 978-0-593-59795-8
Ebook ISBN 978-0-593-59796-5

Printed in the United States of America on acid-free paper

randomhousebooks.com

2 4 6 8 9 7 5 3 1

First Edition

Book design by Elizabeth A. D. Eno

Map by John Jackson Miller

To Ann,
who watched my career with great interest
and offered much wise counsel

THE STAR WARS NOVELS TIMELINE

THE HIGH REPUBLIC

Convergence
The Battle of Jedha
Cataclysm

Light of the Jedi
The Rising Storm
Tempest Runner
The Fallen Star
The Eye of Darkness
Temptation of the Force
Trials of the Jedi

Dooku: Jedi Lost
Master and Apprentice
The Living Force

I — THE PHANTOM MENACE

II — ATTACK OF THE CLONES

Brotherhood
The Thrawn Ascendancy Trilogy
Dark Disciple: A Clone Wars Novel

III — REVENGE OF THE SITH

Inquisitor: Rise of the Red Blade
Catalyst: A Rogue One Novel
Lords of the Sith
Tarkin
Jedi: Battle Scars

SOLO

Thrawn
A New Dawn: A Rebels Novel
Thrawn: Alliances
Thrawn: Treason

ROGUE ONE

IV — A NEW HOPE

Battlefront II: Inferno Squad
Heir to the Jedi
Doctor Aphra
Battlefront: Twilight Company

V — THE EMPIRE STRIKES BACK

VI — RETURN OF THE JEDI

The Princess and the Scoundrel
The Alphabet Squadron Trilogy
The Aftermath Trilogy
Last Shot

Shadow of the Sith
Bloodline
Phasma
Canto Bight

VII — THE FORCE AWAKENS

VIII — THE LAST JEDI

Resistance Reborn
Galaxy's Edge: Black Spire

IX — THE RISE OF SKYWALKER

THE GEM CITIES OF
KWENN

BRIDGES . . . . . .

CASINO DOCK ♦
QUARNEY KEY
NATURE PRESERVE

INDUSTRIAL ZONE
BRAZATTA KEY
▲ SPACEPORT
♦ CASINO DOCK

HARBOR MARKET ♦
LANGDAM KEY
CASINO DOCK ♦

WINDWARD CHAIN

JUDICIAL COMPLEX ⊙
VORAH KEY
GUTSON'S PUB ♦

CASINO DOCK ♦
KINNAWAH KEY
LAMPLIGHTER BOUTIQUE ♦

JEDI OUTPOST

SANCTUARY MOUNT
CAPITAL KEY
MEDIA CENTER ♦
GOVERNMENT TERRACE ⊙
▲ SPACEPORT
CASINO DOCK ♦

RAYLEY KEY
PATHS OF HARMONY ♦
▲ CLINIC

MIDDLE CHAIN

ZYBOH KEY
KWIKHAUL LIVERY ♦

CASINO DOCK ♦
GALA KEY
ARENA ▣
SPACEPORT ▲

MALBAIRA KEY
NATURE PRESERVE

OROKO SPAWNING GROUNDS
CASINO DOCK ♦

PARVA KEY
BIVALL COLONY ♦

LEEWARD CHAIN

OROKO SPAWNING GROUNDS

EDUCATIONAL DISTRICT
ESSAFA KEY
OROKO SPAWNING GROUNDS

ADDOA KEY
RENDILI HYPERWORKS ♦
SPACEPORT ▲

A long time ago, in a galaxy far, far away. . . .

Be mindful of the living Force, young Padawan.

—Qui-Gon Jinn

For generations, the galaxy looked to the JEDI COUNCIL, the most sage Jedi Knights of the Order, for wisdom and guidance. Interpreting the will of THE FORCE, the Council helped bring about an age of unprecedented peace and prosperity.

That time is ending. Riven with corruption, the GALACTIC REPUBLIC shifts vital resources away from many deserving places. The Council finds itself torn between responding to the Senate's desires and its mission to protect all of the galaxy's helpless.

But even as the Order withdraws from some regions, the Council's commitment to the people is unchanged. And just as there are Jedi who believe that the Force expects more from them, there are darker forces waiting to take advantage of their departure. . . .

PART ONE
THE JEDI RETREAT

CHAPTER 1

ABOARD THE *REGAL ZEPHYR*

HYPERSPACE

"Good morning!"

Leaning against the bulkhead of the interstellar transport, Jedi Master Qui-Gon Jinn looked up at the sound of Obi-Wan Kenobi's voice. The words weren't for him. Farther back in the *Regal Zephyr*'s crowded passenger cabin, his apprentice had finally found an open seat and had spoken to the dark-haired human across the aisle. Qui-Gon didn't need to be a Jedi to sense the young woman's apprehension as she tightly clutched her duffel bag.

Obi-Wan noticed it, too, and quickly sought to put her at ease. "I beg your pardon. I didn't know you were sleeping."

"I wasn't," she replied curtly.

"Hyperspace does make that difficult." He gestured to the whirling miasma outside the *Regal Zephyr*'s smudged viewports. "It's hard to know what time of day it is. I sense you don't like flying any more than I—"

She made a sour face. "Look, that seat's taken."

He glanced around. "I'm sorry, I should have—"

"My husband will be here any minute."

Obi-Wan quickly stood. "Excuse me."

He bowed and walked the few meters up the aisle to the forward wall, where Qui-Gon stood near the door to the galley alongside the large metal briefcase that was their cargo. The Jedi Master gently grinned. "Trouble on approach?"

"I wasn't even in the right galaxy."

"I promise you'll make at least one friend before we reach Coruscant, Obi-Wan." Qui-Gon craned his neck to look around the compartment, which contained far more riders than seats. "I would say it's mathematically impossible not to."

Often in the past, Qui-Gon had encouraged his Padawan to use the quieter moments on their journeys to get to know people. To connect with them. It wasn't that the young man had problems making friends; Obi-Wan had a natural ability in that regard. But the structures that turned younglings into Jedi Knights also tended to isolate them—and that could give them the wrong idea about their places in the galaxy. That was why Qui-Gon often chose commercial transport, such as the inaccurately named *Regal Zephyr,* one of a dwindling number of passenger vessels serving the Ootmian Pabol, once a key route leading from the Slice to Coruscant. A seemingly endless flight aboard a ship that smelled like a trash compactor was both humble—and humbling.

Automatic doors opened on Qui-Gon's right. He and Obi-Wan watched as a haggard man entered from the galley, carrying a squirming child in each arm. Ignoring the two Jedi as he trudged past, the man approached the woman Obi-Wan had spoken with. After passing a toddler to her, he displayed a single food pouch, one of the meager rations offered by the galley concessionaire. The reunited family looked exhausted but also hungry. They tore into the pouch and emptied it in seconds.

Qui-Gon walked down the aisle and approached the young parents. He drew a pair of tokens from the folds of his cloak and got their attention. "Pardon me. You dropped your meal vouchers."

"Those aren't mine," the man said, eyeing him. "I just used our last one."

"Then these must have stuck to your shoe. Easy to believe, around here." He looked to the hungry children—and back to their parents. "Please. They shouldn't go to waste."

The wary mother stared for a moment before taking the tokens. She rose. Daughter on her hip, she trotted off to the galley. Qui-Gon retreated to his previous station.

Obi-Wan smirked. "We'll be skipping breakfast, then."

"You wouldn't have enjoyed it."

"You're probably right." He surveyed the surly faces around the cabin. "I'm afraid I lack the common touch, Master."

"There's that phrase again." Qui-Gon shook his head. "Every being is your better, Obi-Wan. Remember that, and service becomes second nature."

"I never tire of hearing that one." Obi-Wan spied another open seat, nearer to where the two Jedi stood. He straightened. "Back into the fray."

"Try a bit more energy this time. The galley's out of caf."

"Done."

Qui-Gon watched as his apprentice gamely stepped over and sat beside a large huddled figure. The Jedi Master had seen him earlier: a massive member of the Houk species, with leathery blue skin and no apparent ears or nose. None of that was visible now, as he was wrapped in a cape and cowl—odd choices, given the warmth in the cabin.

Checking quickly to ensure that the Houk wasn't asleep, Obi-Wan adopted an antic smile and addressed the passenger. "Hello there!"

Beady yellow eyes went wide. The bruiser growled—and abruptly rose to his towering height. The Houk threw off his cloak to reveal a blaster holstered to his chest.

Obi-Wan's eyes widened. "If you wanted to be left alone, you only had to say so."

"Quiet!" The muscular Houk turned to face the rest of the cabin and shouted, "*Now!*"

Two more cloaked passengers rose and shed their disguises. A scar-faced Klatooinian and a horned Devaronian reached for their weapons. The latter had his blaster in his hand first. Golden eyes and sharp fangs flashed as he shouted, "Nobody move!"

Qui-Gon saw Obi-Wan start to rise—only to pause. His Padawan looked instead to him. Qui-Gon had his hand near his lightsaber, still hidden inside his robe—but he, too, waited. He shot a look he knew his student would understand. *No bloodshed. Not with so many innocents about, with nowhere to go.*

"What's the meaning of this?" an elderly passenger demanded.

The Devaronian waved his blaster. "Lemme introduce myself. I'm The Lobber—that's right, *that* Lobber. This ship is now under the control of the Vile!"

The Vile. Qui-Gon knew it as one of several interstellar gangs active in the Slice, the colossal wedge-shaped fan of star systems stretching from the Core Worlds to the Outer Rim. It wasn't an outfit many from Coruscant would have heard of, and it didn't sound like a great name for recruiting purposes. But clearly the passengers knew what it was, given their anxious reactions.

The name also seemed to unsettle someone else: the Houk standing near Obi-Wan. "The Vile?" he asked. "I thought we were doing this for the Skulls."

"The Skulls?" the Klatooinian grumbled in a low voice. "We talked about this, Ghor. The Filthy Cred gang will pay more than either."

"Shut up, Wungo." Lobber waved his blaster at the Klatooinian. "Save it until we're done."

The Staved Skulls. The Filthy Creds. Qui-Gon knew the names. More operations from a regional underworld that was increasingly aboveground. He surreptitiously nudged the case he'd been traveling with under a nearby seat. There was a play here, the Jedi Master knew. He just had to find it.

"This is madness," the young father declared, clutching his wailing son. "We've got nothing to steal!"

"That's obvious enough." Lobber gestured to the ceiling with his blaster. "We're stealing the *ship.*" He pointed to the Houk. "Ghor, you know what to do."

Ghor grabbed an empty canvas bag from beside his seat and moved into the aisle with it. "Any weapons, give 'em." He had turned away from Obi-Wan—a stroke of luck, Qui-Gon thought—but it was still too soon to act. Wungo the Klatoonian was in motion, too, with a sack of his own—only he was demanding valuables.

"You just said you only wanted the ship," a Rodian passenger snarled.

Wungo snapped, "Shut up!"

An elderly traveler began to weep. "What—what's to happen to us?"

Lobber laughed. "We're going to put you all out at the nearest stop."

"Where?" the young father asked. "What's for us there?"

Flustered, the Devaronian raised his voice. "Quit your moaning. You're lucky we don't just space you all!"

Qui-Gon had seen and heard enough. The hijackers had no plan or even any agreement on whom they worked for. Amateurism often meant recklessness and the potential for harm—if he didn't act quickly and smartly. He cast another look he knew his Padawan would recognize and took a step from the bulkhead.

Putting his open hands before him, he spoke calmly. "My friends, there's no need for this."

Lobber glowered at him. "Who are you?"

"Just someone who wants a pleasant ride." Qui-Gon crossed his arms. "I don't want to see anyone get hurt."

"The only person who'll get hurt is *you*," Lobber declared.

Ghor pointed his weapon at Qui-Gon. "All right, brave guy. Where's your blaster?"

"I usually do without one."

The giant guffawed. "You're that good, eh?"

Lobber snarled. "Teach the big hero a lesson—then get to the cockpit."

"You're the one who knows how to fly," Ghor said.

"Just do it!"

Lobber's companions had only started to advance toward Qui-Gon when the door to the galley behind him opened. He looked back to see the mother holding her squirming child. She was three steps inside when she saw the blasters being raised in her direction.

"Leerah, go back!" her husband shouted. Panicked, she took a wrong step back across the threshold and lost her balance, causing her daughter to slip from her hands and tumble toward the metal deck. The woman shrieked.

Righting herself quickly, she stared up in marvel at what had happened to her daughter. The toddler bobbed upside down, floating in the air so close to the floor her hair brushed against it.

"People keep dropping things around here," Qui-Gon said, his hand poised in the air.

The little girl giggled in delight until her mother snapped her up.

The others in the cabin watched, spellbound—but none with more interest than the hijackers. Lobber's mouth hung open. "He's a *Jedi!*"

"Actually," Obi-Wan said, "he's a Jedi Master." He rose from his seat. "And not just *any* Jedi Master. They once asked him to be on the Jedi Council. Have you heard of that?"

Lobber's frown indicated he had. "They're supposed to be the best. The bosses."

Ghor stared at Qui-Gon. "Then what's he doing out here?"

"He told them no," Obi-Wan replied. "He thought it would take time away from his major pursuit."

"Which is?"

"Commercial spacecraft security. There's never been a single hijacking on his watch."

Ghor snorted. "Security! Jedi don't do that kind of stuff." He looked to the Devaronian. "They don't. Do they?"

"Of course not." Lobber sneered. "The Jedi barely bother with this route these days."

"And yet here we are," Qui-Gon said.

Wungo looked in panic between Qui-Gon and the girl he'd rescued. "Did you see how he made her float? I didn't know they could do that."

"Jedi don't go around showing off," Obi-Wan said, stepping forward. "But word gets around. I'm sure you've heard the rumors."

Lobber frowned. "What rumors?"

"Of secret Jedi powers. Some are quite amazing. Disarming you of your weapon with just a few words, for example."

Ghor gripped his blaster more tightly. "Is that so?"

Qui-Gon shook his head. "I won't be doing that. Or anything . . . flashier."

Wungo stared. "Like what?"

"Don't worry yourself." Qui-Gon clasped his hands together. "What was the planet called where you were going to drop everyone off?"

Lobber had the answer. "Randon."

"Wonderful. I'll make sure the pilot stops there. And then *you three* will disembark—and find passage back to wherever you came from." He raised an eyebrow. "Hopefully, on a vessel you have permission to board."

"'Disembark'?" Lobber repeated.

"That means get off," Obi-Wan interjected.

"I know what it—" The Devaronian stopped himself and laughed. "We're not getting off this ship."

"Oh, I think you'll definitely want to."

"And if we don't?"

"The alternative is . . . unpleasant," Qui-Gon said. He looked to Obi-Wan. "My colleague can attest to that."

Ghor followed Qui-Gon's eyes. "You're his colleague?"

Obi-Wan bowed.

"Another Jedi Knight?" Lobber asked.

"Sort of." Obi-Wan flicked at his Padawan braid. "It's complicated."

Lobber swore and looked about. "Great. Any more around here?"

"Forget that," Wungo said. "I still wanna know about this 'unpleasant alternative.'"

"I'm not sure you do," Obi-Wan responded, with visible apprehension. "Master, tell me you're not considering doing what I think you are." He winced and gave a shudder. "I would rather not have to clean up the mess."

"I didn't say it was something I preferred," Qui-Gon said, shaking his head. "It's a last resort."

Lobber looked unconvinced. "Another secret thing Jedi know how to do? Why have I never heard of it?"

"An excellent question," Obi-Wan said. "Is there a reason you might not have heard of it?"

"It doesn't exist!"

"Or?"

It took a beat for the three hijackers to work it out. Wungo had it first. "Nobody you've ever done this thing to has survived?"

"Certainly not." Qui-Gon glanced uneasily at Obi-Wan. "I should say *definitely* not."

Obi-Wan looked sick. "I mean, even if you *did* survive, you really wouldn't want to."

Wungo lowered his blaster. "That's it. I'm out."

"Yeah," Ghor said, following suit. "I'm not doing this."

Lobber was beside himself. "What are you fools talking about? You work for me. We just shoot them!"

"Or maybe *we* shoot *you*," Ghor barked. His blaster rose again—this time, pointed at Lobber. "Who put you in charge, anyway?"

Qui-Gon raised his hands. "There's no need for any of that. There's a way out."

"For starters, we'll need those weapons," Obi-Wan added. He approached Ghor and opened his hand. "For safekeeping."

Qui-Gon nodded. "I assure you we'll give them back."

Wungo couldn't shed his blaster fast enough. Ghor practically shoved his into Obi-Wan's hand.

Lobber looked at them, baffled. At last, he gave a mournful moan before lowering his blaster. Obi-Wan collected it.

"It would also be more comfortable for everyone if you waited in the cargo hold," Qui-Gon said.

"The hold?" Wungo asked. He brightened. "Where all the good stuff is?"

"No, one of the empty bays. It wouldn't do for you to take these people's belongings." He reclaimed the bag of stolen goods from the hijacker.

Lobber objected. "You're gonna lock us in!"

"It's better, I assure you," Qui-Gon said, setting the sack aside. "This way, my associate and I won't have to keep an eye on you. And *you* won't have to be locked in with *us*."

That was enough. Obi-Wan toggled the doorway and made a welcoming gesture. "This way, please."

The trio looked at one another—and grumbled as they made their way to the aperture. "I sure hope the Vile don't hear about this," Lobber said.

"I wouldn't join them anyway," Obi-Wan said. "Terrible name."

Qui-Gon turned and faced the passengers. "Apologies for the commotion, everyone. But you'll find there are a few new empty seats."

CHAPTER 2

THE *REGAL ZEPHYR*

HYPERSPACE

"**D**o the trick, do the trick!"

The toddler was barely old enough to speak, but she could say those words clearly—over and over again. They added to the din in the *Regal Zephyr*'s passenger cabin that had followed the hijackers' departure. A single steward, having finally come to check on the commotion, had quickly found himself fielding a host of complaints.

Qui-Gon refrained from obliging the little girl with any more theatrics. Despite the successful pantomime that he and Obi-Wan had put on, Jedi did not like to advertise their hidden talents. It was a good policy, Qui-Gon thought. Public stunts widened the gulf between the Jedi Order and the people in a way that should discomfit everyone. Still, he hoped that the mood aboard the transport would improve.

Those hopes lasted until his apprentice returned from the hold. "Our would-be abductors are safely stowed," Obi-Wan announced on entering. "It should be a peaceful journey from here."

"A peaceful—?" Leerah stepped forward to collect her rambunctious child. "You're promising a peaceful journey."

Obi-Wan put up his hand. "There's no need for thanks. It's the least we could do."

"I'm *not* thanking you. And it literally *was* the least you could do."

His eyes widened. "I beg your pardon?"

Leerah swiveled with the child in one arm and gestured to the other travelers. "We're most of us coming from Tharben. You do remember Tharben?"

"Why, certainly," Obi-Wan said. "I stayed in the Jedi outpost years ago. A lovely planet."

"It was," her husband said. "The guilds started abandoning the Ootmian route because of all the crime in this part of the Slice—and the Republic subsidies for our planet's security patrol ended." He looked keenly at the Padawan. "You really don't know what happened next?"

Qui-Gon spared him the awkward moment. "The Jedi Order closed the outpost on Tharben last year, Obi-Wan."

"Oh." Deflated, the Padawan cast his eyes to the deck.

"My student isn't apprised of these things." Qui-Gon tilted his head. "What was the impact of the closure?"

An elderly passenger sitting a few meters away spoke up. "Tharben was on the edge of Hutt space, so it behooved both the Republic and the syndicates to keep the planet functioning. A waystation, to do business with the more dangerous places. But now there is no counterbalance." He pointed to the Jedi. "*You* were it."

Obi-Wan looked up. "Wait. If it's along the Ootmian route, there's still protection. The Republic polices the—"

Qui-Gon put his hand up. It was time to listen.

The steward, delighted to no longer be the focus of ire, chipped in. "The star maps don't tell the real story. The Republic boundary beyond the Mid Rim—that's imaginary and has been for years. The hyperspace lanes in the Slice that approach Hutt space get a lot of pirate activity. There's a wide swath where it's gotten too dangerous to operate." He looked embarrassed. "As you've already seen."

Leerah elaborated further as she strapped her daughter into her seat. "I was born and raised on Tharben. Bad things sometimes happened there, but I never saw them. They're in the open, now. When the factories couldn't pay protection anymore, the gangs burned them down—and Vale's and my jobs with them." She rose and gestured to the ship surrounding them. "At least this route's still running." Her eyes darted to the steward. "It *is* still running, isn't it?"

The steward was quick to defend his firm. "The Regal Voyager line has been fortunate—today's trouble was very much an exception. As long as that continues, we'll keep flying. There's still a lot of business traffic out to Ord Jannak and Kwenn."

"To—" Obi-Wan started. He stopped himself and looked back to Qui-Gon, clearly not knowing whether he should say what he knew.

His master answered for him. "Just yesterday, we oversaw the closure of the Jedi outpost on Ord Jannak." Qui-Gon lifted his carrying case. "We're delivering the last effects to Coruscant now."

Tumult followed, as many people spoke at once. "Wonderful," Leerah said, raising her voice. "The whole Ootmian route is collapsing. We got out just in time!"

When he could finally be heard over the chatter, Obi-Wan put up his hands. "These outposts. They aren't police stations—just places for Jedi Knights to stay and study when they visit." He turned his palms upward. "The Jedi were barely there."

"And don't think we didn't know it," the elderly passenger said. "But it wasn't always so. My grandparents said the outpost on Tharben was always busy in their day. The Jedi were often outside it. They were helping people." He shook his head. "But even when the visits slowed down, we knew *someone* would be coming back. The building still meant something."

More voices were raised. One remarked on a new subject. An Ithorian holding a child of her own pointed at Leerah and Vale. "I saw what you did for their family, Jedi. You gave them meal vouchers. Did you bring enough for everyone?"

"And how about tomorrow?" someone else demanded. "What will you do then?"

Qui-Gon struggled to keep the conversation calm. "Once we reach Coruscant, I assure you that the Republic's body that works with refugees—"

"We're not refugees!" someone shouted.

"Pardon, the *suddenly relocated* will work with you to provide housing and sustenance."

A passenger spoke. "I have a medical condition. It can't go untreated."

"They will see to that."

"I had nearly finished my studies," said another. "How will I get my certification now?"

"That, too." Qui-Gon knew it wasn't his role to do everything—nor could he reasonably be expected to. But he would try. He produced a comlink. "I swear to you, I will make the contacts immediately."

"You're passing us off," Leerah said. She threw up her hands. "I always heard so much about the Jedi. I never saw one, but they told me that was because you saved people—*and then you left.*" She looked at Obi-Wan and snorted. "We finally got our turn, I guess!"

"That's not fair," Obi-Wan blurted, before moderating his tone. "I mean, that's not correct."

Rattled by the bedlam, Leerah's children wailed.

Obi-Wan looked overwhelmed. Qui-Gon could well understand why. The galactic scale of their responsibilities meant that the Jedi were focusing more attention than ever on what many called the cosmic Force: the larger picture, involving everyone now and into the future. No one did this more than members of the Jedi Council. Aspiring apprentices who took them as role models sought to likewise spend their time on the galactic astropolitical scene, the bigger questions.

But even though Council members like Master Yoda regularly instructed Padawans to pay attention to the present and where they were, many students tended to forget that concerns that seemed small on a galactic level were often huge for the individual. The hopes and fears of the living came together in an aspect of the Force that Qui-Gon had dedicated his career to better understanding.

And where the living Force was concerned, there was literally no time like the present. Qui-Gon set down the case with a sharp thud that quieted the crowd.

His eyes found the steward. "Sir, how far are we from Coruscant?"

"A ways yet. We have several stops first."

"That's fine." Qui-Gon put his hands before him and addressed the travelers. "It's true we have assignments that keep us on the move. But we are with you now. And my student and I will listen to everything you have to say." He looked to Leerah—and held her gaze. "And I will do more than send messages. You have my word."

She stared back. "The word of a Jedi?"

"The word of someone who wants to help."

After a few moments, she nodded.

The cabin broke up into multiple conversations again, as the passengers sorted out who was to speak, and on what subject. Obi-Wan stepped over, picked up the case, and spoke into Qui-Gon's ear. "I think I miss when people were pointing blasters at us."

"I often tell you to be mindful of the living Force. You've been given an uncommon chance to hear it speak." He put his hand on Obi-Wan's shoulder and whispered, *"Don't miss it."*

CHAPTER 3

CORUSCANT

"One volume of handwritten notes on lightsaber repair. One scholarly work discussing *Poetics of the Jedi*. One code manual, outdated."

In the anteroom to the archives in the Jedi Temple on Coruscant, Eeth Koth observed as a staffer sorted through the case Qui-Gon Jinn had brought from the shuttered outpost on Ord Jannak. The Jedi Master knew there wasn't supposed to be much of value left at that location, and the contents seemed to prove it.

The staffer began speaking again. "One visitor's pass to the Ord Jannak Capital Building, expired. Two datacards, marked PURGED. One—" The staffer paused, peering at a piece of flimsiplast. "One thing I don't recognize." She turned to Eeth. "Master?"

He took the object. Rarities were his specialty—but this was beyond even his knowledge. "You'll have to help me on this one."

"That took a while to figure out," Qui-Gon said, bemused. "It's the catering bill from the time a Hutt was allowed to visit the outpost, centuries ago."

The Zabrak Jedi Master's eyes scanned the list of numbers on the document. "Impressive. I can see why they chose to keep it. A commemoration."

"Or a warning never to spend so much again on a guest," Qui-Gon said.

One of the more recent additions to the Jedi Council, Eeth had taken on oversight of the latest round of outpost closures. Decommissioning was a routine matter in a galaxy where commerce waxed and waned, causing assets to be reallocated for better use. But even small, scarcely used Jedi facilities like Ord Jannak's required special care to close properly. Often, the Order had to formally transfer the outpost building to a planetary government. And in all circumstances, sensitive and historical materials needed to be evaluated on-site, with key items returned to Coruscant, where a member of the Jedi Council gave final say over what belonged in Jocasta Nu's archives.

Eeth had a good mind for spatial information, and an even better handle on where most of the Order's far-flung holdings were. What had started as a temporary task had evolved into a regular responsibility—and, increasingly, a chore. It seemed every time Yoda and Adi Gallia emerged from a meeting with Chancellor Valorum, another outpost closure soon followed.

For Eeth, however, the trivial nature of the materials retrieved from Ord Jannak confirmed the wisdom of the move. "The place was unoccupied for years at a time."

"It looked it," Qui-Gon said.

"Then that is that." After Eeth gestured for his staffers to dispose of the materials, he took notice of the carrying case Qui-Gon had brought them in. A raised emblem on one side of it depicted a golden chalice inside an eight-pointed star. "This isn't one of our containers."

Qui-Gon nodded. "We didn't have one with us when you directed us to Ord Jannak. The Regal Voyager line—that's their logo—provided me one of their security valises before we boarded."

Eeth looked over the interior. "SecuriCase brand. It's very nice." He felt along the corners. "Electronic countermeasures, to thwart scans. Strong ones."

"The line rents them to couriers, bankers—anyone who travels with items they don't want out of their sight. With a voice-activated password lock, as you saw. It was Obi-Wan's idea to choose the mantra from the Jedi Code."

Eeth smiled. "A code from a Code."

"He is not above a play on words."

"I will see it returned to the Regal Voyager office." Eeth closed the case. "That concludes the matter. The two of you are always reliable, Master Qui-Gon. I realize this sort of assignment is less than engaging, but it must be performed by a Jedi of rank, and not a civilian. I appreciate your attention to detail."

"It's good for students to see how things are done."

"Still, there's no need to overdo it. While you remain on call for this detail, you are at liberty until you are reassigned. Thanks again."

"I appreciate that, Master." Qui-Gon paused. "Before I go, I would like to call the Council's attention to something."

Eeth looked up. "Does this relate to the outpost?"

"Yes—but there's more." Qui-Gon's brow furrowed. "It's really a matter for the whole body. When do you next meet?"

Eeth admitted he didn't know. "We are overdue, but I've been so busy here I'm not clear on who is where. Many of us are offworld. That's no impediment—"

"But it takes arranging." Qui-Gon nodded. "I have other things to attend to myself. That case is not the only thing we brought home with us."

"I HAVE REACHED the turbine," echoed a voice from above.

"Excellent," Plo Koon said as he pushed up against the hefty metal grating. "Take your time."

At first glance, anyone looking at the scene in the vehicle maintenance hangar at the Jedi Temple might have thought Plo was trying to catch the enormous transport with his gloved hands. The vessel was suspended two meters off the deck at its lowest point, which was where the Kel Dor Jedi Master stood, hands at the ready. In fact, four repulsorlift jack units aft and forward were keeping the vessel in midair while Plo passed tools into and out of the ventral service hatch.

It was hardly a job for a member of the Council, but the refit of the Jedi's surface fleet had suffered many delays, and Plo thought the best way to invigorate the workers was by example.

The voice resonated again from inside the hatch, above. "I am draining the coolant. Stand by."

Plo assumed it would be another minute, and looked to the side. His eyes widened. A sense of impending danger drew his attention to one of the repulsorlift generators holding up the front of the craft. With an electric flash, the unit stopped functioning. The whole transport toppled, threatening workers on the deck underneath at the far end.

As the massive vessel began to crush downward on his position, Plo reached out with one hand. Drawing on the Force, he blocked the further descent of the vessel. It was only a stopgap; he knew from the start that levitation wasn't the answer. He gestured with his other hand toward the failed repulsorlift generator. Spotting the lever that switched the machine from one power cell to the backup, he pressed with his mind. The Force responded—and the device hummed back to life.

Buffeted once more by antigravity, the corner of the ship surged upward again—too quickly. Spanners and wrenches rained down from the hatch above his head. Mentally manipulating objects for the third time in seconds, Plo caught the varied implements in midair before they struck his head. Unfortunately, the same skill could do nothing against the final thing to tumble from the bobbing ship: an open bucket of drained engine coolant. The sight of it caused him to release the tools with his mind—just in time for the Jedi Master to get a faceful of liquid.

"Master Plo!"

"Stay back," Plo called out to the other workers, in a voice that now sounded like a gurgle. He took care of that first, expelling the fluid from his breathing apparatus. Next he rubbed his goggles clear enough that he could assess the state of the transport. It looked stable.

And he saw something else—a hairless face with downward-pointing horns, peering from the hatch above. Saesee Tiin regarded his colleague coolly. "So that's where you went."

Plo swept coolant drops from his robe. "Do not laugh."

"Have I ever?"

"I suppose not."

Saesee's amber eyes glowered. "You were supposed to hand up my tools."

"Pray tell, Master Tiin, did you happen to notice the ship rocking?"

"I'm working." Saesee looked to the tools strewn about the floor. "They're down there."

It was about all the sympathy one could expect from Saesee, Plo knew. Neither was the most personable of Jedi, but where Plo excelled with handling the logistics for large groups of personnel, starships were Saesee's specialty. Flying them—and fixing them. Increasingly, it meant that most of Saesee's interactions were with contractors and droids—not to mention the students drafted by Plo to repair Jedi transports that needed constant servicing. A frustrating group to lead, to be sure, made more so by its current struggles upgrading the fleet.

"Master Plo," someone said behind him. It wasn't the voice of a worker—but rather Obi-Wan Kenobi. The Padawan offered him a towel.

"Thank you, Obi-Wan." Plo wiped his face. "I see you have returned from the Slice."

"I wish I had been a minute earlier." Obi-Wan knelt and began collecting tools from the floor.

Saesee dropped from the transport, empty toolbox in hand. The sturdily built Iktotchi ably avoided slipping on the fluids underfoot. "Kenobi," he said. It was all the greeting Saesee usually ever gave. "Have you come to join the work crew?"

"Afraid I'm on another mission at the moment, Master Tiin." He piled the tools into the toolbox. "Qui-Gon would like to requisition one of the transport shuttles. There are new arrivals at the spaceport who can't afford the fare to the migrant center on the other side of Coruscant."

Saesee stared. "This is an official request?"

"No, but it relates to something that happened on our last mission. On the way back from it, actually."

"The Republic isn't handling it?" Plo Koon asked.

"There's a funding question. Master Qui-Gon was hoping to sidestep the issue." Obi-Wan straightened. "We are—uh—attending to it in our spare time."

"Good of you," Plo said, before gesturing. "Unfortunately, as you can see, much of the surface fleet is grounded."

Obi-Wan nodded. "It was worth asking."

"A mechanic can only work so fast," Saesee said, "and even a Jedi can only do so much. Patience."

Plo had no illusions about the source of the request—or about how patient Qui-Gon would be, when it came to alleviating the distress of others. Plo approved of the charitable intent, if not entirely of the use of Jedi assets. Nonetheless, he knew Qui-Gon would surely look for a way. "The Force may provide," he said.

"A moment, Master Plo," said an amiable voice from behind.

Plo turned to see that one of their droid maintenance specialists, Heezo, had stepped over to help mop up the mess. The Selonian addressed the others. "My apologies, but I overheard your problem." He looked to Obi-Wan. "There's a chauffeur for a music act who owes me a favor—I repaired her droid once. Would your friends mind riding in a luxury hoverbus?"

"Mind?" Obi-Wan smiled. "They'd love it. They haven't been treated well in a long time."

"I can make the arrangements." Heezo deferred to Plo. "With your permission, Master?"

"Certainly." He took the mop from Heezo. "Please see to it. I'll finish up here."

The worker bowed and dashed for the exit.

Plo gestured broadly. "You see? The Force has *already* provided."

Obi-Wan thanked his listeners—and added one more request. "Master Qui-Gon was hoping to speak with the full Council. Do you expect to convene soon?"

Saesee snorted. "You tell me." He gestured to the disarray surrounding them. Shuttles and repulsorlift craft everywhere were undergoing surgery.

"I see." Obi-Wan nodded and bowed. "As you say: patience."

Standing together, the two Jedi Masters watched as he left. "A worthy student," Plo said. "I hope Qui-Gon doesn't get him into any trouble."

Saesee pressed the toolbox into Plo's hands. "Worry less. Work more."

CHAPTER 4

RIFTWALKER COMPOUND

KELDOOINE

Y ou *can't have a meeting of the minds if nobody attending has one.*

Zilastra had coined the saying early in her career, and it had come in handy far too many times in the decade since. But this was the first time she'd thought of it in the middle of a firefight.

Blaster shots sizzled through the air in the corridor of the freighter *Morleen,* bright lines never to be crossed. Even peeking around the corner was death. All Zilastra could see from her side passage was the opening across the hall, where her second-in-command had just noticed her arrival. A Feeorin, Burlug had head-tendrils like hers; his were blue, while hers were Nautolan green. But he was a much bigger target. Burlug yelled over the incoming fire, "Stay back, Zil!"

"Luggy, what's the story?"

"Tal and Krins got it. Our *surprise guest* popped 'em as soon as they started to parlay."

"Saves me from killing them," Zilastra replied. So much for trying for a peaceful meeting. Her anger grew. *A boarding action, in my own port. What a mess!*

Intake was one of the simplest tasks her crew was expected to handle. In the safety of one of her own landing facilities on Keldooine, newly captured spaceships got the once-over. Valuable cargoes were located and removed, while another team evaluated the vessel's condition using a checklist that would have been the envy of any Republic bureaucrat.

Before all that could happen, however, the ship had to be secured. Capturing and rerouting a large vessel was a hectic affair, and rarely was there time to clear all the occupants while in flight. That tended to just be a formality once in port, where the numbers favored her forces. From there, it progressed as it had since the dawn of piracy. Most captured crewmembers tended to switch sides without much fuss. Joining up was better than unemployment—or a violent death. Even presumably loyal captains of commercial liners would flip once a little pressure was applied.

But owners of independent freighters like the *Morleen* were a different breed: protective of their vessels, and even more in love with their own stories of themselves. One legend-in-his-own-mind after another had refused to give up the ship, some hiding in the ductwork for days, waiting their chance to get taken down by her forces.

Or to do a little damage of their own.

With shots continuing to crackle past, Zilastra adjusted her gloves first, and then drew her blasters. Thermal detonators would be of no use—they'd damage the freighter. And a gas bomb would simply mean an even longer delay before intake could begin. No, this would have to be done the hard way, before—

The shots stopped.

Burlug looked back at her. "Don't. It's a trap."

"You *think*?"

She heard the cockpit door close—and seconds later the low thrum of the freighter's engines starting. *The owner's still trying to save the damn ship!*

Fortunately, there was an option Zilastra had ignored while all the shooting was going on: the intercom, on the wall beside her. She holstered one of her blasters and activated the communications device. "Hey, listen. Up in the cockpit."

Static. Then a husky voice. "I'm not talking to you. Get off my ship!"

"Yeah, I hear that a lot. I'm Zilastra."

A pause. Then the speaker sounded. "You're *Zilastra*? Of the Rift-walkers?"

"I'm glad you've heard of me. That means you know what I'll do."

Silence followed. Burlug shook his head. "I don't think—"

Wait, Zilastra mouthed. It usually took ten seconds.

The freighter owner was ready in five. "Let me keep the *Morleen*."

"The *what*?"

"This ship. It's mine. Just take the cargo."

Zilastra had heard that one before, too. "What are you carrying?"

"Tanks of industrial acid. Four million liters, bound for Introsphere on Gorse."

Ehh. Zilastra's green mouth crinkled.

Still, the engines were really starting to rev. She toggled the intercom. "Okay, you're in luck. We happen to have a buyer for that right here on Keldooine."

"And?"

"I'll give you one of the tanks. You sell it, you can find your way off-world."

"*What?*" The owner was clearly caught off guard. "No! I want my ship!"

"The offer stands. The *Morleen* is mine. You want to negotiate, next time get caught by a used starship dealer." She listened to the engines. "If your ship clears the facility, my people will shoot it down, with me in it."

"What? You'd really order that?"

"I thought you'd heard of me before. You've got ten seconds." Zilastra snapped off the device and redrew her other blaster.

It took the owner all ten seconds to see reason. The engines died. And when the door to the cockpit slid open, the owner died, too—shot once by each of Zilastra's blasters set to kill.

Burlug stepped out and stared at the corpse, which now rested beside the bodies of Zilastra's two former henchmen. "Good old Zilastra. Smile and shoot."

"She was wasting time." Zilastra holstered her weapons. "Get her out of here."

Nearly twice Zilastra's weight, Burlug had no trouble at all picking up the pilot's limp body. "Where to?"

Zilastra pointed a thumb aft. "She owns one of those acid vats in the hold. A deal's a deal." She glanced at the corpses of her fallen henchmen. "Them, too."

"Got it."

Zilastra wanted a bath, herself—if in something a lot less dangerous. Nautolans were at home near water, and while her job kept her in space, Zilastra liked a good soak. But there was more yet to do. "Luggy, where was she hiding?"

"Under the heat exchange manifold. Snuck into the cockpit past everyone."

"Just great." This wasn't supposed to happen. Zilastra looked from side to side. "Where's the kid?"

She started to reach for her comlink—and decided instead on the ship's public address system. Her voice boomed through the halls. "*Kylah Lohmata! Show yourself!*"

A metal bulkhead panel behind Zilastra shot outward, landing on the deck with a clang. A dark-haired human girl of twelve slipped out of a space barely a meter tall. Her face and clothing were completely covered in grease smudges—and her wide brown eyes beamed as she saluted. "Reporting, Your Majesty!"

Zilastra waved a gloved hand. "I'm not in the mood. I've got two dead because of a pilot we missed. Checking crawl spaces is *your* job!"

Kylah got to her feet. "I found something else. I knew you'd want to see it."

"And you thought the way to reach me was to crawl here?"

"People were shooting." Kylah lifted the panel she'd just knocked out. Like most of the corridor, it was pocked with score marks from the pilot's blaster. The kid smiled wide. "Come on! Follow me down to the hold!"

The wiry girl dived back into the maintenance tunnel before Zilastra could grab her. Kneeling, she saw Kylah clambering like a rodent through the tunnel. Unable to fit, Zilastra shouted inside. "What's the matter with taking the stairs?"

"*Shortcut!*"

Seething, Zilastra heard a comment from above. "Smart kid." The pilot's body over his massive shoulder, Burlug snickered at his boss. "Saves her from getting chewed out. I'd follow if I could fit!"

"Get to the hold before I liquidate the lot of you." Zilastra watched him pass and turned to follow. The long way to the hold, down the halls.

There was no place in Zilastra's life for children of her own. It had been hard enough starting the Riftwalkers from the castoffs of the four other gangs working this sector of the Slice. Yet somehow she had become a kind of surrogate parent for Kylah. The foundling had been a stowaway on a merchant ship Zilastra had grabbed; with nowhere to go, she'd stayed on. The skinny kid's talent at getting into places no one else could and finding things no one knew to look for had made her handy to have around.

Still, given all the would-be lieutenants wanting to impress her all the time, an incorrigible orphan made for a change of pace. Kylah was all striving, with none of the conniving. Zilastra wasn't exactly alike in that, but she certainly knew what it was to be on her own—and she respected performance. She'd lately entrusted the stowaway with a very special project, in fact.

She was beginning to doubt the wisdom of that when she arrived in the hold. True to the late captain's word, freestanding tanks stood in the wide area. They were bolted to the deck, and the only way to drain them was at a reservoir facility, using the proper equipment. That was why Zilastra instantly had known the prize was less than useful.

"No kid," Burlug said. "I was sure she'd beat us here."

Zilastra's blood boiled. "*Stowaway!*"

"I'm up here!" came a voice from high above.

Zilastra looked to the top of one of the tanks. Somehow, Kylah had gotten up there and was perched next to an opening in the massive container. "What's the idea?" Zilastra asked.

"You're going to want to see this," Kylah said. "*I'm not the only stowaway on this ship!*"

CHAPTER 5

CORUSCANT

The Great Western Sea on Coruscant was far from the Jedi Temple, but Yaddle felt as if she were drowning nonetheless. Not in liquid, but in details.

"This one again," she said, taking a deep breath for another dive. "Item Fifty-Stroke-Seventeen, in the matter of Yash Helgan, on Corellia."

Her small green frame dwarfed by the semicircular desk in the library annex, she read from the datapad for the benefit of her dictation droid. At least, she assumed it was still standing there. The holobooks she was using were piled high, obstructing her view of the surroundings.

But not off to her right, where she saw a familiar and friendly face. "Master Qui-Gon!"

"Master Yaddle." Qui-Gon bowed. "I'm sorry to disturb you. I was passing through."

She smiled. "I'm always willing to interrupt my day of judgment."

"Pardon?"

"Legal matters." Tiny green fingers gestured to the work surrounding her. "The Galactic Courts of Justice generally hold that Jedi are not liable for events that take place during their official duties within the boundaries of the Republic."

"Generally. But not always?"

"Correct—and there are other kinds of questions." She gestured to the datapad. "Here, for example, are the civil actions for wrongful arrest, all of which involved a Jedi during the investigation or apprehension. The Jedi cannot themselves be made liable, but we do make certain they provide testimony. And that is but one variety."

"Sounds complicated."

"Mmm. One reason I take this duty is I have lived so long, seen so much. There are always precedents. Except when there aren't." She pointed to the latest item. "Consider the plight of poor Yash Helgan, a Padawan who, during air-taxi travel, activated his lightsaber in an attempt to use it as a light source. It went through the seat, impaling the droid driver and resulting in the cab's unscheduled entry in the Remembrance Night Festival Parade."

The dictation droid took a step back. Qui-Gon patted its metal shoulder. "I'm sure the droid was repaired."

"Once they found all of it," Yaddle said. "Let's just say there were a variety of legal claims."

Qui-Gon's comlink beeped. He asked Yaddle's pardon and answered. "Yes, Obi-Wan?"

"I've arranged rides for those who need them."

"Good. Just be careful with your lightsaber."

"*What?*"

"Never mind. I'm still working on my part of the list." Qui-Gon ended the call and made his apologies to Yaddle. "I'm afraid I must be off."

"Like the future, Qui-Gon is always in motion," Yaddle said. She smiled as he disappeared around the tall stack of materials.

Then she looked at the work before her and sighed. *Going places. I remember what that was like!*

WHY IS EVERYTHING so blue?

When it came to having a disciplined mind, Adi Gallia had few equals. It was one reason that her colleagues on the Jedi Council often looked to her on diplomatic matters—and particularly, relations with Senate and other Republic officials.

It wasn't just that she remembered names and titles; any protocol droid could do that. Adi also knew the points of view of those she spoke with. Their legislative records—and the picayune details of their personal projects. Most of the time she didn't need a datapad, though she found it reassured her contacts to see her holding one. Focus, for her, was everything.

Even so, the oddest things could claim her attention. An hour and a half into one of her and Master Yoda's frequent meetings with Supreme Chancellor Valorum and Senator Palpatine on Coruscant, she found her attention increasingly drawn to the walls and the furnishings. Finis Valorum had celebrated his reelection in the usual way, by completely changing the color scheme of the office at great expense. He had chosen an almost hypnotically deep blue, perhaps to put his visitors at ease.

Or to sleep—but then, Valorum's meetings tended to have that effect on their own.

"And there is another concern on the horizon," the chancellor said. Seated in a cerulean chair, Valorum leaned across the enormous desk and spoke with grave intent. "There has been a point-two percent reduction in tourism revenue on Garqi."

"Two percent?" Yoda asked.

"*Point-two* percent," corrected Palpatine, seated alongside the two Jedi Masters. "But it was in excess of what the models predicted."

Valorum referred to a datapad. "The economic working group that Senator Palpatine heads has a theory that it's an indirect effect of the labor action in the caf plant sector, which supplies much of the tourism in the off season."

Adi realized where it was going. "You're suggesting we send Jedi Knights to assist in the labor negotiations?"

"Sending them there on holiday won't do much to help," Valorum said.

Yoda and Adi exchanged a glance. *Patience.*

"There is a similar situation on Chamble," the chancellor added. "Only there it is the local police force that is on strike. The resulting unrest has impacted the market capitalization of Bansche Tech. It has greatly suffered."

Adi made a mental note. "Negotiators to Chamble."

"Oh, no." Palpatine looked up from his datapad. "Chamble's senator says her government will not negotiate for any reason. She just wants the businesses protected."

"We are not police officers," Yoda said. "Nor corporate security."

It was the umpteenth one of these moments, and everyone present took it in stride. "A visit would be enough," Valorum said, idly looking at the back of his hand. "Something where the locals can see you on the corporate grounds. A tour, perhaps?"

"Only if the masters judge it to be worthy of their most valuable time," Palpatine said, smiling mildly at the Jedi. "Such decisions are entirely in your domain. Perhaps you can stage a training mission there. Those make quite a show."

Yoda looked to Adi. "Master Gallia—"

"The note is made," she said, using her datapad this time for show. An ally of the chancellor, Palpatine always seemed to have a suggestion ready for every problem he brought to the Council's attention. It was part of why Valorum brought him into their meetings.

She took a deep breath. "Next item?"

The doors opened behind her. A droid aide walked to the desk carrying a pair of burgundy boots. Adi's first thought was that they didn't match the room. A little too red, and the spangly stone inlays running up their sides were absolutely garish. They certainly didn't look like something Valorum would wear.

"These are manufactures from Hafernia, a new member of the Republic," Valorum said. He ordered the droid to show them to Adi.

She examined them. *Well, maybe the Hafernians like them.* She found a way not to lie. "I'm sure they are proud of their work."

"They are," the chancellor said. "They'd like to send a few pallets to the Temple."

"Pallets?" Yoda asked.

"Of the boots."

The notion caught Adi off guard. "We're happy to convey items to charitable causes—" She stared at the offenses against creation. "If you don't think they're a bit too fine for that."

"Oh, no," Valorum said. "They're not for charity. They're for *you*."

"Me?"

"The Jedi. To wear, of course."

She did a double take. "Jedi. Wearing *these*."

"Just once in a while," he said. "To show Hafernia the Republic welcomes their manufactures."

Palpatine moved his hand dismissively. "They're providing them at no cost, of course."

The boots were suited for a dance hall, not action. "I don't think these will be suitable, Chancellor." She offered to pass them to her colleague. "Would you agree, Master Yoda?"

He tittered. "I am knowledgeable of many things. But I have never worn shoes!"

"No, I guess not." She frowned. "I appreciate the Hafernians' gift, Chancellor, but the Jedi do not endorse products."

Palpatine raised an eyebrow. "Ah, but you do. You endorse the Galactic Republic, and the spread of good governance."

That was true enough, Adi thought, but the whole thing was ridiculous. Valorum had made a number of similarly impossible requests in previous meetings, and it had grown clear to her that he didn't care one way or another about many of them. The chancellor was a pipe through which all the demands of his patrons flowed. Many times, he just wanted to be able to say he made the request.

This appeared to be one of them. "They *are* rather wretched," Valorum said of the boots. He and Palpatine looked at each other and chuckled.

"The Hafernians rarely leave their planet," Palpatine said. "They'll never know the difference."

That's a relief. Adi passed the boots back to the droid and slid a little in her chair. More minutes spent, debating something they were never going to do anyway.

Before it departed, the droid addressed them. "A Jedi has arrived in the antechamber. He said his name is Qui-Gon Jinn."

Adi didn't know he had returned to Coruscant. "That's probably for us," she said.

"Ever things that require attention," Yoda said. He looked to Adi. "Please see to it. Too old, I am, for running back and forth."

She could tell he was trying to rescue her from the meeting, and she wouldn't have it. "I'm sure Master Qui-Gon probably came to see you."

"We should not delay the chancellor. Longer, your legs are."

She couldn't disagree with that. She stood and followed the droid, not knowing how Yoda had handled centuries of meetings.

The anteroom outside the office in the Republic Executive Building was its original color; apparently, Valorum's decorators hadn't reached this chamber yet. She smiled to see who was waiting for her. "Master Qui-Gon. It is good to see you back."

He bowed. "And you as well, Master Gallia." He looked apprehensive. "I told the droid not to interrupt you."

"It did me a favor," she said, before grinning. "What brings you here?"

"I was dealing with some matters relating to my recent trip. But when I heard you and Master Yoda were here, I decided to stop by in case you had concluded. There is a matter I'm hoping to bring to the full Council."

"I'm hoping to survive the day." She cast a glance to the supreme chancellor's door. "Our work here could go on for some time—and I don't expect to be able to contact the other members. But if you see them first, feel free to ask them to set a time for you."

"I will." He bowed again. "I am sorry to have taken you from your meeting."

"I told you, never apologize for doing the right thing." She grinned. "But look who I am telling."

Having watched Qui-Gon depart, she steeled herself and headed back inside. The others had moved on to what had become an increasingly regular phase of their meetings: what everyone had agreed to blithely call reallocations of strength. Valorum and Yoda were in the thick of discussion when Palpatine noticed her return.

The senator from Naboo leaned over and handed her a datapad. "Here is a list of moves we have recommended so far, Master Gallia."

"I will give it my full attention."

But instead, her eyes went somewhere else. Not to the discussion, nor even the vessels flying outside the great rectangular window. Leaning over to Palpatine, she covered her mouth to speak confidentially and gestured to the walls. "Why *this* shade of blue?"

"There's no accounting for taste," Palpatine whispered. "I sometimes wonder what it would look like in red."

CHAPTER 6

RIFTWALKER COMPOUND

KELDOOINE

"Would you look at *these* specimens," Zilastra muttered in the *Morleen*'s hold on Keldooine. Zilastra had called out IK-111, her murder droid, to support her—but it barely seemed necessary for the three shambling figures with filthy clothes and pained expressions before her. They struggled to stand at attention before the ebon droid's blasters. She shook her head. *What a bunch!*

The trio had been fished out of the only tank aboard the freighter that didn't contain acid. The only way in was a hatch at the top; inside was a ten-meter drop. It had taken half an hour and a cable to get the occupants out.

"I heard 'em yelling earlier as I went past," Kylah said. "I don't think they're crew—they smell like they've been in there for a while. I think they got stuck."

"Step back, Eyekay." Zilastra watched as IK-111 complied. "Where was this ship in from?"

"Randon." The response came from Burlug, who was on the stairs beside another tank getting ready to dispose of the pilot. "Kid, you think they're stowaways?"

"I would never hide anyplace that silly," Kylah said.

Devaronian. Houk. Klatooinian. Zilastra snapped her fingers. "You're the guys who tried to 'jack the *Regal Zephyr!*"

The trio said nothing. But like any good card player, she read faces. The Houk was stern, but his eyes were always in motion. He was afraid she was the law. The Klatooinian was afraid she wasn't. Everything *but* his eyes was in motion, thanks to his nervous fidgeting.

But the Devaronian had looked up when she mentioned their attempted crime. That was pride, however misplaced—and it meant something else. He was the boss of the others, or thought he was. Zilastra addressed him. "Who are you?"

"Lobber. *The* Lobber."

"There's more than one?"

Lobber thrust his hand out, drawing an irritated chirp from the droid. The Devaronian pulled his hand back and tried to recover. "I'm the brains."

"How terrible for all of you."

Zilastra began to pace in front of them. Off to the side, Kylah watched her. "You've heard of these guys?"

"Three perps hit a spaceliner on the Ootmian. You can see how well it went by their accommodations here." She peered at the shaky Klatooinian. "Caught the first thing back that had an engine. Do I have that right?"

The Klatooinian cast a glance up at Burlug, dropping a body into another tank with a sickening splash—and nearly fainted.

Lobber spoke up. "Don't bother talking to Wungo, pal. I told you, I'm the mover here." He patted his chest. "I can see you're in the same business. Nice to meet a fellow—"

Zilastra launched herself toward Lobber, her hands lancing out for the Devaronian's horns. She squeezed hard, using them as leverage to wrench his neck.

"Ow! Let go!"

"*Nobody hits ships of the Regal Voyager line!*" Zilastra declared, tightening her grip. Lobber's knees buckled.

Wungo cringed. "Are . . . are they your territory?"

Lobber spoke through the pain. "We—we were going to give the ship to you, I promise. We were talking about it, right, Ghor?"

"That's right!" the Houk declared. "We were going to give the ship to the Vile!"

Zilastra stared angrily at him.

Ghor's lip trembled. "Wait, that's wrong. We said the Staved Skulls."

After she didn't answer, Wungo stammered, "N-no, wait. We said the Filthy Creds!"

Another beat. Lobber, gasping for breath, asked in a small voice: "The Poisoned Blades?"

"*I'm Zilastra*," she declared. She yanked Lobber's horns upward, bringing him face-to-agonized-face with her. "And I run the *Riftwalkers*!"

"That's it!" Lobber said, as if suddenly reminded. "We were stealing the ship for the Riftwalkers!"

Ghor nodded. "Yeah. Like Riftwalker. The pazaak game."

Zilastra winced. "It's *sabacc*, you dolt. And what do you mean, you were stealing it for me?"

"To show you what we could do," Lobber said. "I mean, if it had worked."

"I don't want *anybody* hitting Regal Voyager's ships. For me or anyone else. Everyone working the Slice should know that. Understand?"

Lobber stared at her. "Uh . . . no."

Zilastra certainly wasn't going to explain it to them. She released Lobber, who fell to his knees. She spun and looked up to Burlug. "Three more for an acid bath," she said, snapping her fingers. "And not a moment too soon. Come on, Kylah!"

Still at blasterpoint, Lobber's companions protested. The Devaronian was the only one whose words formed sentences.

"Wait! I don't get it," he said as she started to walk away. "You just told us you didn't want anybody to steal Regal Voyager's ships. Well, we didn't! The Jedi stopped us *before* we took it over!"

Her eyes narrowed on hearing a hated word—and she stopped. She turned around. "Are you saying you three were stopped by a *Jedi*?"

"That's right." Ghor nodded vigorously. "It wasn't just any Jedi, either. It was a Jedi Master!"

"Not just any Jedi Master," Wungo corrected. "He was a *brain doctor!*"

Zilastra stared at him, baffled. "What?"

"You know, one of those people who talks to you, asking why you steal things." The name finally arrived. "A counselor."

Possible explanations ran through her mind. Squinting, she settled on the dumbest possible one. "Do you mean he was on the *Jedi Council?*"

"That's right," Lobber said. "Only he wasn't. He *was* going to be one of those, but he was too dangerous and powerful."

"Yeah," Ghor piped in. "He made blasterfire with his eyes!"

Wungo nodded. "And the other one froze me like ice, just by touching me!"

"Don't be ignorant," she said. She glared at them. "And what do you mean, 'the other one'?"

"There were two," Lobber responded. "I think that one was a consultant, too."

"*Councilor,*" Zilastra corrected. Realizing how she'd spent the last minute of her life, she took a deep breath. "If Jedi really caught you, why aren't you in custody—or dead? And don't tell me you escaped. You couldn't even get out of that tank."

A quiet pause while the trio settled on their tale. Lobber finally gave something like an admission. "They controlled our minds."

"Somebody sure needs to." She didn't believe that story, either. The Jedi were said to be able to influence the simple-minded, but the effect didn't last long. On the other hand, no other explanation made sense. She looked to Kylah. "Kid, look up the report from—"

"Got it." The girl already had a datapad in hand. "Your source on Randon says it was a lone Jedi with a student." She chuckled. "And they never activated their lightsabers."

They've got nerve, Zilastra thought. Even with the Republic and the Order pulling back from the trade route, Jedi still operated with impunity—or thought they could. Fools like Lobber and his buddies made it easy. There was no place for them in any self-respecting outfit—and definitely not in the Riftwalkers.

Still, there was something of concern here. *Jedi aboard a Regal Voyager flight?* That was getting too close. It might be random—but even a small chance that her most hated enemies were nosing around because of her plans meant she had to make a decision she hated even more.

"We're not going to kill you," Zilastra announced. "Instead, you're going to tell us everything that happened. *Every. Little. Thing.*"

Bursting with relief, the three would-be hijackers began talking all at once.

Zilastra put up her index finger. "*After* you help clear this ship." She looked up to Burlug. "Those two bodies still forward?"

"And more corpses aft. The part of the crew that didn't want to join up." Burlug snapped the lid shut on an acid tank. "It got kind of messy."

"Take these characters with you. And if they give you any trouble—"

She didn't need to finish the sentence. The three hobbled off to follow Burlug.

Zilastra looked to Kylah. "You're going over to the Regal Voyager facility at the spaceport again tonight, right?"

"Yeah. Same deal as usual—I can only bring the goods out one at a time."

"While you're there, see if there's anything in the files on the Jedi. I don't want them nosing around. Understand?"

"Got it."

"And be careful—that neighborhood's in the Blades' territory. Has anyone hassled you?"

"Once—but I got out of it. I've got a bodyguard. She helped me scare off a bunch of goons."

Zilastra frowned, and not just over the thought of Kylah being challenged. "What bodyguard? I didn't assign you one."

"I met her on the street stealing a speeder—I call her Hotwire. But you should have seen her fight! I took her on as my driver so she can help me get back and forth."

"It probably helps that she can reach the controls." Zilastra chuckled. "So the stowaway has muscle of her own. Sure you can trust her?"

"Would I be able to trust anyone else you sent to drive me?"

At least someone *remembers my lessons,* Zilastra thought. She grinned. "Get out of here. I have to make sure there isn't a cantina band hiding under the deck plates."

CHAPTER 7

CORUSCANT

"Now, students, we will consider dueling positions when confronted with an opponent of different stature."

Surrounded by helmeted younglings in the training area of the Jedi Temple on Coruscant, Ki-Adi-Mundi took a ready stance and activated his lightsaber. It was refreshing for him to connect with the next generation of Jedi, and he knew it was always a treat for them to learn from a member of the Jedi Council.

Today they were getting two, thanks to Ki-Adi-Mundi's opponent. A member of the Quermian species, Yarael Poof towered over master and children alike thanks to his exceptionally long neck. Yet the alabaster-skinned Jedi wasn't playing his part.

"You have not drawn your weapon," Ki-Adi-Mundi said. "Come now. On your guard!"

Master Yarael reached for his lightsaber—only to wave his spiny fingers in the air instead. *"You don't want to strike me."*

"That isn't going to work."

"No? Well, try this." Yarael faced the oldest group of children, stared, and gestured. *"You don't want him to strike me."*

"We don't want him to strike you," the students droned in unison. *"You want to bar his path."*

"We want to bar his path." Dazed, several of the kids marched in front of Yarael. They turned, faced Ki-Adi-Mundi, and activated their training lightsabers.

Yarael's wide mouth curled into a smile. "And that is how I might defend myself against an opponent with a different stature. Which, for me, is pretty much everyone."

The younger kids that Yarael hadn't spoken to giggled—as did the ones he had attempted to influence. Ki-Adi-Mundi gave him his due. "Very clever. But it is not a reliable method. Not everyone is a member of the Council, able to project a thought to several individuals at once. And it is very difficult to make people face danger against their wills." He gave Yarael a stern look. "It is also quite immoral."

"There's a bigger concern than that," Yarael said. His head lowered on his long neck, and he leered at the older students. "Shame on you. Where's the mental discipline I taught you? I should never have been able to influence you to begin with."

"Oh, you didn't control us," a Rodian girl said. She faced Yarael. "We really didn't want him to strike you, Master."

Yarael's eyes widened. "None of you were influenced?"

The kids broke out into laughter.

"Very kind," Yarael said, patting her helmet with a long white hand. "You see, Master? It pays to be popular!"

Ki-Adi-Mundi deactivated his lightsaber. Yet another group of students had taken Yarael as their mascot. His large spiny frame and huge eyes made him look like a children's drawing, and his joviality only added to the effect. He was also centuries old, and loved regaling the children with tales of Jedi adventures past. Ki-Adi-Mundi was more serious—and seriously irritated over the interruption. "If we might save the hilarity for another time—"

"Excuse me," announced a visitor.

Expecting to be annoyed further, Ki-Adi-Mundi looked up—only to brighten when he saw who it was. "Young Kenobi. You are back from your mission."

"And many smaller ones since," Obi-Wan said, entering. "This is one." He looked about. "But I don't want to intrude."

"We are not doing anything important." He shot a look at Yarael.

Obi-Wan sounded relieved. "There's a young family—several families, actually—with children in need."

"Are they Jedi candidates?"

"I wouldn't think so. Several have reached Coruscant on short notice. They need clothing, bedclothes, toys—items I was hoping could be found here."

"The relief agencies weren't able to help?" Yarael asked.

"Not today."

Ki-Adi-Mundi and Yarael looked at each other—and then at the young man, waiting in hope.

"I think we can do something," Yarael said.

"Better," Ki-Adi-Mundi added. He gestured around the room. "Let us ask our students here what things of their own they are willing to give. It is a teaching opportunity."

Yarael harrumphed. "Nonsense. We can afford to give the children something new—and tailored to them."

Ki-Adi-Mundi raised an eyebrow at Obi-Wan. "My friend has never liked secondhand clothing. Trouble with the fit."

"We could talk about you and helmets," Yarael responded, putting his hands together in a cone mimicking the one atop Ki-Adi-Mundi's head.

The children laughed—and when Obi-Wan saw that Ki-Adi-Mundi didn't mind the joke, the Padawan grinned as well. Clearly, the two masters had an understanding about that sort of humor. "Whatever you decide will be fine."

Before he turned to leave, Obi-Wan asked, "Did Master Qui-Gon speak with you about addressing the Council?"

"It would have to come after our lessons." Ki-Adi-Mundi shot another look at Yarael. "For some reason, today we are behind."

TWO BEADS. MANY gems.
A cloak, abandoned.

Hands. Transparent—no, invisible.

A cup, overflowing with pain.

Boots.

Mace Windu opened his eyes, and exhaled. *Where did* boots *come from?*

The Jedi Temple complex had been built over what was once a soaring mountain peak—home to the original cave chapels and a sacred spire. As Coruscant's artificial surface reached ever skyward, the modern Temple overtopped the original one, leaving only the sequestered pinnacle at its center—and a new, modern spire atop it, surrounded by four other columns.

High in the central Tranquility Spire, in the same meditation chamber where years earlier he had spent the night before the ceremonies raising him to the rank of Jedi Knight—and then Jedi Master—Mace communed with the future. It wasn't his normal setting for contemplation, but something about inhabiting his life before his duties expanded appealed to him.

But his thoughts had been disordered all day, clouded with routine cares and random elements that didn't amount to much. Never one for futile exercises, Mace recalled the words of Master Yarael: *The Force cannot be forced.* He stood and made his way down from the chamber through the spire.

He exited at the base, where he found Qui-Gon Jinn on one of the ancient balconies surrounding the original peak below, seated in quiet meditation of his own. Or—

"Master Qui-Gon—are you *asleep?*"

Qui-Gon opened his eyes. "I apologize, Master. I had a long journey—with no rest since."

Mace nodded. "I'm told you and young Kenobi saw some action."

"Thankfully, action was not required." Qui-Gon's eyes went to the spire above. "I didn't want to interrupt your meditations."

"You didn't." Mace shook his head. "I'm afraid we'll never replace what Master Sifo-Dyas could do when it comes to sensing the future. There are too many threads on this planet." Qui-Gon rose, and they began to walk toward the great staircase. "Master Rancisis is offworld,"

Mace said, "trying to commune with the Force in a more peaceful place. I envy him."

"You could have gone elsewhere as well, Master."

Mace wanted to believe that. But he shook his head. "Too many responsibilities here, of late."

"Master Yarael has a saying about too much work—"

"I was there when he first said it." Mace regarded Qui-Gon. "I was also told you have something to bring to the Council's attention. By more than one person, in fact."

"Between myself and Obi-Wan, we have managed to encounter a quorum of the Council since we've returned. But I would prefer to speak to you all at once."

"And you sought me out." Mace considered it. "We do need to convene."

"It touches on the events that took place on our route back from Ord Jannak."

"That's the corridor where Master Billaba is working," Mace said. He thought of his former student, now fellow Council member, absent for many weeks on assignment. He had not spoken to her, not since—

Mace stopped on the top stair and closed his eyes. *Two beads—the marks of the Chalactan culture, which Depa Billaba wore on her brow. And an abandoned cloak . . .*

Snapped from his trance, he saw Qui-Gon had paused beside him. "Master?"

"All right, it's time," Mace said. "The word will be given. The Council will convene."

THE DRIVER IN the cab of the speeder truck looked into the lengthening shadows of Keldooine's largest city. Somewhere in that mass of dying industry was the planetary port for the Riftwalkers. One could easily see that from the vessels—mostly captured—flying in. But the ground entrance to the facility was hidden within a warren of covered alleyways.

Young Kylah Lohmata had never asked to be let out of the speeder truck at the same place, and she had never invited her driver to join her. The pickup locations also changed every time. It was remarkable that someone so young had picked up so much tradecraft.

"Hey, Hotwire!" Kylah called out. The adolescent emerged from a doorway nowhere near the direction of the purported location of the Riftwalker base.

"Not where I expected to see you."

"We're like that." Kylah opened the passenger door and rapped on the dash. "Move." The speeder truck was under way before the girl was fully in her seat.

All of it was to be expected. It wasn't fear of the authorities that motivated such care; the Republic's rule of Keldooine had been a trivial detail even before the Jedi outpost closed. The rival gangs were another story. Everything on the world was a zero-sum game; spies and turncoats were everywhere. It paid to be careful.

That especially applied when it came to new talent, like the woman Kylah called Hotwire. She looked the part of a gearhead speeder thief, from her big goggles and ancient leather helmet to her grease-smeared face and clothes. She'd only been on Keldooine a couple of days when she first encountered Kylah; the girl was in over her head, and in need of a quick escape from a group of thieves. The driver had provided it and more protection, since, earning a modicum of trust. Not enough to get inside the Riftwalkers' spaceport, but that wasn't really something a surface driver should be interested in.

"I need you to drop me near the East Spaceport again," Kylah said. "The alley behind the executive complex."

"Don't you ever sleep?"

"Wrong planet for that." Kylah reached into her jacket and plopped a small bag on the dash. "Here."

"Republic credits?"

"They're good. For a while. Double that when you pick me up. Let's go!"

The sun set during the drive, a ride during which Kylah hardly stopped talking to the driver, whom Kylah kept referring to as her "new employee." The girl desperately wanted to be a pirate—*why* had not yet come up—and was delighted to show someone more than twice her age her mastery of the streets. The driver herself was new to Keldooine, and more than willing to listen.

The speeder truck pulled up to the alleyway in darkness. "Are you sure *this* is where you want out?"

"This time, yeah." Kylah opened the door. "Be a few hours again. I'll signal you. Can you make yourself scarce until I call?"

"No problem." Before the driver could say more, her comlink beeped. She looked at a message on it. "I've even got something to do. My friends back home get together every so often for a call."

"Must be nice to *have* a 'back home.'"

"We're all over the place—these sessions aren't easy to arrange." It wasn't the best time for it, either. She nodded to the teen. "Stay safe— *boss.*"

It was perhaps more care than most gangland drivers might have exhibited, but Kylah tended to bring that out, and she seemed to appreciate it. The kid vanished into the night, while the driver found a new parking spot blocks away.

There she entered the back of the vehicle and set up her holographic communicator. Finding a seat on a crate, she removed her helmet and goggles, revealing long loops of black hair—and two beads on her brow. She spoke in a tone much more refined than she had used before with Kylah.

"This is Depa Billaba, on assignment, responding to summons."

"This is Temple Comm Control. Welcome, Master Billaba. Stand by to join the Council, already in progress . . ."

CHAPTER 8

CORUSCANT

When Master Windu finally convened the Jedi Council, Qui-Gon was without his Padawan, having set Obi-Wan at liberty after seeing to the requests from the *Regal Zephyr* passengers. Everyone deserved personal time after a long assignment, and while bringing one's student to important meetings was educational for them, Qui-Gon thought this was a good session for him to attend alone.

He had time for second thoughts about that—and third ones, and fourth ones—while waiting outside the Council Chamber. His request was at the bottom of the agenda, and from the sound of it, a couple of the traveling members had been slow to call in. Worse, Adi Gallia had darted in and out of the meeting several times, passing Qui-Gon in the antechamber to find out some fact that the others required. "This feels familiar," she said to him.

"I admire your endurance."

Eventually, his time came. But somewhere during the fifty steps Qui-Gon took into the round room, things changed again. Master Even Piell holographically appeared, bringing the number of Council members, real and virtual, to the full dozen. Mace appealed to Qui-Gon for further patience and spoke to Piell. "Do I understand you're on Yitabo by senatorial request?"

"That's right," the long-eared Piell replied. "Two agricultural corporations here are in a tussle with the civilian government. Chancellor Valorum requested Jedi intercession."

Mace scowled. "And we sent a *member of the Jedi High Council*?"

"I was in the neighborhood. And I knew a couple o' the people involved. It's been exactly as exciting as you'd imagine."

Ki-Adi-Mundi shook his head. "Next they will have us settling parking disputes."

"Let's hope it never comes to that," Mace said. He looked to Qui-Gon. "You had something to share?"

Qui-Gon nodded. "Master Piell is actually in the region I've come to discuss. I have firsthand evidence that our recent outpost closures in the Slice are making life more difficult for the people there."

He described what he and Obi-Wan had seen on their recent junket—and, more important, what they had heard from those on the *Regal Zephyr*. "Every time a corporation relocates from the Slice, the region loses power in the Senate, and becomes less secure," Qui-Gon said. "The people move, and it begins again."

"I can confirm this," Depa Billaba said. Her holographic image was of poor quality, and her voice had an echo. "I am in the Slice now, investigating the roots of piracy with the help of the Judicial Forces' Diplomatic Fleet. I have seen firsthand how lawlessness spreads. Even the young are impacted."

"*Especially* the young," Piell said. "There's a generation at risk out here."

Adi reacted as if it was nothing new. "Places fall out of favor. We serve the Senate."

That produced a buzz from several of her colleagues. Mace spoke for them. "We are independent."

"Your pardon, Masters. I mean we take their needs into account when making our plans." She gestured to her datapad. "A tremendous amount of information goes into these decisions. They are not made lightly."

From another planet, hairy-faced Oppo Rancisis concurred. "We are not charged with changing the laws of economics. Opportunity ebbs and flows, and seeks its level."

"Of course," Qui-Gon said, turning to face the white-haired sage. "Yet there was a time, Master Oppo, when the Jedi sponsored works that did change the lives of many."

Mace frowned. "Take care, Qui-Gon. Those who envy the past may lose sight of where they are."

"I agree, Master Windu—but this speaks to my point. Decisions are made here with the best of intent, strengthened both by what we know of the past, and what the Force tells us of the future. We are well guided. But we seldom see the results of our actions in person."

"That is what we send Jedi into the field for," Saesee interjected sharply.

"And as one of them, Master Tiin, I am duty-bound to report what I see."

The Council's gruffest member stared for a moment. "Fair."

Qui-Gon took a deep breath. Speaking to the Jedi Council was literally dizzying. The room's circular design was intended to mean all were equal—but those given an audience were definitely not. Comments could come from any direction, forcing the interviewee to spin, searching for the speaker—by which time another voice would sound off from behind. Adding to the disorientation were the windows facing out in every direction, presenting a panoramic view of space and air traffic over the galaxy's busiest planet. The ancient Jedi Order may have been on to something, meeting in caves.

The biggest hazard, Qui-Gon thought, was the temptation to pace the room. This was no court and jury, no sales pitch. One had to stand firm. Ideas, not theatrics, were important. He centered himself and struck a humble pose as he rejoined his appeal.

"We know our work touches billions. We stop menaces, some before they even develop. We save whole star systems at a time." He focused on an empty spot on the floor. "And yet, when was the last time one of us counseled someone who was bereaved? Helped someone overcome self-destructive behavior?" He looked up. "Told anyone that *their* decisions, *their* lives are important?"

Silence.

Yoda broke it. "From small sparks, grows the light."

Gratified, Qui-Gon bowed his head.

Adi shook hers, with evident sadness. "There is simply not the time to do these things. Not at our level."

"But we ain't at a different level," Piell said. "Least, we ain't supposed to be. We're like anyone else."

"With a greater charge, Master." Adi waved her datapad before her. "We have worlds of responsibilities. What we want doesn't enter into it. It's what the Force wants of us."

"Ah, but is it?" Qui-Gon lifted his head and raised an eyebrow. "Even as we look across space and time, the living Force asks us to look right before our eyes. What do you see there?"

"Not much," Eeth replied. "We are very much rooted here, of late."

"Our cares are dictated by what is before us." Qui-Gon's eyes moved from one face to another. "The people Obi-Wan and I met thought little of the Jedi because they felt we thought of *them* too little."

"Nothing could be further from the truth," Mace said.

"It is *their* truth. The truth they see, in their daily lives. And as outposts close, what they do not see—is *us*." Qui-Gon paused to take a breath. "It is more than an oversight on our part. Indeed, I think it could be quite dangerous."

Several members of the Council spoke at once. Ki-Adi-Mundi declared, "This is an extreme conclusion."

"I agree," Plo Koon said. "Just because they do not see—or understand—our actions, it does not mean we do not care. Or that we haven't done anything."

Qui-Gon shook his head. "With forgiveness, Master, to a person in crisis, it means *exactly* that. We are known by what we do. A galaxy in which the Jedi are increasingly unseen allows a different picture to form in the void. And that *is* dangerous."

Yaddle agreed. "These people think poorly of us. What worse thing could they think?"

Or be made *to think?* Qui-Gon thought to add. But that was an incendiary thought, and he decided it was best to stay on course. "I am not here to question this body's great wisdom or to challenge the way things are done—"

"But you *are*," Yoda said. "You, Qui-Gon, we have met before."

Several of the Jedi Masters chuckled, and Qui-Gon was relieved to hear them. Humbled, he flashed a grin and looked down. "I will put this another way, then. We spend a great deal of time seeking balance—and we do this because we inherently know when something is out of balance. Well, something *is* out of balance, for each of us." He looked up. "Fortunately, it requires no grand plan, no great work. And this wise Council already knows what is needed."

Scanning the faces around him, Qui-Gon could tell they had heard him.

Mace nodded gently. "Thank you, Master Qui-Gon."

"And I thank all of you." Qui-Gon bowed. He started to turn to leave—only to gesture with his hands. "*Help one person. A Jedi needs no permission for that.*"

CHAPTER 9

CORUSCANT

"It seems we have been given a challenge," Mace said with no little amusement after the doors closed behind Qui-Gon. "I can't imagine how improving lives never occurred to us."

Light laughter followed—but not from everyone. "We all respect Master Qui-Gon," Ki-Adi-Mundi said. "But we have heard this before from him, many times." He crossed his arms. "The Jedi Order serves society—but it is not a government agency."

Yoda looked up from his contemplation. "Not of the Order does Qui-Gon speak. He means individual Jedi."

Ki-Adi-Mundi nodded deferentially. "It is true—stories of Jedi who are isolated from the Order have always fascinated him. And his master, too, if I recall. They show what good could be done without our cares of state. But members of the Jedi Council are capable of considering the galactic and the local. Indeed, it is our job."

Saesee shrugged. "This is classic Qui-Gon. Nothing new."

"I disagree," Mace said, pausing a moment as he mused. "This was different. *We* are different."

The others stared at him in surprise. Depa looked at him searchingly. "Go on, Master."

Mace looked around. "You all know I protect the traditions of the Order. There is wisdom in them. And yet even I can see it: We rarely act as individuals. Our responsibilities mount—but this body remains the same size. Members of the Council are bound to Coruscant more than ever before." He gestured to the holographic figures. "Just three of us are away—and only Master Billaba is undertaking investigative work."

"And I have spent three hours in hiding attending this meeting," Depa said. "And forgive me—but only now, near the end, have we come to the productive part."

"A part that was never on the agenda," Yaddle said. She looked to the center of the room. "Qui-Gon sees our condition clearly. But I am not sure what to prescribe."

Adi Gallia raised her datapad and spoke with hesitation. "I'm reluctant to bring matters back to business, but the chancellor's office provided us this year's final list of suggestions regarding Jedi assets."

Piell snorted. "Final as a politician's promise."

Mace waved his hand. All the members had a good understanding of the nature of the Senate, and a healthy skepticism. He quite agreed with Piell. But calling attention to that served no purpose at the moment. "Continue, Master Gallia."

"We covered the locations where the Senate expects growth," Adi said, "where its requests for Jedi aid are likely to expand. As usual when that happens, we compile a list of outposts that Jedi no longer frequent, either for research or for other activities, to balance the need."

"Our study has been completed?" Mace asked.

"Just now." She read as information scrolled across her datapad screen. "Janaus. Lesser Tontakoh. Barayfe."

Yarael chortled. "Does *anyone* live in those places?"

Adi paused, and her eyes widened.

"What is it?" Mace asked.

She looked up. "*Kwenn.*"

Stunned silence.

Oppo was the first to break it with a half-whispered "*No.*"

His shock was shared by Council members young and old. "That one's been open for nearly two hundred years," Piell said.

"Almost exactly," Eeth responded. "This would have been the bicentennial of its founding."

"Present, several of us were," Yoda said. "A symbol, at the edge of Hutt space."

Plo nodded. "A grand gesture. It showed there was no place we would not go."

"And it crowned what was yet another great achievement, on the planet itself," Yaddle said. "A monumental work that this Order— including one of us here—had much to do with."

Her eyes turned to Oppo—as did those of several others who knew his role. But the holographic figure appeared lost in thought. "Many were involved," he finally said, before looking away.

Even the more taciturn members seemed affected by the news. "I first visited Kwenn as a Padawan," Saesee recalled.

"We have *all* visited," Ki-Adi-Mundi added. "Some, many times."

Yarael seemed thunderstruck. "I loved the repertory theater there."

Mace couldn't argue with the others' concerns, but he also couldn't help but notice something. "Our experiences there are many. But how recent are any of them?"

"Not very," Adi said after consulting the study. "The surrounding systems haven't had active relic excavations in years, and our missions in the area have declined just as trade has. And leaving facilities in unstable regions unattended for too long puts the materials inside them at risk."

Mace nodded. "That's why we closed Tharben and Keldooine—and just now, Ord Jannak. Those I understood. But has Kwenn changed so?"

Adi tilted her head. "Between pirates and taxes, the Ootmian route is out of favor. Traffic at the Kwenn Space Station is down; I suspect the same for the planet below. Corporations leave, then the people. That's what Master Qui-Gon saw."

Piell raised a holographic finger. "You missed a step. We leave. *Then* the people leave." The eye-patch-wearing Lannik spoke about his recent experiences. "Qui-Gon's not the only one who's witnessed it. I've seen people flocking toward the Core on that route the whole time I've been on Yitabo."

Mace was going to ask Depa for her observations when he noticed his onetime student looking behind her. "Is something wrong, Master Billaba?"

"I may be called away here at any minute," Depa said, speaking quickly. "But I fear the closure of the Kwenn outpost may embolden the criminal element there. It happened when we closed the site at Keldooine—and I am seeing the result now." A beep sounded from her location. "I must go."

"May the Force be with you," Mace said, but her image disappeared before he finished the sentence.

Eeth took a breath. "If we close the Kwenn outpost—"

"That has not been decided," Oppo interjected.

"Of course," Eeth corrected himself. "I simply meant to say that if we agree with the study suggesting closure, it would affect one who is not a Jedi: the caretaker."

Several reacted with recognition, including Yarael. "Ah, the seneschal. I haven't seen him in years." He looked to Adi. "Wait. The site *isn't* unattended!"

"True," she said, "but our report finds he is nearly incapable of continuing his duties. And no suitable alternative is likely to be found. It is a solitary existence."

"Voh has been there most of his life," Yoda said. "Hard news, this would be."

Oppo nodded. "If anyone deserves to learn of it directly, it is Seneschal Voh."

Yaddle looked to the space vacated by Depa's image. "So many of our meetings were once face-to-face." She bowed her head, and a pall fell over her companions.

Part of Mace's mind was still on Depa's abrupt departure, and what that might portend for her mission. But he had been listening, and struggling with all the issues that had been put before them.

His eyes widened, and Yoda saw it. "I know that look, Master Windu. A plan, you have."

"Indeed." Mace clasped his hands together. "Let us visit the outpost on Kwenn."

The others stared at him.

Adi responded by consulting her datapad. "That . . . could be difficult. But let me see who's available. Maybe someone can get away."

"Not someone," Mace said, raising his index finger. "*All of us.*"

His words startled many. "*All?*" Oppo asked.

"We will reconvene there, in person. We will meet the people, learn about their lives, and show our support. Both individually—and collectively, in public commemoration of the anniversary of the outpost's founding."

Saesee looked puzzled. "Celebrate the founding of the outpost—just to close it?"

Eeth pointed out what he'd just been reminded of—that no decision had been made. "But are we being honest? Closure has been recommended by our own researchers."

"People we trust," Ki-Adi-Mundi said. "Sentiment and nostalgia should not lead us to ignore them. Nor is it right to deceive the people of Kwenn."

"There is no deception," Yaddle said. "We truly wish to celebrate— and we might learn something that alters our view."

Yoda nodded. "Change, Kwenn's destiny could."

Adi looked concerned. She spoke tentatively. "The chancellor will have received a copy of our study. It's a courtesy. You know the Senate wants us committing our attentions elsewhere—and they know we always follow our researchers' leads. They might not understand why we're not doing so now."

Saesee snorted. He looked around. "I don't seem to see the chancellor's seat in here."

Yaddle nodded. "The Senate and the Jedi are allies. But we keep our own counsel."

Mace agreed. "Master Tiin is correct—we *can* do more than one thing at a time. Even as we meet the people of Kwenn, we can identify the artifacts we need to retrieve in advance of any closure."

"It *is* a big outpost," Yarael said. "Room for all of us."

Plo glanced about. "I doubt there will be enough provisions for a group our size."

"No problem," Piell said. "I'm nearby, remember? Yitabo is the larder for half the worlds around. I'll stock up here."

Yaddle clasped her hands together in delight. "Answering the call. It feels right."

Her trepidation passing, Adi concurred. "It *would* be good to get away from this thing for a while." She plopped her datapad in her lap.

Mace heard nothing but agreement from the others. "It is decided. We will make our own ways there—arriving as we can. Master Depa will be apprised as well."

"We will see the people of Kwenn—and they will see *us,*" Yaddle said. "And they will hear our message: *The Jedi stand with you.*"

CHAPTER 10

SHIPPING DISTRICT

KELDOOINE

Where is that girl?

Depa Billaba didn't know the answer, but it was far from the only question on her mind. The impromptu Jedi Council meeting had given her a lot more to think about. It was the first time she'd ever attended one while seated in the cargo area of a speeder truck. At least now she was in the front seat, though she was still in the dark, both literally and figuratively.

The Slice extended inward from Hutt space, stretching along the trade routes toward the Core like a dagger pointed at the heart of the galaxy. No sensible Hutt would act directly in the region, but all the local privateers seemed to be auditioning for jobs with them, banking on a future without the Republic and the Jedi to interfere. The Hutts were inevitable, the thinking went. It was just a matter of time before the gangs in the region became their subsidiaries.

But tantalizing intel had been developed by a student Depa had once tutored, the late, lamented Xaran Raal. One pirate band in the region alone had no ties to the Hutts at all, overt or otherwise: the Riftwalkers. The newest and, from all reports, the most intrepid of the gangs, led by someone called Zilastra. Most in the local underworld knew her name, if little beyond that—other than that she played for keeps, while also reportedly playing a blisteringly good game of sabacc.

Depa had committed to remedy that lack of information. There was no question of a single Jedi, even a member of the Jedi Council, bringing a multiplanet operation like the Riftwalkers to justice. But the leader of such a group could not remain a cipher. Maz Kanata, who had ruled from her castle for centuries, had shown that a pirate state was not always the worst neighbor to have. Whether a "Queen Zilastra" would be another Maz was in the vital security interests of the Republic to know.

And Depa's best connection to find out was twelve years old. And running late.

Where is she? Depa checked the vehicle's monitors for the umpteenth time before deciding to stand outside the vehicle. *This must be what it's like to be a parent waiting to pick up a child.*

Then again, the trash-filled backstreet outside the spaceport after midnight was no educational institution, and Kylah was no student—unless larceny was the subject. And the blaster shots Depa now heard signaled that school was still in session.

"*Hotwire!*" Kylah yelled.

Depa saw the girl dashing toward her through the darkness, a big bundle in her hands. Behind her, the alley was lit with red searchlights emanating from the bodies of at least half a dozen droids. They were private patrol units—light on intelligence, heavy on aggression. They shouted in unison, their voices amplified: "Halt, thief!"

Depa had her blaster out in an instant. The droids disregarded her warning shots, charging ahead while a frantic Kylah raced for the speeder truck.

Knowing that using her lightsaber would blow her cover, Depa reached out through the Force and brought a wave of abandoned shipping containers into the droids' paths behind Kylah. The girl didn't see the feat, but did benefit from it, reaching the hovertruck just as Depa opened its passenger door.

Kylah shouted, "*Go, go, go!*"

"Get down!" Depa yelled. Blaster shots peppered the side of the closed door, which Kylah shrank behind. The Jedi herself was already on the move, making for the driver's side. Within seconds, the speeder was in motion.

"Look out!" Kylah yelled as two of the droids blocked their path.

"Hang on," Depa shouted. Gripping the control yoke, she plowed the vehicle right through the attackers. Red lights pinwheeled as the droids went flying noisily end-over-end. Blaster shots continued to strike the vehicle's frame—but from behind, as she gunned it forward.

Doubled over the large cloth sack she was carrying, Kylah cheered. "*Whee!* That was fun!"

"Not the word I'd use." Depa accelerated until she could no longer see the droids behind her. "We're clear," she announced.

The girl looked up—and smiled. "Home. No running lights."

"Got it." Depa took a breath. Squinting in the darkness, she regarded the bundle in Kylah's lap. "Get what you were looking for?"

"You don't need to know."

Depa straightened. "Whatever you say."

As the vehicle drove farther from the spaceport, Kylah relaxed—and said a lot more. "I was perfect."

"You were?"

"Going in is never a problem. I wait until dark and hop over a fence. Then I shimmy up this post with a rotating security cam—"

"You climb a post with a cam on it?"

"Isn't it great?" Kylah practically bounced in the seat, pleased with her cleverness. "Just below the cam I can hop onto this roof nearby—where there's a vent that's about this size." With her hands, she traced a shape that wasn't much larger than the sack she was holding. "I slide down, and I'm inside."

"And you came out with that."

"Yeah, but I can only grab one in a trip, and there's only ten minutes each day when I can get in the stockroom, during the shift change."

"Looks like they noticed this time."

"Only on the way out. As long as I can keep getting in, we're in business."

Unsure what the business was, Depa eyed the sack. "Must be worth a lot."

Kylah laughed. "That, you *really* don't need to know."

"You're the boss."

In the days since Depa's arrival on Keldooine, the Jedi had insinuated herself into the life of the largest megalopolis. Finding a way into its burgeoning underworld hadn't been easy. Competition among various pirate bands had driven all of them into defensive stances, making them paranoid about newcomers. Posing as a speeder thief for hire had gotten her no ins at all. The only thing close to a break had come from her chance rescue of a child on the street being chased by bandits. Realizing Kylah was a courier for the Riftwalkers, Depa had made herself indispensable as driver and bodyguard, to the point where Kylah offered to share her hovel with the woman she called Hotwire.

Depa parked behind it and exited, checking the alley for threats. Before she was done, Kylah bounded out. She worked a lock and let them both inside a darkened flat, abandoned by one of the many residents who had left Keldooine in a hurry.

As she had after her other nightly forays, the girl carried her sack toward a storage room. "Back in a minute."

"Right." Depa locked the door behind them—and quickly slipped next to the opening Kylah had entered.

She listened—and heard Kylah speak. "*Wowee bowee zip zap shoo!*"

Depa tilted her head. It was a child's phrase, nonsense. But then she heard a mechanical voice from the storage room. "Lock phrase initialized." A light click followed.

There was no time to think about it. Depa quickly stepped away from the aperture and made a show of double-checking the front door.

She looked back to see Kylah throwing the empty bag on the floor. "I'm a sweat monster. I'm going to change."

"You have had a long day."

After she saw Kylah disappear into her personal space, Depa crept into the storage room. The girl's apparent prize sat upon a table: a carrying case with an emblem on its side. A chalice inside a star.

Depa began to understand. It was from one of the passenger lines—Regal Voyager. The case had weight, she found on lifting it, but did not make noise when she shook it. It was also locked tight. She wondered about the contents. *Money, gems, weapons? Or something worse?*

Examining the mechanism, she understood what Kylah had just done. "Hope I get this right," she whispered, before speaking to the case itself. "*Wowee bowee zip zap shoo.*"

The lock clicked and the case sprang open. Depa flinched, on her guard—but there was no threat. Indeed, there was nothing inside at all. Struck curious, she lifted the container again. The heft, she realized, came from the interior plating that worked as a countermeasure against scanners.

It took no trained Jedi senses to know Kylah was almost ready to return; the girl made so much noise at home it was hard to believe she was a successful burglar—much less Depa's best hope to connect with her quarry, the Riftwalkers. Depa quickly shut the case and exited the room.

Kylah appeared in brighter, lighter clothes than her work garb. "Let's go eat. They're still serving at Jammah's Place."

"A restaurant? Kind of expensive, isn't it?"

"You're buying. I just paid you, remember?"

Her memory jarred, Depa nodded. "I left the money in the truck."

"Some pro you are." Kylah laughed as she unlocked the door. "Stick with me. You'll learn!"

Depa watched the girl head back into the alley. That had been their dynamic: someone the age of a young Padawan, treating *her* as the student. But the kid's loose talk had already told Depa a lot, and she sensed that it would pay to continue playing her part.

Closing up the flat, the Jedi noticed that a message had come in on her muted comlink while they were driving. It was from Mace—a lengthy hologram, the timecode advised. Depa decided to wait to watch it until she was alone again. Odds were it was just more about the closure of the outpost at Kwenn. That was one debate her mind was made up about. She was already seeing what life was like in a place without Jedi. Homes became hovels—and children became gangsters.

But out here, I can do something about it.

"You coming?" Kylah called out, already in the passenger seat and holding up Depa's credit pouch. "Another minute and I'll start emptying this. If I don't eat it first!"

"On my way." Depa pocketed the comlink and made for the truck.

DEPA HAS NOT responded, Mace thought as he examined his com-link on Coruscant. It wasn't unusual. She was on assignment; it might be a long time before she checked in again. Repeatedly attempting to contact her could compromise her position. It could wait.

The various Council members' departures to Kwenn weren't happening immediately anyway, thanks to the work going on in the Jedi Temple hangar. Plo Koon and Saesee Tiin had moved there from the surface fleet garage, and the latter's mood had not benefited from the change of scenery.

"Whose bright idea was it to upgrade the surface and space fleets at the same time?" Tiin growled.

"As I recall, it was yours," Mace responded.

"Hmph." Saesee shook his head. "I've been trying to forget."

Several of their colleagues had already visited the hangar, arranging passages to Kwenn that matched their schedules. Even with many of their personal vehicles temporarily out of action, ships could always be arranged—but few wanted to take available vessels from Jedi with more urgent needs.

Saesee pointed out to Mace the others, already on the hangar floor, making their plans. "Is there any concern over *all* of us leaving the Jedi Temple?"

"It is hardly unattended," Mace said. "Countless Jedi are present. It is the safest place in the galaxy." But he saw what Saesee was getting at. "You would prefer to remain to finish the fleet upgrades."

"Yes—but I remember Kwenn, as we all do. Master Plo and I will get as much done as possible before we join you." Saesee turned to where Heezo was patiently waiting, holding the upper half of an astromech droid in both arms. Saesee pointed to a fighter. "Over there."

"Of course, Master." The Selonian lugged the equipment past Mace, pausing long enough to smile. "Everyone appears to be leaving. This must be a great adventure!"

Saesee looked back at him and scowled—enough to get his assistant moving again. A Padawan who had failed his trials long ago, Heezo still had talents, and thus had been given various jobs in the Jedi Temple. He was liked by most, but Mace knew Saesee's patience had its limits.

Crossing the deck, Mace saw Yoda and Adi Gallia ending their conversations with a worker. "All settled?" Mace asked.

"Master Yoda and I will be along to Kwenn later," Adi replied.

Yoda nodded. "We have matters to finalize, from our meeting with the chancellor."

Mace raised an eyebrow. "You're not seeing him again before our trip?"

Adi shook her head.

"Perhaps that's best," Mace said. "We're not concealing anything, but where the Council meets is our prerogative."

As Adi departed to return to her backlog, Mace walked slowly, matching his pace to Yoda's. The wizened master gestured to the shuttle he'd reserved. "Will you travel with us?"

"No," Mace said, indicating his starfighter. "Master Depa is already in the area. I will join the Republic task force she is working with."

Yoda stopped and stared up at him. "You have not heard from her."

"Not yet."

A hum from Yoda. "Concerned, you are, for your former Padawan."

"She has not been that for a very long time," Mace said. "She has grown beyond, in the way of all students who succeed. I only wish to ensure that she attends the meeting on Kwenn."

"And if she is in trouble?"

"You would agree that she is equal to any difficulty we can imagine." Mace's brow furrowed. "But if there is something we cannot imagine— something that would detain even a member of the Jedi Council—it might require the presence of two."

Yoda studied him. "You have sensed danger to her."

"I cannot say for certain. But she took on this antipiracy mission after the death of Xaran Raal—and she has stayed on it longer than most Council members would."

"A tragedy." Yoda bowed his head. "A hard thing, the loss of any Jedi is."

"Ambushed on his first mission, by forces unknown."

"She knew young Xaran?"

"He was one of many initiates who learned meditation techniques from her—and once he was knighted, it was she who sent him to investigate the situation on the Ootmian route."

"Ah," Yoda said, looking up. "Conflicted, you feel her intentions are."

"Not at all. She is beyond attachments—as all of us on the Council are. But she felt the mission Xaran undertook was worthy—else she would not have sent him on it. It required closure."

"Good." Yoda began walking again. "I will see you both on Kwenn."

Mace bowed. "The Force travels with you."

"Traveled faster, it once did." Yoda looked to the massive expanse of the hangar floor ahead of him and laughed. "Heh! Much faster, yes!"

PART TWO
GOOD WORKS

CHAPTER 11

JEDI SHUTTLE

APPROACHING KWENN

Memory, Oppo Rancisis thought, was a magical thing, able to vividly bring back the past with a mere thought. In long-lived species, such as his own Thisspiasian kind, memory could reach across centuries in an instant. It was not always cooperative—and often it preserved things people wanted to forget. But at its best, memory was a gift: an asset available to all, regardless of their relationship to the Force.

Traveling through hyperspace toward Kwenn, Oppo guessed that he remembered the planet better than almost anyone alive. Certainly, among the older members of the Council, he had spent the most time on the frontier world. Indeed, it had been his personal project, his fixation for years at a time.

Kwenn's population had grown swiftly in the era before the High Republic; its trove of precious gemstones was so close to the surface, no mining firms could resist the place. They leveled mountains, tore up the plains, and relocated oceans. After digging up everything of value, they left the unwanted remains in colossal piles of tailings, mountains of slag looming around once-busy manufacturing centers. In kind, the planet's climate, broken by abuse, had returned some cruelty of its own, flooding the low areas with a toxic brew.

A far younger Oppo had seen the misery after the miners left, and heard the cries of the people who remained, incapable of reviving their world. Relocating an entire civilization seemed an impossible challenge. But leaving it in place was a death sentence for millions. Something had to be done—and as a member of the Jedi Council, Oppo was in a position to do it.

He led many missions to the planet, importing the brightest minds and the most responsible financiers from the Republic, encouraging them to look for answers. With the Jedi inspiring them, they together achieved what came to be seen as one of the Great Works of the High Republic era: the Grand Renewal.

While colossal machines purified seas and skies, mountains of rubbish were decontaminated, covered, and reshaped into clusters of artificial islands that became known as the Gem Cities of Kwenn. Taller landforms were ringed by populated terraces, while in the shimmering sea between them, lower-elevation keys provided parklands in abundance. Majestic bridges that would have been architectural marvels on any world traversed the many straits.

Near-dead industries were resuscitated with an eye to protecting the ecosystem. Spaceports, sensibly placed, flourished. Even the use of airspeeders was limited, keeping most transports centimeters off the ground and the skies between the islands open. Within a few short years, Kwenn became a choice stopover for travelers in the Slice.

Even at the time, Oppo privately knew that Kwenn was a showpiece, receiving a disproportionate amount of attention when there were other worlds in need elsewhere. But fair or not, he thought it was important to show what was possible not just to the corporate sphere, but to Jedi Knights, as well.

The latter drive led to the creation of the artist's signature, one of the few Jedi outposts with a name: Sanctuary Mount.

It was the title both of the natural feature—a promontory high over Capital Key, tallest of the mound cities—and the elaborate stone structure carved into it, larger than many other outposts. There was nothing ostentatious about it during the day. But just after sunset, every night for two hundred years, a great brazier was lit on the uppermost level. The light the outpost cast was visible from all the surrounding islands. The galaxy might have lost a similar symbol in the Starlight Beacon space station in that era, but Kwenn's Unquenchable Fire served the same role in microcosm, reminding citizens that they had allies against the night.

And for a long time, that was true, as Sanctuary Mount was regularly occupied. Countless Jedi stopped there for its library and inspiring views of a world brought back from the brink. Oppo remembered it well.

"I *have* been away too long," he mused aloud as his small vessel neared the end of its journey. Other duties had kept him elsewhere for what he now realized was decades. He had briefly considered Kwenn as the site for his truncated meditative retreat, deciding against it only because he assumed being on so lovely a world would tempt him away from his solitude. Good memories were powerful, but they sometimes made focusing on the future difficult. Now, though, more new memories could be made.

His long serpentlike form felt the jolt from his ship's emergence from hyperspace. Passing Kwenn's gigantic space station, he looked down on a memory from another time: the *wrong* time. The dark clouds near the urban centers, first seen on his visit centuries ago, had started to return. The arc of the horizon had a slightly orange pallor. Startled, Oppo guided the vessel down for a closer look.

Some of the haze came from smokestacks he didn't remember from his last visit. Some of the keys set aside as nature preserves were afire, with forests smoldering. The world was still alive with activity, but vehicular traffic was snarled—in part, by landspeeders sitting abandoned on bridges and roads. Bringing the shuttle down for a closer look at the vehicles, he saw many of them had been gutted for parts.

This is still Kwenn. But the gems are tarnished.

At least Sanctuary Mount looked unchanged. He set down just before sunset on the landing pad that sat at the bottom end of a long and winding stone ramp that spiraled upward. That feature had been his idea, too; opting against stairs was a Thisspiasian's design prerogative. He'd made his way partway up when light appeared from above. The Unquenchable Fire was lit.

He let out a deep breath. Some things remained the same.

It drove him to ascend faster. At the top, he reached the front door and used the heavy knocker. The loud echo from it gave way to the sound of hurried footsteps on stone. "A moment!"

The door creaked open, revealing a figure a little over a meter tall. An elderly Bimm, he had floppy ears and tiny black eyes—and he was as bald on top as the Jedi was hairy. His elongated jaw dropped open momentarily, only to resolve into a broad smile. "Master Rancisis!"

"Seneschal Voh." Oppo drew all four hands from his cloak and clasped them around the short caretaker's wrists. "It has been too long."

"An age."

"The fault is mine." Bimms lived more than a century, Oppo knew; the seneschal had minded Sanctuary Mount for the greater part of one.

"Come in, come in!" The little figure made way. "I had just lit the brazier."

"I saw it. Ever on duty."

"'Kwenn's Unquenchable Fire' was always a misnomer—it never burns during the day. But of course, you know that."

"Indeed, the name was mine. I liked the rhyme."

Oppo snaked his way through the reception area. The foot of a ramp was to his left; it spiraled up the inside of the structure, going to higher floors and terminating at the beacon level. Scaling it was exhilarating exercise for the Jedi who stayed here; he couldn't imagine Voh handling it daily at his age.

Yet the robe-clad keeper seemed spry. "Please excuse the dust— I haven't had visitors in a long while."

Oppo had noticed. There was plenty of a Thisspiasian's body in contact with the floor at any given moment. But despite a bit of grit, Voh seemed to have kept the place in good order.

That was especially true of the library. More than a hundred cubbyholes had been worked into the colossal stone pillars holding up the high ceiling of the central room. An outpost might normally have just a few texts available, given the fact that Jedi rarely stayed there for long. But this collection came not from Coruscant, but from the visitors. Travelers over the centuries brought with them texts and personal histories stored in a variety of media, from common datapads and datacards to the occasional scroll or book; often, they left them for others. If visitors wanted to find what Avar Kriss had been reading during her travels in nearby Hutt space, there was a nook where they could find out.

It was not Oppo's idea, but he had treasured watching it develop over the years. Voh clearly had, too, adding to the collection while respecting the building's history. Oppo spotted a piece of that now. "Is that what I think it is?"

"Oh, yes," Voh said, walking over to the wheeled book cart. "A handcraft made by the oldest resident on Kwenn prior to the Grand Renewal, presented at the outpost's founding." He pushed it back and forth. "It still works!"

"And you still use it, I see."

"I once tried a repulsorlift cart for carrying to the higher levels, but they're not designed for spiral ramps. It kept scuffing the walls. Sometimes the old ways are better."

"Indeed." Oppo looked around with admiration. "I could spend days in this library, Seneschal. A wonderful collection."

"It may seem smaller than you remember," Voh said with some trepidation. "I have consolidated somewhat—I no longer have the reach I once had. And there are not many visitors, so there are few new materials since you were last here." He looked Oppo over. "Did you bring anything, perchance?"

"In fact, I have come with news."

Voh took a breath and straightened—only for his shoulders to droop as the life went out of him. "I suppose I knew this day would come."

"How so?"

"It's been clear to me for some time that the outpost would be shuttered." Voh looked around and shook his head. "Keldooine and Kwenn—these were the keystone worlds in this region. But Keldooine has already fallen to chaos, and the businesses that remain here refuse to maintain

Kwenn's network of atmospheric cleansing towers even as their industrial practices tax their performance. No one cares to . . ." He trailed off, looking away in shame. "We have squandered the promise you brought forth on this planet."

"You have done nothing of the sort, Seneschal—and you have mistaken my meaning." He looked up. "Before any such decision is made, the Council has elected to stage a celebration on Kwenn, commemorating the Grand Renewal."

Voh was startled. "You . . . are here to organize this? All by yourself?"

"You again mistake me, my old friend. I, too, am past the days of slithering around, doing everything myself." Oppo chuckled. "The entire Council is coming."

The caretaker's eyes went wide. "*All?*"

"Just so. We will all work together, to raise Kwenn up."

Voh put his hands to his forehead and began to pace. "This is outstanding, of course. But if you had contacted me, I could have planned for your arrival." He looked to another doorway. "The food stores must be replenished!"

"Master Piell is handling that."

"Master—?" Voh gathered it all in for a moment, before breaking into a smile. "It will be wonderful to see everyone again. And to have them here." He stood a little taller. "How may I be of service?"

Voh's reaction gratified Oppo. *Help one person,* Qui-Gon had said. This was clearly not what he'd had in mind, but it felt good to bring life to old friends. Organic—and architectural.

"We have much to prepare," he said, snaking between towers riddled with the knowledge of the ages. "Let us begin."

CHAPTER 12

SHIPPING DISTRICT

KELDOOINE

Kylah splashed through the midnight rain, yet another stolen Regal Voyager case in hand. "Let's go!"

Depa obliged by accelerating. "I didn't hear any shots."

"They couldn't see me. Our plan worked!"

Since the incident after the Jedi Council meeting, the sentry droids inside the Regal Voyager hub facility on Keldooine had been aware of Kylah's nightly invasions. Finding that no amount of persuasion could keep the girl from facing danger, Depa had shifted toward eliminating threats instead, employing a new tactic each time. This one involved devising and placing smoke bombs of the sort Master Windu had once employed during a mission on Dallenor. Kylah had made it through the haze without a shot fired at her. The two had gone from strangers to an effective team in less than a week.

While no stranger to undercover work, Depa still felt odd participating in the thefts. She had even secretly paid for the speeder truck she claimed to have heisted. Kylah, meanwhile, had no such compunctions. Her burglaries were always for the same thing: the same SecuriCase brand valises, all empty. No longer hiding them from Depa, Kylah said there were hundreds of the cases at the hub; the Keldooine facility disinfected, serviced, and supplied them to all of Regal Voyager's routes. The girl confessed she'd been stealing them for the Riftwalkers for months. The firm had finally recognized the break-ins, as the droids demonstrated, but it appeared to have no idea what exactly was being taken.

After all, who would steal empty cases?

The girl wrung raindrops from her hair. "Did you put the other cases from my storage room in back?"

"All four." Depa adjusted her goggles. "I take it we're not going back there tonight?"

"Nope. Head west." Kylah pointed to a location on the monitor.

Depa recognized it as being near the suspected pirate den—and chanced a direct question. "Why do the Riftwalkers want these things?"

"I don't ask. I do what Zil says."

A name. *Now we're getting somewhere.* "Think they're using them for smuggling?"

"The Riftwalkers don't smuggle. They *hit* smugglers—*pow!*" Kylah punched her hand with her fist. "Who cares what they want them for?"

I do, Depa thought as she drove. There was something in this—a possibility for mischief, or actual menace. She didn't know which yet, but it meant something that it was at the gang leader's behest. Depa had won Kylah's trust, and was finally getting closer to the center of operations.

Yet her thoughts were clouded. Instead of anticipation, Depa found herself worrying more about what moving up in a criminal organization meant for someone so young. Kylah loved to playact the brash criminal, but she was no Padawan, trained for danger. Depa was certain there was a child in there somewhere.

The idea was to use Kylah to get into the gang. Now all I think of are ways to get her out!

Rain continued to pour as she drove toward a crossroads. "Just up here?"

Kylah checked the map. "Yeah, it's—"

"*Hold on!*" Depa sensed it before she saw it: a black speeder van, careening through the downpour toward them from the alley on the right.

She banked the truck sharply, protecting her passenger from a potential impact—only to wind up in the path of an identical machine racing toward them from the other side.

The blow was a glancing one, but still enough to send the truck spiraling on its repulsorlift cushion. Depa grabbed hold of a screaming Kylah with one hand even as she fought to regain control with the other. A row of parked vehicles ended that attempt, the resulting collision launching the truck into the air. There was nothing for Depa to do as it rolled but hang on to Kylah.

When the vehicle came to rest upside down, the Jedi saw nothing. The problem was her goggles, knocked askew. Depa released Kylah and adjusted them—only for the frantic girl to roll over and scramble out the open window.

"Kylah, no!" This was no accident, she knew. The Jedi hurriedly righted herself and followed.

On her hands and knees in the puddle outside, Depa looked both ways. Another scream had her on her feet and rounding the wreck. There, in the rain, a group of several shadowy figures stood before the black speeder van that had just missed her earlier. The tallest attacker had captured Kylah, holding her by her jacket collar. The girl squealed. "*Hotwire! Help!*"

Depa felt for her lightsaber just inside her vest. She could have it out in a second, but the blasters pointed at the girl advised extreme caution. A series of lightning flashes overhead illuminated the scene, showing her that Kylah was bruised from the crash, with a cut on her forehead. A Rodian with a metal spike atop his head, halfway between his antennae, aimed his blaster at Depa and snarled, "Don't move."

"I won't." She showed that her hands were empty. "Don't hurt the girl."

"You should be worried about *you.*"

Noticing that the spike theme was repeated with the Rodian's companions, Depa spoke calmly as thunder rolled. "The Staved Skulls, I presume." She touched the top of her head. "Are those decorative? They look like they hurt."

"Shut up!"

Keep them talking. "What do you want?"

"What you're carrying. We know who the brat works for—and we've seen her sneaking into the spaceport." The Rodian directed two of his companions to the wreck of the truck. "Whatever she's stealing's got to be worth plenty."

"Would you believe me if I said you were wrong?"

"No."

Given the misshapen frame of the vehicle, Depa didn't think the cargo doors would be easy to open. They weren't, prompting the Rodian to send another of his number over. The Jedi's mouth crinkled. It was an opening. Depa just needed to make sure that she didn't get—

Another blinding lightning strike was accompanied by a shout from above and behind her. "*Kid, duck!*"

Depa didn't recognize the voice, but Kylah clearly did. The girl squirmed out of her jacket, leaving the collar in the hands of a startled Skull. It was the last surprise of his life, as twin blaster shots sizzled over the girl's head and struck the would-be captor in his face.

The Jedi dived toward the girl, unable to tell thunder from the sounds of laserfire as shots peppered the street. Tucking Kylah beneath her, Depa grabbed the fallen Skull's blaster from the ground and fired at the nearest target. Another spike-head went down, even as his companions confronted attackers on all sides. Depa stood—only to have the Rodian try to grab for her. Depa delivered a roundhouse kick that stopped his attempt—and another that put him on the street, his blaster flung away. Kylah scurried for cover behind the black van.

The girl safe behind her, the Jedi turned to see Kylah's initial savior: a Nautolan woman atop the smashed truck, firing blasters with both hands. With precision, she took down every Staved Skull that her companions hadn't dealt with. The job done, she stood, lightning flashing behind her as she did.

"Zil!" Kylah cried out, smiling.

The rescuer's warriors on the ground turned toward Depa and Kylah, weapons drawn. The Jedi didn't drop her blaster. "Wait. I'm with Kylah!"

A colossal Feeorin snarled in response. "Move away, kid!"

"You heard her, Luggy!" Kylah moved in front of Depa. "She's with me!"

The Feeorin glared at Depa—and then glanced back at the Nautolan woman, who'd just hopped down off the truck. "What do we do here, Zil?"

"Stand down, Burlug." The woman sauntered up without a care in the world—and glanced at the blaster in Depa's hand. "You have plans for that?"

The Jedi studied her—and dropped the weapon on the ground. "They called you *Zil*. You're Zilastra. *The* Zilastra?"

"As opposed to *The* Lobber?"

"The what?"

"Forget it. Relic of an encounter with a fool." One of the Staved Skulls stirred, and Zilastra fired a killing shot into his back. "Seems to be my week for them," she said, holstering her weapons.

Merciless. Depa made a mental note of that and checked on Kylah. "Are you all right?"

The kid touched her forehead. "Just shaken up."

Zilastra strolled around them. "You must be the bodyguard. Hotwire, is it?"

Depa shrugged. "That's what she calls me."

"Anybody call you anything else?"

"Hotwire is fine."

Zilastra turned her attention to Kylah. "You're late, Stowaway."

"It's not my fault." Kylah's voice went up an octave. "The mark's on to us."

"What are you talking about?" Zilastra asked.

"I nearly got pinched earlier this week when you asked me to check out the story about the Jedi aboard the *Regal Zephyr*."

The pirate frowned. "You didn't tell me that."

Kylah stammered. "Sorry," she finally said. "They spotted me leaving the data center."

Depa nodded. "They've chased her out every night this week."

"And she helped me get away each time," Kylah said, indicating Depa. The girl's head drooped in guilt. "But I think tonight might have been the end. They saw me leaving the cage the cases are stored in."

Zilastra's eyes widened. "Tell me you got what I asked for!"

"No problem!" Kylah pointed to the smashed hover truck. "Four in the back, one up front." She glanced at the bodies lying in the rain—and quickly looked away. "The Staved Skulls were on to us, too."

"That, I knew." Zilastra strutted over to the wreck. "There's always a leak somewhere. I figured they'd try something." She gestured to her associates. "Get my cases."

"On it," Burlug declared. He and his companions went to work on the battered rear door of the vehicle.

The pirate boss turned back to Depa. "Good driving—and fighting."

"Just doing my job."

"If the runt was paying you, that's that. Don't expect a reward."

"I was hoping to join up," Depa said. "Lot of options on Keldooine. But Kylah says you're the best."

Zilastra laughed. "And you're taking the word of a kid?"

"Is she wrong?"

"I don't need any more drivers—or speeder thieves, or whatever you do."

"You've seen me fight."

"I've seen a lot of people fight. But I've got no shortage of personnel. I'm literally fishing people out of tanks." Zilastra looked Depa over. "You don't seem hungry. Come back when you've starved some."

Depa inhaled. Hands slickened with rain meant Zilastra's goons were having trouble with the battered doors, just as the Staved Skulls had. There was time to make a play—but she'd also need to hide her lightsaber and comlink.

An idea occurred to her. "Let me get in there. Least I can do is finish the delivery."

Zilastra shrugged. "Go for it."

She passed the pirate leader and rounded the vehicle to the open passenger window of the upside-down cab. As Depa knelt, Kylah called to her. "Hey, I can do that!"

"You're hurt. Stay put." The Jedi crawled in.

After a minute of fumbling in the dark, she had found what she needed to find—and done what she needed to do. She used the Force to push against one of the doors to the cargo section from the inside. The instant the door started to give way, she kicked it, causing it to fly open.

The abrupt act caught Burlug in the side of his head, knocking him to the street.

Depa glanced down at him. "Sorry," she said, not sounding like she meant it. She faced Zilastra, holding a case in one hand. She'd lined four others up, two on either side of her. "Your delivery," Depa said.

"Now we're talking!" Zilastra said.

Kylah stepped past her. "Is that the one I stole tonight?"

Depa handed her the case. "No dents. I'm impressed."

The girl handed it to Zilastra. "This one should be open," Kylah said. "I never initialized it."

Zilastra fumbled with the latch—and frowned. "Something's wrong. It's locked."

Startled, Kylah took it back—and fiddled with it in vain. The case was impenetrable.

"Could you have gotten one that was already activated?"

The kid shook her head. "None of the others were. It doesn't make sense." Her eyes went to the other four cases, now sitting outside the wreck. "These will open, I know."

"They'd better."

Zilastra and Depa watched in silence as Kylah spoke her nonsense code phrase. Nothing happened. She repeated it again and again. Her voice pitched high. "Someone's changed the codes!"

"Oh," Depa said, wandering to the side. "That would be me."

"What?" Zilastra blurted.

Kylah looked at her, befuddled. "When?"

"Just now in the truck," the Jedi said. "I knew your code, so I reinitialized them."

"You did *what*? Why?"

"You were stealing these for your boss, here. But the delivery isn't done until I give the word. *Or words.*"

"Your *employee* is a real comedian," Zilastra said, drawing her blasters. "I don't like jokers." She gestured with one of the weapons toward the cases. "They're no good to me this way. Speak the code. Now."

"I don't think I will. I've taken a good look at these cases. Without the code phrase, you're not getting them open without a thermal detonator."

Zilastra glared. "I'll just send the stowaway back to get more. Right, kid?"

Kylah, still looking betrayed, sank. "I don't think I can. The droids saw where I was tonight. I think those are all I'm gonna be able to get."

Growing more enraged, the pirate called to one of her associates. "Tokchi, can we get into them any other way?"

An Ithorian wearing a shiny golden translator collar shook his enormous head. "Not without breaking the mechanisms."

"Consider it a signing bonus in reverse," Depa said, nonchalant. "Bring me in and I'll open one a day."

Zilastra spat into a puddle. "Who says I won't shoot you on Day Five?"

"Maybe you will. But I'll have earned my place by then." Depa picked up the first case, the one from that night. "I even think I'll just hang on to this one until last."

The Nautolan stared at Depa, smoldering—only to start laughing. She smiled at her lieutenant. "You believe this one, Luggy?"

"No." Massaging his jaw, he glared at Depa. "No, I do not."

Zilastra lowered her weapons. "Okay, I'm dealing you in. A day at a time." She gestured to her fallen rivals. "But we're frisking you first. In case you are a plant."

"Be my guest." Depa looked to Kylah and smiled. "Looks like you're a recruiter now."

Kylah watched in confusion as Burlug frisked Depa. He wasn't gentle about it, but the Jedi didn't mind at all, knowing where her lightsaber and comlink were: right by her side, locked inside a case only she could open. She'd be able to reach her weapon in a jam, and she expected the case's shielding would protect it from scans.

Of course, it also meant the Council wouldn't be able to reach her. She hoped they would understand. Some things were more important than meetings.

CHAPTER 13

ESSAFA KEY

KWENN

"Where do I go if I want to get socked in the jaw?"

The adviser at the tourist information station outside the speeder bus stop on Essafa Key squinted at Even Piell. "Can you repeat that?"

On Kwenn or elsewhere, Piell was accustomed to people not understanding his thick accent. "Socked in the jaw," he repeated. "Belted. Beaten. Smacked around."

"That's what I thought you said." The adviser stared down at the diminutive newcomer with obvious distaste. "I'm sure I can't help you."

"You live here, don't you?"

"I'd rather not discuss where I—"

"I mean on this island. The mound cities of Kwenn—they're not all alike, are they?" Piell grinned. "Gimme the bad part of this one."

The adviser's face lost all emotion. "I hate this job," he finally said, before turning and walking away.

Piell leaned over the counter and shouted after him. "Hey, now, thanks for your help!" He pivoted and headed out into the crowded street.

The Jedi Master didn't know why he had such trouble with strangers. He wasn't *that* frightening to behold; he was built like a hovertank, but one that only stood a little over a meter tall. And among his kind, his long pink ears were considered fetching—even if the way they stuck out sometimes made automatic doors a hazard.

Maybe it was because the scar over his bad eye always made him look like he was scowling, just as his voice always sounded like he was growling. Whatever the reason, it was his lot in life. He loved people, but they seldom knew what to make of him.

Like most Jedi, Piell had left the planet of his birth at an early age. Younglings with Force potential were brought to the attention of the Order, which offered to raise them; they infrequently returned home. But even amid the mix of species at the Jedi Temple, Piell had spoken differently than his companions—blunter, more colloquial. And when he finally did return to visit the Lannik homeworld, it changed his consciousness. The place was in a constant state of political unrest; his parents probably thought they had done well in sending him away. Yet he saw himself in the hard faces of those he had lived apart from. It only took a minor leap to understand that all beings were his kin.

For that reason, he felt he was probably the member of the Jedi Council closest to Qui-Gon in terms of his attention to the living Force. That was no easy call, however. The views on the current Council were nuanced; on a spectrum. Even those focused on galactic concerns still cared about individuals. They just arrived at those feelings from a different direction. It was good that was the case, Piell thought. Jedi Councils historically tended not to have factions, and those that did weren't very effective.

The Council's response to Qui-Gon's challenge had pleased Piell. True, going to Kwenn gave him an excuse to wrap up the mind-numbing deliberations on Yitabo; he'd have happily left to celebrate the anniversary of a stewed fruit pit. But the chance to help the general public was nectar to him. He wanted to start where the suffering was most obvious. With no help from the guide, he made his way down the hill, following a lesson he'd learned years before during his Padawan days.

Trouble finds its own level—usually near the waterfront.

He was halfway there when he heard a commotion down a side street. A patrol officer was just standing there, doing nothing about it. Piell called out. "Hey!"

"What?"

"Is this where you keep the violence?"

The burly guard stared down at him. "What are you on about?"

"I'm in from offworld, and I've got a few days before my meeting," Piell said. "I wanna see where the trouble is."

"You've come to the right place." The sentry gestured with his baton. "Essafa Key is the island that houses several of the local schools."

"Why is *that* trouble?"

"Because the kids aren't in them. They've been running wild, harassing people and businesses."

"You should get a truant officer."

"We had one. He just quit." The officer removed the badge from his uniform and handed it to Piell. "I'm going to try something more relaxing, like hauling explosives."

Piell heard glass breaking far away. He craned his neck to see the source of the noise—and pinned the badge on his tunic. "I'll take it from here."

He began marching toward the plaza. The now-former officer called out after him, "Hey, I wouldn't go over there. With those ears and that topknot, they'll eat you alive."

"Keep the baton," Piell called back. "Souvenir."

Kids ran back and forth across the plaza, a busy quadrangle set between rows of marble buildings. A massive plinth sat in the middle of the area, home to a group of statues that was no longer there. The dates engraved into the buildings' cornerstones marked them as having been erected in the first wave of improvements during the Grand Renewal. But that wasn't all that had been carved into—or painted over—the walls of the structures.

Piell chuckled as he read the graffiti. "Somebody's got some opinions."

He looked over his shoulder and saw the approach of a dozen or more raggedly dressed youths of various species. They ranged in age, but the shortest was as tall as he was.

No one seemed to be in charge, but a gangly Twi'lek male stepped to the fore. "Admiring my handiwork?"

"This yours?"

"So what if it is?"

Piell pointed to the wall. "You misspelled *poodoo*."

"You a professor?"

"Not of poodoo." Piell looked again at the graffiti. "Although I see you were actually referring to a teacher here where you used it."

"*Former* teacher," another kid said. "He went out the window."

"Bottom floor, I hope."

"He wound up there, yeah."

The others laughed. Piell decided to, as well. "This a holiday or something?"

"*Is it a holiday*," the Twi'lek mimicked, distorting his voice so he sounded ridiculous. "Is it a holiday for you? Because you're clearly in the wrong place."

"I am?" Startled, Piell began looking around. "Kwenn. Essafa Key." He made a comical show of it, prompting laughter. "No, I'm in the right place."

"Hadaro says you're not." The Twi'lek advanced, sticking out his chest. "I'm Hadaro!"

"Guess having your name on half the walls helps you remember that," Piell said. "School's good for something."

"Funny guy." Four of Hadaro's companions flanked him, two on either side.

The Jedi reacted mildly. "Oh, I see. You think 'cause you're taller than me, you can push me around."

"Nobody's pushing you," Hadaro said. "Now, we might *carry* you somewhere!"

The kids swarmed, each grabbing for a piece of Piell—a limb, or his clothing. Nothing but his pride endangered, Piell decided to let them have their fun. A parade carried him around a corner into the space between buildings.

"To the trash compactor!" someone yelled.

Jostled atop their hands, the Jedi responded, "Thanks, but I'd rather not."

"Don't worry," another kid said. "It doesn't run. They're all over-stuffed."

"Then there's no room for me." Face up atop the hands of those bearing him, he spotted a pipe spanning the space between buildings. Having a good idea what it was, he reached out through the Force and snapped it in half at its seam. White foam exploded from it, part of the linked fire suppression system that protected the academy here. He closed his eyes and mouth quickly as the cascade came down, causing wild squeals from the kids.

His bearers headed in every direction trying to escape, and their hold on him faltered. He tumbled until he reached the foam-sodden pavement—whereupon the fun really began. Clearing the spray from his eyes, Piell burst forth from the scrum like a greased animal. Would-be pursuers slipped and fell as he bolted back toward the plaza.

By the time Piell approached the two-meter-high plinth at the center of the quad, he realized that not a single adult had been attracted by the chaos. No matter: Half the children in the galaxy seemed to be here. When a group tried to block him, he used his Jedi skills to bound over them. He did a double somersault before landing on the plinth.

Safe for the moment, the foam-soaked Jedi turned, standing in the place where statues once had been. The hullabaloo had given way to oohs and aahs over his feat. The shock increased when he removed his cloak to wring it out, revealing the weapon tethered to his uniform.

"That's a lightsaber!" Similarly drenched, Hadaro looked to Piell in awe. "How'd *you* get it?"

"I went to school."

Hadaro sneered. "You're no Jedi!"

"Yah, you're right," Piell said, folding his cloak. "I'm just really good at pretending."

The crowd buzzed. "The Jedi only go to the outpost," one child said. "Mom says none of them have come down from there in years."

"I heard they're all dead," said another.

"Here's a lesson," the Jedi said. "Believe your eyes." He smiled. "Some good fun you have here."

A chime sounded from the tower across the quad, and Piell looked to the sky. "Noon. Why don't you go inside and take a lunch break?"

Hadaro frowned. "What lunch?"

"Don't they feed you here?"

"Where have *you* been? Rendili Hyperworks stopped sponsoring the cafeteria a month ago."

Piell frowned. "A company was subsidizing this?"

"Until they weren't. The Mercantile Guild runs the school—but they cut the funding when people started moving away."

So they're not just wild. They're hungry. He found his comlink and spoke into it. "Yah, I need a pickup."

Hadaro rolled his eyes. "What are you doing, calling for help?"

"I don't need help. I thought we'd established that." He focused on Hadaro. "What about your classes?"

"What about them? Half don't even meet anymore. I told you—"

"The Mercantile Guild. Got it." It was that way on many planets; early education existed mostly for the children of workers, and relied upon corporate largesse. But those commitments were always subject to the market.

Piell strolled around the plinth, thinking—while the kids buzzed among themselves, deciding what to do. They were still doing so when sound overhead announced the arrival of a small spaceship.

The *Limulus*-class courier was a squat half-moon of a vehicle, capable of carrying cargo. The droid in its copilot's seat could perform simple jobs like flying a short distance. Piell spoke a few more commands into the comlink, prompting the ship to settle down next to him. It was just able to fit on the plinth.

More cries of amazement came from the kids marveling at the Jedi ship. But not Hadaro. "So that's it? You're gonna leave?"

"Wrong again. You really *do* need to go to school." Piell rounded the vehicle and unlatched the cargo hold. He removed a container and pitched it into the crowd. "Catch."

He was unloading more when Hadaro opened the first one. "It's food!"

"Not just any food," Piell said, passing down another container. "Catered meals, from Yitabo. This here's the grub I was bringing to Sanctuary Mount for the Jedi to eat."

"You eat a lot."

"It ain't all for me. Actually, none of it's for me. It's yours." He calculated that at a minimum, he had enough for the kids present for the day. "It sounds like they don't teach you much about the Jedi—when you go to class, that is. That right?"

Holding the container while smaller kids grabbed for its contents, Hadaro nodded. "We don't hear anything."

"Tell you what. Once everyone's got something to eat, I'll answer any questions anyone has about the Jedi. Anyone interested?"

Overlapping shouts of approval drowned one another out.

"Fine." Piell gestured at the buildings and smiled. "If anybody asks, we're having class outside."

CHAPTER 14

ABOARD *ASSURANCE*

THE SLICE

"Hard about!" the captain ordered.

The corvette *Assurance* lurched. The asteroids filling the forward bridge display port moved out of view, to be replaced by a slightly clearer area. There, at its center, sat a single vessel several kilometers distant.

Mace saw the captain clench his fist. "Target those thrusters," the man said. "Disabling fire!"

Having just arrived on the cramped bridge, Mace knew it was already too late. With audible reluctance, *Assurance*'s young weapons officer announced the obvious. "Target has just gone to hyperspace, Captain."

Pell Baylo stared. "I gathered that, Lieutenant. But this time it's not your fault." He turned and pointed at Mace. "*It's the Jedi's fault.*"

Unflinching, Mace looked over at the tracking station. "Captain, there's a chance you can still find—"

"Forget it. We're at the edge of our operational area anyway." Disgusted, Baylo stormed over to look at a display.

The engagement had been short. *Assurance* had been in the asteroid belt when Mace's starfighter arrived; it exited it to accept his arrival. His fighter had barely connected to the docking ring of the Corellian Engineering CR56 corvette when the target ship had raced back into the belt. But the battle was not to be.

Mace spoke calmly. "Who were they?"

"Privateer," Baylo said without looking up. "We've been chasing her all day. Aligned with an outfit called the Vile. After we scored some hits, she crept into this mess to hide." He turned away from the display and glared at Mace. "We'd have taken them down, but we had to hightail it out of the belt to pick *someone* up."

Mace felt the ice in his words. "If you had apprised me when I called, I could have waited—or assisted."

"There wasn't time for a conversation. We got back after 'em, but I guess it was enough time for them to repair."

"I never intended to interrupt your operations."

Baylo sneered. "You're not even the first member of the Jedi Council to interrupt my operations this *month*." He looked again at the rocks ahead of the vessel and swore. "Nellis, get us out of here."

His helm operator responded, "Yes, Captain."

If there were a database entry for a model military officer, Mace imagined that Pell Baylo would have been the illustration. A human in his late fifties, he was sharply attired in the slate-gray garb of the Perlemian Commercial Defense Force, a defunct body that had existed just long enough to generate some really fine uniforms. Black gloves and a hat with insignia Mace had never seen completed the ensemble. The others aboard the ship were similarly—but not identically—dressed. It was as if everyone who joined up had to supply their own gear.

Then again, Mace thought, that might not be far off the mark. *Assurance* itself was in a class of its own. That wasn't a statement about its quality, but rather one about its uniqueness. In a Republic with no organized military, standardization wasn't to be expected—and the most unusual thing, by far, was the ship's crew complement. For every lifer like Baylo, Mace had seen two officers who were younger—usually, much younger. The bridge crew on duty at the moment included several uniformed teenagers—as well as trainees who seemed even younger.

The youngest person Mace had encountered, a sandy-haired human of eleven at most, stepped onto the bridge, breathless. In a high voice, he called out, "Captain, Master Windu has—" He saw the captain's expression and stopped speaking.

"Go ahead," Baylo growled. "You were going to tell me that Master Windu had arrived, and I was going to say that someone who's never been on this ship before beat you to the bridge by three minutes."

Mace put up his hand. "I hurried here when you went into action."

"Don't make excuses for him, Master. This ship may be an antique, but its internal communications system works fine." He pointed a thumb at the downcast cadet. "If there's a proper navy someday, young Veers here will be in charge of it, mark my words. I have so many people who can tell you what's already happened that I could start a holofeed." He gave the kid a glance. "Comm station. Shadow your mentor for an additional shift, starting now."

Mace watched as the boy hurried over and relieved another trainee.

Recognizing the sort of person he was dealing with, Mace took the opportunity to get to the point. "You mentioned another member of the Council. Is Master Billaba aboard?"

"Still out on her mission," Baylo said. "We rendezvoused with a civilian shuttle ten days ago—she was going to take that to Keldooine."

Mace nodded. That made sense, if she was traveling undercover. "When is she due back?"

"A couple of days."

Mace was relieved to realize she'd be done in time for the commemoration on Kwenn. "You've been acting in a support role for her?"

"Transport, and on call if she needs anything. Seems to me there are cheaper taxi services, but I don't make the decisions."

Baylo began walking aft, and Mace joined him. Three times, the captain stopped to castigate a bridge officer for some detail or other. Somehow an action that had lasted mere minutes had generated a lot for him to complain about.

They stepped off the bridge into the corridor. "Many young people in your crew," Mace said as they walked. "And this vessel sees combat?"

"When we're not called away. And I've seen the kids you Jedi drag around."

Mace raised an eyebrow. "The cases are not similar."

"I need crew—but more than that, I need resources. And that means courting the favor of aristocrats who want to build political résumés for their kids—or just plain get rid of them. If I have to nursemaid the no-good spawn of families willing to put up something to keep *Assurance* flying, I will."

Mace understood. "You do work them hard."

"I'm going to keep things to naval standards if it kills me."

The comment puzzled Mace. "There is no Republic navy."

"Don't I know it. But those of us in service—any service—act as if there is. And *Assurance* is part."

"I notice you don't call it *the Assurance.*"

"The parlance is part of the training. You don't want the crew thinking their ship's an inanimate object. They've got to get personal. Do people call you *the* Mace Windu?"

"Point taken."

Baylo led Mace into his office. It was sparsely furnished, but the walls were festooned with plaques recording different actions the captain had been a part of—awarded by just as many commands, it seemed.

"I've walked the decks of ships since I was the same age as that kid back there," the captain said. "Most of that time, on this one." Pouring himself a beverage, Baylo gestured to the section of wall Mace was looking at. "Those are all the outfits *Assurance* has been a part of."

Mace deferred the offered cup. The plaques told a fascinating story. "I assumed your ship was part of the Judicial Forces' Diplomatic Fleet."

"It has been—for exactly three weeks. *This* time."

"This time?"

"Oh, *Assurance* gets around, Master. This ship has operated as part of the Diplomatic Fleet, as part of nine different planetary defense forces, and as commercial security for eight different corporations. And it'll go back to one of them as soon as this round of funding runs out."

"You sound sure of that."

"Already booked," Baylo said, plopping himself in his office chair. "In two weeks we'll be running escort on the Hydian Way for Chokoll Indemnity."

"The insurance company?"

"*Assurance* is very big with underwriters. They like the name."

No Jedi could assist the Republic against piracy and not know the piecemeal nature of the forces that protected the interstellar space lanes, but Mace had to admit he was surprised. "These operational periods— they've grown shorter in this region?"

"You'd better believe it. When someone yanks the Senate's leash, everything gets pulled with it." He took a drink. "The Jedi, too. But look who I'm telling."

Mace didn't like the implication, but he wanted to stay positive. "I suppose it falls to us to make the best of the opportunities for cooperation we get."

Baylo snorted. "I don't miss them. Believe me."

"Captain, you don't care for working with Jedi, do you?"

"What would make you say that, Master Jedi?" Baylo flashed a look that was not meant to endear. "You can't have discipline with passengers prancing around the bridge."

"We are not mere passengers."

"But you're not mere observers, either." Baylo put down his cup and stood. "You've seen my crew—and you know where many of them come from. Not one of them has ever known any discipline. So I spend every waking moment trying to impress on this lot the importance of respecting the chain of command. And then someone *not in uniform* strolls onto the bridge and undercuts my orders!"

"You would have Jedi dress as members of your crew?"

"I'd have you find your own damn ships. You Jedi just go blithely by, expecting everyone to drop everything—and then you're gone, and we're left to repair the damage."

They eyed each other for a long moment. Mace helped lead one of the most important organizations in the galaxy—and yet he wasn't sure how to handle Pell Baylo. It was clear the captain was an exceptional representative of his trade. But it was a trade that had been constrained by politics to an even greater extent than the Jedi Order had been.

He was glad that when they stepped back out of the office, the captain grew more conciliatory.

"I guess it's a necessity," Baylo said. "It was probably Master Billaba's mission that caused us to get this contract. Fighting pirates only matters to the Republic when someone gets interested enough to pay for it—but I can still get something done here, even when she's gone." He stopped and stared at Mace. "Unless you have something else for us to do."

"I am simply here to meet Master Billaba. Once she joins us, we will take our leave."

"That, I like the sound of." They continued onto the bridge.

Mace looked at the space outside—and suddenly stopped. He moved toward a tactical display terminal and looked over the shoulder of the officer running it.

"What now?" Baylo asked.

Mace studied the board, which displayed star systems and suspected pirate contacts. He pointed. "That region. Something's not right."

Baylo pushed his way in and studied the scope. "I'll be—" Baylo shook his head. "Looks like a frigate—out of Keldooine, on that vector."

Mace stared at the contact that had been detected. It was larger than they were. "Is there any official traffic that size?"

"Not at all." Baylo snapped his fingers. "Could be the *Randomizer*— that's the Riftwalkers' flagship!" He rubbed his gloved hands together. "I've wanted a shot at these guys."

"They're much larger."

"Chances like this don't come along often. And we've already lost one today." The captain stood and turned toward the helm. "Nellis, get after them. *Assurance*, clear for action."

Mace stood off to the side and clasped his hands together. He wasn't going to impose his help on Baylo, but he certainly wasn't going to shy away from a situation where he might be of assistance.

But the corvette had not moved when the nervous boy from before called for the captain.

"Now what?"

"Incoming communication." The kid's eyes bulged as he looked at the display.

"Spit it out, Veers."

"Sen-senator Palpatine and the chancellor, for the Jedi Master."

The captain threw up his hands. "Wonderful."

Mace was confused. Valorum's office hadn't been informed of their plans to visit Kwenn. He'd expected the chancellor would hear eventually; it was no secret, and word traveled fast on Coruscant. All the members of the Council hadn't yet left Coruscant, but enough had that someone would notice. Even so, this was speedier than he had expected. "Captain, we may need to—"

"On it," Baylo declared. He was already directing his crew. "Call off the hunt—again. Get clear of the belt so our *passenger* can take his call." His words became a sullen growl as he stomped off the bridge. "This is no way to run a navy!"

CHAPTER 15

CAPITAL KEY SPACEPORT

KWENN

"Message from Master Windu," Plo Koon said, comlink in hand. "The chancellor is aware of our venture here on Kwenn. He is . . . curious. So is Gabban, Kwenn's senator."

Saesee Tiin frowned. "We landed three minutes ago. How is this possible?"

"No hyperdrive can approach the speed news travels on Coruscant."

"A sufficient reason to get away."

As Saesee retrieved their baggage from the Jedi shuttle they'd flown to the spaceport in, Plo adjusted his breathing unit for the local atmosphere. Kwenn had been a frequent stop for him in past years, but he was not surprised to find that the air quality had worsened; the view of the planet on entry had prepared him for that. But the air was still better than Coruscant. The oceans, unpolluted as yet, surely helped.

Saesee arrived beside him, carrying a duffel over either shoulder. "I can carry mine," Plo offered.

"I'm sure you can." Saesee walked in front of him. "Where to?"

"Out of the spaceport would be a start."

"Hmph."

. While finishing their work on the fleet had led to them traveling to Kwenn together, Saesee was not one of Plo's more frequent companions on journeys. That was by design, rather than a lack of friendship; their skill sets called them to different kinds of assignments. Saesee could fly or repair any vessel ever made; Plo's strength as a tactician meant he always knew which ship was the right one to take. And while every member of the Council had extensive experience with diplomacy— even Saesee—neither of them was a particularly big talker.

One thing was unfamiliar for both of them, however: playing tourist. Plo had expected to follow the lead of other arriving travelers in exiting the facility, but there weren't many. On the other hand, he saw quite a few families lined up with their baggage ready to depart the planet. The area was noisy, and he got the sense that the passengers there had been waiting a long time.

Saesee didn't speak again until they were on the street. "We are out of the spaceport. Now what?"

"We are to give aid."

"To whom. Where?" Capital Key Spaceport's departure plaza was empty, save for a number of landspeeders idling nearby. The Iktotchi Jedi Master frowned. "I prefer a mission."

"Rendering aid *is* a mission," Plo said. "But I agree it is not well defined."

"Do we stand on a corner? Will you hold a sign?" Saesee smirked. "Master Yarael suggested last month that someone should start a chain of Jedi stands."

"I know you are not serious, my friend, and neither was he. Certainly you are no long way from your days as a Jedi Knight or a student. It wasn't *all* fighting. Didn't you help people then?"

"I flew. I drove. I fixed. I consider that helpful."

"Not to the people who did those things for a living, perhaps."

Saesee stared. "Now *you* are trying to be amusing."

"Not very hard." Plo spotted a vehicle up ahead. "Let us provide someone with gainful employment now." He hailed the cab.

It made its way to them quickly, its driver's head gleaming in the sun. "So much for that idea," Saesee said. "It's a droid."

"Droids need labor, too." Plo pulled one of the duffels away from his partner and loaded it atop the back of the landspeeder. He greeted the driver. "What is your designation?"

The droid responded in a pleasant voice. "Esskay-Aytnine."

"I visited a place here long ago, Esskay. Do you know the Bivall Colony?"

SK-89 chirped. "It is on Parva Key. It is far, several bridges away. There is a surcharge."

"Take us." Plo settled in the back seat and looked to Saesee. "The island was settled by victims of the solar storm on Protobranch. That was decades ago, but it has since served others in need. Where there are refugees, there is want."

"From the look of the people flying out, Kwenn's generating refugees of its own."

"All the more reason to pay a call."

"Hmm." Saesee climbed in and they were off.

The vehicle drove in silence for several minutes. Plo and Saesee took in a Kwenn that, while still recognizable, had seen a lot of recent change. Several buildings bore the silhouettes where corporate logos had once been affixed. The farther they got from Capital Key, the more of those they saw. It wasn't blight—not yet. But Plo could feel something was missing.

His colleague noticed it, too. "This is foolishness," Saesee muttered. "You really think we can do much for Kwenn with a few days' walkabout and a party?"

"The Force should guide our—"

Plo didn't finish his sentence. Their vehicle zipped through an intersection, threatening to strike a speeder bike. He used the Force to divert the smaller craft and its rider just in time.

"Careful!" Saesee called out.

SK-89 quickly admitted she was at fault. "I apologize, patrons."

Plo knew that Kwenn's bridges and terraces weren't the easiest to navigate. "How long have you been driving in this area?"

A pause. "You are my first fare."

"On this route, you mean."

"Anywhere."

The Jedi looked at each other.

"You're a general-purpose model," Saesee said, frowning. "Driving isn't your specialty."

"I function at the pleasure of Kwikhaul Livery Corporation. My last assignment was as a tour guide, but there is not much demand for that. So this is my task now." SK-89 made a turn, more cautiously. "Would you like to hear about the sculptures on the bridge to our left?"

Plo caught Saesee giving him a sideways glance. The most expert pilot he had ever met, Saesee was unlikely to think much of anyone who considered driving a task for the unskilled. But it was not the droid's fault.

Plo tried to sound accommodating. "Esskay, we are in no hurry. Exercise all the caution you want."

The landspeeder's slower pace and the droid's previous job weren't the worst things, as the Jedi saw more of the surroundings—with the droid filling them in on the place's more recent history. Plo figured they were about halfway to the Bivall Colony when another speeder raced up behind them.

And then two. And a third and fourth, on either side. The vehicles had nothing in common, other than that their operators seemed to have animosity toward the cab. It was easy to tell, given the scant few centimeters that existed between their speeders and SK-89's.

"Friends of the person we nearly struck?" Plo asked Saesee.

"Not likely." Saesee glared. "Someone is trying to kill us."

"Is there organized criminal activity on this planet, Esskay?" Plo asked.

"It is not a thing I would discuss with tourists," the droid said.

"Override that protocol. Say what you know."

"Every major pirate group in the Slice has a foothold somewhere in the islands. I know because I am told where to avoid."

They were bumped by the speeder behind. More glancing blows came from the vehicles on either side of them. He looked to the droid. "*Now* we are in a hurry."

SK-89 froze up at the controls. "I must obey all traffic regulations."

"There was a time and a place for that." Saesee began to crawl over the seat. "I'm taking over."

"I am not authorized to allow passengers to drive."

"I am sorry." Plo reached his arms under the droid and began pulling her over the seat into the back. "Esskay, do you know what the Jedi Council is?"

"No."

"Then you will have a lot to tell the other droids."

There was indeed a lot to see once Saesee was behind the controls. He gunned the landspeeder, racing ahead. But even as he lost two of the vehicles tailing them, more emerged from intersections. By the time the Jedi crossed the bridge to Zyboh Key, the vehicles were running five wide, much to the panic of oncoming traffic.

"Blast," Saesee said, as the lanes narrowed on the other side. "Plo, you planning on anything?"

In fact, Plo was already standing in the back of the open cab, over the safety-related protestations of the droid. His hand went for his lightsaber—only to hover over the hilt. There was something off, here. Few people had even seen them arrive at the spaceport. And while the chancellor and Senator Palpatine also were aware of their visit, it was ludicrous to consider anything of concern in their regard. He was unwilling to use deadly force against assailants when he didn't yet know who they were.

A sudden lurch sent him off balance—and took the matter out of his hands. The landspeeder slowed, bleeding off some of the lead Saesee had just built. "The controls aren't responding!"

As the landspeeder took a corner, Plo noticed a red light flashing on the dashboard. "Are we out of fuel?"

The droid spoke up. "Kwikhaul has detected our aberrant operation. We are being directed back to the depot."

Saesee didn't believe it. "This model speeder doesn't have a smart autopilot. That's why *you're* here!"

"It works for short distances. The depot is within sight."

Plo shifted from looking behind him to looking ahead. His arms hung limp as he saw what awaited. A sprawling jungle of vehicles, parked around and in front of the gates of the Kwikhaul complex, waiting for them. Within moments, their landspeeder was enveloped within the jam. A cacophony of engines, warning signal bleats, and shouts came from all around. Many drivers and passengers exited, many holding crowbars or other implements. No blasters that Plo could see—but in a crowd this size, it hardly mattered.

The engine died. Saesee looked back. "I can't get it going again."

Plo was greatly concerned, but more confused as the mob closed in. "What did we do to merit this?"

He didn't expect a response from the droid—but got one. "They are not after you, patrons. They are after *me*."

CHAPTER 16

ABOARD THE *RANDOMIZER*

THE SLICE

abers, staves, coins, flasks.

Zilastra sat in the gaming parlor that served as the nerve center of her starship, the *Randomizer,* as it waited near an asteroid belt on the Ootmian route. With practiced care, she riffled through her deck of sabacc cards. Her gloves were extremely thin, specially tailored so as not to interfere with her shuffling or card handling. She was oblivious to the activity around her. No matter what madness was going on in her life, no matter what dangerous confrontations of importance were taking place near or far, she had always been able to rely on her deck.

When she was a refugee in Hutt space, the curious pictures on the cards her mother left her provided the young Zilastra with comfort and company. Learning the game as a young adult kept her out of bad situations in places where money meant control. And since her rise to power over a gang of her own, the deck had helped her organize her thoughts—and strategies.

Interstellar pirate bands rose and fell in importance, merging or disintegrating. As far back as she could remember, those in the know along the Ootmian route had referred to the Big Three—or Two, or Four, depending on which gangs were in ascendance. Purely by chance, the most active outfits when Zilastra struck out with her own crew had names roughly corresponding to the four sabacc suits.

She played cards to the table, noting that some of the better-known fortune-telling meanings for the suits mapped pretty well to the gangs:

Sabers. The Poisoned Blades, backstabbers of the worst kind.

Staves. The Staved Skulls, blunt and incendiary.

Coins. The Filthy Creds, who bought loyalty when they weren't being bought.

Flasks only fit when Zilastra realized the word *vial* sounded like the Vile, a vicious group that always lived down to its name.

Fanciful connections, of course—but ones that allowed her to visually model the relative powers and positions of her rivals. A solitaire game for the conquering kind, it passed the time while she waited to hear how her latest plays went down.

She dealt one card after another. *Flask. Flask. Flask.* Then Demise, one of the face cards.

Fate, you're being interesting today.

"Boarding party returning," Burlug announced as he walked past. "Hotwire's flying the shuttle."

"Huh. So she survived her mission."

She had to hand it to Kylah: Her bodyguard was indeed something. It had taken mere hours for Hotwire to make her own mark. With Kylah's thefts on Keldooine complete, Zilastra had headed for space in the *Randomizer*, the older-model *Pelta*-class frigate that had served as her flagship since its "liberation" from the Trade Federation years earlier.

Not long into the flight, the *Randomizer* had been scanned by one of Zilastra's many enemies, Pell Baylo of *Assurance*. But the Republic ship had departed, never getting close enough for a fight. Hotwire theorized Baylo must have been there hunting someone else. Hotwire then detected a ship of the Vile, moving slowly through an asteroid belt. Reluctant to risk the *Randomizer* in that locale, Zilastra sent Hotwire on the boarding shuttle, accompanied by crewmembers she considered expendable. The Vile never gave anything up without a fight.

Zilastra heard a commotion she recognized and picked up the cards. "Where have *you* been, Stowaway?"

Kylah practically bounced in. "I went with Hotwire!"

"To board a Vile ship?" The pirate looked at her, stunned. "You have a death wish?"

Hotwire entered. "I didn't know Kylah was with us. My former boss has an affinity for maintenance lockers."

"I'll lock her in one next time," Zilastra said.

While Kylah initially had been upset over her one-time bodyguard making a play for herself, that had lasted about five minutes. That was as long as it took Kylah to decide that having her driver-slash-protégée inducted into the Riftwalkers was a mark of distinction. Kylah rounded the table, gleeful. "You won't believe what Hotwire did!"

Hotwire stepped in. "We closed on the target in the belt. I was right—it was a modified Sienar IPV-1, probably a planetary defender somewhere, captured and repurposed by the Vile."

"Pretending to be the law? That's more of a Blade trick."

"Not when you paint obscene drawings all on the outside." She offered Zilastra a datapad. "You'll probably want to scrape that stuff off, by the way."

"And disinfect the interior." Zilastra studied the images of the vessel. "It was a derelict?"

"Not yet, but they were headed that direction. They said their hyperdrive survived one short jump away from that Republic corvette when everything blew up. All systems, including life support."

"Who said this?"

"The Vile, as soon as we got close enough for them to get our signal. We took the ship without a shot fired. We tractored it back here."

Zilastra's eyes bulged. "Just you and the kid?"

"And your attack droids—and the new crewmembers you sent on the boarding action."

"*The Idiot Three?*"

"Ghor, Wungo, and The Lobber."

"Don't call him that. Don't let him think he's famous!" Zilastra grew flustered. "And they're not in the crew! I was expecting the Vile would kill them in a heartbeat. If I whack them now, people will think I don't reward performance."

"Isn't it better to keep them alive if they're accomplishing something?"

"*You* accomplished something. If the other bosses see those guys working for me, they'll die laughing."

Zilastra looked again at the images on the datapad and smiled in spite of herself. Hotwire, whoever she was, had succeeded in a mission nobody had expected her to survive—with oafs and a youngling for a crew. She had not yet killed anyone in Zilastra's service, but there hadn't been an opportunity for that. That would come later. It always did.

The woman had shared enough parts of her story that it was easy for Zilastra to fill in the rest. Hotwire had been someone's partner on the Ootmian route, either romantic or business—and had been abandoned and left with nothing. *Shades of my mother,* Zilastra thought. Unburdened by children, Hotwire had tried to make an honest living until that wasn't possible anymore.

It was clear her getup—the goggles and flight helmet she wore day and night—was a disguise, but Zilastra saw nothing odd about that. Lots of soft-looking people she encountered were afraid to be seen as such, while others harbored fantasies about getting back to the law-abiding world one day. Masks came with the territory. Jodak, her pilot, still wore one everywhere despite the fact that he was likely the only Yinchorri wherever he went. It was hard to travel incognito when you were a snub-nosed, mean-eyed reptilian taller than a Wookiee.

She put down the datapad and dealt the cards again. Kylah noticed. "I forget. Which suit are we?"

"I keep telling you, we're the *game.* Riftwalker is a variant from Valnoos."

"What's so special about it?"

"A lot of things—but the big one is that whoever calls it doesn't ante up. They get in the game for free."

"I can see where that would be appealing," Hotwire said. She glanced at the table. "Solitaire or divination?"

"Both," Zilastra said. She invited the women to sit. "Have you noticed all the fives?"

Kylah nodded. "Does that mean you're losing?"

"No. Think about it. There are five big criminal syndicates in the galaxy—but there's also five families in the Hutt and Crymorah syndicates themselves."

"And we're the fifth outfit in this part of the Slice!"

Hotwire touched the girl's shoulder. "I doubt anyone planned that," she said.

"Didn't they?" Zilastra rearranged the cards into two piles. "Look at the math. Games with two players are balanced—stroke and counterstroke. Add one, though—"

Hotwire caught her drift. "Tripolar systems are unstable. The weakest defects from one partner to the other."

"And back." Zilastra split the piles. "Four splits evenly. You end up with two cartels, and things freeze again. If a third joins the other pair, the smaller of the two just flips sides."

"Because nobody wants to be the junior partner—but especially not in third position."

"Exactly." Zilastra broke the cards up into five piles. "But five—now, that's the *evil* number."

"Evil?" Hotwire asked.

"Guy in a card game told me about a study someone did. Planets with five major powers had the most conflict. Three-on-two fights spread a lot of destruction but rarely ended conclusively. Nobody wants to be the odd power out, so they're always realigning—and third-position players are constantly jumping ship."

"What about more than five?" Kylah asked.

Zilastra split the piles again into shorter stacks. "There's more fights—but they're smaller, less destructive." Fingers working too fast to be seen, she sorted them again and again. "An outfit—*any* outfit—is just a way to bring order from chaos, to make what we do more efficient. But we profit from everything else remaining a mess, so there's still territory to grab, ships to steal. And so no matter how many different gangs you start out with, we always land . . . at five."

Hotwire nodded. "Five, so there's always a fight somewhere. Five, so nobody ever really loses."

"Oh, I don't know about that." Zilastra cut the deck into five piles and dealt the top card in each. Fives in the four suits—and a special card.

"Nice trick," Hotwire said. "The Queen of Air and Darkness."

"That's a title I don't mind claiming." Zilastra looked up at her new recruit. "Now I'm going to claim something else. The second case."

Hotwire stood up. "Back in a minute."

She stepped out and returned holding one of the Regal Voyager cases. She opened it.

"You can reprogram the code phrase as you like. That's two of them I've unlocked. You get the next one tomorrow, as we agreed."

"That timing works perfectly," Zilastra said. She rose from the table and took the case. "Have Keldooine send someone to haul off the Vile ship. I'll be in Tokchi's workshop. There's a very important meeting coming up, and I want to be ready!"

CHAPTER 17

ZYBOH KEY

KWENN

Outside the gates of Kwikhaul's compound, Saesee Tiin stood back-to-back with Plo Koon atop their stalled landspeeder. The two Jedi had ignited their lightsabers earlier, provoking the angry mob's shock and then confusion. Nobody had gotten any closer to them or to the terrified SK-89, but quite a few people had thrown things at them.

"So much for helping people," Saesee said.

"We are helping this droid," Plo replied.

And ourselves, Saesee thought, *in case they decide to tear us apart, too.*

From his vantage point atop the landspeeder, he could see several other cabs stalled amid the madness. Their droid drivers had all been torn to pieces. The metal bars he thought he'd seen in the hands of the rioters were actually limbs. The rocks thrown at the Jedi had included more than a few heads.

A silver skull hurtled toward him. Saesee caught this one in mid-flight.

Already the electronic equivalent of apoplectic, SK-89 looked into the disembodied head of a member of her own model. "Oh, no! Oh, no, oh no!"

Plo Koon understood her response. "Perhaps you should put that down, Master Tiin."

Saesee tossed it to the ground. He looked over his shoulder to his companion. "About time for us to say something."

"I agree. You have the louder voice."

"I knew you were going to say that." Looking down, Saesee saw the control for the landspeeder's alert signal near its shifter. He stomped on it and held his boot there. The landspeeder let out a deafening bleat that continued until he released his foot. "*Silence!*" Saesee boomed.

The crowd went momentarily still.

"We are Jedi," Saesee continued. "Our job is to keep the peace. *This is not peace!*"

"This is none of your business!" a human woman shouted. "This is between us and the droids!"

"What droids? You've ripped them all apart!"

"Not all," a Togruta said, pointing at SK-89. "And there are dozens of craft out on the streets right now being driven by them!"

"So?"

"These people are the drivers," the droid said. "Or were."

Saesee looked to the droid—and then to Plo. "What is this?"

Plo gestured toward the fenced compound. "I think we are about to find out."

From the garage facility inside the fence, a tall, alabaster-skinned Muun stormed toward the gates. The mob began shouting again and throwing droid parts, though this time not aimed at the two Jedi. The Muun's face was nearly featureless, but her rage was unmistakable. As several droid parts clanged against the fence railings, she outstretched her spindly arms before the Masters. "Thank goodness you're here, Jedi. Arrest these people!"

Saesee looked around. There were easily a hundred people in the crowd. "How do you expect us to do that?"

"I don't care. They're destroying private property!"

"Yours?"

"Yeah," called out the woman who had spoken to Saesee first. "She's Fraxa—the owner!"

Several managers joined Fraxa at the gate. She surveyed the destruction the crowd had wrought. "Look what these people have done, Jedi. I say again: You have to arrest them!"

Plo shook his head. "We aren't police."

"Then why are you here?" Fraxa asked. "What good are you?"

"We keep the peace."

"It doesn't look like it."

"We also do justice," Saesee said. He pointed to SK-89. "She said you replaced these drivers with droids. Is that true?"

"Just this morning!" someone shouted. "The whole fleet." Others joined in yelling.

By the time Fraxa could be heard again, the executive was in the middle of a tirade about the business conditions on Kwenn. "Tourism is down. The livery business has cratered. I can't afford organic drivers!"

"You can't afford not to have them," the Togruta said. "I'm Teeler—I've been driving here for decades." He pointed at SK-89. "I saw this one earlier. The droid nearly ran over somebody!"

Fraxa waved her hand. "Nonsense!"

Plo corrected her. "It is true."

"You put an untrained droid on the streets," Saesee added.

"I'm in the middle of a labor action," Fraxa said. "How am I supposed to keep the fleet running?"

"By paying us!" Teeler shouted. "We know you pay yourself. I've seen that hangar of yours in back with that old starfighter you're restoring."

"An antique, hauled out of scrap—and I haven't spent a credit on it in a year. A third of our daily traffic was running executives back and forth to the spaceport. You may have noticed that a lot of them took their companies with them. And the rumor is Rendili Hyperworks is next to go!"

As the Muun and the mob traded insults through the fence, Saesee leaned in and spoke to Plo. "You're the great organizer—and you wanted to help."

There was consternation in Plo's voice. "We settle large disputes. This is smaller—but no more simple, for it."

Saesee nodded in agreement. "It's not the sort of thing we do."

Plo's head tilted.

"What?"

"Perhaps," Plo said, "the situation requires the sort of thing *you* do, instead." He clapped Saesee on the shoulder.

Amid the din, Saesee took a look at the landspeeder he was in—and realized something. He pointed and yelled. "*You've got boats!*"

The parties stopped their quarreling. "What?" Fraxa asked.

Saesee bounded off the landspeeder and landed next to it. "You've been running this model on city streets. But a lot of the bridges are in disrepair, and some are out of service altogether." Saesee turned and faced in the direction of the wharf. "These units could function as water taxis with just a few tweaks."

"And oceanic observation vehicles," Plo added as he joined Saesee on the ground. "From what I saw on the ride in, this is an area of tourism you have not developed."

Fraxa raised a finger. "No airspeeders are allowed on Kwenn."

"But hovering repulsorcraft *are* permitted," Plo said. "It makes no difference whether a vehicle cruises centimeters above land, or above water."

Saesee agreed. "What about that big sail barge I saw when I flew in? It hovers over the water."

"The *Pelagic*?" Fraxa scratched her chin. "It's a casino. We always assumed they had an exception."

"If an exception is needed," Plo said, "we know a little about negotiation."

Teeler raised his hand. "That kind of retrofit takes fine adjustments. Our mechanics aren't up to it."

"I am," Saesee said. "And I've been upgrading speeders with novices for years. We can get it done in a couple of days."

The owner shook her head. "It wouldn't be enough," Fraxa said. "The travelers are just not here—and you've seen what some of the islands are to look at!"

"Then change that." Saesee pointed across the yard at a group of parked speeder buses. "Do those work?"

"The touring craft?" She shrugged. "We haven't been able to fill them in years."

"Fine. I'll show you how to chop the tops off."

"What?" Fraxa's tiny eyes went wide. "Why would you do that?"

"So they can carry refuse off the streets."

Exclamations of shock from the crowd—but Plo seemed to catch Saesee's drift. "I know some of the authorities here. I'm sure I can negotiate a contract."

Laughter from the crowd. Teeler spoke for all of them. "We're drivers, not trash collectors."

"And the droids are laborers and not drivers," Plo replied. He addressed SK-89, still cowering in the back seat of the speeder. "Could you take that role?"

"Certainly. We can fulfill that function—and more safely—if others drive." The droid looked about. "But—er—I seem to be the only one left."

"Not a problem," Saesee said. He gestured to the droid parts strewn on the ground. "We'll fix them, too."

The guffaws this time came from the owner. "Now you'll tell me you're experts at droid repair, as well!"

"We know people who are." Saesee indicated his comlink. "Heezo, back at the Jedi Temple, does droid repair for the Jedi. Get him on the holo and he can guide us through anything."

Shamefaced, one of the drivers lifted a droid's arm. "I don't know—they're pretty far gone."

"We have faith in Heezo," Plo said.

The crowd calming at last, Saesee turned toward the gate and used the Force to snap the lock holding it. It swung open and the Jedi Master walked into the courtyard. He picked the broken lock off the ground and handed it to Fraxa. "I'll fix this, too," he said, before striding purposefully toward the garage. There, and in the yard beyond, he noticed several other things that, with a little repurposing, could help Kwikhaul through its hard times. Towing wrecks off the bridges for salvage would even resolve two problems at once.

His eyes lingered for more than a moment on the contents of the small hangar in the back: the aforementioned starfighter that Fraxa was restoring. Even in its sorry shape, the ARC-8 from the High Republic era was a rare and welcome sight for Saesee. He had taken a tentative step inside the hangar when a hand rested on his shoulder, stopping him. Plo's words nudged him back to reality. "Not now, my friend. You are needed."

"Hmph." Saesee turned from the hangar and saw the drivers interacting peaceably with the owner and her management team. He inhaled deeply. "You realize," he told Plo, "we have crossed the stars to do the same work we were doing at home."

"Not the same," his colleague said. "No, it is not the same at all."

"This will be difficult to complete before the celebration begins."

"On that, my friend, you are correct. We had better get started."

CHAPTER 18

ABOARD *ASSURANCE*

THE SLICE

Depa Billaba was officially overdue.

Mace Windu stood on the bridge of *Assurance,* doing his best not to get in the way. He had borne several resurgences of Captain Baylo's incendiary temper, despite the fact that he had been helpful to the pirate-hunter on several occasions since his arrival. Baylo would grow tolerable for a time—only to find some reason to remind Mace that he was an unwanted guest.

The worst thing he could do was to ask after Depa, and he had avoided doing so. No communications had come in from her, over either the Jedi comlinks they shared or any other means of communication *Assurance* could receive. Baylo had not agreed to retrieve her at any particular location, the assumption being her mission would keep her on the move. He had further discouraged Mace from traveling to the surface of Keldooine on his own, advising that there was no place for him to start in the morass of criminality that world had become.

Mace was certain his investigative skills were up to the challenge, but the fact that Baylo argued for staying aboard swayed him. A captain who despised Jedi being on his bridge wasn't likely to stop one from

leaving, unless such an act was truly futile. Or, as Baylo had more color-
fully put it, "If I lose two members of the Jedi Council, I can kiss this
ship's future goodbye."

So *Assurance* had stayed in orbit near Keldooine, and stayed visible.
Mace hoped that would make it easier for Depa to find them, even as
Baylo saw value in showing force along the trade route. As civilian vessels approached in normal space, the corvette played escort for them for
a few hours. It was the sort of gesture that was sure to get back to corporate headquarters.

"What's this one?" Baylo asked as a cargo ship emerged from hyperspace.

A crewmember responded. "The *Regal Hopper.* Grains from Yitabo,
bound for Keldooine."

"Regal Star Freight." Baylo snorted. "They don't need any help."

Mace heard something worth asking about. "That's connected to the
passenger line, correct?"

"Same firm," Baylo responded. "We've escorted a few. I was sure they
were ripe for a hit. They haven't been struck in months. The damnedest
luck."

"Luck rarely enters into things, in my experience." Mace looked out
at the cargo ship. "Are they doing something better than the other
lines?"

"Not that I can tell. I mean, there are the countermeasures all transport lines practice. Minimizing time not in hyperspace. Looping down
from orbit to cut down on the surface area they're crossing during descent. Transponders off during stops in deep space."

"Do these work?"

"For anyone else, not so much. Even the Staved Skulls are on to those
tricks, and they've got holes in their heads." He looked at the transport.
"Regal Voyager's pilots lead charmed lives."

Mace looked Baylo in the eyes. "Have you known many people with
charmed lives, Captain?"

"You think a fix is in?" Baylo shook his head. "Impossible. Paying for
protection doesn't work, not out here. You might make a deal with one
gang, but then another would hit you."

"I would tend to agree. But it is worth investigating."

The captain stepped over to a terminal. Mace stood and watched as he searched the records.

Baylo pointed at an entry. "Looks like their luck ran out a few days ago. *Regal Zephyr,* hijack attempt during a run to Coruscant." Noting a symbol, he studied it more closely. "Says here, *Attack unsuccessful: Jedi intervention!*"

Mace stepped to the screen. "May I?"

"See for yourself." Baylo stepped back. "Their luck continues."

Checking further into the entry, Mace realized why the name of the firm had caught his attention. "I spoke with the Jedi involved just after this. But the details of the attack are not here." He looked up. "Captain—"

"If you're going to ask permission again, it'll get on my nerves more than if you didn't," Baylo said. "Set up a call to Coruscant for Master Windu," he ordered.

Mace nodded. "I appreciate that."

"At least we don't have to leave anything important this time."

The connection was made after several minutes, with the Jedi Temple rerouting Mace's call. A holographic image appeared on the bridge, but it was not of the party he expected.

"*Master Windu!*" Obi-Wan Kenobi said.

"Your Jedi Knights are getting younger all the time," Baylo mumbled.

Mace ignored him. "Obi-Wan, where is Master Qui-Gon?"

"We are at the immigration center." Obi-Wan gestured behind him. "He is inside, speaking on behalf of a few of the passengers from the *Regal Zephyr.*"

"The very ship I want to ask about. I'm unable to find your report on the attack."

"I'm sorry to say we haven't filed it, yet. It was a minor incident—and we have been busy with other tasks."

"And they are worthy ones. But procedures have purposes. Tell me about the attack."

Obi-Wan smirked. "It wasn't much of one."

"How so?"

"As I said, it was minor. There were just three assailants. Complete amateurs. It would have been comical, if they hadn't been threatening people."

"What pirate group were they affiliated with?"

"None."

The answer startled Baylo. "Repeat that?"

"None. They mentioned groups they might sell the ship to, but they hadn't even agreed about that. They were novices, full of bluster but easily frightened."

"I'll bet." The captain looked at Mace. "Local losers can't take a ship that size."

"What happened to the hijackers?" Mace asked.

"We released them on Randon."

"You let them *go*?" Baylo turned around and threw his cap on the deck.

"They'd harmed no one, and Qui-Gon thought it right." Obi-Wan blanched a little at the captain's reaction. "Master Windu, did we make a mistake?"

Mace dismissed the matter. "I have full trust in Master Qui-Gon's evaluation of the situation." Another question occurred to him. "How did the *Regal Zephyr*'s crew respond?"

"As you would expect," Obi-Wan said. "I spoke with several of them. They hadn't faced threats like this lately, but were resigned to it happening eventually. They were relieved that we were aboard."

"I'm certain." Mace nodded slightly. "I appreciate the information. Tell Master Qui-Gon he may consider the report filed."

Obi-Wan bowed. "I was told you were on retreat, Master. I hope it is going well."

"For some of us, it has yet to begin." Mace gave a hand signal, and the communications officer signed off. Then the young trainee beside him, Veers, dashed over to hand Baylo his hat.

The captain put it on. "You take anything from all that, Windu?"

Mace clasped his hands together. "The Regal Voyager line has rarely been struck. But it is not immune to piracy, and its employees do not expect it to be."

"So?"

"It has to do with that luck you speak of." Mace turned toward Baylo. "An honest gambler seeing a bad die roll after many good ones is upset, but not angry. But a cheater becomes enraged, because his devices were defeated." He looked to the cargo ship in space. "If there is something protecting this line's vessels, even its workers are unaware of it."

Baylo caught his drift—and chortled. "Why pay to protect your ships if you're still going to fly scared all the time?" He pointed outside, where *Regal Hopper* had begun its quick, cautious descent to Keldooine. "So why pay, then? What's the point?"

Mace didn't know. But he wondered if Depa Billaba did.

CHAPTER 19

SANCTUARY MOUNT

KWENN

*T*hese numbers don't add up.

Standing in the library within Sanctuary Mount, Eeth Koth squinted at the figures on his datapad and rubbed his eyes. He'd need to go over everything again, he realized. It wasn't how he'd intended to spend his precious time on Kwenn.

Eeth supported the Council's missions on the planet as much as anyone. Having lately managed several outpost closures, he knew the full scope of the Jedi Order's drawdown along the Ootmian route. He believed what Depa Billaba and Even Piell had said about the conditions in the region. The Zabrak Jedi Master further supported Qui-Gon's call for more personal interactions on behalf of the Jedi. Eeth certainly hadn't gotten to have many of those doing bureaucratic work.

And yet his personal interactions since arriving on Kwenn had been limited to conversations inside the outpost with Oppo Rancisis and Seneschal Voh, both of whom were busy managing matters related to the bicentennial celebration. That event wasn't Eeth's responsibility, and he'd hoped to descend to the city to begin the walkabout he'd promised himself.

But he had never been able to escape his sense of duty, and that had told him to get ahead on an inventory of Sanctuary Mount's library on the chance that the facility had to be closed. It was a small matter. Knowing Voh's reputation for precision, he expected to be on the streets in under an hour.

With an afternoon, and evening, and most of the next morning gone, he still hadn't left the outpost. The simple job had become a difficult one.

There had been some shrinkage in the collection over the years as Jedi took more items than they left. Voh had consolidated the collection to nooks that he, given his small stature and advanced age, could reach. But Eeth nonetheless found the materials count was off by a large percentage. The missing items covered a range of subjects: some of historical significance, others chronicling Jedi lore, still others trivial. Several were unique to Kwenn, being held nowhere else.

News that Yoda and Adi Gallia were approaching Kwenn in the next few hours made Eeth realize his time for exploration was limited. He had no choice but to disturb Voh. "Seneschal, are you certain the records are correct?"

Voh seemed startled. "*My* records?"

"Yes. Is your inventory accurate?"

The caretaker stared blankly, as if not knowing what to say.

Instead, Oppo broke from his other matters to respond. "Master Koth, the good seneschal has maintained Sanctuary Mount since long before you joined the Council. His knowledge of the place is peerless."

"I certainly agree. I only seek answers." Eeth handed the datapad to Voh. "These materials are missing."

Voh's eyes fixed on the data—and as he scrolled through the report, his face fell. "I know these items, of course. They are not here?"

"Unless they are somewhere I have not looked." He looked to the ceiling. "Are there more stored above?"

"No."

Eeth nodded—and patted the seneschal's arm. He didn't want to alarm the old fellow. "I'm sure there's a simple answer. Could some have been loaned out to local scholars?"

"I should think that would be in the records," Oppo volunteered.

"It is not."

Voh shook his head. Then his breath seemed to catch, and he spoke in a small voice. "*There were the mites.*"

"Mites?"

The seneschal looked down. "It embarrasses me to say this, but there was an infestation of egralla mites on this island a few years ago. It happened when the spaceport began skimping on decontamination protocols. The insects made for higher elevations, seeking anything they could consume. They are to data devices what mynocks are to starships."

Eeth was alarmed. "Technovores consumed multiple storage devices? Wouldn't you have noticed the uneaten remnants they left behind?"

Voh bit his lip. "Yes, I probably would have, wouldn't I?"

"Most assuredly." Eeth took back the datapad—and sensed something. He glanced down at the caretaker. "You think there is another explanation."

Voh took a deep breath. "A related one."

Oppo spoke kindly. "Do tell us."

"The mites were endangering the collection, and it was well beyond my ability to stop. So I hired an exterminator from the city below."

"A sound response," Eeth said. "This ended the threat?"

"It did. But . . . I was forced to absent myself from the library for days at a time while she was doing the work."

"You left the building?"

"I had access to the ramp to the brazier, so I could light it. But yes, the exterminator was alone in the library."

Eeth raised an eyebrow. "You did not remain?"

Oppo looked sternly at him. "He has answered you, Master."

"No, it's all right." Voh's words came more quickly. "The exterminator said the pesticide would have been harmful to me. Only she had the proper protection." He looked around at the cubbyholes, rattled. "I can't believe she would have stolen from this place—of all places. And that I would not have noticed!" He hung his head in shame.

"If true, the fault is hers, not yours." Oppo put two of his arms around Voh's shoulders.

"Perhaps I am too old for this work."

Oppo laughed. "Say that when you reach my age!"

Eeth was quick to appear conciliatory. "There are many people in need below and on the surrounding islands. This must be the explanation." He glanced at the shelves. "Can you identify the pest control firm, Seneschal?"

Voh could not. "It may not be in business—and it was some time back. But I don't know what value the works would have to anyone besides Jedi."

"You never know." Eeth bowed. "Thank you. Please return to your duties."

He did, and Oppo followed Eeth out through the anteroom.

"What do you think?" Eeth asked.

Oppo cast a sideways glance at him. "I think that you were given a wonderful opportunity to get to know this planet and its people—and you turned it instead into a bureaucratic chore. And now you have made it into a mystery you can solve." He looked back inside. "I suspect that good old man simply lost count over the years."

"I'm sure you're right."

"Go and see the world, my friend. Help someone, as Qui-Gon suggested."

"I will." Eeth's eyes narrowed. "I must start somewhere. Perhaps there is someone in the city below who deals in rare materials."

Oppo shook his head. "And people say *I* am stuck in my ways." He laughed as he slithered away. "You will be a wonderful attraction for the celebration, Master Koth. Come, people of Kwenn, and meet the youngling who is older than I!"

CHAPTER 20

ABOARD THE *RANDOMIZER*

HYPERSPACE

"Hotwire, wake up!"

Depa Billaba was accustomed to sleeping on bare floors. She'd done so as a Jedi on many occasions. Her explorations of her people's Chalactan heritage had added even more asceticism to her Jedi philosophy. Humble lodgings didn't bother her at all.

What Depa wasn't accustomed to was being prodded awake by someone's foot. She opened her eyes and glared up at Kylah. "Can I help you?"

"Sorry, but you wanted to know." Kylah pointed. "We're in hyperspace!"

Depa sat up on the deck of the *Randomizer*. Her goggles had slipped in the night, and she repositioned them. Not the most comfortable of disguises, she'd realized. But she'd slept so deeply she never noticed the jump. "Where are we going?"

"Nobody will say. I haven't seen Zil."

Another morning, another mystery.

Depa had earned her sleep. Her mission had become an odyssey—

and though she didn't know the destination, she'd made the most of her time as it was going on. Anywhere else, trust took months to build. But in a world where life was cheap and associations were fleeting, things moved at a faster pace. And the terms of her tenure had forced her to act even more swiftly.

Almost immediately after meeting the Riftwalkers on Keldooine, Depa—still known to the pirates as Hotwire—had started proving herself, winning the chance to accompany Zilastra when she left her lair for her next hunting mission. She'd thought the mission would end quickly when the *Randomizer* lucked across *Assurance;* the corvette had even scanned the Riftwalker ship. But before Depa could get to where her comlink was hidden, *Assurance* left the scene. She was sure Captain Baylo had a good reason, but it was a missed opportunity to take down the Riftwalker flagship, from within and without. Even so, the sequel was significant, as Depa captured the derelict ship operated by the Vile.

Taking a prize without a shot fired made her someone of stature. Yes, it had taken her beyond the moment of her intended rendezvous with *Assurance,* but she sensed it was worth it. Baylo was the least understanding person in the galaxy, but even he should see the value of the intel she was gathering.

Yet Depa had struggled to understand the last couple of days. After the captured Vile ship had been sent on its way, the *Randomizer* had jumped to deep space. The Jedi had seen Zilastra a couple of times after that. Once, she was in furtive conversation with Tokchi, her resident engineer of considerable talent; the golden translator collar was of his own design. And another time Zilastra was dealing with a group of protocol droids. *Odd servants to have,* she'd thought. It was during that peculiar encounter that Depa delivered the fourth, penultimate Regal Voyager case to Zilastra.

And it was the last she had seen of the pirate leader.

Depa readied herself for her day. She was down to the last of the cases, and she decided to keep it by her side at all times. There were several hours to go before she was due to provide it to Zilastra; she wasn't going to allow it to leave her sight. She felt the same way about Kylah. The Jedi might have to leave the *Randomizer* at any minute, and she didn't want to leave alone. She decided that while she had some freedom, she might as well see what vessels were available in the twin landing bays.

The next time I "hotwire" something, it'll be for a good cause.

On the starboard landing deck she and Kylah encountered three of the Riftwalkers' other new recruits. Ghor, Wungo, and The Lobber had not matched Depa's quick rise in stature; instead, the three were moving crates from one side of the hangar deck to the other under the supervision of IK-111. They were just finishing when Depa arrived.

"That's it. We're done," Lobber declared, panting after having shifted the last mammoth container.

"Congratulations," declared IK-111. "Now move them back."

Groans from the trio—which ended when the droid fired his blaster into the ceiling. They got back to work.

Kylah whispered to Depa. "I don't see the point in this."

"That *is* the point in this." She didn't know where the Riftwalkers had picked up the three, but she had no illusions about their worth in Zilastra's eyes—or their likely future. In any organization that practiced violence, cannon fodder was a position that needed constant filling. They'd be kept alive until then. No later.

Satisfied to see work resumed, the droid clanked its way into the corridor. Depa approached the three. "How long have you been at this?"

"Long enough for me to name the things we're carrying," Wungo said. The beleaguered Klatooinian glanced at the barrel in his arms. "This is Sarla."

Depa saw the swirling tunnel of hyperspace streaking past the magnetically sealed entrance to the hangar deck. "How long ago did we jump?"

"Two trips across the deck ago," Ghor said. "But the life pods took off way earlier."

"Life pods?"

"They weren't life pods," Lobber snarled. "They were just small ships. They went out of the other bay."

Depa was considering what that could mean when Ghor elbowed Wungo in the ribs and pointed in the Jedi's direction. "That look familiar?"

Wungo turned toward Depa—and winced. "I've been trying to forget it."

"What are you talking about?" she asked. She followed his eyeline to the case in her hand. "You mean this?"

Lobber nodded. "Regal Voyager logo. We hit a ship of theirs just the other day."

That surprised Depa. "You did this for the Riftwalkers?"

"Naw, before. Right before, in fact," Ghor said. "It—uh, didn't go well."

"You shut up," Lobber said. "It was fine before the Jedi got involved."

Depa's eyes widened. Qui-Gon had told the Council of such an event. "You say you *weren't* working for Zilastra then?"

Wungo nodded. "If we had been, it never would have happened. Zil told us she didn't want us to hit the ship."

"Because she wanted it for herself?"

"No, she just didn't want *anyone* to hit it." Abashed, Wungo spoke in a smaller voice. "*She yelled at us.*"

A theory arose in Depa's mind. Perhaps Zilastra was extorting the Regal Voyager line. Graft in commercial transport was not unheard of, sadly. It explained the pirate leader's response to the trio.

But not this. Depa looked at the case in her hand. *Where do the cases enter into it? Why does she want them?*

She heard Zilastra's voice. "There it is," the boss said, stepping around a corner and looking at the final case. She glanced at her overworked henchbeings. "Get lost, fools."

"Lost it is," Lobber responded. He, Ghor, and Wungo unceremoniously dropped what they were carting and made a quick exit.

Before Depa could say anything, the ship lurched—and a yellow flash replaced the streaks of light outside. It took her a moment to realize she was looking at a bright, nearly featureless planet.

"Now orbiting Valboraan," announced the pilot over the public address system.

Zilastra touched the intercom. "Take us in, Jodak."

"Aye aye."

Depa had never visited Valboraan, but she knew it wasn't far from where she'd started. Kwenn and Keldooine were a short distance away. But unlike those planets, Valboraan appeared uninhabited from above.

"Popular destination?" she asked.

"Not unless you like spelunking," Zilastra said. "It's shot full of caves. But that has its appeal." She turned. "Follow me."

Depa and Kylah did as ordered. They saw more of Valboraan as the ship descended. Keldooine, chaotic as it was, made sense as a hub; a place to eat and refuel and sell stolen goods. Valboraan, meanwhile, was a true pirates' nest. A stronghold, a hideaway. The only indication anything was on the planet at all appeared when a section of the desert floor irised open, allowing a transmitter array to mechanically rise from beneath the surface. Depa saw it only for a few moments, however, as the ship made for a nearby mountain outcrop—and the dark caverns that dwarfed even the *Randomizer*'s massive size. The ship found a large aperture and cruised into it.

With Zilastra busy in conversation with her crew, Depa turned to Kylah, glued to the window beside her. "Have you been here before?"

"Never." The girl smiled. "We're really on the inside now!"

In more ways than one, Depa thought. Darkness interrupted by occasional fleeting artificial lights outside took away whatever bearings she might have had. There was no telling how far inside the cave system they'd gone—just that the prospects of getting Kylah away from the Riftwalkers were as remote as could be.

"I wish you'd stayed on Keldooine when we went back," Depa said.

"What was I going to do there? That place was dying." She pointed outside. "This is where it's happening."

Depa was going to say she didn't know what *it* was—but then she returned her gaze outside. More lights appeared. A massive landing complex in the middle of the mountain, where dozens of ships were parked. Very few looked alike. Some were commercial craft; others appeared to be patrol vessels of some stripe. The Riftwalkers' Keldooine facility was smaller, in the middle of an urban area on a contested world. Here on Valboraan, Zilastra could store her ill-gotten gains out of sight while deciding what to do with them.

The *Randomizer* deployed its wings before it touched down, a maneuver that allowed it to put more landing struts on the ground. Between the frigate and the base, the Jedi Master had to admit she was impressed. Zilastra had achieved a lot. Depa wondered what she might have become, in a different walk of life.

And what is all this for?

Zilastra turned back to Depa and gestured. "That the final case?"

The Jedi clutched the handle tightly and calmly took a breath. "I take it we're at the end of our bargain. But I thought you were going to keep me on."

Zilastra shrugged. "Don't worry about that. I don't even need to open it. I just need you to bring it."

Good, Depa thought.

The pirate stared at her—and then at Kylah. "Follow us, Stowaway. You might learn something."

CHAPTER 21

KINNAWAH KEY

KWENN

Permanent media, Eeth Koth thought, held a curious place in galactic culture. One reason that electronic means had long been the standard when it came to communicating was that most storage devices could be altered, allowing updates—or easy erasure and reuse. But other devices and materials were locked, the thoughts recorded on them never-changing.

The *most* permanent media weren't electronic at all. Flimsiplast was often used in locations without reliable power and by criminals who wanted to prevent computerized access to their records. Far less common were scrolls and bound editions, byproducts of cultures disconnected from the modern galaxy.

In Eeth's experience, those who preferred permanent media—from the common content-locked datapad to the rarest stone tablets—tended to have a philosophical bent. They were comfortable with the idea that the knowledge stored within would never change, even if it was one day proved wrong or otherwise overtaken by events. And more than anything, owning such items suggested ample leisure time—and sufficient means to have space for things.

Eeth had quickly learned that the exterminator who had worked at Sanctuary Mount likely had no space to spare. Kwenn's governmental records showed him that she had emigrated from the planet with her family soon after her work at the outpost. The Jedi reasoned there was a fair chance any goods taken from the building were still on the planet— and everyone he spoke to told him there was only one place to go to sell printed works. If materials had been stolen from the library, a possible place to find them was the Lamplighter Boutique, an emporium on the fourth terrace of Kinnawah Key owned and operated by one Hadden Shrag.

Unfortunately, it was no longer a place to find Hadden Shrag himself. His wife, Pogee, informed Eeth of that fact when she met him at the door. The Jedi heard her, but it barely registered. Instead, surprise completely overwhelmed his famous politeness and he responded with the same question anyone would ask: "*What is on your head?*"

Pogee Shrag cackled with laughter. She and her husband were Nosaurians, and like the other members of that bipedal reptilian species, their heads were crowned with scaly spikes. That wasn't a foreign concept for Eeth; his Zabrak people had horns of their own, though not so prominent. But Pogee's spikes were hidden by fur. White, writhing fur. She smiled. "Grand, ain't they?"

"They?"

"*They!*" She shook her head back and forth vigorously, and Eeth saw she actually had half a dozen long, slinky rodents curled around her spikes. Her shaking sent them into movement, as they wound from one spike to another, slipping underneath and over one another.

Eeth couldn't stop staring. "What *are* those?"

"Boolah kits. Orphans, the poor things. I'm raising them." Pogee gave a warbling call in her species' native tongue and put out her arms. One after another, the creatures hopped onto her shoulder and descended along her arms. At last, she had three hanging from each wrist by their prehensile tails. "You want to hear their names?"

"Just seeing them is experience enough."

She smiled. "Come on in!"

Eeth couldn't find fault with her hospitality. Her family's housekeeping was another story. The Jedi Master saw dozens more boolah kits inside, squirming back and forth from place to place. He spotted a number of larger specimens hanging from fixtures; he assumed them to be adult boolahs.

Contrary to his expectations, the house had a decent floral smell, not offending his senses in the least. But the boolah kits immediately saw him as something new to be explored, and in seconds he had his own supply.

He tried to be respectful of what he assumed were her pets. "Why so many?"

"Oh, they ain't mine," she said, starting to cackle again. "Boolahs are one of the few native critters on Kwenn. Every child wants one—and everybody who moves off the planet wants to leave them behind."

A kit on his head wagging her tail past his eyes, Eeth began to understand the émigrés' rationale. He gently plucked the beast from his pate and remembered what he'd come for. "You said Hadden Shrag isn't here?"

"My husband went to one of the moons to recuperate. Low gravity, you know."

"He is unwell?"

"He ain't been well since I've known him." She cackled again.

Eeth didn't know where she had picked up her accent, but it seemed normal coming from her. "I do have the correct person? I'm looking for the dealer in ephemera."

"You mean junk?"

"I'm not sure. What do *you* mean?"

"Come on." She plucked a kit off her wrist and threw it over her shoulder like she was discarding trash. The thing landed on its feet and bounded away.

The creatures, which Pogee said feared the outdoors, would not follow them across the Shrags' side yard to the larger building beside. That was good, Eeth thought, since she said that was where her husband's store was. But it was clear from the way the door didn't want to open inward that the Lamplighter Boutique hadn't had customers recently.

"There is nowhere to stand," he said, once the door was open.

"No, there ain't. I told you, he's a mess."

Outmoded datapads. Dusty holobooks. Boxes overflowing with flimsiplast cels. Framed documents, centuries old. Even the odd book or scroll. The mummified ideas of a hundred worlds seemed to be everywhere, stacked to the ceiling. In some places, literally, with the rafters bracing what was beneath. Eeth couldn't see any shelves or bookcases anywhere, but he wouldn't have sworn they weren't there, either.

Receiving Pogee's permission, he stepped gingerly inside, trying not to damage anything as he passed between the pillars. Eeth half wondered if her husband had a psychological problem, but he would never ask such a thing. Instead, he said, "He must have had an insatiable appetite for knowledge."

"Hah! His problem was he saw credits in everything that came in. But nobody could ever offer him enough to get him to part with anything."

Eeth had met the type—but never anyone like this. "You say Hadden is rehabilitating?"

"The cooking section fell on him." Standing on the threshold, she pointed to a darker area across the room. "Took folks a day to get him out of here. But it wasn't my cooking that got him, at least!" Pogee hooted at her joke and slapped Eeth on the back. It took all his Jedi reflexes not to pitch forward into a calamity of his own.

He took another cautious step inside. "Is Hadden due home soon?"

"I tried to get him to take the bacta treatment like anyone else, but he said he wanted time to read. I don't think he's ever coming back."

Eeth didn't think Pogee sounded too unhappy about that. He did know that *Lamplighter* was a poor name for the place. A candle would send the whole building up in a heartbeat.

"I am looking," he said, "for materials that would have been sold by a former exterminator from the northern shore. It would have been a couple of years ago."

She snorted. "No idea. All I can say is if they brought a boolah with them, it's probably got grandkits by now." She crossed her arms. "You can't have those."

Eeth shook his head. *This is madness.*

He started to turn to leave when one of the datapads shifted underneath his feet, its gilded case flashing in the light from the open door. He carefully knelt to inspect it.

The Wisdom of Master Fogo Charu, Jedi.

Eeth activated the device and studied its contents. While written by a Jedi, the "wisdom" was entirely related to fishing. Fogo Charu, whoever he was, knew what he liked to do. It was a lesser work, to be sure, but it bore the imprinted symbol of having circulated through the Sanctuary Mount library.

He looked about for more in vain. There was just too much of everything. Still, it was evidence he was in the right place.

Eeth rose and stepped back outside. He faced her. "This datapad. It was taken from my people."

"You can have it—and everything else. You're welcome to all of it." She grabbed him by the collar of his robe and fixed her giant eyes on him. "*Please, take all of it.*"

"I cannot do that—but I would like to keep searching. I would need to straighten up a bit, if you don't mind."

She hooted again. "Take all the time in the universe." Then her expression changed, and she crossed her arms. "Just don't take any of my precious boolahs. I can't part with them."

"I fully understand." He fully did not, but he bowed anyway.

As he watched her leave, Eeth remembered that he did not have all the time in the universe. There were already several members of the Council on Kwenn, and there was nobody better to evaluate what belonged to the outpost.

But the responses to his calls over the next hour were not encouraging.

"No, no, Master Piell. Your work with the children is definitely more important," he said in the first conversation. "No, please don't send any of them over. I doubt a lesson in identifying ancient Coremaic script would be of service to them."

"Never mind, Master Tiin. The workers of Kwenn are better served with you where you are. But I do appreciate the offer of a garbage hauler. Perhaps later."

"Thank you, Master Yoda, but you have just arrived. And to be honest, I would be afraid for you to walk into the room."

Resigned, Eeth stared at the comlink. Any good deeds of his on Kwenn would almost certainly be limited to helping Pogee clean up after her husband. Of course, it was probably not what Qui-Gon had in mind when he challenged the—

It dawned on him. There was a way. He stood clear of the building and used his comlink to call offworld.

Qui-Gon answered. "Master Koth. What can I do for you?"

"An apt question," Eeth said. "Are you aware of the mission your words inspired?"

"The Council's visit to Kwenn? I learned of it from Master Yaddle." Qui-Gon sounded a little discomfited. "I didn't intend to put everyone to such trouble."

Eeth thought that was at least a little debatable, but he never would have said it. "If you would see the results of our visit, you have the chance. I am recalling you to duty. The library at Sanctuary Mount requires your attention."

Qui-Gon sounded confused. "It was in perfect order when last I visited. Certainly Seneschal Voh can assist—"

"You'll just have to see for yourself." Eeth looked around the room. "And bring your Padawan. We need all the help we can get."

CHAPTER 22

RIFTWALKER HEADQUARTERS
VALBORAAN

"This is neat!" Kylah declared.

Not how I would have described a deadly criminal's under-ground lair, Depa thought, but she kept her mouth shut. She wasn't happy about Kylah joining her inside Zilastra's retreat on Valbo-raan, but neither had she wanted to lose sight of the girl. In this place, she might never find her again.

Despite Zilastra's darker tendencies, Depa had to salute her inven-tiveness. No attempt had been made to hew corridors or rooms into the stone walls of the Riftwalkers' lair within the Valboraan cave system. Rather, office and living spaces had been created by gutting pirated star-ships and fusing them together. Power and ventilation systems, some-how restored to functioning, made the hodgepodge livable for the dozens, if not hundreds, of people Depa saw.

"It's no Maz's Castle, but it's mine," Zilastra said.

She led them farther inside, where Burlug and IK-111 joined them. There was also a droid of another kind—a basic protocol model of the sort Depa had seen Zilastra and Tokchi working with earlier belowdecks. The Jedi grew more curious by the second.

At the end of several corridors, the group came upon a room that Depa figured must once have been an observation dome on another ship. There was little to see outside but rock walls, and little furnishing inside, either. Just a captain's chair near the outer circumference, turned so it faced the middle of the room.

The protocol droid stepped up to her. "The case."

The request startled Depa. "You said I didn't have to open this one."

Taking a seat in the chair, Zilastra waved off her concern. "I told you, it's just for show."

To whom? Depa didn't know, but she couldn't see the harm, either. Only she could open the lock. She passed it to the droid, who walked with it and took position at Zilastra's left.

Burlug and IK-111 took stations of their own, and more toughs filtered in to do the same. Depa joined them near the wall and tried to figure out what was happening. *Why does this seem familiar?*

Zilastra beckoned for Kylah to come closer. "You want to be in this business, kid? Here's an education, for real."

Mesmerized by the mysterious goings-on, the girl stood a few steps away, off to the right of the chair.

Tokchi's voice came from a speaker in her armrest. "They're in the room."

"Hit it," Zilastra said.

One by one, four other images flickered into holographic being, forming in a ring around the center of the chamber—a Jedi Council in microcosm. But there, the similarities stopped. Each image depicted two beings: one standing, one seated. The standers in each case were protocol droids, just like the one beside Zilastra; each held a sealed Regal Voyager case.

The seated figures were another story. Each looked different, as did their chairs.

Zilastra spoke first. "Riftwalkers," she declared, saying her name afterward.

"Poisoned Blades," cooed a slinky Twi'lek woman in a plush chair. "Venom Vee here."

"Skulls," growled a massive bald Iotran with half a dozen metal spikes protruding from his head. The bloodstained thing he sat in looked like it might also serve as a torture device. "I am the Eviscerator."

"Chief Executive Darwoh," announced a well-dressed older human seated on a gilded antique chair. "For all the Filthy Credits."

"The Vile," said a frightening-looking Sanyassan, his voice dripping with malice. Golden eyes glared from a scaly face smeared with something black and oily. It was hard to tell where his shock of hair ended and the furs he wore began. Clasping his hands together, he leaned forward in his iron throne. "Call me Bobo."

The disjoint between the latter participant's name and mien produced laughter from the others. All but Zilastra, who evinced concern. "What happened to Jupas? He's the leader of the Vile."

"*Not anymore.*" Bobo flashed a surplus of teeth. "I'm in charge now."

Zilastra shrugged. "It happens. Doesn't change our deal."

"Fill me in on this deal." Bobo thumped the case the droid was holding. "This droid showed up and said I had to call in."

Venom Vee groaned. "Here we go. Every time someone gets knocked off, we have to go over it all again."

Depa was glad of the change in personnel, just because it meant she got an explanation. Darwoh provided it with an elegance that clashed with the company he was speaking in.

"It's very simple, my fearsome friend. Droids came to us months ago with a proposition from Regal Voyager. All five of our organizations agree not to attack any of their ships—either the passenger line or their freight service."

"I know about that," Bobo said. "Damnedest thing, but Jupas made us all swear to it. Wouldn't tell us why."

"These cases are why," Zilastra said. "Payoffs. Big payoffs, in the exact same amounts to be delivered at the same time each month."

The Vile representative eyed the case. "This thing holds money?"

"Credits, gems, precious metals—whatever we request," Darwoh said. "But the values are equal. I insisted."

"We all insisted," Zilastra said. "Regal Voyager's deal only holds so long as none of us break the agreement. If any one of us reneges and hits their ships, the deal is off."

"I wasn't able to open mine," Bobo said. "We couldn't even scan to see what's in the thing."

"That's the catch," Venom Vee explained. "To ensure everyone gets their share—and their share alone—each of the droids knows one word of the code phrase that opens the cases."

The self-proclaimed Eviscerator spoke up. "It's a good deal. The Staved Skulls do protection rackets all the time—but nothing on this scale."

"Indeed," Darwoh said. "Regal Voyager is a huge conglomerate. Their freight traffic alone is worth a fortune. Safe passage through the Slice is vital for them."

"And they thought of it," Zilastra said. She seemed pleased about the arrangement.

Depa listened—and marveled. The gangsters were right. Corporations were extorted all the time. One extorting itself, for competitive gain, was a different story—and unheard of on this kind of a scale.

But then her eyes went to Kylah, kneeling and watching in rapt amazement. These were the exact sort of cases she'd been stealing from the Regal Voyager hub for months. And Depa had just helped her get four more—plus the one held by the droid beside Zilastra.

Four.

Depa's eyes darted from one holographic image to another—and then to Zilastra, who looked directly back. "That's enough talk," the Riftwalker leader declared. "Let's get to it."

"Quite right." Darwoh clasped his hands together greedily and addressed the droid beside him. "It is time, droids. The phrase!"

The droid next to him spoke. "Wookiee."

"Spoon," said the one beside Bobo.

"Turbo."

"Lightning."

Depa's eyes widened as she put it all together. She had to say something—

But Zilastra spoke first. "*Demise!*"

"*No! Keep them shut,*" Depa shouted. "*Keep—*"

It was too late. At the sound of the fifth word of a code phrase heard both there and in rooms across the stars, snaps came from the cases in the holographic images. Blinding flashes followed, accompanied by horrific screeches that were both organic and electronic.

And just as quickly as they had appeared, all four rival pirate bosses vanished. Meanwhile, the case in the hands of the droid beside Zilastra remained locked. And the pirate didn't seem at all surprised.

"What happened?" Kylah asked. "Where'd they go?"

"Away—forever!" Burlug shouted with glee. "There was enough baradium-357 in those things to take out whole ships!"

"But nothing happened here!"

"I wouldn't say that." Zilastra drew her blasters and pointed them at Depa. "You had something to say . . . *Jedi*?"

Kylah's eyes went wide—and so did Depa's. She didn't know how Zilastra knew—but she knew what she had to do. "Yes, I do have something to say. *Peace, knowledge, serenity, harmony, Force!*"

At her recitation of the last words of the lines of the Jedi mantra, the case in the droid's hands—the one Zilastra had not unlocked—popped open, startling her. The comlink inside tumbled toward the floor. The other item there did not: Depa's lightsaber, which she drew to her hand through the Force. She ignited the blue blade—and needed to, as the pirate chieftain started firing.

Depa deflected the shots in the directions of Burlug and the assassin droid, who had been reaching for their own weapons. No furnishings in the dome meant no cover—except for Zilastra's chair, which a terrified Kylah scrambled behind, and the bodies of her assailants.

Depa tried to use that cover, leaping high into the air and landing behind two of the other Riftwalkers. Slashing one's weapon and striking another down, she used their bodies as a screen to allow her to get closer to IK-111 and Burlug. She threw the droid back with the Force and assaulted Burlug, knocking him off balance and bisecting his weapon. The only way to escape from the melee was to be the last person standing.

But there was another person, whose scream she now heard over the din. It came from Kylah, huddled behind the chair.

Zilastra had her by her hair, with a blaster to her head. "It's over, Jedi!"

The point of Depa's blade glistened at the nape of Burlug's neck. "Let the girl go!"

Zilastra pulled the girl's hair tighter, producing tears. "Not happening. It's hopeless." More of her guards appeared in the doorway. "Stand down, now!"

Depa wanted to yell back that she didn't think Zilastra would do it—but she remembered the way she'd dealt with the attackers back on Keldooine. Kylah squealed.

There was nothing else to do. Depa took a step back, deactivating her lightsaber. She kept it in her hand until she saw Zilastra call out to her minions. "Take her alive. I have questions!"

So did Kylah, whom she released. The girl scrambled away and wiped her eyes. "Why'd you do that?" she cried to Zilastra.

"I had to. I told you. She's a Jedi."

The girl blinked, still processing. She looked to Depa. "You're a Jedi?"

Depa stood motionless as Burlug stepped up and took her lightsaber from her. She stared at Zilastra. "How did you know?"

"I didn't—not at first. You put on a good act. But it's like any game—I needed to find the one play that'd make you tip your hand. And you just did." Zilastra smiled at Kylah. "No hard feelings, kid. Four bosses and a Jedi in thirty seconds—we've made history today!"

CHAPTER 23

RAYLEY KEY

KWENN

"What is it, Master Yoda?"

Standing in Kwenn's most famous park, the Paths of Harmony, Yoda opened his eyes and looked at Adi Gallia. "A thought, I had. Many people, suffering great and sudden pain."

Adi's face grew serious. "Here on Kwenn?"

"No. That much is clear."

Yoda exhaled. For all the gifts that close kinship with the Force provided, the warnings he felt through it could come at any time, and in any place. Even here, in a place he had come to love years before. He had learned to live with it.

"Path pause," Adi said, and beneath their feet, the section of automated walkway they were on stopped moving. "Master Windu is traveling with Depa's escort," she said, comlink in hand. "Should I alert him?"

"Sensed it, he surely has. Closer, he is."

Adi put away the device and shut her eyes. A few seconds later, she opened them and shook her head. "I see distress in many places at once. But this region is known for it." She let out a deep breath. "That's all. My mind is too cluttered."

Yoda knew that part was his fault. The Jedi Order had a well-established structure for dealing with the mundane complexities of life, so its more wizened members could focus on the mysteries of the Force. But a number of matters were so delicate that only a member of the Jedi Council could attend to them—and after hundreds of years of service, his appetite for minutiae had waned.

Adi was a talented master in her own right, both as a fighter and as a diplomat. She did not deserve to spend so many hours assisting an elder colleague when she could be forging her own future. Yoda had told her so, many times. Yet nothing could dissuade her from wanting to help—even if it came at a cost.

But if any place could restore the spirit, it was the one they were in. Yoda gestured to the gardens. "To where we are, our attention belongs."

One of the first things the restorers of Kwenn had needed to consider during the Grand Renewal was how to address differences in elevation on the taller keys. Terraces became the major topographic element, and they worked around what were once mounds of debris in clever ways, employing techniques not found anywhere else in the galaxy. The most interesting expression of it was the Paths of Harmony, a park on Rayley Key that combined technology with horticulture.

"Path resume," Adi said, and they began moving again. "I see why you like this place."

Yoda chuckled. "Suggested it, I did!"

The Paths of Harmony were automated walkways disguised as natural trails, so everyone who stood upon them moved at the same pace. Visitors had the ability to control the speeds of the subsections they were on with spoken commands. Another clever innovation awaited visitors at the many observation points that interrupted the walkways. The area inside the observation rail was broken up into multiple sections that rose from the ground, equalizing the heights of everyone who stood there. People could see the natural beauty of the restored Kwenn—while to either side, they could look into the faces of their neighbors regardless of their differences in stature.

Gimmick though it was, Yoda appreciated the effort that had gone into it. "I am accustomed to life at my size. But here, all who walk are equal."

"And the beauty is everywhere around," Adi said, gesturing to the flowering trees in bloom. Families walked up ahead, children alongside their parents in wonder. Adi sighed. "How could such a place be in distress?"

Yoda knew she already had the answer. Adi had read the statistics about Kwenn in the recommendation from the chancellor's office, had seen the signs of decline during their flight in. But it heartened him to hear she had seen past that.

Beyond the foliage, their path ended along with several others at an overlook. The wharf could be seen, farther below. Islands and their connecting bridges looked lovely against the horizon. Kwenn's sun was starting to slip behind Capital Key, the island the Jedi outpost was on. A dozen or so people had lined up before the outer wall to watch, giving vocal commands to activate the risers that elevated their feet. The viewers looked out as one.

Yoda noticed that the person to his left was looking not at the sun, but down at the water far below. He was Sullustan, roughly halfway between his and Adi's heights—and the Jedi Master could sense his turmoil.

"A beautiful place," Yoda said.

For a second, the Sullustan acted as if he didn't hear. Then he looked to his right and stared into Yoda's face. Seeing kindness, he spoke. "It *is* beautiful. Only two weeks of the year does the sun pass behind Sanctuary Mount from here."

"Fortunate, we are, to be here today. I am Yoda. This is Adi Gallia."

The Sullustan bowed. "I am Lyal Lunn."

"On Kwenn, you live?"

"All my life." Lyal gestured to those watching the sea. "We used to have fifty people or more for the sunsets. On regular days."

"I remember," Yoda responded. "There were not enough paths for all."

"But people would line up anyway. They would come from other planets." Lyal smiled wistfully. "My father especially loved to come here. His hobby was making holos of Kwenn's sights—but never here. He said there was no capturing the beauty. I'm afraid he doesn't get out anymore." He sighed and shook his head—before looking at the Jedi. "I take it you're not from Kwenn?"

Adi smiled at him. "We are from Coruscant."

"And I thought I came a long way." Lyal pointed to the faraway island, now dropping into shadow. "I work performer relations at the arena on Gala Key."

Yoda knew it. "Saw it being built, I did."

Lyal chuckled. "*That* was a long time ago. It's pretty old now, like so much here. Our systems have deteriorated—we can't even get parts for some things."

"Has it hurt attendance for events?" Adi asked.

"We can't even *get* the events. We can't put on any of the modern operas. A lot of musical acts won't do Kwenn anymore just because of where it is—we practically have to give them the world to get them here. And we can't guarantee the audiences like we once could. People are on the move."

Yoda felt the worry pouring off Lyal. Evening was when the arena did most of its business, yet here he was, watching the Gem Cities sink into darkness.

Adi apparently sensed the same distress—and saw in it an opportunity. "Lyal, do you think there would be an opening for an event at the arena in the near future? I know it is short notice."

Lyal snorted. "Name the day, it's probably available." He looked over at her. "What is it, a birthday celebration? Anniversary?"

"Both."

"The facility is really too big for those, but that's all we've been getting lately."

"How many does it hold?"

He chuckled. "Well, twenty thousand. But of course, you won't need to accommodate that many."

"On the contrary," Adi said. "We'll need more."

"More?" Lyal was flabbergasted.

"Is there room outside?"

"Well, there are festival grounds surrounding it."

"Fine. We will supplement with electronic means for those on the farther islands—or for the homebound."

Yoda smiled. "Yes, all are welcome. After all, Kwenn's anniversary, it is."

Lyal laughed. "A party for Kwenn? That's impossible." He recoiled, starting to take offense. "You're making fun of me. Who do you think you are?"

"Jedi," Adi said. "It is the Jedi who wish a celebration."

Lyal stared. "You two work for the Jedi?"

Yoda nodded. "We work for everyone."

Lyal looked out across the water—just in time to see light coming from the beacon atop the Jedi outpost. A smattering of applause came from the others at the observation area as the Unquenchable Fire glowed anew.

Fortuitous, coincidental timing—and it seemed to dizzy the Sullustan. "You are really Jedi?"

Yoda and Adi looked at each other. It would be an easy thing to display a lightsaber or do a trick. But he had something else in mind. "The seneschal is still by the brazier."

"On it." Adi toggled her comlink. "Seneschal. Blue, please."

"Of course, Master."

She gestured for Lyal to cast his eyes again to the outpost. After a moment, the light atop it blazed a brilliant blue, the result of a handful of powder tossed upon the flame by the caretaker. An old signal, and one that worked wonders on Lyal.

The Sullustan beamed. "It's true!"

His change in expression warmed Yoda's heart. "We are in earnest. We would like your arena."

Now taking it seriously, Lyal appeared to concentrate. "I don't know if it's possible to put on such an event, not at our place. It would take much work. And the promotion—"

"We are not alone here," Adi said. "We are skilled at making things happen."

"You'd have to be." Lyal shared with her the contact information for the arena's booking officer. "Call now—but then I'd go in person. I don't think she'll believe you if you don't." He gestured to the outpost. "Unless you have more tricks like that!"

Adi thanked him and stepped away.

Yoda observed Lyal. The news had momentarily lifted his spirits, but the Jedi Master could sense a cloud returning. "Something troubles you?"

"It's nothing."

"You grew angry earlier."

"Sorry about that. I thought you were making fun of me."

"Not then." He peered at Lyal. "You reacted when my colleague said 'homebound.' "

Dark eyes looked down at the enshrouded shore below. "The hospital has sent my father home."

Yoda nodded. "He is very ill?"

"He is old. Every sickness threatens him—and it has been costly. He cannot go to the places he once loved, like this. I have taken him to my house."

"And your family."

"He *is* my family. And I am his. But he requires constant care." He looked up. "I guess we all did, once. But still . . ."

"Began your life, he did. And paused your life, he has. You know your duty—but you also feel guilt over being upset by it."

He looked to Yoda and nodded.

Yoda spoke with understanding. "Difficult, it can be, to think beyond ourselves. No acclaim, do we receive. But in such acts, the poorest soul finds nobility." He gently poked Lyal in the chest. "You are a good son."

A warning bell sounded, and lights went on across the park. Lyal's height advantage over Yoda manifested slowly as the cantilevered observation platforms moved back to a flattened state so that everyone could depart safely. The Paths of Harmony were done for another day.

The other visitors departed, but a cloaked figure remained beneath one of the lamps far from their location. Lyal looked in that direction before turning to Yoda. "There is someone I must see here. But I appreciate your talking with me—and definitely your business." He looked over to see that Adi had finished her call. "I hope we will meet again."

Yoda bowed. "Good night."

As Lyal walked slowly over to where his companion awaited, he looked back through the shadows to them more than once.

Adi approached Yoda. "The call is made. Lyal's word is good. We have a meeting this evening."

"So fast?"

Adi nodded. "It is as you have said. The Force sometimes provides."

Sometimes it does, Yoda thought. But as he watched Lyal, he wondered if this was indeed one of those times.

CHAPTER 24

ABOARD *ASSURANCE*

AKLASIAN NEBULA

"*Fire! Fire! Fire!*"

Mace barely heard Captain Baylo's words as he rushed back onto the bridge. While hunting pirates in a nebula, *Assurance* had finally seen the action that Baylo had sought—and several decks of the corvette were burning as a result.

Initially, their venture into the nebula off the Ootmian route had looked like another waste of time as they continued to wait for word from Depa Billaba. A scout ship belonging to the Poisoned Blades had been snooping about in the cloud. Baylo had expected it would go to hyperspace before *Assurance* got into weapons range. But it had lingered past the time when it should have sensed the corvette's presence. Mace and Baylo realized something was amiss at the same time, but too late. A Poisoned Blade warship struck from within the nebular mass, in keeping with the gang's reputation for deceit.

While well-led, this iteration of Baylo's crew was green—and damage to *Assurance* had quickly mounted. Danger escalated so quickly that the captain thought nothing of Mace relieving an injured weapons officer. The Jedi's actions held off the enemy vessel—up until the bridge lost all fire control. With the thrusters damaged, the only question that re-mained was whether the Blades would go for the capture or the kill.

The Jedi called out, "Captain, we've sealed off the landing bay. We are no longer venting into space."

"Cauterized the wound." Baylo hunched over a sparking control panel vacated by a helm officer who still lay unconscious on the deck. "I need these weapons and engines back online, now!"

Mace looked out the forward viewport. For whatever reason, the Blades had stopped firing—but Baylo was anxious to reengage. Mace said, "You can't mean to continue the fight. We must get to safety."

"Don't tell me what to do!" Baylo punched keys, trying to make some-thing happen. "I've got casualties. They're not getting away with it!"

Mace knew that the Poisoned Blades would have the upper hand in any renewed engagement, but there was no telling the captain that. He knelt and began tending to the injured crewmember. "Nellis is alive."

"Keep him that way—or his parents will kill both of us!"

Mace considered the few options left to them. A boarding action, he could deal with. The other prospect was one he wasn't sure how to—

"Something's happening," Mace said, his senses alive. "Something's changed."

Baylo gawked as the Blade vessels turned hard about. "What in the—?"

Mace had no answers for the captain. For some reason, the Blades had abandoned them and were screaming toward the edge of the nebula.

"Target has gone to hyperspace," an officer said.

"You say that all the time," Baylo snarled. He gave up on the console and pounded his fist on it. "Damn them!"

He stepped away from the panel. A junior officer, bruised and black-ened by smoke, took the helm promptly and asked for orders. Baylo ordered *Assurance* to leave the nebula under whatever means of propul-sion were available. "Open a hatch if you need to."

"*Captain,*" Mace said, looking up from tending the wounded officer. It wasn't the right thing for Baylo to say—not with depressurized cabins and suffering crew aft. Mace said no more, simply holding his gaze on the elder man.

Chastened, Baylo lowered his voice a little. "You were below decks earlier. How were the kids back there faring?"

Mace wanted to be diplomatic. "They're trying."

"They were never going to hold it together under fire."

"But they did, as we have survived. Your crew has performed admirably." Mace looked around the bridge. "Especially here."

"That's because they can see me." Baylo glanced at him. "And you."

Mace didn't know what he thought about that. But the captain did help him get Nellis to a waiting litter.

Assurance had been out of communication with the outside world not because of the nebula, but due to a hit to its receiving array—an event producing explosive feedback injuring its communications officer. Young Veers had taken his mentor's place there, but there wasn't much he could do. The damage meant there had been no communication with the pirates attacking them—nor any explanation as to why they had fled when victory was within their grasp.

"I don't get it," Baylo said as the medics took Nellis away. "They had us. They had us!"

"Hyperdrive available in five minutes," came a call from over the intercom.

Mace looked forward. *Assurance* was just limping out of the nebula. "Captain, we are nowhere near ready to—"

A cracking voice came from starboard. "Communications are back up."

Baylo and Mace turned toward Veers—only to see the recruit looking much less confident. Baylo frowned. "*Well?*"

"Sorry, Captain—we're receiving many alerts at once. Flash traffic for us on many different channels."

Mace nodded. "The backlog."

"Looks like two—no, three—pirate stalkers in the sector disengaged from ships they were hunting and left," Veers said.

"Good news."

"A SoroSuub freighter reports witnessing an explosion at a private space station. Many casualties."

"Let me see that," Baylo said, moving to the youth's side but not pushing him away. He stared. "I'll be damned. That's in Poisoned Blade space. No wonder they left so fast!"

Mace thought it a sufficient answer—but things grew more complicated when the trainee found something else. "Republic traveler distress channel reports that a ship in orbit around Ord Jannak blew up."

"Ord Jannak? Was it under fire?" Mace asked.

"Not according to the report."

"Malfunction?" Baylo asked.

Mace frowned. "At another time, I might entertain that. Now I am not so sure."

Veers saw something that made him blanch. He cleared his throat. "A skytower on Keldooine exploded."

The news hit the bridge like a torpedo. "*Exploded?*" Baylo asked.

"Yes, Captain. The upper ten levels."

Mace sprang toward an adjacent set of terminals. The other disasters were bad. This was potentially catastrophic for thousands—and for one.

"Master Billaba was last on Keldooine." Mace worked the controls. "Get us feeds from the planet, quickly!"

Mace watched the carnage—and the firefighting droids struggling to respond. "Urban area. Horoja District?"

Baylo scratched his chin and thought for a moment. "I know that city. The corporations pulled out of there two years ago. It's Filthy Cred territory now." He looked at the display and back to Mace. "Eight city blocks afire. Could she be there?"

Mace concentrated. He had sensed anguish through the Force during the attack on *Assurance*—which had then spiked around the time of the reported explosion. Now he could no longer tell. He very much wanted to go, to respond to the crisis—but the Jedi Order didn't rely upon him because of how he responded to his wants. It wanted something else from him.

Surety.

Baylo saw him staring into space and shook his head in bewilderment. He walked behind the helm operator. "Set navicomputer for coordinates to Keldooine!"

Mace looked over at him. "Belay that order."

"What?" Baylo erupted. "That's not your call, Windu!"

Mace knew instantly he had forgotten himself. But something larger was happening, and it wasn't just on Keldooine. "Captain, we should hold station."

"Hold station?" Baylo sputtered. "I knew you were a cold customer, Windu, but there are people in jeopardy there. Including the person I was hired to escort. Sure, it's probably a lot of pirates burning up, but Master Billaba—"

"May not be there. And if she is, she is already on the scene, helping people—whether they are pirates or not."

"And if she isn't?"

"The local authorities—"

"Are a joke. And why is that?" Baylo glared at him. "*Because you left.*"

Mace locked eyes with the captain. He felt the danger to the people on Keldooine—but he could also feel the other flashpoints. Reason had always driven his actions, and it did so now. Calm words were the only response.

"Captain, your crew is hurt—and whatever it is, it isn't a rescue team. You must see that there is something more going on. *And it is not just on Keldooine.*"

Baylo's eyes narrowed. He called over his shoulder without turning. "What are you hearing, cadet?"

The young man spoke again. "More traffic from the convoy channel. Reports of firefights at various locations in space. Participants unidentified."

Baylo looked again at the images of the fires on Keldooine.

"Systems restored, Captain," the relief helm officer told him. "Heading?"

Baylo swore at Windu. "You're right, dammit."

Mace raised an eyebrow. "I am?"

The captain scratched his chin. "People like me have been gaming out crises for centuries. A firefighter goes to a fire. A doctor goes to a patient. But a military vessel—"

"Doesn't go straight to what may be a provocation." Mace considered all the incident reports. "We don't even know which is the provocation."

"When we don't know, we don't go." Baylo stepped forward and turned to face the bridge crew. "*Assurance,* we're standing down. Let's tend the wounded and fix this tub."

Mace exhaled and checked his comlink. It was rare for the Jedi Master's calm to slip, and it had almost never happened since he joined the Jedi Council. But this incident had tested his reserve. He wasn't sensing Depa, and there was still no message from her. But that didn't mean the worst.

He toggled the device. "Some of my colleagues are still en route to Kwenn. I'll alert everyone to what has transpired. If Keldooine needs them, they'll respond."

"I hope you know what you're doing, Windu."

"So do I, Captain. So do I."

CHAPTER 25

LANGDAM KEY

KWENN

"I will have the ice mound."

"One Tasty Comet ice mound." The frozen treat vendor in the harbor market on Langdam Key looked up from his trolley at Ki-Adi-Mundi. "What flavor ice mound will that be, sir?"

"Ice."

"Ice?"

"Yes, I said this," Ki-Adi-Mundi replied. "An ice mound."

The Jedi Master knew of Even Piell's occasional problems in being understood. He had no such issues. His diction was flawless. Here on Kwenn or anywhere else, if a person understood Galactic Basic, they understood the Cerean Jedi.

The operator of the Tasty Comet cart was still having problems, however. "You just want ice. No flavoring."

"Ice *is* a flavor."

"If you say so." The vendor sighed and scooped a mound of ice crystals from his hovercart into a conical container. He handed it to the Jedi. "That will be—" He paused.

"Is something the matter?"

The vendor scratched his head. "We charge by the flavor. There isn't a price for ice."

Ki-Adi-Mundi looked at the signage on the cart. "That *is* an oversight. One you should probably correct." He placed a credit in the vendor's hand anyway. "Toward making a new sign."

The Jedi Master strode away from the vendor, feeling good about having helped someone. He didn't understand what Qui-Gon Jinn was always on about. Members of the Council were helpful wherever they went.

The harbor market at Perro Quay still seemed thriving. Wind conditions here made the sunny day more apparent, and several families milled about enjoying it. And if there were not so many visitors as he had seen in earlier years, they seemed happy enough.

Ki-Adi-Mundi enjoyed the respite it offered even as he cast his thoughts toward other, less fortunate places. He was aware of stories of turmoil in nearby systems, but the one that had surprised him was the building explosion on Keldooine. Master Windu had sent out an alert about it from *Assurance,* the patrol craft he was aboard—and Yarael Poof had diverted his shuttle to the planet to offer aid.

From what Ki-Adi-Mundi had heard, Master Yarael's attempt to help had been roundly rejected by the surviving members of the Filthy Creds. That hadn't surprised Yarael—or anyone else. The criminals were reeling from what was very probably an attack. It was no surprise that they'd closed off access to their territory. Frustratingly, the Republic itself had issued no alerts whatsoever in regard to these places, leaving things in local hands. As such, none of the Jedi on Kwenn had left the planet, or their preparations.

As concerned as he was over events on Keldooine, he was glad Yarael hadn't arrived with him. The two had been thrown together overmuch of late, and the Quermian's disposition had grown more antic over the centuries. Ki-Adi-Mundi wasn't made of stone, but he thought the office required a little more decorum. And Kwenn needed serious attention. It was a world the Order had not abandoned—not yet—and that made the event they were planning more important than ever.

Around the bend, he found several mobile stands specializing in prepared lunches. Ki-Adi-Mundi was no aesthete, but he could infer popularity from the numbers at each stand, competence by how fast the lines moved, and satisfaction from reading faces of those leaving. Determining the best option, he bowed to one of the operators, a Snivvian female. "I am seeking a business to cater an event to be held shortly."

"Very good," the woman said. "What is the date?"

Ki-Adi-Mundi shared the information, which she entered in her datapad. "That should be no problem," she said. "How many are we serving?"

"I wish to be precise. Approximately twenty thousand inside. Another hundred thousand at various external viewing sites across the islands."

She stared at Ki-Adi-Mundi. "You're out of your mind."

"I assure you both my brains are in proper working order, according to my last physical."

"You want a hundred thousand lunches?"

"A hundred twenty."

"A hundred twenty thousand lunches."

"We may require dinners, as well. We do not know how long the event will last." He looked around. "Can you provide this service?"

"Not alone." She stared at him. "Are you sure there are that many people who'd pay to eat?"

"Oh, the lunches will be free."

She laughed. "No, they won't."

Ki-Adi-Mundi's voice soared. "A celebration of the kind we intend should be open to all. We want our message heard—and to attend to the needs of our listeners both worldly and spiritual."

"Worldly and spiritual." She scratched her head. "And who's paying?"

"The Jedi Order."

She closed her eyes and rubbed her forehead.

"Is something wrong?"

"No, it's just been a long morning." She opened her eyes and made a mark in her datapad. "I'm going to have to see a form of identification."

Ki-Adi-Mundi thought for a moment. Nothing else occurring to him, he unclasped the lightsaber from his belt and ignited it.

" 'Jedi Order,' " she said as she made her note. "Well, as long as your credit's good."

After he deactivated the weapon, she took the rest of his contact information. "I'll talk to some people and get back to you." She looked down at the cone in his hand. "Your ice is dripping."

Indeed it was, he saw. Ki-Adi-Mundi righted it and ventured back out into the crowd.

He was about to try the ice mound when, without warning, a tall Yarkora woman in a floral gown burst forth from the crowd. Well-coiffed hair framed her long snout and wide nostrils—and she wore an enormous smile. "*Hello!*" she cried.

Ki-Adi-Mundi looked up at her with mild disinterest. "Greetings."

She looked back over her shoulder before facing him. "And what's your name?"

"Ki-Adi-Mundi."

"You say the most wonderful things!" Long tan arms grabbed the surprised Jedi, pulling him into an embrace.

He looked past her to the street. "I have dropped my ice mound."

"You'll buy another one." She released him. "You'll buy me one, too. Won't you, sweetheart?"

Ki-Adi-Mundi tried to pull away. "I am afraid you have mistaken me for someone else."

"Oh, I could never want someone else. Such a profile you cut. That rugged frame. That beard." She stroked the side of his face. "That head!"

The Jedi Master looked around, embarrassed by the display of affection. It was fortunate that no one knew him here, and that his fellow members of the Council were not around. That would have been a fate worse than death.

Still, he preferred not to act abruptly. If she was experiencing mental or emotional instability, that might cause her a setback. So he took care in trying to escape her. "I'm sorry, but you must—"

"All right, that's enough!" A rugged-looking Yarkora male charged from a storefront in their direction. He stopped before the pair and looked Ki-Adi-Mundi over. "Aha! A Cerean!" He faced the woman. "The truth, Varralis! Is he the one from that sales conference?"

"I'm not telling you anything!" The female clung to Ki-Adi-Mundi more tightly. "Leave us alone, Aptorr!"

The Jedi put up his hands. "Good citizens, I have no—"

The man she'd called Aptorr yelled, "A likely story!"

"I told no story."

"That's it!" Aptorr punched his hand with his fist. "I don't know who you think you are, but let's go!"

"Go? Go where?"

"Right here." He pointed at the ground. He stomped on the fallen ice mound and pulverized it with his shoe. "That'll be your head if you don't let Varralis go!"

This time, the Jedi succeeded in freeing himself from her. There was quite a crowd around by now. "I tell you, I have never seen this person before."

"Then what are you doing, harassing her?"

"Harassing?"

Aptorr pointed to Varralis. "She and I are having a disagreement. This has nothing to do with you, and I'll thank you to keep out of it."

"It would be my profound pleasure," Ki-Adi-Mundi said.

Varralis reached out, preventing him from leaving. "You leave Kee-Odee-Modee alone, Aptorr. We're finished."

"Finished?" Aptorr stomped on the ground again. "What about the children?"

With difficulty, Ki-Adi-Mundi reclaimed his arm. "Am I to understand you two have a family together?"

"Family, yes; together, no." Varralis glared at Aptorr. "I've been his business partner for twenty years. We've got a house together. We've got five children."

Aptorr put his hands on his hips. "You forgot the mortgages, the business loans, your father in the attic, and a tree full of boolahs!"

Ki-Adi-Mundi blinked. "Boolahs?"

"And not a one housebroken!"

The Cerean put his hand on the back of his cranium. "I am missing vital information."

The couple continued to rage at each other. Ki-Adi-Mundi considered taking flight. There was a ledge off to the left, over which a twenty-meter drop led to the shore below. But there were vines he might use to make his escape. That was what Master Tiin would do in a heartbeat—and not a few other members of the Council.

Then another thought struck. *What would Qui-Gon do?*

He stepped closer to the couple, who were now nose-to-nose, screaming. He worked to get into their eyelines and raised his hand. "You don't want to argue."

They looked at him and spoke in unison. "What?"

"I didn't think that would work." Ki-Adi-Mundi put up his other hand—and used it to gesture for peace. "Please listen to me."

Aptorr spat on the ground. "Why should we?"

"Quiet," Varralis barked. She looked to the Jedi. "What is it, beloved?"

Ki-Adi-Mundi shifted uncomfortably at the name—but plowed ahead. "You," he said, indicating her. "You feel neglected. Hence these theatrics."

"You see?" she said to her partner. "He understands me. Not like—"

"And you," he said, pointing to Aptorr, "you struggle with the demands of work and family. I see by your attire it has been a long time since a new wardrobe."

Aptorr looked at his tatty clothes. "I make sacrifices, yes. What of it?"

Ki-Adi-Mundi continued. "You have apparently seen so little of Varralis that when she accosted me, you entertained suspicions because you have not been present."

Varralis crossed her arms. "He's been gone every night this month!"

The Cerean looked to Aptorr. "Is this true?"

Aptorr stared in anger—and then hung his head. "I have."

"I knew it! He's been seeing someone," Varralis said. "Who is it?"

He spoke in a small voice. "A Wookiee."

"A Wookiee?" The word came not just from Varralis but also from several of the eavesdropping shoppers.

Ki-Adi-Mundi put up his hand. "I don't think—"

Aptorr looked both ways—and gestured for Varralis and Ki-Adi-Mundi to follow him out of earshot from the passersby. Reluctantly, the Jedi complied. Varralis stomped after them.

Away from others, he spoke quietly. "I have been training a Wookiee after hours to operate my plant on Brazatta Key."

Ki-Adi-Mundi stared at him—and at Varralis's shocked response. He saw no lie in it. "And why were you keeping this a secret?"

"If anyone learns Gartabba is running things, I could lose my franchise." He gestured to the storefront behind him. "Aptorr Industries products are advertised as one hundred percent Yarkora-made!"

"But why not tell *me*?" Varralis said.

Aptorr laughed. "Then *everyone* would know!"

Ki-Adi-Mundi saw Varralis's ire rising again. He gestured for patience from her. "I do not agree with dishonesty," the Jedi said. "Why can't you tell the truth?"

"Commerce on Kwenn is on the edge of a blade," Aptorr said. "The world of quality-made fabric chairs, umbrellas, and camping equipment is cutthroat. It's kill or be killed!"

That was three more violent metaphors than Ki-Adi-Mundi thought necessary, but he soldiered on. "Tell me what you get from it. You are not mistreating the Wookiee?"

"Oh, no!" Aptorr looked up. "Gartabba receives a fair wage. From his presence I get added security for the plant—you've heard about the protection schemes popping up there."

Ki-Adi-Mundi had not. "What else do you receive?"

"Time, which is most precious."

"It would surely be precious for your spouse." The Jedi glanced at Varralis. "She *must* receive some of the benefit."

Aptorr looked off to the side—and then at Varralis. "Yes, I can make sure of that," he said. "You will see me more—if that is what you want."

Varralis took his hands and smiled. "Thank you, Kee-Olee-Molee."

The Cerean decided not to correct her. He hadn't even mentioned he was a Jedi—much less a Council member—but he'd made an impact.

Now it was Aptorr who grabbed his arm. "You will not tell anyone about Gartabba?"

"I think that is between the two of you. You may be able to train your clients to regard Gartabba-made goods as superior." Ki-Adi-Mundi scratched his beard. "And I may have the very event at which you could debut them."

"That's wonderful!" Varralis said. "It's amazing that I found you!"

"The Force—" he began, only to change his mind. People would learn that soon enough. "Things have a way of working out," he said as he squinted at the sun. "But I may require another ice mound."

CHAPTER 26

RIFTWALKER HEADQUARTERS
VALBORAAN

"Where's that blasted kid?"

Kylah Lohmata watched through the grating of the vent as Burlug stomped around the Riftwalkers' secret base on Valboraan. It was about time somebody noticed she was gone—but being mistreated and then forgotten about was the story of her life.

She'd been born in Hutt space, on a world that had never seen peace or justice. Kylah had barely known her father at all before he died in a blaster fight over something he had nothing to do with; at least, that was the story her mother told her. Arduous travels followed, culminating with her mother's remarriage and a few months of relative peace in a migrant community on Chalacta. But after her mother suddenly died, that family wanted nothing to do with Kylah—and when the migrant colony broke up, she was left behind.

She had just turned nine years old.

What followed was life aboard one starship after another, never as an official passenger. Vessels were always going back and forth along the Ootmian route, and there was always a meal to be had for a sharp-witted person who could get in and out of small hiding places. She'd stayed in the Slice during it all; it was a place she knew well, and while she had no home she was never lost. Discovery or capture, when they happened, were just chances to change ships. Kylah thought nothing of either danger, after a while. A person either rode the waves or got swept underneath.

That was why Kylah had thought she'd found a kindred spirit when she met Zilastra. She'd been left behind somewhere, too—or so she'd said. Kylah had witnessed her doing violent things, even cruel ones. But until the standoff with Hotwire, the pirate had never raised a hand to her, instead treating her like an important part of the Riftwalker family.

That was what it was to Kylah. Or it had been.

She looked again out at Burlug—her big, cranky Feeorin uncle who loved putting the scare into people, most of whom deserved it. He'd stopped looking for her and had moved on to something else. Kylah turned around, creeping farther back through the vents. If the Riftwalkers were no longer a place for her, so be it. There'd be some way off Valboraan. There always was.

One thing still bothered her. She hadn't seen Zilastra since the incident in the dome, and she hadn't wanted to. But Hotwire—*a Jedi*? She didn't know what to think of that at all. Presumably, the woman was a prisoner now. Why hadn't Hotwire told her the truth? It seemed like one more betrayal, but she still had questions.

She heard a commotion down a tunnel to the right. A section she hadn't entered, it was dark, and it stank. Such conditions had never stopped her before, however, and they didn't stop her now. A faint light appeared beyond a grating at the end. When she saw who was beyond it, she kicked open the vent cover. "Guys!"

Three soot-faced figures looked at her in the low light of a glowing lantern. Ghor, Wungo, and The Lobber were filthy as they stood surrounded by what had probably been the mechanical bowels of a much larger ship. They all had tiny brushes in their hands.

"Hey," Ghor said to her, without enthusiasm.

Kylah scrambled to her feet. "What are you doing?"

"Eyekay says there's fungus growing in the vents. Something that was on one of these ships they built this place out of. He's got us scrubbing everything down."

"We've got the trash compactor next," Wungo said. "We're moving up."

In contrast with his miserable companions, Lobber seemed energetic. If his confidence had been shaken at all by their latest chore, the Devaronian's face didn't show it. "You've got the right idea coming here, kid. This place is the nerve center."

Kylah didn't understand. "Nerve center?"

"Yeah, the brain!"

Ghor winced. "It's one of the organs, for sure."

"You're lucky," Wungo said to the Houk. "You don't have a nose."

Lobber was unperturbed. "We're hearing *everything*. Everywhere in this whole base. Stuff's going on all over the place."

Kylah nodded. "You heard what happened to the other gangs?"

"Yeah, they've all gone wobbly. There's one opportunity after another. I'm telling these guys, this could be the start of something big."

The girl wasn't interested. "Have you seen Hotwire?"

"What, your driver friend?"

"She's your friend, too. She gave you credit for catching that Vile ship when Zil was ready to do away with you."

"That's true." Wungo looked to his friends. "That is true."

"Nonsense," Lobber snapped. "Nobody did anything for us. Why should we know where she is?"

"I thought you heard everything," Kylah said. "I haven't seen her since Zilastra caught her."

"Caught her? Why?"

"*She's a Jedi.*"

Wungo's eyes went wide. "Zilastra is a Jedi?"

"No," Kylah said. "Hotwire is!"

She explained the fight that had transpired in the round room. She couldn't tell if they believed her or not—but she could tell they had a healthy respect for the Jedi and what they could do.

What they *thought* they could do, anyway.

"That was close," Ghor said. "Being in the room with an angry Jedi? She could have turned you into a tree. Or worse!"

"What's worse than a tree?" Lobber asked.

Wungo was dazzled. "She really had a lightsaber? Our Jedi didn't even have those!" The Klatooinian clasped his hands and looked at Kylah. "Ghor's right. You're lucky you're alive."

"All right, that's enough!"

Everyone's attention went to an open hatchway. Zilastra stepped through it. A second after seeing her, her three lowliest underlings were back at the walls, scrubbing away. "We're working," Lobber said. "We're working."

Zilastra looked to Kylah. "Burlug thought you were down here. You're not as quiet as you think."

The girl crossed her arms. "You've hunted me down to finish me off, I guess."

The pirate leader shook her head. "I told you, I did what I had to do. I was up against a Jedi."

Ghor and Wungo looked at each other. Lobber spoke for both of them. "So it's true. She *was* a Jedi."

"And I said 'that's enough' because I have had it with you three when it comes to the Jedi." Zilastra's eyes filled with rage. "Everyone treats the Jedi like they're gods, but they're not invincible. They can do fancy tricks, but they're just people. People who can be beat."

Kylah shrugged. "How should we know? I've only heard stories. I've never even seen a Jedi before."

Zilastra scowled—and came to a decision. "Fine. The only way anyone in this organization is going to learn is if people see for themselves what they're up against. Might as well start at the bottom—and there's nobody closer to the bottom than you three. Follow me." Zilastra looked at Kylah. "You, too."

The three underlings filed out after Zilastra. Kylah followed them through a maze of corridors to a section of the pirates' nest she hadn't seen before.

A high-pitched sound up ahead suggested they were getting close to something, but it didn't sound mechanical. "What's that screeching?" Ghor yelled.

Lobber covered his ears. "Whatever it is, it could drive a Wookiee mad!"

Zilastra ignored them, leading them inside the room the sound was emanating from. The IK-111 droid stood sentry before a figure suspended a meter off the ground in an immobilization beam.

"Hotwire!" Kylah uncovered her ears and hurried to the imprisoned woman's side. Hotwire's goggles and helmet were gone, revealing that her hair was dark and braided in loops—and that she bore two small beads on her forehead between her eyes. Her eyes were shut, even as Kylah's were wide. "Is . . . is she dead?"

"No. We're trying to find out who she is and why she's here." Zilastra indicated the table and chair nearby. "But she's putting up a fight."

Wungo shouted over the din. "What's this noise for?"

"In case she wakes up. It's not enough to keep her in stasis. Jedi can do things with their minds. Manipulate people, objects." She glared up at the suspended figure. "I only want her able to concentrate when I have something to ask."

Lobber stared. "She doesn't look like much."

"That's what I'm telling you. The things they can do can all be defeated. It just takes some smarts." She turned and faced down the trio. "You've seen her. Now get back to work."

Lobber and his companions hurried back up the corridor. Seeing a message on her comlink, Zilastra headed for the exit. "Come on, while you can still hear."

Kylah took a mournful look at Hotwire and complied.

Zilastra spoke to Kylah over her shoulder as they walked. "I don't want you scurrying around anymore," the pirate boss said. "I explained about earlier. I just had a big win, and you were part of it. But if you want to stick around, don't give me any attitude. I don't have the time."

Kylah looked back to the room where Hotwire was imprisoned. "What will you do with her?"

"I told you. I'm going to find out who she is, and why she's here. And then I'm going to kill her."

"But she's my friend! Or—she was."

"Friendship is overrated, kid. It's not for people like us." Zilastra stopped and turned to face the girl, eyes afire. "No. This will be a pleasure."

CHAPTER 27

ADDOA KEY

KWENN

"Excuse me!"

Yaddle directed her speeder bike around a parked vehicle and zipped up to the intersection. Stopping there, she drew the attention of a ruby-colored patrol droid at the center of the crossroads.

It called out, "Children's conveyances are not allowed on the thoroughfare!"

"Oh, dear, I'm older than every bolt in your body." Yaddle waved as she put the bike back into motion. "Have a good day!"

Yaddle couldn't remember the last time she'd ridden a speeder bike—or when she'd had as much fun. When finding a conveyance outside the speederport had been impossible—some kind of labor action was still being resolved, she'd been told—she'd contacted Master Piell for help. He'd responded by sending her a speeder bike, of all things. A Rodian child of perhaps eight arrived on the souped-up craft, handed it off to her, and left on the back of an older child's speeder.

Every safety protocol on the little machine had been bypassed, she soon realized; its engine came from some other vehicle altogether. As far as Yaddle knew, podracing had never taken hold as a serious sport on Kwenn, probably there was no space for it—but that hadn't stopped the youth of the planet from wanting to live fast and fly young.

Young was how Yaddle felt, cruising down and around the winding terrace roads. Sometimes fast, sometimes slow, crossing from one artificial island to another. Rayley, Malbaira, Addoa—all names she knew from centuries ago. Master Oppo and the brain trust behind the Grand Renewal had considered naming the islets after the major systems in the Republic. One would travel by bridge from Little Coruscant to New Corellia, and so on. It certainly had encouraged investors, who saw whole neighborhoods springing up celebrating the cultures of faraway worlds.

Yaddle had led the opposition to that. Kwenn wasn't an amusement park for outsiders; it belonged to those who had lived there before and had remained during the planet's ecological collapse. And so location names from the world's past were chosen for the islands. She'd even forestalled the use of *New* before any place-names. A "new" city could become an old one quickly with lack of care. Better that the people feel the places they lived were everlasting, connected to both the past and the future—and always in need of renewal as they passed from one custodian generation to another. That was the circle of life.

People had forgotten that. Yaddle's travels had taken her across pretty islands with parks and harbors with street vendors. That was the part of Kwenn that was still working. The farther she rode, however, the more she became convinced it was vestigial—an echo of the past. Decline was in the air. Whose fault it was made no difference to her. There was still a chance to turn things around.

Yaddle crossed another bridge leading to Addoa Key, the most industrial of Kwenn's islands. That once hadn't been a bad thing. Manufacturers on the planet during the Grand Renewal had improved their practices voluntarily, answering the Jedi's call to action. But Yaddle had seen on her approach to Kwenn that something had changed. With that earlier leadership absent, local regulations had filled the void; now, it seemed from the smoke, neither was having any impact. She fully expected to find harsh conditions as she drew closer to the first of many factories.

What she didn't expect to find was a veritable army of school-aged children outside the walls of the Rendili Hyperworks factory. The walls were something Yaddle definitely didn't remember seeing before on her last tour of Kwenn. As near as she could tell, the children were painting them.

She pulled the speeder bike to a stop just outside the group and dismounted.

"Master Yaddle! You made it!" a familiar voice called. Yaddle followed it and watched Even Piell emerge from the crowd carrying an armload of containers. He placed the canisters on the paved ground, revealing that the front of his robe was covered with spatters of paint. "Welcome to art class!"

Yaddle looked at him in disbelief. "The children told me you wanted to see me, but they didn't say what you were doing." She stared at the kids. "What *are* you doing?"

"I told you. *Art.*" Piell led Yaddle through the crowd. "Make way for another Jedi," he called out.

Cheers rose as the kids cleared a path for the new arrival. Yaddle saw that the wall was relatively new—an ebon barrier, stretching tall and wide to the edge of the terrace. But the area where the children worked had come alive with color. Below were whimsical animals and fantastic islands, while above, planets, stars, and aurorae broke up the monument to monotony.

"Wondrous," she said, clasping her hands together. She looked again at the painters—youths of all species and ages. "You found them here?"

"I brought them here."

"There's a school on this island?"

"Nah," he said. He walked her from the group and pointed a thumb at a hoverbus. "Plo Koon sent that over."

Yaddle stared. "Plo has access to a speeder bus?"

Piell chuckled. "You really did just get here, didn't you?"

"I admit I'm a little late. I thought for a moment the employment problem here was worse than I imagined!"

Piell explained that Rendili had stopped funding programs at the educational facilities on Essafa Key, owing to what it called a deteriorating business climate on and near Kwenn. It had used the same rationale to turn the factory into a fortress. They'd done that in such a way that made the island ugly—and less like the Kwenn that Yaddle remembered.

She saw Piell's motive—and wasn't entirely happy with it. "I'm not sure it should be incumbent upon children to work for a corporation to get fed."

"All I know is they love to paint and draw. They were gonna do it somewhere. I suggested here." He pointed out to sea. "This morning, we were over by the Mercantile Guild headquarters—they run the schools on Essafa, or are supposed to. We were planting trees."

"Botany class." She glanced at the speeder bike she'd driven and smiled. "I suppose you've also taught mechanics for a bit."

"That was Master Tiin when he dropped off the bus. It's good for them to know a trade."

A speeder truck pulled up. For a moment, Yaddle was concerned it carried someone from the factory—or some other authority here to put a stop to the children's efforts. But a hoot from Piell told her it was something else.

"They came!" He clapped his hands together. "They're from the Kwenn Holofeed."

"Reporters." She looked to him. "Your doing?"

He pointed to the painters. "A kid over there named Hadaro knew them. Apparently he tried to decorate the outside of their studio one night. They'd already heard about what we're doing."

"And if other people hear, *that* could put pressure on Rendili to stick around." Yaddle nodded. "Well done, Master Piell."

"Problem is, I'm not the prettiest face—or the best voice. That's why I told the kids to send you here."

Yaddle was a little surprised. "You could have just asked me directly."

"You'd have said we should consult Mace or Yoda or Adi instead—and given me some guff about you not being a spokesbeing. But you are exactly who they need to hear from."

She took that in. Neither of them cut the most imposing figure, at least as far as the general public was concerned. Yaddle had always been aware of that, and had never been self-conscious about it. It didn't matter what the public imagined about Jedi. But then she remembered the whole reason they were there, on Kwenn.

They will see us—and our works.

She strode toward the parking area. Several other vehicles were arriving. More members of the media, from the looks of the devices they carried—but also a local government vehicle. Two of Piell's young friends brought a crate and placed it before the holocam setup. Yaddle leapt nimbly atop it, drawing grins and chuckles.

They can laugh if they want—as long as they listen. "Greetings, my friends. I am Yaddle—a member of the Jedi Council. Welcome."

There were several eager-looking journalists in the scrum that had developed, but Yaddle's eyes went to a Woostroid woman holding a holocam. With black oval eyes and a slender purple face, she seemed rattled to be in the middle of the pack. Yaddle called on her. "You have a question?"

"Oh, I don't ask questions," she said in a small voice. "My reporter hasn't arrived yet."

"What's your name?"

"Uh—Morna." She looked around awkwardly, and as others around her started loudly beckoning to Yaddle, she shrank.

"I'm happy to take *your* question, Morna." Yaddle smiled politely until the others settled down.

Morna gulped, clearly not accustomed to public speaking. "Master, word has spread that the Jedi have returned to Kwenn after a long absence. More than one, in fact. What do you have to say about that?"

"Quite a lot, Morna." Yaddle lifted her arms and gestured to the sky. "You know, the Jedi may not frequent the outpost so much anymore, but we never truly *leave* you." She lowered her arms and drew them wide apart. "In the same way, Kwenn remains with those of us who've visited. Now, I know there have been some hard times. But this remains a special place for us—and while all places are special for Jedi, it fills all of our hearts with joy to be back."

"You said 'all.' Who all is here?" Morna asked.

Yaddle smiled. "Is there a chair available? The list could take some time to get through."

CHAPTER 28

RIFTWALKER HEADQUARTERS
VALBORAAN

"Twenty-two beats twelve. I win again."

Depa Billaba opened her eyes. Whenever she had done so over the past several hours—or was it days?—she'd regretted it. The Riftwalkers didn't have interrogator droids; their means were more primitive—and painful. The earsplitting sound being deactivated usually meant more questioning was at hand.

Not this time. The immobilization beam gave her just enough range of motion to see that Zilastra had set up a table with the cards she so enjoyed. Only she wasn't playing solitaire.

"Kylah," Depa muttered.

The young girl turned from the table and looked up at her. "You're awake!"

"A matter . . . of opinion."

Zilastra gathered the cards. "Sorry for moving into your space. While we waited for you to wake up, I was teaching our friend some more about sabacc. Including how fast things can change."

Depa said nothing.

The pirate shuffled the deck. "There's something called the sabacc shift—I'm sure you've heard of it. The values change. You can be holding a great card, and suddenly it's worthless. Or you can discover you suddenly have a winner, made from nothing." She glanced at the girl while pointing at Depa. "Take *her*, for example. What's her name?"

Reacting uneasily to Depa's condition, the girl spoke. "She's Hotwire."

"Hilarious." Zilastra stood up, intercutting the cards nimbly with her hands over and over again as she did. "I'd like you to meet Depa Billaba. She's not just a Jedi—or even a Jedi Master. We've got ourselves a real, live member of the Jedi Council here."

Depa was surprised to be identified, but she still said nothing.

"What's the Jedi Council?" Kylah asked.

"The fools in charge of the fools." Zilastra made a sour face to Depa. "You look rough, Master. Seen a mirror lately?" She cut straight to a single card in her deck. "Here's one."

Depa looked at the face card. The Idiot.

Zilastra laughed.

Depa tried to ignore her, and focused on breathing. There had to be some way out, something in the room she could manipulate. But her ragged condition precluded anything fancy, and Zilastra kept pacing, distracting her.

"It wasn't hard to discover your name," she said. "We've been hunkered down since the big meeting, so we didn't have the transmitter deployed. Once we were able to make contact with our network it took about five seconds." She stopped and looked up at Depa. "What happened? Did you get bored sitting in your tower up there on Coruscant, swiping children and getting in other people's business?"

Depa's eyes shifted to Kylah, who looked at her plaintively.

"You lied to me," the girl said, pain evident in her voice. "You told me you were from around here."

"I didn't lie," the Jedi replied, her voice strained. "I was . . . born on Chalacta."

"She just didn't stay." Zilastra smirked. "None of them do. Whisked off to their silver tower in the center of everything—leaving people like us with nothing."

Kylah looked confused. "Then why would you come back?"

"I was trying to find out what happened to someone," Depa said. "Someone I met when he was not much older than you. Xaran was his name. I was one of his teachers. He was killed in this region."

"And you came here to find his killer?"

"No." Depa took a deep breath. "I came here to understand the place that produced his killer. I can't protect every member of the Jedi Order. But if bad things are happening to people like us, they are most certainly happening much more often to people like you."

Zilastra sneered. "Nice way to put it—*you*, and *us*." She pointed to Kylah. "I'm the best thing to happen to the kid. I actually offer her something. A life."

"Of what?" Depa asked. "Of murder? Or is it mass murder, now?"

"I'm just playing my hand."

Depa wanted to argue it further, but her head hurt too much.

Zilastra strolled back to the table. "See, Stowaway, I play as many hands as it takes to understand who's in the game with me. To establish my persona. To get them to think I don't know any more than they do about the game."

"But it's all a bluff?" Kylah asked.

"She doesn't bluff," Depa responded. "She cheats." Her stay in suspension had given her the time she needed to figure something out. "There never was any arrangement with the Regal Voyager line, was there?"

Zilastra grinned. She put her deck back on the table and leaned behind it. The final case was there. She lifted it. "I'm sure you remember this."

Depa did. She also knew her lightsaber wasn't in it anymore. She wondered where it was.

The pirate ran her fingers over the raised emblem. "I got the idea when I killed a courier traveling with one of these. I never got it open—or found out what was inside. It's the spoken code or nothing."

"So you started stealing ones that were already open."

"Oh, I tried to get them the easy way—sending travelers on flights and renting them. But there was a hitch. Travelers could keep the cases for a week after arrival, but after that the locks would seize up."

"Regal Voyager's way of preventing people from keeping the cases."

"You got it. There was no way I could get the cases and turn them around in time. That's where Kylah came in. When I found out the carrier was sourcing the cases out of the depot on Keldooine, I took over a landing pad nearby. Nobody else was small and wiry enough to sneak in there."

Depa had already figured out what happened next. "You booby-trapped the cases and sent them to your enemies. But you had to bait them, first."

"Nobody was just going to open a case and go boom," Zilastra said. "Not even that dolt from the Vile. That's where the droids came in. I sent one to each gang, carrying a message from Regal Voyager's president, wanting to set up a relationship."

"The messages were fake," Depa said, watching Zilastra. "But the bribes inside were real. *You* put up the money."

Zilastra rolled her eyes. "I put a fortune into those cases. Call it seeding the pot. For the first few months, the bosses refused to open them on their own—they had their droids or lackeys do it. But the rules never changed. All five cases had to be opened at once, on holo-cam."

"You baited them—and put them to sleep. When did the bosses start opening the cases?"

"A few months ago. It took forever. Venom Vee was the last to buy the cover story." Zilastra smiled. "But I got her. I filled their hands with winning cards again and again. And they all split the pot, taking my money every time."

Depa understood it all. The need for Kylah to keep supplying the Riftwalkers with empty cases, first and foremost. But she also now understood why Zilastra didn't need to be able to open the final case. That time, she wasn't planning on showing her rivals what was inside her container. They would all be dead.

Kylah understood, too. Her eyes widened as she stared at the case in Zilastra's hand. "So the things I took killed all those people?"

The pirate passed the case to her and smiled. "Kid, you made it all possible."

Depa could tell from the way the girl looked at the case that she wasn't comfortable with the thought. She sought to assuage her. "You didn't know what you were involved with, Kylah."

"She was involved with the biggest takedown ever in the Slice," Zilastra retorted. "I'd say she did pretty well." She sat down to finish her drink. "Pot's yours, kid. We're done here."

Depa had only one thing left to ask. "So now what?"

Zilastra looked back. "What do you mean?"

"To what end? All that strategizing you do with the cards. You've decapitated the other regimes. What now?"

"I won."

"And that's *it*?"

"You're starting to tick me off."

"I'm serious," Depa said. "You trumped the top card in every other suit. But the next-best in each is in line. New bosses."

"Not yet." Zilastra picked up her deck and smirked. "From what I'm hearing, I took out a *lot* of cards. And while they're sorting things out, I'll sweep up a lot of new territory. There'll be breakaway crews looking to join up with someone solid."

"But you're laying low now—probably pretending you got hit, too. When they realize you didn't, they'll come gunning for you."

"I'm waiting to see the lay of the land, that's all." Zilastra fanned her cards. "I can take care of myself. Sure enough nobody else ever did."

Depa looked to the girl. "Let Kylah go."

"What?"

"You're done with her. She's done what you asked."

"She doesn't want to go. What are you going to do, take her away?" Zilastra glared at her. "That's what you people do, isn't it?"

Depa frowned. "You've mentioned that before. What do you know about it?"

"What do I—?" Zilastra dropped her deck on the table and looked at Kylah. "Picture this, kid. I'm in a hellhole colony the Republic has abandoned. My mother, desperate to earn enough to get us out, dies in a mine collapse, leaving me with nothing but a deck of cards to remember her by. I wind up at an orphanage that's falling apart—there's just a nanny droid running it, and I'm one of only three kids there. But I'm not alone, because I'm with my two best friends in the galaxy."

She rose from the table. "Now, oh, here comes a Jedi. Someone's going to save us, make our lives better, right?"

Kylah stared. "What happened?"

"To my friends? Everything. The Jedi took them away—and left me to rot!"

Depa felt Zilastra's anger through the Force. Such animosity, more than she'd sensed in a long time. Her only defense was reason. "The Jedi didn't steal your friends, Zilastra. They only could've gone with their guardians' permission."

"Guardians? There was just a broken-down old droid that didn't last another month. The droid begged the Jedi to take me, too—but I wasn't wanted. I wasn't good enough. I wasn't *worthy* of a better life!"

Kylah looked at Zilastra—and then Depa. "Is that really how it works?"

Depa had to admit it. "Sometimes. The Jedi should have done something to help her." She spoke lower. "But it doesn't always happen."

"'Doesn't always happen,'" Zilastra repeated. She stood abruptly, knocking over her chair. "I spent a lifetime in places you left, Master. The people you call criminals were the only ones who helped me, gave me a home. And when Jedi did show up, it was to try to destroy me. Me, and the people who took me in."

"Because of what those people were doing. Because—"

"Because now I was with the enemy. I *was* the enemy!"

Depa looked to Kylah and spoke quickly. "This is what I mean. You can't stay here. There are other people who can help you, can give you a hand."

"You want to talk hands?" Zilastra grabbed the chair and turned it around in front of Depa. She stepped onto it so she was face-to-face with the suspended prisoner. "I'll show you the hands of your enemy."

Zilastra removed one tight-fitting glove, and then the other. Depa watched, mesmerized, as she saw that, in contrast with her green Nautolan skin, both of Zilastra's hands were pinkish.

"Like them, Jedi?" Zilastra turned them backward and forward in front of her eyes. "I know what you're thinking. They're not my color. But it was as close as the surgeon droids could get."

Depa stared. She knew there was something else, something deeper. "A Jedi did that to you."

"That's what you think, isn't it? And you'd forgive whoever it was, because they were fighting the nasty pirates."

"Tell me."

Zilastra stared at her—and laughed. "I was with another gang then. A Jedi boarded. There was a blast. I got hurt from that—bad. I still crawled forward, after him—but I was too late. He tore through the place, ripping it apart."

Zilastra turned and faced Kylah. "Things were flying everywhere. And that blade of his—I'll never forget it. Murdered the boss, his wife—everybody who'd helped me."

Face twisted with rage, she turned back to Depa. "I got to my knees and found the weapons locker. When he was on the deck below, in the middle of a fight, I did it. I threw myself down the catwalk onto him."

Depa pictured the scene—and understood. "He cut your hands off."

"You do that a lot, do you?" Zilastra shook her head. "Not that time. Because I wasn't like the others. Because when I landed on him—I had a thermal charge. A grenade. I lost my hands, but he lost everything. *And it was worth it!*"

Depa heard Kylah gasp. Her own eyes went wide. "Your hands. *You* did it."

"No. *He* did it, by boarding us. What I did—I did because it was worth it. I had a good cause! That ship was ours. That territory was ours." She hopped down from the chair and found her gloves on the floor.

Depa saw that Kylah was bunched up on the chair, looking in horror at Zilastra. The pirate glanced over at the girl. "It's not bad, kid. They're great for playing cards. You've seen me shuffle. And they're good for other things."

"Other things." Depa's eyes narrowed. "Xaran Raal died investigating the Riftwalkers—by strangulation."

Zilastra shrugged as she put on her gloves. "I don't remember names. But it's a funny thing, Master. Jedi make the same sounds when you strangle them as everybody else. I guess you're not so special after all."

"Xaran would have fought you!"

"And you already know I don't fight fair. Once we're done questioning, we switch to the paralytic gas. And then the fun begins." She smiled as she backed toward the door. "See you again soon."

CHAPTER 29

CAPITAL KEY

KWENN

"Master Yaddle," Morna said. "Is that your only name?"

Yaddle chuckled at the young holofeed engineer's question. "If the people of Kwenn can't identify me on sight by now, I don't think any other details will help!"

Her impromptu press conference outside Rendili Hyperworks had launched her on a whirlwind of interviews. About the Jedi Masters arriving on the planet—Yarael was soon to bring the total to ten—and also about some of the activities they'd already taken part in.

The major news, however, she'd decided to save for this moment, now that the details had all been worked out. The holofeed program with the largest regular audience on the planet, *Remember Kwenn*, was hosted by Reezingrom Abbayav, a member of the two-headed, four-armed Troig species. Two individuals attached at the neck, Reez and Grom agreed on absolutely nothing, making them loved and hated in equal measure by their viewers.

They'd showed nothing but kindness and courtesy to Yaddle when they set up the interview, although she could tell by the expression of Morna, their technical engineer, that living with them on a daily basis could be a trial.

Pointing to the desk onstage, Reez snapped at the engineer. "Monah, where's my favorite cup?"

"Working on it," Morna responded.

Grom added his own complaint. "Morrena, I said I wanted the blue lighting on my side!"

"Working on that, too." Morna said.

The harried engineer remained in motion, dutifully taking care of needs that Yaddle imagined weren't part of her job description. Finally, she led Yaddle onto the stage and adjusted the height of the Jedi's chair. She whispered in her ear, "*Good luck.*"

"Thank you," Yaddle said. "Morna, wasn't it?"

The engineer seemed surprised to hear it. "I've been here three years and they've never gotten it right."

"I don't know why. It has a beautiful sound."

Morna saw her bosses stepping onto the stage and made a hasty descent.

"Good to see you here, Master," Reez said in a higher voice. She offered one of her hands.

"You ninny," responded Grom in a deeper voice. He grabbed the hand by the wrist and pulled it back. "You don't shake a Jedi's hand!" He tried to bow instead, a movement that Reez's half of their shared body resisted.

Yaddle didn't know whom to respond to, so she simply grinned. "A pleasure."

Reez rolled her eyes and nodded toward her other half. "Sorry for my partner. I keep talking about breaking up the act, but nobody believes me."

Grom chuckled. "That's why the company thinks it can get away with paying us just one salary."

"I don't know that even a Jedi could help you there," Yaddle said.

"Going live now," Morna said.

The music and pleasantries were over in seconds. "Everyone has heard the stories," Grom said. "Jedi are on Kwenn in numbers not seen since the Grand Renewal. And not just any Jedi, but members of the High Council, like our guest, Yaddle."

Yaddle smiled sweetly—but didn't get a chance to say a word before Reez attacked. "Admit it, Master. The Jedi are here now for the same reasons you were at Keldooine. And then Ord Jannak. You're here to shut down Sanctuary Mount."

Grom was softer, but no less pointed. "Everyone is afraid, Master. You're going to put out the light—and truly leave us in the dark!"

Yaddle had expected the question. It had been asked of her many times since that afternoon at the wall; each time, she had sidestepped it. She took time to choose her words carefully. "The Jedi Council has made no decision regarding the outpost, other than that we are all visiting it."

"To close it," Reez said.

"We have a celebration to stage. Even Jedi Masters need a place to sleep."

"Celebration?" Grom asked. "What celebration?"

"The bicentennial of the Grand Renewal, of course."

Yaddle could see their surprise. She glanced at Morna, as well, and read her expression. It suggested Reez and Grom had never been rendered speechless before.

That was helpful for Yaddle, who spoke at length of the plan that had been coming together. Inside the arena on Gala Key, the Jedi Council would hold a meeting before thousands of members of the general public, while many times that number would gather in the terrace parks outside and on other islands, watching the feed as they picnicked. The event would culminate with the Jedi walking to the top of Sanctuary Mount, where the Unquenchable Fire would be lit for another evening.

"People who have never seen a Jedi before will see the entire Council at work," Yaddle said. "It is the sort of thing we did long ago, in places like Kublop Springs on the planet Tenoo, where Jedi emerged from the outpost to join the local festival."

Her hosts were amazed—but also confused.

"Master Rancisis is here," Grom said. "He launched the Grand Renewal. Why isn't *he* before us speaking about this?"

"Just as my friend Oppo coordinated many things two centuries ago, he is doing so again now," she said. "Even as I've been speaking with the public, he's been making arrangements with local authorities. But I guarantee that by the time we depart, many people will have had the chance to get to know one of us."

Having regained her bearings, Reez went on offense again. "Pardon my ignorance, but who's protecting the galaxy while you people are here, celebrating? What about all these disasters that have been taking place? Like the one on Keldooine?"

She shook her head in sadness. "So tragic. But we have responded." Yaddle did not add that Yarael had been rebuffed. The intentions were the important thing.

Reez kept on. "All right, well, how about this business of running around with a gang of urchins?"

"The young artisans?"

"That's what *you* call them. Troublemakers is more like it. Jedi have also meddled in a labor dispute, taking the side of the Kwikhaul workers against an honest businessperson—"

Grom called his other half on that. "That's not true, and you know it. They were helping management!"

"Here comes the exploitation thing again!"

Yaddle looked pleasantly at the holocam as they bickered. Behind the device, Morna had her hand over her face.

Reez finally returned to the Jedi. "There are countless reports of Jedi encounters this week. Receipts are down at the *Pelagic* casino barge after a Jedi Master talked to a crowd about gambling."

"Someone convinced three members of a local music act to seek treatment," Grom chimed in. "A member of the Council has practically moved in with one poor woman, cleaning her house."

"And word is one of your number was even seen eating ice mounds at the Langdam Harbor Market and offering relationship advice!"

Yaddle had no idea about some of the incidents the hosts were referring to. But it didn't matter. "The responsibilities of a Jedi go far beyond the basic protections we provide. Seeking peace—that can take many forms. The same is true for justice."

"But you can't be everywhere and do everything," Grom said.

"That's absolutely so," Yaddle replied. "And part of the job of the Jedi

Council is to determine exactly who goes where, and for what reasons. But our charge includes helping individual people, as well as individual planets. And if a Jedi Knight or Jedi Master in the course of action has the opportunity to act on a smaller scale, we want them to do so. We also seek to encourage those we meet to effect change in their own lives. You all have that power. Everyone does."

Her voice was warm and calm, and she hoped she was winning people over in the audience. But the hosts were very much invested in conflict. Reez challenged her. "Tell me again, who do the Jedi serve?"

"The people." Yaddle lifted her hand for a pronouncement. "It is why we have chosen these as our words to open the celebration from the arena stage: *The Jedi stand with you.*"

"Pretty," Reez responded. "But who *else* do you stand with?"

"We protect peace and justice. And the Galactic Republic."

"Those are in contradiction," Grom said. "It's like I've said for years. The Republic *is* the problem."

"Here we go," Reez responded. "Another rant about corporate greed. All the good people of Kwenn want is a decent place to—"

Yaddle spied Grom making a hand signal.

"—break for some messages of commercial import," Reez said, without missing a beat. "But when we come back, we'll be joined by a surprise guest on hologram: Kwenn's own Senator Gabban, speaking from Coruscant about this amazing news we've just heard. Stay with us!"

The program paused. Yaddle was startled. "The senator? Already?"

Reez tapped her earpiece. "Old Gabban was watching, along with everyone else on our interstellar feed."

"Yeah, if something's even slightly popular, Gabban the Gabbler is right there, on the spot, taking credit." Grom rolled his eyes. "I hate him."

"Me, too."

It was the one thing Yaddle had heard both halves of Reezingrom agree on.

"Stretch your legs," Reez said to her. "We'll have you back in here when he's done talking."

"How will I know when that will be?"

"When the sun explodes," Grom said.

She lowered her chair and stepped off. Crossing the dais, she saw that the engineer had let another worker take her place.

Yaddle found Morna in the outer hallway, looking out the studio building's bank of windows at the darkness creeping across the harbor. "Is there a problem, my child?"

The engineer looked back at her, huge dark eyes glistening. "I'm sorry. Just hearing you talk about this place—and helping people help themselves." She shook her head. "I'm sorry," she said again. She looked back outside again.

"You keep apologizing." Yaddle walked until she stood beside her. "What do you have to be sorry for?"

"For being miserable." Morna dropped to her knees, crying.

Startled by the outburst, Yaddle placed her hand on the woman's forehead. "No one is at fault for a thing like that."

"But I am. I should be happier."

"You should be *you*. To deny how you feel would be to deny your very self." Yaddle glanced back toward the studio. "You have a difficult job managing those two. Your work is exemplary."

Morna shook her head. "They're no worse today than any other day."

Yaddle found that dispiriting. "Have you looked for a better job?"

"There isn't one. And it wouldn't matter." Morna wiped her eyes and stood. "You don't need to hear this."

"But you need to be heard. I am here."

Yaddle walked alongside her, ready to listen.

After a long silence, Morna opened up. "I came here from Hutt space, thinking things would be better. I'd always heard Kwenn was the prettiest place out here. The keys, the oceans, the Paths of Harmony. The beacon on the tower."

The Jedi outpost. "The things that drew you to Kwenn—did they turn out to be what you believed they were?"

"No. I mean yes—they looked like the holos I'd seen, mostly. But it's true that things are getting worse. People say in a year, Kwenn will look like Ord Jannak. That Ord Jannak is turning into Keldooine."

"So it's about safety."

"Yes. And no." Morna sighed. "I've been scared all the time, no matter where I've lived. It's all the same everywhere. Nobody cares about anyone else. They get mad if you *do* care, as if there's something they know that you don't."

"And you fear that, as well."

"I know, it sounds silly." She shook her head. "Maybe I'm imagining all of it."

Yaddle shook her head. "Your world is the one you perceive."

"But I *have* thought it's just me. That I'm just not going to be happy anywhere." Morna took a deep breath. "I have seen the company's medical droid, and I've sought other help. I have been through it all before." She looked off into nothingness. "A couple of years ago, I felt like things just started falling apart. Like gravity stopped working."

"Even gravity is not a constant," Yaddle said. "What *have* you held on to?"

"Nothing, much. My job, I guess. But you've just seen what Reezingrom is like. Imagine it for five years."

"And people say we Jedi take on difficult challenges."

"There is that." Morna looked outside—and pointed. "*That*—that's been the only constant. The Unquenchable Fire. It's still there. It's made me less scared. It's why hearing you talk sort of made me—"

She stopped.

Yaddle reached up to take her hand. "That light, Morna—that's outside you. There's a light that's within."

"A light. What am I supposed to do with that?"

"The Jedi spend their whole lives trying to see that light—in themselves, and in others. It's part of something larger. *You* are part of something larger."

"It's something that doesn't want me."

Yaddle shook her head. "The Force exists for everyone, because it *is* everyone. The Jedi—some may think we are favored, because we have a closer relationship with it. But all we do is ride the wind. The air, the sun—that's everyone else."

"I'd like to feel I was part of something like that. I just can't imagine ever feeling it on this planet."

"I know. There *is* anguish on Kwenn. Of the everyday kind—and the kind that has crept up on Keldooine and those other planets. It's all real. Suffering lies at the end of a chain that begins with fear—and fear is something we carry with us, from world to world, job to job, home to home. But there is something else."

"What?"

"Another chain," Yaddle said. "Courage leads to peace. Peace leads to love. Love leads to healing."

Morna looked down at her—and then was startled when a chime sounded through the halls. "Senator Gabban's segment just ended. You'd better get back there." She dabbed her eyes. "You have so many more people to speak to."

"The Force decides who I need to speak to. And I will decide when I am done." Yaddle started to walk with Morna, leading her away from the studio. "I'm sure that 'Gabban the Gabbler' can fill all the time he is offered."

CHAPTER 30

RIFTWALKER HEADQUARTERS
VALBORAAN

"*After the snow and then the rain, the sun always comes back again . . .*

"*After a hurt and then the pain, both do go, while you remain . . .*"

It was a rhyme from her very earliest years on Chalacta. A child's couplet, for skinned knees and elbows. Depa would have learned more of them then had she stayed, but the Force had other plans for her. It would be a long time before she absorbed more, and after years as a student of Master Windu's. By then, Chalacta was like many other planets along the Ootmian route: a world with many pains—and the illumination many of its residents sought had grown elusive.

And yet, for all the mantras used by Jedi to shut out pain and disharmony, during her imprisonment it was that child's rhyme that she repeated to herself, over and over. It wasn't clear to her how long she'd been imprisoned by Zilastra. Just that the woman seemed to take a perverse glee in keeping her in suspension for most of the day, bombarded by sonic torture.

As near as Depa could tell, Zilastra was using her as a prop. A teaching tool, to convince the members of her band that Jedi—even those who belonged to the High Council—were not invincible, even as it demonstrated the pirate's power and ability. Depa couldn't remember all the faces she'd seen. What she did know was that the last visit portended that it might all soon be over. Zilastra had recorded a holovid in the room, apparently addressing Riftwalker members who were not on Valboraan. That was it, then: the last of her educational value. The end must come soon.

There was no way around it. The droid, IK-111, had no trouble functioning in the chamber when it was filled with the screeching electronic sounds; she wished she had the same auditory off switch. Since awakening from another half sleep, she had watched it go about the business of preparing a tranquilizer spray. The canister was different than they'd used before, suggesting a stronger dose. Zilastra might get her sadistic finale after all.

The droid looked up from its work. It turned and departed, leaving the sonic menace operating. *I guess we're about ready,* Depa thought.

Sadly, she already knew that solitude offered no opportunity at all for escape. The strains of her captivity had gone beyond the superior endurance of even a Jedi Master. There was no switch to manipulate, no item to project against an electronic lock. Not in her condition, and not that would be likely to work. She just couldn't concentrate.

"*After the snow and then the rain . . . hurt and pain?*" That wasn't right, she realized. She'd made a mistake. Just as she'd made a mistake by being reckless, taking an interest in a region she'd left as a child. She'd tried to remain responsibly aloof, following Master Windu's lead; she'd sent Xaran Raal to investigate the area instead. It had become personal after that, no matter what her protestations were to the contrary. And Kylah had made it even more so.

"Kylah," she muttered, her eyes closed. "Kylah . . . you need . . . to get away. You need to go."

"But I just got here," came a shouted response from below.

Depa opened her eyes and struggled to focus. There was Kylah, off to the right. The girl scrambled over to the controls for the sound generator and deactivated the noise.

Kylah rubbed her fingers in her ears. "That's enough of that!"

Depa found the strength to speak. "How—?"

The girl pointed to a newly opened ventilation duct to Depa's left. "It wasn't hard to find a way in here. I just followed the sound."

"Zilastra doesn't know . . . you're here?"

"No. I wanted to talk to you again." She peeked around the corner. "If Eyekay's gone to get Zil, it'll take a while. She's finishing a game."

"Is . . . she winning?"

"Everyone works for her. Anyone who beat her would wind up scrubbing fungus off the walls with the boys. Or worse."

Such a mundane pursuit, right before an execution. Depa had gone up against many masters of mayhem in her career. All of them had big plans for the days after masterstrokes, had they been successful. Zilastra had followed up her coup against the other gangs with a stay-at-home vacation with occasional breaks for educational brutality. She could imagine some members of the Council being offended at the idea of dying at such a person's hands. Not Depa. Death was death.

She saw Kylah at the wall, attempting to work the suspension beam control panel. Attempting, but not succeeding. "I can't turn this off. Zilastra enters a code. I don't have it."

Depa hadn't gotten her hopes up. "What matters is that you came."

Kylah looked over at the cabinet where the medical sprays were secured. "I could steal all of those!"

"Delaying the inevitable. Zilastra will just hurt you, then."

The girl's face fell. She began to cry. "She's really going to do it."

"Don't be here. She'll make you watch."

"Why?"

"The same reason she had you in here before," Depa said. "So you'll become like her. Cruel and heartless."

"But you heard how she grew up."

"I can't help that. All three of us came from this region. It didn't make either one of us turn out like her."

Kylah looked up at her with eyes glistening with tears. "Did the Jedi really take her friends away?"

"I have no reason to doubt that. We do that with younglings who show promise. As you heard, the droid approved."

"Where are they? Her friends?"

"I don't know. We probably wouldn't have raised them together. They would have been split up early on."

"What? That's terrible!"

"Connections—personal ties—make it hard for us to do our jobs. We have an entire galaxy to care for. Attachments compromise our judgment."

"So you have no friends? No family?"

"We have the rest of the Jedi Order—and they are our friends, our family. But we don't allow that to rule our decision making. The responsibility we've been given is too great for that."

Kylah stared at the hole in the wall, still not understanding. "So you really didn't come out here because your friend was killed?"

"I did—I admit it. But I also wanted to know what it was about this place that it could make someone do such a terrible thing—so that I might stop it from happening again." Depa's face drooped. "Poor Xaran is gone. Revenge won't bring him back."

Kylah shook her head. "I'm glad I'm not a Jedi."

Depa thought it was a strange statement. "Why?"

"I don't think I want to trust the judgment of anyone who isn't tied to other people." Her words hung in the room for several moments. Then she added, "I don't like Zilastra killing Jedi either. What if she runs into one of her friends from the orphanage and doesn't recognize them? She might kill them by accident!"

And how do you think she would feel if she did? Depa wanted to ask the question, but it was all too horrible.

Kylah looked back again down the corridor. "You're going to die unless I help you."

"And if you help me, *you'll* die." Depa put what little strength she had into a final appeal. "I need you to go. You stow away on ships all the time. Go." She locked eyes with her. "*I'm begging you.*"

Reluctantly, the girl toggled the sound control and covered her ears. *Goodbye,* she mouthed. Then after one last look at Depa, she scrambled into the vent and closed the grating.

The sonic attack lasted less than a minute, this time. The assassin droid reentered and deactivated it. Zilastra followed soon after that, leading a large entourage. Burlug set up the holocam again.

"Welcome back," Depa said.

"Hey, you can still talk!" Zilastra gave a thumbs-up. "That's the spirit, Master. Talk their ears off until the end."

Depa surveyed those in attendance. They oozed menace. Just Zilastra's captains, this time; no soldiers or underlings. "Quite an audience."

"I'd wanted Kylah to see, but she's vanished again." Zilastra smirked. "Little squirt had better get a stronger stomach." She gestured to the cam. "She'll catch it later. I'll make sure of it."

"I'm surprised you've never brought The Lobber and his friends by."

"Oh, I did, while you were out. But don't look to them for help. They know strength. They don't have it, so they're drawn to it. They'll follow it—anywhere." She winked to her captains. "Just what we want, right?"

Depa's eyes narrowed. "Seems to me strength isn't drugging someone to kill them."

Zilastra stared at her. "Are you done?"

"It's all right. I'm ready. The Force is with me. I have a clear conscience."

"And *that* is why this galaxy will be better off without you." She nodded, and IK-111 obtained the prepared spray.

Depa knew how it would work, next. Nothing she did mentally would knock it from the droid's magnetic grasp; the suspension beam would have no effect on the droplets at all. Zilastra and the others were masking up, in case anything went wrong. Protective garb in place, the pirate leader put her gloved hands together and cracked her knuckles. "See you on the floor."

The Jedi had one last play. Something, anything, the Force could do to foul the electronics. The lights in the room, the workings of the droid, anything. But she was too weak. All she heard was a light buzz.

"What now?" Zilastra growled. "Always just when the fun's about to start."

She drew a device from her vest pocket and read a message on it. "*What?*"

Zilastra read it again—only to show it to Burlug. "Can you believe this?"

He read it twice. "That doesn't make any sense."

"Unexpected guests?" Depa asked.

"No—you don't get off that easy." But Zilastra took the device back with some urgency. Whatever was on there had mesmerized her. The Nautolan narrowed her eyes, just as she did when she was calculating.

This is the longest execution ever. "What?" Depa finally asked.

"Wait." Zilastra took off her mask and instructed the droid. "You wait, too. I'll be back."

Burlug looked at her in astonishment. "You're leaving her?"

"I'll deal with her later," Zilastra called over her shoulder as she hurried for the exit. "You wanted me to see the big picture, Master? Well, I just saw it. Hang around—I want you to see it, too!"

CHAPTER 31

BRAZATTA KEY

KWENN

*L*ast to arrive again! Predictable.

Yarael Poof didn't really have a persecution complex. He just pretended to have one. As one of the longer-standing members of the Jedi Council, the Quermian had earned his place a hundred times over. His ability to persuade people through the use of the Force was second to none, and he wielded his lightsaber with consummate skill. But while Yarael was still in peak physical condition, a consequence of his extremely long life span was that he'd seen it all. He bored easily.

Increasingly in the last century, he had sought to entertain himself by responding to events differently than he might have before. The most extreme expression was a new fondness for pranks, but there were other elements. He now engaged in banter, something he'd once considered a waste of time and focus. He also reacted to slights with feigned dismay, just to see what others would say.

In truth, it was by happenstance that he tended to arrive to meetings last. Occasionally his distractedness was to blame, but many more were the times he was busy doing something altruistic. His Kwenn arrival fit the latter case; it had been delayed by his well-meaning—if futile—trip to Keldooine.

So when he landed at a small pad on Brazatta Key, where Ki-Adi-Mundi had said he could be found, Yarael determined that he wouldn't mention his late arrival. Ki-Adi-Mundi had little patience for repartee, and that included attempts at provocation. *He is a good and hardworking person,* Yarael thought, *and I must not vex him.*

Ki-Adi-Mundi saw him approach. "Greetings, Master Yarael."

"Say what you mean." Yarael crossed his long, bony arms. "I'm always the last to arrive."

"You told me you were going to stop provoking arguments."

"That was my plan—until five seconds ago."

"This is progress," Ki-Adi-Mundi replied. They began walking the streets of the industrial area, overshadowed by factories on either side. "You are not the last to arrive, anyway. Master Windu is still searching for Master Billaba. And Master Koth told me he had sent for Master—"

"Everyone we know is a master. You'd think we could just use people's first names."

"You simply want your *own* first name to be used."

"Poof is a grand and historic name among the Quermians. It's not *my* fault that when it translates into Basic it sounds like the end of a magic trick."

"Nonetheless," Ki-Adi-Mundi said, "our colleagues deserve their honorifics. They have earned them."

"And I earned mine long before you drew breath." Yarael shook his head. "Never mind."

He saw Ki-Adi-Mundi manage the faintest trace of a smile. "You initially intended not to needle me this time. That is progress. And while the bicentennial celebration is announced and our time grows short, you have arrived in plenty of time to assist me."

"Assist you—in finding entertainment?" Yarael smiled. "I helped fund the amphitheater for the local repertory group, you know."

Ki-Adi-Mundi waved his hand. "I seek no diversions. I told Master Rancisis that I was looking into a problem the locals are having."

"I spoke to him when I arrived in orbit. All he said is you'd been on one of the resort islands. If this is one, it's going to lose its endorsement from the tourism bureau."

Yarael gestured to the dilapidated buildings lining the lane. He'd visited Kwenn many times, but he didn't remember it having anyplace that looked like this.

Ki-Adi-Mundi pointed to the south. "A couple I met own an industrial concern on this key. The goods they manufacture are really quite impressive. Their main product is a tent that protects campers against sun, wind, fire—they claim it would reflect a blaster shot, and I do not doubt it. Very useful on the keys where fires have been prevalent."

Yarael had seen a few of the fires during his descent. "Sounds like a good idea."

"It is—and I have confirmed what else they told me: There are people going about threatening business owners and residents."

"And you thought it an opportunity for some fieldwork." Yarael patted his lightsaber within his cloak. "I've been in a shuttle all day. Direct me to the rapscallions!"

"That would be unwise." Ki-Adi-Mundi ticked off some of the other factors they had to reckon with. That the troublemakers were armed was not of great concern, but the number of civilians around was. There were children and elderly people in the streets, as well as beings of small stature. They, too, were being victimized by the roving nuisances.

Ki-Adi-Mundi pointed to a leatherbound bald human with spikes somehow driven into his head. "He is a member of the Staved Skulls. One of five working this street."

"Out here. During the day."

"Yes, the farther one travels from Sanctuary Mount, the bolder they become. I have been puzzling most of the morning over how to extricate these people from the populace."

"Is that all?" Yarael craned his head until he was at his tallest and waved to the tough. "Hey! Over here!"

The hooligan turned away from the merchant he was harassing and walked in their direction. Ki-Adi-Mundi's eyes shifted from left to right. "I told you, battle here would be—"

"Unwise. Leave it to me."

The Skull wore blasters in a double holster and carried a club, which Yarael thought was overkill. He stepped up to Ki-Adi-Mundi and Yarael and grunted. "You're new."

Yarael bowed his head. "I'm actually very old, but thank you."

"You haven't paid your taxes."

Yarael was about to say something when Ki-Adi-Mundi interceded. "My associate and I are tourists."

"Good for you," the Skull said. "There's a twenty-credit tourist tax." Letting the club hang on a chain at his side, he opened a pouch. There were Republic credits inside. "Pay up."

Ki-Adi-Mundi raised a white eyebrow. "Why was this tax not assessed when we landed?"

"An oversight."

"How terribly sad." Ki-Adi-Mundi shook his head. "Perhaps if you showed us your credentials, we could contact someone who could clear the matter up."

"Clear *what* up?"

Yarael put his hand over his face. *We could do this all day.*

Ki-Adi-Mundi was about to speak again when Yarael leaned over and waved his hand before the gang member. "*You don't want our money.*"

The Staved Skull froze. "*I don't want your money.*"

"*You will leave us alone.*"

"*I will leave you alone.*" Seemingly confused, he turned and ambled away.

Yarael put out his long arms and smiled. "You see? Simple."

"Well done." Ki-Adi-Mundi nodded in the direction of the next business. "What will you do about *that*?"

The Skull had gone back to bothering the merchant from before.

Yarael saw that and strode over to him. "Hey!"

"What?"

"*You have already collected from him,*" Yarael said.

"*I have already collected from him.*"

The rest of the interplay continued as it had before—and the Skull moved on up the block.

Yarael turned to see Ki-Adi-Mundi tapping his foot against the pavement. "As you informed the younglings back in the Jedi Temple, it is not possible for us to affect his decision making beyond these brief interactions. Do you intend to follow him around all day?"

"I'll tell him he's already collected from everyone." Yarael snapped his fingers. "An early day!"

"And what will you do when he reaches his employers—for he surely has them—with no proceeds?"

Yarael frowned. "I guess we could give him some credits of our own." He reached for his credit pouch, only to say, "How much have you got?"

The cold stare was answer enough.

Ki-Adi-Mundi was right, Yarael knew. Subsidizing all the mobsters on the island was probably not a workable solution, and certainly not a long-term one. Nor were any of the pranks he could imagine going to be of use.

The Cerean paused as he noticed several other roaming hoodlums. This part of Brazatta Key appeared to be Skull territory, for sure. "Perhaps if we entered a building. Confined the action to a space where no one will be harmed, or even see."

Yarael rubbed his chin. "When Qui-Gon suggested we meet the people, I doubt he meant for us to drag them off the street." He thought for a moment. "The better option would be to find out what drives someone to drill a hole in his head, and address that."

"Which I would be happy to do," Ki-Adi-Mundi said. "But I suspect the answer may vary from individual to individual, and while I said we had plenty of time before the celebration—"

"There's not *that* much."

"You have captured my thoughts succinctly."

"'Succinct' is not in your vocabulary—but you're right on this one." Yarael sighed. "Would it save time if we followed that money—and found out what motivated whoever's running this operation?"

Ki-Adi-Mundi stared. "It would potentially have a greater impact. And at a minimum, it might be a more appropriate place for combat."

The Staved Skulls who had evidently completed their rounds headed toward a brown landspeeder parked at the end of a bridge leading off the island. One by one, they handed off their credit pouches to someone inside the enclosed cabin.

"Now," Ki-Adi-Mundi said, reaching for his lightsaber. "Let us get these poor people their money back."

Yarael tugged at his robe. "Or!"

"Or what?"

Yarael was already walking. "You there!"

The Staved Skull they'd talked to earlier looked back at him. "What now?"

"Where do we go to sign up?"

"Sign up?"

"With your order," Ki-Adi-Mundi said.

"Order?"

"Your organized chaos," Yarael replied. "Whatever you call it. Where do we join?"

The bald man looked him up and down. "A Quermian Skull? Ridiculous!"

"You wound me." Yarael pointed to Ki-Adi-Mundi. "How about my friend here? Imagine that prominent crown, festooned with spikes. He'll be running the neighborhood in no time."

Ki-Adi-Mundi got into the act. "Yes, I would like to . . . do whatever you do." He proffered a handful of credits. "And these would be for you."

"Thanks from a tourist—and a future co-worker," Yarael said.

The Skull shook his head. Then he took the money. "Your funeral. The boss runs things out of Gutson's Pub, over on Vorah Key." He stomped off.

Yarael clapped his hands together. "Vorah!" Then he remembered something, and his lips curled down. "That's the next island over. How do we get there?"

"The same manner in which I got here." Ki-Ad-Mundi reached for his comlink. "Masters Plo and Tiin are operating a taxi service."

Yarael chuckled. "You mean they've got the only speeder and Saesee is stuck driving all of us around."

"I spoke precisely. *They are operating a taxi service.*"

Baffled, Yarael called out after him. "Are you going to tell me what you're talking about?"

"I cannot explain everything." Ki-Adi-Mundi started to walk. He looked back over his shoulder. "Try arriving earlier next time."

CHAPTER 32

RIFTWALKER HEADQUARTERS
VALBORAAN

Zilastra hurried through the halls of the Riftwalker base on Valboraan, with Burlug trailing behind her. He'd nearly caught up to her when she skidded to a stop and abruptly started scaling a ladder.

"Zil, wait up!" The Feeorin began to climb. "Where are you going?"

She didn't answer. Arriving on the upper level, she headed for the makeshift command center. There she found Ventner, her resident know-it-all, hunched over the terminal through which he kept tabs on the region. She slapped the back of his scaly Rodian head. "Wake up!"

Ventner groaned and looked at her. "What is it, boss?"

"What do you have on the other crews?"

"Our crews?"

"No, nerf herder. The other gangs!"

"Not a lot." He rubbed the back of his head where he'd been struck. "I'd have more if you let me put up the receiver array for more than a minute at a time."

"*Ventner!*"

"Fine, fine." He shook his head and pulled up a status screen. "Here's what we have."

Zilastra pored over the information. Burlug arrived as she was reading.

She chuckled. "Yeah. They're still tearing the flesh off each other," she said. "And lashing out, looking for anyone to hit."

"We knew that." Burlug crossed his arms. "I thought you were gonna kill the Jedi!"

"*The Jedi*," she muttered. "How could they be so foolish?"

"What are you talking about? What do we do with Billaba?"

"Oh, I'm going to kill her. Don't doubt that. But there's something else—and it can't wait another second." Zil pointed at the screen. "That's enough of this. Show me the other gangs' personnel."

Ventner yawned. "Why?"

"*Personnel!*"

"All right, all right." The Rodian made the adjustment and looked to the Feeorin. "What's this all about?"

"You got me," Burlug said.

Zilastra scanned the names. They all belonged to high-ranking members of the other four gangs—or people that the Riftwalkers suspected to be in those positions, at any rate. "These red ones are confirmed dead?"

Ventner shrugged. "To the extent anything can be. It's from intercepts and rumors passed from our people, so it's spotty."

Zilastra nodded. She didn't know if she was alone among pirate bosses in keeping tabs on such information, but it had certainly benefited her. Without it, she never would have been able to pull off the scheme with the cases that had started the chaos to begin with.

"The cases," she said. "Months. Months we put into collecting and filling those silly cases!"

"What's your problem?" Burlug's patience was long gone. "It was genius, Zil. It was a great idea, and you got what you wanted. We blew a hole in the sides of the other four gangs, so we could have easier pickings. Maybe we can sweep up some of the goodies they dropped in the wreckage. It was worth the investment."

"But I haven't collected that pot yet. Nobody even knows for sure that I was responsible. Do they?" She grabbed Ventner's collar. "*Do they?*"

"What? No!" He shook his head. "No, no. They think you're dead, too."

Zilastra nodded as she stared at the screen. "They don't know I did it."

"Well, you sure can't tell them you did," Burlug said. "You'd have everyone against us. Four against one usually wins."

"Not against the Queen of Air and Darkness." She stood straight.

"What, the sabacc card?"

She didn't give Burlug an answer. Zilastra was off again—this time, on the way to the workshop lair of Tokchi, her technical expert.

She arrived there just as he did, breathless, having just returned from the interrupted execution. The Ithorian looked to her. "What's going on?"

"That holovid we did earlier with the Jedi. Have we sent it out to our crews yet?"

"Of course not," Tokchi said. "You said we were gonna wait until you croaked her and put that on the end."

Zilastra thought for a moment. "We'll save that part, in case we need a sweetener."

"Need a what?" Burlug had arrived behind her, looking flustered. "I'm not getting where you're going here, Zil."

"I want the council room ready for me to make a call," she told Tokchi. "Cue up the vid for when I ask for it. Ventner's got the contact list."

Tokchi shook his head and looked for his headset.

Zilastra spun again, ready to dash off—only for Burlug to seize her by the shoulders. "Stop!"

She gritted her teeth. "Get your hands off me, Luggy."

"Not until I know what you're doing!"

"There's no time."

"Time for what?"

"It's like I said. The pot's still on the table. But I'm going to let it ride. Parlay it. Go bigger—much bigger."

"I don't know what in blazes you're talking about."

Burlug released her—and she took a breath.

"The channels we were using to reach the other gangs," she said. "We still have those."

"Yeah, but there's nobody on the other end. We blew them all up!"

"The people on top, Luggy. The red ones on Ventner's list. But the outfits still exist. Somebody's gonna answer. And odds are it'll be whoever's on top at the moment."

"I don't know about that. They're all still reeling. They're going after one another, sure—but that's to cover their weakness. And to keep their own members from trying to kill one another." Burlug shook his head. "You did more of a number on the other gangs than you know."

"And so it's still my play."

She watched as he stared at her. She'd known him longer than anyone in the Riftwalkers; indeed, *he'd* been the leader of the band in its earliest days. But he had wisely recognized her skill as a tactician—and her readiness to do anything to succeed. That was rare among the gangs. She trusted him, and had kept him alive as a consequence, where others might see a potential usurper. He trusted her, as well—and appeared to do so again now. "What do you have in mind?"

"You remember the thing we talked about back on Aggarda? With the old guy who'd been in the racket for a century?"

He scratched his chin. "You don't mean—?"

"Yeah, the *thing*!"

Burlug clearly remembered. "Zil, but that was just wishful thinking. An old campaigner, drunk and half dead, moaning about what might have been."

"I don't drink—and I'm alive."

"It's a dream. A pirate's dream. That's all it is. You've got a better chance of herding—what are those things on Kwenn?"

"Boolahs."

Tokchi lifted his headset and spoke up. "I've made some of those connections you asked for."

Zilastra smiled. "They answered!"

"They're, uh . . . surprised." He winced. "And swearing."

She poked Burlug in the chest. "It'll work. Watch me."

"But what about the Jedi?"

"Just bring me the case!" She pointed to Tokchi. "And you—afterward, get ready. I'm gonna need you to make a trip!"

"Me? Where?"

"Later. The call, first!"

She ignored their further pleas for information as she dashed down the hall. There was no time to change, to find something suitable to wear for the next play, the most important one of her life. Every second she wasted increased the odds of failure. She had to act while the memories were fresh.

She stepped into the round room. The score marks from the shots the Jedi had deflected were still visible on the wall. "Tokchi, is the cam on?"

His voice came over the intercom. "You're on, boss."

She settled into her chair—only to change her mind. "I'm going to walk while I talk. Is that a problem?"

"I'm only connecting you to four different parties light-years away, none of whom want to hear from you. Sure, I can improvise."

She took a breath, composing herself—and then smiled when Burlug entered with the final Regal Voyager case from days earlier. It was still open, and had not lost its value as a prop. If anything, its importance had grown.

She took it from him. "Thanks. Now get out of my shot."

"Gladly." Burlug stepped to the round wall.

"All four parties are on," Tokchi announced.

Zilastra looked from spot to empty spot. No holographic chairs, this time—or anything else. "I can't see anybody."

"Nobody's willing to go on holo. They're just watching and listening. But they're there."

"That's fine."

She began strolling in the middle of the chamber. "You're all new here, so if you haven't heard, I'm Zilastra of the Riftwalkers. As you can see, I'm alive." She held up the case and showed that it was open. "And I'm alive because I did this to all of you. The bombs that were in these— they all came from me."

Silence. And then a voice could be heard from the empty space to her left. "You're lying."

"Yeah," said someone to her right. "Likely story."

"Oh, I'm telling the truth. I'm guessing you already figured out these were what killed your bosses. Maybe some of you geniuses have even retaliated against Regal Voyager."

Silence. Until someone said, "No, but that's a good idea."

"It's a *stupid* idea. But that's okay. I'm here to think for all of you."

She cast an eye to Burlug. He was covering his face with his hands. But there was no stopping now.

"I did all of this," she said. "One big hit, taking out all your bosses. The fact is, all of you owe me. I made moves some of you were probably already thinking of doing. The difference is, I moved first."

Still nobody appeared. But someone said, "Go on."

She continued pacing in a circle. "You've probably been hunting the Riftwalkers along with everyone else you've been chasing. Maybe you've noticed we're scarce. That should be proof enough that I'm telling the truth. Some of you are thinking even more about hitting me now."

"*All of us!*" It was a yell sure to have come from the representative of the Vile.

She wasn't intimidated. "Sure, you can waste time doing that. But think: If I was able to get baradium-357 right under your bosses' noses, what other little surprises have I planted? I must have people everywhere, right?"

A Twi'lek woman in a three-piece suit holographically appeared. She, too, was standing. Zilastra made her immediately as a Filthy Cred.

"I am Chief Executive Linn, successor to Darwoh," the woman said, guarded. "Where are you going with this?"

"I'm saying if I can do whatever I want to you, whenever I want, then the Ootmian route is a whole new game."

A Staved Skull member appeared by hologram. He clutched a blood-covered chain, clearly something that had just seen some use. "You think you can extort us? Make us your slaves?"

"Cool your jets," she said. The guy looked much like the Eviscerator, his late leader. *They must get these guys from the same factory,* she thought. "I never said anything about slavery. I just described our relationship—our new relationship—in terms you should understand." She raised the case in her hand. "I've already given you a very vivid example, just a few days ago."

A black-clad Trandoshan appeared in the space reserved for the Vile. "You're bluffing," he said with a snarl.

"Someone very important—someone I'll show you in a moment—says I never bluff." Zilastra paced to the center. "And that gets to the reason I've called you today. I said the game has changed. I meant to say there's a *new game*—if you're interested." She raised the case again. "Really, whether or not you're interested."

The final member appeared, representing the Poisoned Blades. "What are you offering?"

"An old pirate's dream. One pirate band for the whole route. United—*under me*—and making all of you wealthier than you've ever imagined." She smiled at Burlug. "But we're going to have to act fast. *Very* fast."

CHAPTER 33

MALBAIRA KEY

KWENN

"Stand by," Plo Koon called out. "Now!"

The Kel Dor watched as Saesee Tiin gunned the engines of the repulsorcraft. It was a ridiculously dangerous thing they were trying. Civilians were not allowed airspeeders on Kwenn, but Saesee had used girders to connect several surplus Kwikhaul engines together into an open-framed flying platform, capable of lifting something large a meter off the ground.

The item to be hoisted was truly colossal: a teal oroko. The nine-pointed echinoderm was flattish—just two meters tall—but it made up for that in surface area. Plo Koon thought it would cover most of the open floor of the Jedi Council Chamber on Coruscant. It sat limply on the beach on Malbaira Key, unresponsive but still alive.

Through the framework of the hovering lifter, Plo could see the cables he'd carefully looped around the beast's dorsal fins. The repulsorlift's movement brought the cables taut, but the massive beast didn't budge.

"Stop! You must stop!" Oppo Rancisis yelled up from below. "Cease before you do harm!"

Plo relayed the order and looked down. "What is it?"

"It is no good." Covered in spray from the sea, Oppo stood beside the creature. "Kooroo-coo is terrified. His hold on the ground below only increases as the cables tug on him."

Plo looked to see if Saesee had heard the instruction. He had. The engines slowed down, allowing the makeshift platform to hover a few meters over the slimy creature's body.

The teal oroko had been native to Kwenn before the ecological calamity, centuries before. Well before the Renewal, the zoological academy on Alderaan had judged Kwenn a lost cause, removing a school of oroko to a lagoon preserve on that planet. They later returned the creatures to their native habitat, thanks to the efforts of Master Oppo and the Jedi. The reintroduction of the oroko to Kwenn had been the crowning moment of the multiyear rescue effort. Oppo himself had swum with the beings then.

The species had flourished, but now it seemed to be in danger again. Yoda had reported seeing a beached oroko while a passenger aboard one of Kwikhaul's new water speeders. Such events were happening more often lately, according to the well-meaning people gathered nearby. Without a swift return to the water, the oroko's death was inevitable. It had been enough to get Oppo away from his event preparations and into the action.

Oppo pressed his hands and cheek against the slimy surface of the creature. "Yes, my friend. All will be well."

"Your friend?" Plo asked.

"Kooroo-coo I know of old," the Thisspiasian Jedi replied. "He is the proctor, and by that I mean he leads the school."

"If he is intelligent, ask him to release the ground," Saesee said.

"He is an old friend, but we have not conquered nouns."

They had already considered and rejected the idea of moving the oroko with the Force. The naturalist they had summoned from the university suggested that flying might cause a fatal panic reaction.

Plo adjusted his breathing filter. He looked at the meters the creature had traveled up the shore before he became entrapped. "What caused him to be beached?"

Oppo closed his eyes as he held on to the oroko. "I sense loss. Confusion. Sorrow."

"Something close to him died?" Saesee asked.

"Or will." Oppo opened his eyes. "I cannot say more."

"What are those?" From his perch atop the flying platform, Plo pointed out the small pits up and down the beach. "It looks like someone has been digging."

The naturalist hurried from the crowd to take a look. "Those were orokite nodule deposits," she said. "These could be troves!"

"Troves?" Oppo asked—and as he did so, the oroko shuddered.

"He responded to that," Saesee said.

"Or to my thoughts." Oppo slapped his forehead. "Curse me for a fool. The proctor's body accretes minerals from the seabed into large polished nodules, which he deposits in the sand. They dry out over the course of decades."

The naturalist chimed in. "He was trying to return these to feed the young. The oroko must be birthing out there!"

Oppo touched the oroko and concentrated again. "Yes. Someone has dug up Kooroo-coo's troves. When he could not find them, he stayed too long—and the tide went out."

"Poachers," the naturalist said with a scowl. "People sell the nodules to the Filthy Creds over on Quarney Key. They go for thousands on the illicit market."

"We know how to take care of that," Saesee said. "But that water is meters away yet."

"Then we must turn the tide," Plo said. He cut loose a cable and moved to another one.

His action alarmed his colleague. "What are you doing?"

"We cannot bring him to the sea. But we can bring the sea to him!"

It took a few moments before Saesee understood what he had in mind—but he appeared game for it. He guided the flier a few dozen meters out to sea. "After all our repair work, it'll be a change to destroy something!"

Briefed on what to do, Oppo ordered the onlookers to move farther inland. He removed his outer cloak and slithered up and on top of the oroko's body. Meanwhile, Plo and Saesee nimbly stepped along the girders holding the turbines together, making key—and destructive—alterations to the engines keeping them aloft.

The latticework flier began to spin. Slowly, at first, but with engines roaring faster and faster. At the same time, the hodgepodge craft lost altitude. It was barely a meter above the surface when the Jedi dived from it. They stayed in the water for mere seconds, swimming away as fast as they could. Behind them, the would-be oroko carrier spun crazily, the vortex from its rotation kicking up water from below.

Plo glanced to see that Oppo was on Kooroo-coo's back, clinging to one of the fins. What he yelled could not be heard over the din, but all three knew what was to come next. Plo and Saesee turned in the water.

Saesee had set the flier for a short ride—and it abruptly ended when the whole contraption suddenly lost the little elevation it had left, a plunging pinwheel. The turbines exploded on schedule, a shallow depth charge sending a colossal plume of seawater high in the air.

But *not* in all directions. Treading water, Plo and Saesee simultaneously lifted their hands and directed the cascade inward with the Force. A wall of water screamed toward Oppo and the oroko, smashing down upon them. As more poured down, the creature lost its death-clench on the beach and caught the outgoing wave.

Plo looked to Saesee, as waterlogged as he was. "You see, Master Tiin? I could have redirected that coolant you spilled on me back in the hangar."

"*I* spilled?"

They heard a happy animal bleat. Soaked and clinging, Oppo spiraled along with the creature, whirling on an eddy created by the explosion. Plo called out, "Do you require aid, Master?"

"Not at all," Oppo said. "Kooroo-coo is always glad to be in the sea—and ready to find his other troves. I will ride with him to ensure he comes to no harm!"

Saesee looked at Plo—and cupped his hands to call out. "You have an event to plan!"

Oppo did not respond, unless hooting like a Thisspiasian one-tenth his age counted. It delighted Plo to see it.

Drenched, he waded back to the shore, where the onlookers applauded. "That is not necessary," he said, wiping his goggles. "The crisis is over. Malbaira Key is a nature preserve. Let it again be at peace."

As the civilians headed for their vehicles, Plo saw that his companion was still in the water, having found a turbine blade from the exploded platform. "You could have asked them to help us haul this debris out of here," Saesee said.

Plo did not respond. Rather, he joined his companion in fishing pieces of wreckage out of the sea.

Saesee spoke as they worked. "So the Filthy Creds are set up on Quarney Key."

"Among other places." Working with Kwikhaul had been for the benefit of the workers and business owner, but it had given them lots of intelligence about who was where on Kwenn. "Everyone has recruits here, if not an actual base. It is as if they are waiting for something. Or *someone* to leave."

"There you go again. Blaming us." Saesee lifted a twisted engine panel from the muck. "We did not tell these people to move here and rob a sea mammal."

"*Echinoderm*," Plo corrected. "And let us be clear. Criminals did not simply spring up here organically as opportunities on this planet waned. The parent organizations have observed our movements elsewhere—the Jedi's and the Republic's—and they predict that we will depart."

"They're prophets, now?"

"One does not need to be able to prophesize. One needs only to believe a thing to act accordingly."

"Fine thoughts, Plo Koon. But the Jedi must not defy reality by keeping the outpost open. We have done much to revive one business here—and several associated ones—but it only delays the inevitable. If the Senate no longer sees value in Kwenn, there will eventually be fewer people here to serve, no matter what the Jedi might prefer." Saesee dragged part of an engine onto the beach and dropped it. "One does not service a vehicle no longer in use."

"You speak of a world as you would a freighter?"

Saesee knelt over the debris. "Machines have life cycles, just as sen-

tient beings do. Just as every speeder operator understands obsoles-
cence, you and I see death as part of the natural order of things." He
stood and gestured to the verdant land behind them. "The Order two
centuries ago took the extreme step of bringing this entire planet back
from the edge. But we may do it no favors by trying to prolong its life
span." He peered keenly at Plo. "You and I would agree anyone attempting to use the Force to lengthen life would be committing a crime of the
highest order."

"Of course." Plo could not imagine anyone even trying, much less
how they could succeed. But looking at the beauty around them, he rejected the analogy. "We are helping this planet, these people, to heal."

"Jedi are not healers."

"Perhaps not. But we are teachers. And those people today saw something."

CHAPTER 34

KINNAWAH KEY

KWENN

"Master Qui-Gon, are you there?" Eeth Koth looked at his comlink to confirm it was working. "Obi-Wan? Anybody?"

Standing in the courtyard outside the Lamplighter Boutique on Kinnawah Key on Kwenn, Eeth Koth looked to the evening sky. Sometimes solar activity interfered with signals, but Kwenn had a large space station that acted as a relay. He was sure his messages were getting out.

Perhaps the interference is on their end, he thought as he deactivated the unit. Eeth's nature was to assume everything but incompetence or insubordination, and certainly Qui-Gon and Obi-Wan had earned the benefit of the doubt.

Still, Eeth wished he had someone to blame as he glanced back through the advancing shadows at the building full of ephemera. Sorting had kept him from all other activities, and with the celebration now announced, his chances of seeing anything other than the Lamplighter while on Kwenn were growing fewer. The great triumph of his long day was clearing the boutique's front door to the street enough so it could open.

"Master Reeth!"

He didn't need to turn; the bellow could only have come from Pogee Shrag, ruining his name as only she could. She stood in the side doorway of her house, boolah kits crawling all over her. "What can I do for you?" Eeth asked.

"Your friends are here to see you. Yoddle and Odd Peel."

It took Eeth a second to work on that one. "Yaddle and Even Piell?"

"That's what I said!" She poked at the side of her head. "Your ears are on the outside. I'd figure they'd work!"

She stepped aside, revealing the guests in her home.

Oh, no. Eeth's breath caught as he saw his colleagues. Yaddle cradled a boolah kit in her arms like a baby. Piell was less fortunate. A pair of kits were trying to hang from his ears, which, while prodigious, could not hold their weight, giving the effect that he was wearing long white sideburns. Eeth did not need the Force to see that Piell was not at peace within it.

"Thank you for inviting us into your lovely home," Yaddle said to Pogee. Yaddle released her kit, which squirmed up its owner's leg. "They're charming animals."

"Yeah," Piell said, detaching one creature and then another. "I'm running a food drive. I'm sure these things would go good in a soup."

"Master Piell!" Yaddle whispered.

Rather than take offense, Pogee laughed loudly. "You're a pip, Master Pile!"

The Nosaurian woman turned back inside, followed by her skittering creatures.

Eeth offered his friends an apology—and some good news. "The creatures will not follow us into the courtyard."

Yaddle looked back to see the door close. "Pogee is something, isn't she?"

"She fits that definition, yes."

"Generous," Piell said, massaging his ears.

Eeth was glad to see them, but confused. "Why are you on Kinnawah Key? I thought you were working with schoolchildren."

"They have to go home sometime. Even though some of them need to be convinced of that." Piell shook his head. "Some of their home lives—well, they're more than we could address in a year here. But there's enough troublemakers at work on Kwenn that we can't have them out at all hours, either."

Yaddle nodded. "A difficult puzzle. And one that speaks to the urgency of our mission."

Eeth finally noticed the setting sun. His work had caused him to forget the time again.

He faced Yaddle. "I assumed you'd be continuing your publicity work."

"I have been," she replied. "I've also been counseling a young woman through a hard time."

"And I've got a hundred new students," Piell said.

Eeth smiled. "So you both have answered Qui-Gon's challenge!"

"You could say that," Piell replied.

Eeth could not say the same, in many ways. He looked at his comlink before putting it away. "I am happy for you both."

Yaddle nodded. "I sensed you were feeling a bit abandoned."

"I can handle it." Eeth brightened.

"You don't fool me a bit, Eeth Koth. We've traveled parsecs to an archipelago packed with people to meet, and you're back in an archive."

"Utility comes in many forms," he said.

"Yeah, I have to be reminded about that a time or ten." Piell stepped over to the storehouse. "How goes your search?"

Eeth gestured inside. "I have found nine works belonging to the outpost library—far short of what the seneschal's list led me to expect." He stepped inside for a moment and brought out a stack of materials. He showed them to his colleagues.

Piell read the titles in the fading light and snorted. "Dull stuff. These'd put my kids to sleep for sure."

Eeth nodded. "All minor texts, I agree. I keep expecting to find the more valuable material farther in." He stared at the piles. "But I am running out of time."

"*We* have time." Yaddle walked to the threshold. "You have lights we can use?"

Eeth was startled. "Yes, but—"

"Then make way." Piell strode past him, and Yaddle followed.

"I appreciate this," Eeth said, joining them. "But you have more important work—"

"We are all equal," Yaddle said, "and we will share in this work." She looked up at him. "The Force doesn't ask us to martyr ourselves for it—to commit ourselves too entirely to the humblest jobs, staying ever in one place. We should move, experiencing life. These rote duties can be shared."

Eeth looked with trepidation at the pillars of datapads and other materials as his short companions worked their way in. "Really, it is safer if I am the one—"

"Bah!" Piell glanced up at the towers surrounding him. "I think we can handle getting whacked in the head."

"Hadden Shrag couldn't," Eeth muttered.

"What?"

"Never mind." He stepped around some of the nicer stacks he'd made. "If you both will manage these lower piles, that would be of great service."

"Not a problem," Piell said.

"And there is water beside the entrance."

Yaddle smiled pleasantly. "That's nice, Eeth, but what are you still doing here?"

That startled Eeth. "Excuse me?"

"We aren't just helping you. We're *relieving* you."

Piell clapped his lower back. "Go out. See Kwenn. Do something."

Eeth started to object—only to smile. "Thank you, my friends."

He stepped through the recently unblocked door and onto the street. It was a side of Kwenn that he hadn't seen in years. The buildings along the walking plaza on Kinnawah Key came alive with light, and people settled in at outdoor tables to dine. He couldn't tell the tourists from the local residents, and he liked that. This Gem City was still shining. Perhaps there was hope for all of them.

Eeth soon lost track of time again, but this time, he didn't resent it. He circled several blocks, just observing people—and feeling their contribution to the Force.

Thank you, Piell and Yaddle, he thought.

By the time he remembered his hunger, outdoor table service was wrapping up. But the casino barge *Pelagic* was in at Kinnawah, and that meant there was still activity near the dock. He found an open-air bar on the ground floor of a small hotel and settled in, ordering a meal and continuing his people-watching.

The bartender explained to him that unlike other parts of Kwenn's economy, gambling had prospered in recent years; as large as it was, the barge had been forced to limit how many boarded at once, bringing people to and from *Pelagic* in its excursion skiffs. Those here in the bar still had their money—and were willing to spend it as they waited for their turn to board the skiff.

That was the way many people spent their days, Eeth thought. Living, while they waited to live.

He had nearly completed his repast when he saw a woman looking at him from the other side of the room. Her hair was dark like that of other Falleen, but the way she wore it was not. Instead of a topknot, she let it hang down, festooned on one side with a bright-yellow flower that stood out against her green skin. She was attired fancily, though not out of place given the number of well-to-do tourists he'd seen.

Indeed, I am the one out of place.

She sidled up next to him as he worked on his meal. "Hello, hello."

"Greetings."

"Your line is 'greetings'?" She grinned. "You don't get out much, do you?" She leaned in beside him. "Inisa."

"Like the flower." It was not the type of flower that was in her hair, but he decided not to mention that. He stood and bowed. "I am Eeth."

Inisa startled him by reaching out to touch the side of his face. "Zabrak. I like it. Spiky."

Eeth eyed her. "I carry few credits. I am assuming that is why your hand is in the pocket of my cloak."

She registered what he'd said—and then quickly removed her hand. She scrunched her face. "Pooh. Everyone's always broke."

"When they don't belong to ascetic sects."

She did a double take. "Come again?"

He quickly rephrased his statement. "I belong to a *sect*—the Jedi Order. We have money, but we don't often carry it."

"Got it." She shrugged. "Well, carry on." She started to move away.

"You don't have to go." Eeth gestured for the bartender to approach—but glanced at Inisa before ordering. "With your permission?"

She looked surprised. "You're ordering for me?"

"I can afford that much."

"These Jedi—they let you buy drinks for strangers?"

"It is already done." His credits were on the bar.

Soon the drink was in her hand. She smirked at him through her glass as he finished eating. "I don't believe you for a second. I've heard a little about Jedi. You don't seem to fit."

He gestured to a Twi'lek at the opposite corner of the bar. "Is that your associate over there?"

Inisa looked in that direction. The Twi'lek was laughing hard, his arm around a well-dressed companion. "What makes you think I know him?"

"He just placed something in the drink of the businessperson next to him."

In full view of Inisa, Eeth flicked his hand in the unsuspecting victim's direction—and the glass in question leapt over, spilling onto the Twi'lek. It caused a minor scene.

"Hey, you *are* a Jedi!" Inisa looked dazzled. She pointed to another glass on the bar. "Do that again."

"I've made enough of a mess." Eeth glanced over to see that the mark was safe. "But if your friend tries it again, I will intervene."

Leaning her back against the bar, she stared at him—and smiled, a new respect forming. "So. A real Jedi, huh?"

"Correct."

"I heard you people were here. For a celebration."

"Yes. Will you attend?"

Inisa chortled. "What do I have to celebrate?"

Eeth spoke with reverence. "We celebrate life."

"While living a life where you don't have to worry about money. I'd celebrate that, too." Inisa turned and took a swig of her drink. "I'm afraid the sect that *I* belong to cares about it a lot more, Jedi."

"Tell me about this sect. What do they offer you?"

"A place."

"To live?"

"To belong. Among other things."

"But not a place worth celebrating." Eeth looked around—and then back at her. "This island seems well off. What brings you to this kind of activity?"

"This kind of activity brings me to this island." She put up her hand. "If you're going to judge—"

"Jedi are called upon to act as judges—and more—in many situations. This is not one of them. But I am willing to listen."

She stared at him, evaluating. "I wasn't expecting to meet a Jedi."

Eeth took it as a compliment.

They spoke more over the course of the next hour. Eeth learned that Inisa and her friends were stringers for the Poisoned Blades, a group slowly starting to assert itself on Kwenn. Less brazen but no less dangerous than some of their rival outfits, they had worked their way into society on Kwenn's more prosperous islands, like Kinnawah. The people they drew upon lacked hope and opportunity—and while none of them were as imposing as the Staved Skulls or as depraved as the Vile, they had other weapons at their disposal. Including, Eeth could see, an endless supply of people willing to sacrifice their ideals for the promise of status.

Eeth understood—and he counseled. "Whatever your situation, Inisa, your actions bring sorrow to others."

"I just steal—and find marks for the higher-ups. I don't—"

Eeth put up his hand. "That doesn't matter to me. What matters is that you recognize when you add to the darkness. And that you care."

"I assume you're going to talk me into a normal life and a dead-end job," Inisa said. "Well, I had one. I'm pretty sure a Jedi could never imagine how soul destroying it is sifting through administrative minutiae all day."

"You might be surprised," Eeth said. "But it's who that work helps—and what you do the rest of the time—that matters."

He didn't say anything after that. She watched him. "I was kidding, but you really *don't* get out much, do you?"

"Not lately." Eeth looked past the bar. "I came to Kwenn because I had allowed my responsibilities to the Jedi to make me forget what it meant to *be* a Jedi. And then I immediately went back to doing it again."

"What *does* it mean to be a Jedi?"

"Oh, that's easy. I'm one with everything. I know that the universe has meaning—and that what people do matters. And my role is to help people see that."

"But you've avoided that, even here?"

"Every step I have taken forward in the Order has shown me how big and complicated the galaxy is—and how necessary the Jedi are, acting as a group and across immense distances. And I cannot stray from that." He looked up. "Still, I miss when I was more *Jedi* than *Order*."

She chuckled. "I don't want to be a part in someone else's machine. You want to forget the machine."

Eeth mused over that. But only for a moment.

"Do you have a comlink?" he asked. "If you have need to talk again, I want you to have the opportunity."

Inisa's eyes widened with disbelief as he provided his data. "A Jedi is giving me his contact information?"

"Obviously I work someplace else. But there are a lot of us. And if you find yourself needing to exit the life you're in, we can find someone to help."

" 'Someone to help.' " She smirked. "But not you, huh?"

"We don't do—"

"Yeah, yeah, yeah."

Eeth stood back, thanked the bartender for the meal, and bowed. "I have much still left to do before—"

The device in Inisa's hand buzzed—as did at least three others Eeth could hear around the room. Including, he saw, the one belonging to the Twi'lek he'd spilled a drink on. Inisa read the message. "Oh," she said. "Something's come up."

"Your *sect* calls, I take it."

She looked across the room at her associate—and then placed her hand on Eeth's wrist. "I have to go, too. But I appreciate your talking to me, Eeth." She stepped back and smiled. "Or do I call you Master Eeth?"

"Call me," he replied, "if you need help."

He watched as she stepped outside into the darkness.

CHAPTER 35

ABOARD *ASSURANCE*

OOTMIAN ROUTE

"Get those cannons online, Windu!"

Mace wasn't accustomed to being spoken to in such a manner—but protocol had been left well in *Assurance*'s wake. He responded to Captain Baylo with a look the other now understood: *he was working on it.*

In the days since the encounter in the Aklasian Nebula, *Assurance* had been partially repaired when it happened upon a new target: a twin-cockpit hunter vessel belonging to the Staved Skulls. The starship was festooned with so many cannons that Baylo doubted it carried enough personnel to operate them all. A first pass had resulted in a lucky shot from the Skulls damaging the corvette's shields—and causing Baylo to once again entrust the weapons station to Mace.

It was no failing of the Jedi's that caused things to turn the Skulls' way; *Assurance*'s main turbolaser cannon had overheated from use, a consequence of the incomplete repairs. That had forced the ship into evasive action—which wasn't working, either.

"We're not going to make it," Baylo said. He glanced at Mace. "At least they're not the Vile. Those lunkheads destroy half their catch out of sheer incompetence. The Skulls will board us."

The Jedi Master rose. "I will buy us time for repairs—with your crew's help."

"You'll have it." Baylo spoke into the ship's communicator. "Stand by to repel boarders!"

Mace had reached the exit when he stopped. He turned and looked back out through the main viewport at space.

"What now?" the captain yelled.

"There!" Mace pointed. A cruiser emerged from hyperspace just ahead of the corvette. The ship's unmistakable markings—the lurid graffiti of the Vile—were visible as it approached. The vessel opened fire, but not at *Assurance*.

"New contact is targeting the Skulls, Captain!"

Baylo was bewildered. "Did the Vile just come to our rescue?"

Mace stepped to the center of the bridge beside him—and realized the drama wasn't done. He pointed out the starboard portal. "Another!"

The vessel that arrived from that direction was similarly easy to identify: a silvery sleek cruiser belonging to the Filthy Creds. The ship similarly ignored *Assurance*, strafing the Skulls' ship on the way to attacking the Vile.

"Cannons ready," said the officer who'd taken Mace's place. "Who do we target, Captain?"

Baylo studied the scene. "I'm sure there's something about this in the histories somewhere. But I'm damned if I ever read it."

Mace felt his confusion. "I suggest we take station nearby to repair and observe."

"Observe. Yeah. For all the good that'll do." Baylo gave the order anyway.

Patient observation had benefited Mace often in his time on the Jedi Council, but he wasn't born with it as a default. When he was a younger man, he might have responded differently to the array of events that he and *Assurance* had learned about. He probably would have rushed to those in jeopardy on Keldooine. He also would've gone if the only person who was threatened was a close associate, like Depa. But in more recent years, Mace had learned to reckon with the wider scheme—with what the Force wanted from him. It had advised caution and watchfulness time and again. That had always paid off.

He wasn't sure either choice would have worked this time. The fires on Keldooine were out; Master Yarael had deployed there but ultimately had not been able to help. Nor did Yarael find Depa, though there was evidence she had been there: a demolished speeder truck she had rented from an intermediary Baylo knew had turned up in territory contested among multiple gangs, groups that were now in all-out war with one another. Depa's trail was cold.

But Mace remaining with the patrol hadn't been the answer, either. The shock of the events that had sent the various pirate crews reeling had given way to acts of reprisal in space, as well. It was clear from reports that several groups had lost their leadership in a concerted act of terrorism, but nobody knew exactly who yet survived. That made everyone a potential suspect—and target. The spaceways mirrored what was happening on Keldooine's surface, and likely elsewhere across the Slice. The gangs had all turned on one another.

With *Assurance* out of weapons range of the raging conflagration, Mace and Baylo walked over to where Lieutenant Nellis, still recovering from his injuries, was stationed before a stellar display indicating reported confrontations and the parties involved. "Guess this is a new one for the board," Baylo said.

Nellis made a record of the ongoing battle—and directed their attention to earlier reports. "These markings here were Blade-on-Vile battles. Vile-Creds are here. And the Skulls—well, you can see they're just swinging at anything."

Mace took in all the data. He saw no pattern at all—but did note the relative absence of something. "How often have Riftwalker vessels been in these actions?"

"Not often." Nellis pointed to some symbols—a smaller number. "They've been fleeing a lot."

Baylo chortled. "I guess they really are the smartest."

The captain had shed no tears over seeing others doing his job, but Mace knew chaos on such a scale could come to no good. People were dying. He could feel it happening on the three warring ships as they traded blows.

And then he felt something else.

"Something's happened."

Baylo looked to him. "What?"

"Wait."

The captain looked back outside—and saw all three ships disengage. They all fled, heading for hyperspace as quickly as they had arrived. He turned back to Mace, flabbergasted. "They all just ran away!"

Mace headed over to look at a status display. *Assurance*'s last scan of the three ships had shown that none of the vessels was in imminent danger of destruction, and he said so.

Baylo threw up his hands. "I've got forty years and I haven't seen anything like this. What's happening, Windu?"

Mace stared back outside. "I don't know. But something changed."

He concentrated on the Force. "Whatever it was, they all found out about it at the same time."

Baylo looked to his communications station. "Did we pick up any intercepts?"

The young cadet, Veers, shook his head. "Systems still rebooting, Captain."

Baylo let out an exasperated sigh. "Maybe they all got an invite to a luncheon." He removed his hat and wiped perspiration from his forehead. "Forget it. I've been paid already. I don't care anymore."

Mace looked at him. "You care."

Baylo looked back at Mace, his eyes narrow slits. Finally, he spoke. "Damn!" The captain straightened his hat and put it back on.

As word that repairs had been completed arrived, Mace and the captain strolled across the bridge, which now looked out onto empty space. Mace stopped. "I have a quandary, Captain. I am due at the bicentennial celebration on Kwenn. But I don't want to leave without having found Master Billaba."

"There's not a lot you can do here," Baylo said. "Us, either. Our commission's about to run out, remember?"

"I can have your superiors extend your detachment to us."

"I can't believe I'm going to say this—but you'd be wasting your credits. And my time." Baylo shook his head. "When the day comes that anyone can make sense of this area, the Hutts will be running it." He shrugged. "Maybe they're running it already, and we just haven't gotten the word."

Mace took a deep breath. It was not in his nature to quit—especially when nothing was making sense. But just as in the meditation chamber on Coruscant, he knew when he wasn't getting anywhere.

"I won't risk any more of your personnel," he said. "Captain Baylo, I request passage to Kwenn. Upon my arrival, I declare *Assurance*'s obligation to the Jedi Order fulfilled. For its part, I'm sure the Republic will agree."

"So I'm back to the insurance game. That's that." Baylo spun and strode toward his helm officer.

He was preparing to give a command when the cadet at the communications station spoke again. "Coded interstellar signal coming in. Relatively strong, not far away."

"*Now* it works," Baylo said.

Mace felt for the comlink in his robe and removed it. "The call is for me."

He didn't get his hopes up. It was more likely to be from one of the Jedi on Kwenn than from Depa. He patched it through the bridge's holographic projectors.

"Qui-Gon?"

"Greetings, Master Windu." The headset Qui-Gon was wearing indicated he was piloting a small spacecraft.

"Master Qui-Gon. I have Captain Baylo of *Assurance* beside me." Mace frowned. "Why are you not on Coruscant?"

"Master Koth summoned us to help him in a project on Kwenn."

That's unusual, Mace thought. "Then why are you not on Kwenn?"

"We were on the way. But we paused when we were passing the Valboraan system, dropping out of hyperspace for a mechanical check. And then we heard it, about ten minutes ago."

"Heard what?"

"It was on the Jedi emergency channel, but we could only receive a very faint transmission. Nobody who wasn't passing by the system could have received it. We made a recording."

"Put it through."

Qui-Gon's image disappeared—and a human girl appeared in a flickering hologram. Her voice crackled with static.

"—name is Kylah Lohmata. I'm friends with Depa Billaba. The Riftwalkers on Valboraan have her, in the big caves. They're going to kill her!"

Mace and Baylo looked at each other.

"This communicator was in the stuff they took from her. I stole it, but I only have a few minutes. Jedi, if you're out there, please come. She needs you!"

Baylo peered at the frozen image—which was soon replaced by Qui-Gon's visage. "It's a fake," the captain said. "Just the sort of thing the Poisoned Blades would pull."

Qui-Gon answered. "I had my suspicions as well, Captain. I did not immediately answer—and the call was not repeated."

Mace's brow furrowed. He stepped over to check Qui-Gon's location. "Captain, no one else would hear that transmission. There's nothing nearby." He looked over at the hologram. "The message only played once?"

"That's correct, Master. That makes deceit unlikely—or at least, unlikely to reach any potential targets. I think the message is in earnest."

Baylo snorted. "How can you know that?"

Qui-Gon paused before answering. "I hear it in her voice."

The captain stared—and threw up his hands. "*Jedi!*"

Mace continued to study the location. Valboraan's features made it look more and more like a place the Riftwalkers might frequent. He traced a course and showed the captain. "We emerge here. Correct?"

Baylo looked—and nodded. "I still think you're wrong, Windu. It's another damn thing like the Poisoned Blades pulled on us back at the nebula."

"Yet everything we have observed suggests the Blades are leaderless and directionless. Whereas the Riftwalkers have been spared in the current outbreak of violence." Mace nodded slowly. "I agree with Qui-Gon."

A beat. And then, Qui-Gon said, "What would you like us to do, Master?"

"You and Obi-Wan will remain near Valboraan. If anyone departs, or another transmission is sent, alert us—and use your own judgment about following. But do not land. If it is the Riftwalkers' base, charging in alone will only lead to more dead Jedi. An assault this size requires support." He looked up—and over to Baylo. "*Naval* support. What do you think, Captain?"

The suggestion startled Baylo, who raised an eyebrow. "Combined operations?"

"Why, Captain, I thought you were a man of history. You should know the Republic Defense Coalition once engaged in combined actions with the Jedi." He eyed Baylo. "They worked out well, as I recall."

The captain considered it. "A joint action. But I would remain in command."

"I insist. Unless, of course, you'd rather work for Chokoll Indemnity."

"Close that communication, Veers." Baylo pounded his fist on the console and flashed what Mace thought was the start of a grin. "*Assurance*, all hands—get this tug running. We've got a job to finish!"

CHAPTER 36

VORAH KEY

KWENN

The tall and imposing Trandoshan bouncer outside the nightclub on Vorah Key stared up at the still-taller Yarael Poof and hissed, "I don't want you hanging around here."

The Jedi waved his hand. "*You want me hanging around here.*"

"*I want you hanging around here,*" the green-skinned tough droned.

But the guard's job was to remain at his post, and Yarael did not depart from his position a few meters away. So after twenty seconds, the bouncer spoke again. "Wait. *Why* do I want you hanging around here?"

Another wave. "*You don't need to know the answer to that question.*"

"*I don't need to know the answer to that question.*"

This produced ten seconds of calm, followed by growing consternation for the Trandoshan.

And then: "What question was that, again?"

Yarael put his hand over his face. They'd been going at it for fifteen minutes, ever since Ki-Adi-Mundi entered Gutson's Pub across the street.

Time for another tack.

He extended a long arm toward an eatery a few doors down. It was extremely late, but that didn't seem to matter on Vorah Key. The lights were still on inside. "You see that place?"

The bouncer stared. "What of it?"

Yarael gestured. *"You'd really like a curried nuna-roll."*

"I'd really—" The behemoth paused. "That's too spicy."

Yarael put his hand on the bouncer's shoulder. "Ask for the children's menu." He gave him a push. "Bye now."

The Jedi Master relied a lot upon using the Force to persuade people, but it wasn't because he was afraid of fighting. He just wasn't partial to it. Lightsaber combat might be elegant for some beings, but even with weapons tailored for him, Yarael's great height always made him feel like he was prodding an animal with a broom. And Quermians' olfactory senses were in their hands, meaning it was impossible for him to engage in fisticuffs without learning what his opponent had for lunch.

There was, of course, a moral dimension to pushing people to action against their wills, regardless of the motives involved. Abuse of that power was a sure path to the dark side. But countless days interacting with other beings had shown him that will was a multifaceted thing. In the recent case, he suspected the Trandoshan really was hungry—and may well have had a history of leaving his post. The Force just eased him to a decision he was likely to make anyway.

Regardless, Yarael had staked out his position on the walkway and he wasn't going to leave it. The hour was late, and he'd had his fill of side trips. Going to the pub named by the Staved Skull member would have been a relatively simple matter, had their call for a ride not resulted in another detour. Plo Koon had asked them to visit Quarney Key and check out the market for illicit mineral nodules, which he'd said were highly valuable. Sea creature dietary supplements did not spell treasure to Yarael, but they'd agreed to go.

They'd caught some of the poachers red-handed in the middle of a sale. After a brief battle ended as it inevitably had to, Ki-Adi-Mundi had spoken to the criminals in stern tones. He could probably give lessons in scolding. The Cerean had inveighed against desecrating natural places so strongly that Yarael himself started to feel guilty about walking on the grass earlier.

The two Jedi emerged from the incident with a cab full of recovered orokite nodules worth thousands of credits on the black market, even dripping in slime as they were. It meant they had recently been dug up, and that they were certainly the ones stolen from the oroko on Malbaira Key. But "fresh" didn't really seem like an apt word to Yarael, as he'd discovered to his lingering horror after picking the rank things up. He had no desire to learn how the oroko carried them around. He'd been relieved to send the speeder and its cargo on its way.

Another Trandoshan poked her head out of the nightclub. "Where'd Blaask go?"

"He stepped away for a bite."

She groaned. "Typical." Then she focused on Yarael. "Don't hang around here."

The Quermian's face twisted in annoyance—but only for a second. The door to Gutson's Pub opened, allowing the sounds of raucous music to escape. A hooded figure emerged as well. Unless he had a melon sitting on his head, there was only one person it could be.

Yarael met him in the street. "Come on, let me see."

Ki-Adi-Mundi was emotionless. "I would rather not."

"Come on. You insult me, my friend."

Reluctantly, Ki-Adi-Mundi lowered his hood, revealing a head festooned with small spikes—decorations in the Staved Skull manner. "Are you satisfied?"

"They stayed on!"

Yarael had indeed supported the repertory theater company—and while he had been disappointed to learn it had disbanded due to hard times, he'd been able to look up its veteran makeup artist. She had been their stop before Gutson's—and her appliqués appeared to have held.

"You should have gone over well," Yarael said. "The number of spikes is a signifier of success among the Skulls, isn't it?"

"And also, apparently, an indicator of brazen posturing. It was difficult to gain anyone's confidence," Ki-Adi-Mundi said. He looked back at the pub. "I do not know why I had to be the one to infiltrate."

"Yaddle announced that members of the Jedi Council were on the planet. Every pirate on Kwenn has to be on the lookout. They'd spot me in a heartbeat."

"Ah. Because you are so much better known."

Yarael peered at him. "That was almost a joke. Very good, Master. I mean there aren't many Quermians in the underworld. I'd stand out."

Ki-Adi-Mundi soldiered on. "I did see some of the Skulls' extortion agents from Brazatta Key—and the local boss they were making payments to. But it would have been difficult to reach her. There were dozens of criminals present."

"I've been seeing people going in all night. You think it's just the day they make their payments?"

"It strikes me that you would see them going out. But it only grew more crowded."

Yarael saw the lights of an approaching landspeeder. "It's about to get even busier. Come on." He gestured toward an alley.

Ki-Adi-Mundi pointed at the sidewalk in front of the nightclub. "We could just stand there."

"No." He reached out and tugged his colleague's robe. "Come on!"

The black speeder had an armored hardtop and fancy neon lighting around the frame. A luxury vehicle for those who needed extra protection. "The Filthy Creds had one like that on Quarney Key, right?" Yarael asked.

"You are correct," Ki-Adi-Mundi said. "The orokite nodule buyer had one."

It pulled up before Gutson's Pub. Yarael spied a couple of armed Staved Skulls emerging from the building. "This could be trouble."

He was aware of the gang war taking place along this part of the Ootmian route, but it hadn't infected Kwenn, as yet. Part of it, he and his colleagues had surmised, was the distance that the straits put between the islands where the various outfits had adherents. The reports of members of the Jedi Council being on the planet had also likely made a difference. Yarael thought it was a good argument for keeping the outpost open.

Still, it looked like a bad place for the Creds to stop for a drink—and yet the driver got out and exchanged words with the Skulls. "They are bitter rivals," Ki-Adi-Mundi said. "My disguise notwithstanding, we may need to intercede to keep the peace."

But to the surprise of both Jedi, the driver opened the rear door and escorted two well-dressed humans—almost certainly captains from the Creds—out of the vehicle. The Skulls flanked them as they all headed inside the pub.

Ki-Adi-Mundi started to move toward the entrance, but speeders arriving from both directions on the street caused him to pause. The graffiti covering the first vehicle gave away its ownership: the Vile. Neither master recognized the second machine, though the way its cloaked occupant furtively skulked from it into the pub suggested a connection to the Poisoned Blades.

"Here's another one," Ki-Adi-Mundi said as yet another speeder running without lights appeared. "What goes on here?"

"Maybe they're holding a dance." Yarael shrugged. "Could the Skull boss herself be paying the other gangs?"

"Or are they paying her? Ransom? A peace offering?"

Yarael knew it was just the sort of puzzle that would captivate his companion. He stared at the building and sighed. "We're going to sit out here watching all night, aren't we?"

"Determining what these miscreants are up to accomplishes just what Master Qui-Gon challenged us to do. It helps the people." Ki-Adi-Mundi arrived at a decision. "I will return to the establishment and redouble my efforts."

"Wait here a few minutes. If you're going back inside and I'm to stand lookout, I'm going to help myself to a curried nuna-roll."

CHAPTER 37

GALA KEY

KWENN

Yoda liked sunrises, whatever the planet—and seeing Kwenn's from Sanctuary Mount had been invigorating. Even with the unwelcome introduction of pollution, he had marveled at its serene beauty. The Force was here, as everywhere.

A consequence of the outpost being at the highest point on the planet, however, was that seeing the sunrise meant he was awake before every other Jedi on Kwenn—including several who had, according to the seneschal, gotten in extremely late. Yoda was sure there were many stories to hear, but his mission for the day was clear. He was happy that his partner in it, Adi Gallia, was also an early riser.

"It's as I suspected," she said outside the door of the Gala Key Arena. "It's not open yet."

Yoda clasped his hands together. "A time for all things. We will walk."

There was no sense allowing their eagerness to turn into impatience—and eager they were to finish the preparations for the celebration. Adi had been her usual amazing self, rounding up a variety of special guests from Kwenn, including many long-lived people who could testify both to the state of the planet before the Grand Renewal and to the actions taken during it.

"There will be holograms on display in the foyer," she said, looking at her ever-handy datapad. "People will be able to see Kwenn as it was—and the efforts to change it."

"Some of us will be hard to recognize. Changed, we have."

"Never you, Master!"

Yoda chuckled.

They walked around the circumference of the arena. A number of abutting parks were starting to turn into festival grounds, with people camping out in advance of the celebration, either to get in or to get a good space. Gala Key was slow coming to life, in the lazy ways of an island paradise.

Adi gestured to the clouds. "The only other wrinkle is the weather. Given the declining state of the climate, tropical rains come up with less notice. I've been working with the meteorological teams to alert me to anything damaging."

Yoda grinned. "Thought of everything, you have. Here, as—"

An Ithorian emerged from a side door of the arena, nearly stumbling over Yoda as he did. The tools on his utility belt clanked against one another, and something fell from his hand. It clattered to the ground in front of Yoda.

The Ithorian apologized nervously. "So sorry," came the words from his golden translator collar. Behind him, the door to the arena closed. "We're, uh, not open yet."

"We know," Yoda said. He picked up the errant item, which appeared to be some kind of control mechanism. He passed the Ithorian what he'd dropped.

He took the mechanism, turned, and pointed it toward the door. He triggered it. Yoda heard the clang of clamps as the door locked. "Mustn't lose that!"

"We look forward to working with you soon," Adi added.

"Hmm?"

She nodded to the door. "In the arena."

"Oh, yes, of course." He nodded before walking hurriedly in the direction Adi and Yoda had come from.

The two glanced back at him. A speeder truck pulled up on the street. He got in and it drove off.

Yoda and Adi looked at one another for a moment and resumed walking. Soon another vehicle arrived from a different direction. The LiteVan stopped two blocks from the arena, alongside an alley. There it disgorged two burly-looking figures. The Besalisk with tattoos up and down his four arms looked menacing enough, but his companion was something else: a massive feline Cathar with a completely hairless head and studs screwed into his skull. They strode purposefully toward the opening and disappeared between the buildings.

No words passed between the Jedi. Something was wrong—and it was in that alley. As Yoda and Adi approached, the driver in business attire stepped out of the parked van and barred their path.

"You'll need to step away," the human said. "Safety inspection."

Yoda had seen no markings on the vehicle—and certainly, the vehicle's passengers looked nothing like the well-dressed driver. And what he'd sensed told him not to offer the benefit of the doubt.

Next to him, Adi's eyes suddenly went wide, suggesting she felt the same danger. "Master!"

"I know." Yoda reached through the Force and shoved the driver against the hood of the speeder van so hard that it knocked the wind out of him.

He began running, and Adi turned the corner with him. The driver's two associates were halfway down the long alley, approaching two more figures at the far end. One of them was a male Twi'lek in a cloak; the other was shorter, and too obscured to make out.

A voice that sounded familiar to Yoda came from the pair. "This wasn't the plan! You were supposed to—"

A horrified yelp finished the sentence. The shorter figure fell to the street.

Adi was yet unnoticed by the toughs, who hurriedly closed on the Twi'lek and the other person. The Besalisk spoke to the bald Cathar. "Hurry, get him into the speeder!"

As Yoda rushed forward, Adi was far ahead, closing the distance with the assailants within seconds. She stopped running and used her powers to yank the two large opponents whose backs were to her off their feet. She activated her lightsaber and shouted, "Stay where you are!"

The Twi'lek, facing her direction, had seen her approach and withdrew a blaster from his cloak. He fired over his beefy companions, who both rolled over, astonished looks on their faces as they saw the Jedi. Yoda spotted a body slumped before the Twi'lek's feet.

Between deflected shots, Yoda saw Adi pause to glance back to him. It was the look of someone completely in control of the situation. He'd come to expect no less from Master Gallia. "See to the victim," she said. "I've got this!"

The shots stopped as the Cathar, from his knees, sprang toward Adi. She leapt higher, doing a flip over him and landing behind him. A precise low swing of her lightsaber took off the top of one of the attacker's head-spikes.

"Yield, or you'll lose another!"

Yoda had not watched Adi in action in some time. Indeed, he didn't know how long it had been since she'd seen any. But the Jedi Master had fallen into a perfect rhythm fending off attacks from multiple directions: volleying the blasts from the Twi'lek, while avoiding the brawler moves of his two companions.

The Twi'lek's focus on Adi was such that he never noticed Yoda—not until the Jedi Master charged. Between shots, Adi reached out and gave Yoda a lift through the Force, making his intended high jump truly prodigious. He came down behind the Twi'lek and telekinetically threw him forward, away from the fallen victim. Only then did Yoda activate his lightsaber, taking a defensive posture over the body on the ground.

At once, more blaster shots filled the alley, though not from the Twi'lek, who had lost his blaster. Rather, they came from behind Adi. Yoda looked back to see the LiteVan now blocking the exit—and the driver, recovered from his fall, standing in the doorway, firing. Adi and Yoda repelled their bolts in a whirlwind of parries that sent their three assailants scrambling for cover that did not exist.

"I'm on it," Adi called out.

Indeed, she was, Yoda saw. Even as she deflected shots from the van with her lightsaber hand, she used the other to knock out the Besalisk and the Twi'lek, one after the other, by telekinetically hurling them into the walls of the surrounding buildings. The Cathar got farther, leaping onto the hood of the LiteVan as its driver started to back away. Adi charged after the vehicle and its impromptu rider.

Yoda looked down at the victim—and rolled him over. It was Lyal Lunn, the somber Sullustan from several nights earlier at the Paths of Harmony. The handle of a dagger stuck out from his chest.

Lyal looked up at him in a daze. "Yoda?"

Yoda leaned over his body. "I must help you."

The Sullustan shook his head. "It's not possible. You can't be here, not now—"

"But here, I am." Yoda thought him delirious. It was clear Lyal was in bad shape. The Jedi Master triggered an emergency call on his comlink and set to work doing what he could.

He realized something black was coated on the blade. If it was poison, it might be overkill. Yoda worried he was engaged in a losing effort, able to dull the pain but little more. But it was important to keep Lyal talking. "Who attacked you?"

"I don't know, I don't—" Tears welled in Lyal's eyes. "Yoda, I'm so ashamed." Lyal's voice cracked. "I've been selling illegal drugs for the Vile."

Yoda had suspected something back at the Paths of Harmony, but not that. It jarred with his image of the Sullustan. "You work for the arena."

"I do. But . . . I told you. Acts were hard to find—and I had to pay for my father's care." He sobbed. "I was going to buy a droid for him."

"Help is coming. Rest," Yoda said. Lyal's struggling was making the bleeding worse. He tried to use the Force to calm the Sullustan.

But he would not stop writhing. Between coughs, he kept talking. "I never used them. But the music acts, their parties—there was always demand."

People had unburdened themselves to Yoda many times—including in their last moments. He wanted to tell Lyal this was not one of those times, but he didn't know for sure.

Lyal's body wrenched as he tried to move. "My pouch."

Yoda found it. It bulged. "Credits."

"Swear . . . you'll take this money to my father on Addoa Key. I can't leave him alone right now. See . . . that he gets the droid."

Yoda had every reason to suspect it was money from an illicit act, but there was no mentioning that now. He held Lyal's hand. "Visit your father, I will."

"You're so . . . kind. And that, after . . ."

More, there is. But Lyal was fading fast.

With unexpected exertion, Lyal lifted his head from the alleyway and clutched at Yoda's sleeve. "So . . . sorry. It was a mistake. I can't . . . let you . . ."

That was all the energy he had left. Lyal's head drooped to the ground. The Sullustan was still breathing, Yoda saw to his relief.

He looked back to see Adi trotting up the alley.

"The LiteVan's wrapped around a streetlight," she said. "Constables are already there." She noted the conditions of the two fallen assailants in the alley. They were still unconscious. "No funerals today." Then she saw Lyal and said his name in shock. "Is he—?"

"Barely with us. But help comes."

Adi knelt beside them. "Poor Lyal. What was this about?"

Yoda told her what Lyal had said, and Adi's face fell. "I guess they decided not to pay him—and did this instead."

"He was paid." Yoda held the pouch of credits in his hand.

"Why would they pay him and then kill him?"

It didn't make any sense to Yoda, either. "Something else, there is." He glanced back up the alley. "The four assailants were not the same."

Adi stood and walked to one of the fallen. "This one has the Vile's markings," she said of the Besalisk. "And the Cathar for sure was a Staved Skull."

An ambulance speeder arrived carrying medics. Yoda stood and pointed them to Lyal. "There is little time. Poisoned, that blade may be."

As the medics went to work, the Jedi saw police vehicles approaching, carrying the people who inevitably had to deal with the aftermath of such incidents. But there were wider ramifications to consider.

"This is bad timing for the celebration," Adi said. "I know Lyal wasn't directly involved in organizing it. But so close to the date—and the arena—"

Yoda knew he had something to deal with as well. "Learn what you can of what happened here. To Lyal's father, I must go." He held the pouch in his hand.

Adi stared. "Isn't that evidence?"

"Of a promise. Keep it, I will."

CHAPTER 38

RIFTWALKER HEADQUARTERS
VALBORAAN

*T*o live your life, prepare for death. Depa had learned that saying long ago, not from Master Windu or any of his colleagues, but rather from the journal of a Jedi who had lived centuries before. Working in a remote region, the young woman had been cut off from all hope of assistance—but she had never stopped fighting. Once she understood the role of death in the natural order of things, she had no complaint giving her all.

After days of hanging in a stasis field and enduring sonic torture, the quotation was all Depa had left. On other missions when she'd been held captive, it had been part of some grander scheme; her captors usually needed to keep her alive to make their plans work. But Zilastra lacked inspiration. Like the assassinations of the pirate leaders, Depa's captivity was a display of pure brute force with no second act. The cruelty was the point. That, and Zilastra proving that it took no special effort to destroy a member of the Jedi Council. It took only patience—and pain.

But while Depa could scarcely think clearly anymore, the saying about life and death was foundational to her being. She had lived her life always prepared for death. So when Zilastra entered the chamber and deactivated the screeching sound—and when Depa realized it was not a trick of her mind—she was unconcerned. The Force was with her.

Her eyes lazily followed Zilastra as the pirate crossed the room. Even the assassin droid was gone. "Where's . . . the audience . . . this time?"

"They're busy. But I can do this myself."

So the execution is on again. Depa realized she had no idea how long it had been since the last attempt was interrupted. "Was this delay . . . just more torture?"

"I told you, I finally saw the big picture. Everything I've done? It was prologue, and I didn't know it." The pirate found the can of knockout spray. She looked back at Depa. "I was startled at how easy it was. It just took a few calls. It's all in motion now, everywhere. You can't stop it!"

"Stop . . . *what*?"

"Oh, no. You're not buying more time that way." Zilastra found a face mask. "I've got somewhere to be." She looked up at the ceiling. "I'm done hiding in holes. Those days are over. But I wouldn't miss this for the galaxy."

Zilastra crossed back toward Depa and saw the table where she'd once played cards. Memory seemingly jarred, she put the can down. "Oh, and I'll need one of these." When she turned, she brought a handful of sabacc cards out of her pocket and fanned them. "Pick one."

"No."

Zilastra flicked her thumb—and one of the cards leapt from her hand. She turned it around. Of course, it was The Idiot.

"Calling . . . card," Depa mumbled.

"It's yours. So they'll know you when they find you."

"You won't . . . be able . . . to play without it."

"Funny, Master. But no. It's not my mother's deck. I wouldn't waste a card from that on you." She placed the card on the table and put the rest back in her pocket. Then she stepped back to examine the holocam on the stand near the door. "Just making sure our connection is still feeding back to the ship."

Depa made one last stab, using her mind to reach out for the stand, the table, the canister, anything—trying to move something through the Force, to weaponize it. All she was able to do was to knock the can of knockout spray over.

Zilastra laughed at that. "Weak, Master, weak." She put on her face mask and picked up the fallen spray. "Time to go to sleep."

"You . . . won't need that."

"Probably not. But I'm no fool."

Zilastra stepped around in front of her, raising the can toward Depa's face. Depa summoned the energy to glare at her. "You're . . . a coward."

"It's rich, a Jedi wanting a fair fight. You're not going to bait me."

"*I have friends.*"

Zilastra lowered the can long enough to laugh. "There's a funny story there. But you'll never—"

The lights flashed—and the whole room went sideways. Literally, with a sound that battered Depa's abused eardrums.

Groundquake!

Zilastra, the table, and all the room's equipment tumbled away from Depa. A cabinet fell over and rolled. It struck the pirate, pinning her against the wall.

Depa blinked. The flickering lights showed that the doorway Zilastra had entered through was now beneath the Jedi's level, having shifted forty degrees downward. The paralysis beam still operated, keeping Depa suspended—but now she was hovering, angelic, over the pirate.

With a pained grunt, Zilastra shoved the cabinet off her. She looked up at Depa—only to lose balance as something loud cracked. The floor began to list further, forcing Zilastra to scramble like a rodent against a slick wall.

The quaking slowed. The Jedi watched, amazed, as Zilastra worked her way across the slanted surface to the intercom on the wall. She ripped off her mask. "Luggy! Did some of Tokchi's hot stuff go off?"

The response, when it came, was garbled. "—firing on the—"

"What?"

More static, as the lights flashed. Another boom sent another shock wave. Everything shifted again, this time in a different direction.

Depa recognized what it was even as Zilastra said it: "That was a turbolaser hit!"

Burlug spoke again. "—last shot brought part of the cave ceiling down on the complex!"

"Shot? By who? What?" The room shuddered. Zilastra struggled to remain at the control. "Why did everything go sideways?"

"—cave floor might be damaged. We might be—"

The audio cut off. Depa remembered that the pirates' nest was actually a series of interconnected starship decks inside a grotto. And on a planet as shot full of holes as Valboraan was, a cave-in might well take whatever structure they were in down. Down, to who knew where.

Unable to get the intercom to work anymore, Zilastra swore at it. And then at Depa. "You're still dying here!" She drew one of her blasters—only to lose hold of it, as the ship lost its own hold on whatever precarious position it was in. With an angry groan, the room tilted back in the opposite direction. The room's contents crashed with the screaming pirate into a corner. The entrance, once below Depa, was now tilted partly above her.

The lights went out, and with them, the stasis beam. Like a wilted leaf, Depa's body fell away, slamming against a bulkhead that had become a floor. She could hear Zilastra somewhere, also struggling.

That was confirmed when blaster shots sizzled past, fired blindly into the dark. Zilastra still lived—and had one of her weapons. Others might have been tempted to say something, to taunt—but Depa knew any sound would give away her position. There was no fighting here, for sure—not in Depa's state, presuming the wayward structure would even allow it. But while her days of imprisonment had been interminable, they had provided her with ample time to memorize the room she was in.

The vent!

Kylah had entered the room through it, opening and closing the grating. Depa felt along the wall for it—and found the lattice in the dark. She found the strength to yank the grate open. More shots fired, directed this time at the noise. But with the room gone sideways and plenty more noise about, the shots went astray.

Still, Zilastra continued to yell. "*Die!*"

Entering the vent was a risk; Kylah's entire franchise with the Riftwalkers had been her ability to traverse areas that no adult could fit through. It also stood to reason that shocks that could upend a starship deck could mangle a ventilation shaft with ease. But she had to take the chance.

She heaved her body into the opening, the blaster shots continuing behind her. They continued until another metallic creak evidently changed the pirate's mind. Remaining in the structure was madness—for both of them.

"You're still going to die here," she heard Zilastra yell. "One way or another, Jedi. You're going to die here!"

Depa knew she may well be right. But she was also prepared to live. She found the energy to crawl.

CHAPTER 39

OVER VALBORAAN

"New turrets, northeast!"

Mace Windu's starfighter screamed ahead of *Assurance* through Valboraan's atmosphere. Down in the dusty desert sameness, another cannon had appeared, rising mechanically from a position on a ridge.

"They're locked on you," Baylo said in Mace's headset.

"That's the plan, Captain."

Crimson fire lanced up from the crest, directed at Mace. Guided by the Force, he banked left and then right, anticipating and evading the shots.

He sensed no intelligence behind them. "The fire is automated."

"It'll still hurt like hell."

"Then we strike first."

Mace sent the Delta-7 interceptor into a dive heading straight for the cannon emplacement—only to veer off in the last instant. Laserfire far more powerful than anything his vessel could generate cut the air beneath him, striking not the turret, but the ridge it was implanted in. A landform that hadn't been struck by anything more than wind in eons went into motion, with gravity taking the cannons down in an explosive burst.

"My compliments to your gunner," Mace said.

"Save 'em," Baylo replied over comms. "That was off by a parsec." Mace heard the captain yell, more faintly, at someone on his own bridge. "Shape up!"

The Corellian Engineering Corporation hadn't designed the CR line for combat, but that hadn't stopped Baylo and others from using its ships for that purpose. *Assurance* had been tricked out with a formidable dorsal turbolaser emplacement, but that was of no use for ground bombardment unless it performed a banking maneuver allowing it to bring the guns to bear. That meant difficult runs at a lower altitude than either Mace or Baylo was comfortable with—and the Jedi's decision to run interference for the corvette.

With *Assurance* following, Mace banked back around. Since their surprise arrival over Valboraan, a circle of gun emplacements had emerged, all within a few kilometers of a central mountain range; more turrets had appeared on the outcrop itself. Several of them were out of commission, but the territory was still hotly contested. The ring, Mace was sure, circumscribed something important down below. And one of his allies in the air knew more about it.

"We're seeing several openings in the central range," Qui-Gon signaled. "Definitely caves there, Master Windu."

Qui-Gon and Obi-Wan had come from Coruscant in a Jedi T-5 shuttle, having been ordered to Kwenn on some mission Mace still didn't know about. Whatever it was, their decision to take a shuttle meant they expected no trouble; the ship was without armament. But it could watch from a safe altitude—and also aid in evacuation.

The latter was on Mace's mind as the map on his monitor populated with the cave openings Qui-Gon had marked. "You're sure Master Billaba is still down there?"

"We've only seen a one-person shuttle depart since we got the girl's message," Qui-Gon replied. "We remained here, as instructed."

Mace agreed. If Depa had escaped in that ship, someone would have heard by now. He called out to *Assurance*. "Captain, we must exercise care with any further strikes on the central range."

Baylo laughed. "Like the care they're showing us?"

"We don't know who is down there." There was a small chance that the ground emplacements were associated with settlers or someone else having nothing to do with pirates, but the fact that the guns had opened fire without warning made that remote. And there was another concern: "If Master Billaba is present, we don't want to bring a mountain down on top of her."

"If we haven't already," Qui-Gon interjected. "You've struck a lot of batteries."

"Correct. Our next steps must be on the surface."

"*Your* next steps," Baylo corrected. "I don't have a ground assault team. Tell the Republic to pay for one next time."

Mace could have told him that the Republic had no intention of creating an armed force, but Baylo was no Sifo-Dyas. The captain knew better. But he was right about whose boots were to touch the ground.

Mace was working on a plan when his comlink buzzed indicating a message on the Jedi's dedicated channel. He thought about not answering it: Flying under fire was hardly the best time to respond to anyone on Kwenn about the impending celebration. But he piped it through to his headset anyway. "Windu."

A surprised squeal. "Are you a Jedi?"

Mace's eyes widened. It sounded like the girl from the earlier message. "Are you the person who called us?"

"Yes! And everything's falling down here!"

The girl sounded terrified. Mace's brow furrowed. "You're hearing this, Master Qui-Gon?"

"I am," Qui-Gon said.

"Caller, is Depa Billaba with you?"

"No—I mean, I don't know," the girl said. "But I need your help!"

"You'll have it. Keep broadcasting, if you can." Mace adjusted his fighter's controls. "Captain Baylo, I need you to buy us some time. Master Qui-Gon, after the next pass, we will head for the stratosphere. Join the formation behind *Assurance*—and on our next run you will break off and land at the following coordinates." Mace signaled for his astromech droid to share the information. "I'll see you on the ground!"

PORTABLE LIGHT IN hand, Zilastra ran on the wall of what had once been the corridor of a starship. Tilted sideways, it had become an obstacle course. Every so often, an open passageway required a leap—and every time she landed, she felt the metal beneath her feet shake. Building a cavern base out of spacecraft salvage had been a great idea; the hull had probably saved her life. But she'd never considered that the cavern floor beneath the ships might give way under fire.

That was a lesson. *You can lock in a sabacc card's value so it doesn't change. But everything else in life is up for grabs.*

After taking time to get her bearings. she realized the corridor leading to the next section of the complex opened onto nothing but rock. Two ships had sheared from each other where they connected, and her portion had fallen downward. That meant there was no exit that way—but by going up, she might find her way out.

A maintenance-hallway-turned-shaft offered promise. No ladder or lift could help her, but the exposed pipes on what had been the ceiling made for excellent footholds. She climbed, her rising anger competing only with dread from the sound of every remote blast.

Finally, she kicked open a hatch and emerged into what seemed like a junkyard. It was not, of course; rather, it was a faintly lit jangle of durasteel beams and boulders. A path around and over them existed, however, and she made her way up with speed.

Her clothes were tattered by the time she clambered out onto a still-standing portion of cavern floor. It took her a moment to realize the light above wasn't coming from the fixtures they'd installed. Those weren't functioning. Instead, a portion of the cavern ceiling was gone, its remnants now sitting on top of the upended part of her metal complex. Somewhere in the lofty heights, light was entering through a new sinkhole.

Motion lay ahead. In the intact portion of the complex, she saw frantic Riftwalkers running in all directions, trying to save their skins or salvage something. Initially, nobody noticed her, covered in dust.

Then someone did. "Zil!"

Zilastra turned to see Burlug approach. His stoic reserve was gone; he looked more flustered than she'd ever seen him. "What's going on?" she asked.

"What's going on?" He pointed to the new skylight. "I told you. We're under attack!"

She'd heard part of that earlier, and it had worried her. It meant her whole gambit had failed. "Which gang hit us?"

Burlug sputtered. "What difference does it make?" He raged at her, something he hadn't done in years. "You just had to call everyone with your big plan. The transmitter was deployed outside all that time for anyone to see!"

"That was the only way."

"To do what? Tell everyone where we were, so they could kill us?" Burlug looked about at what was left of their base. "This is a nightmare. Why did we do this?"

"Get over it. There was *always* a chance the other gangs would find Valboraan. That's what the turrets are for."

"Well, half of them are gone. I *think*. We lost the data hookup when the roof fell in!"

There was nothing to be done for it. Zilastra hurried from one chamber into another, bound for the main landing area. Her first sight of it took her breath away. Several parked ships had been demolished. Others had fallen through the cave floor, at least partially. And the rest—including her flagship, the *Randomizer*—had been struck with rubble. Jodak, the massive reptilian pilot, led the other Riftwalker members in working to remove the debris.

"It's still upright," she said. "Hull looks okay."

"For now," Jodak said, pausing to wipe dust from his blunt snout. He gestured toward the ship. "I'm afraid starting the engines could bring the whole works down!"

"Who wants to live forever?"

Both Jodak and Burlug were animated, for sure—but neither they nor the others had left without her.

Ventner ran down the ramp of the *Randomizer*. He stopped in front of her, looking frantic. "There's a call coming in."

"From whom?"

"He says they're the ones shooting at us." Ventner passed her the portable unit.

The crew cleaning the rocks off the *Randomizer* paused, listening as Zilastra toggled the unit. "You have something to say?"

The voice she heard wasn't that of any of her gangland adversaries—but she knew the name. "This is Captain Baylo of the Diplomatic Fleet corvette *Assurance*. Your installation is suspected of pirate activity. Under the authority of the Judicial Forces, I'm authorized to instruct you to stop firing and surrender!"

Zilastra had never been so happy to hear anyone in her life. She beamed as she responded. "Hello, Pell Baylo. Under my own authority, I'm authorized to tell you to go eat a brick!"

"Nice. You'll like it when we bring the rest of the mountain down on you."

"You're Republic. I'm not sure you could hit the mountain range twice in one day." She smirked. "I know you, Baylo. You've got a ship nobody would take for scrap, crewed by rich people's children and run by a staff of toothless never-weres—with you as the fossil in chief. Any of this sound familiar?"

"I'm going to enjoy this. Baylo out."

"You were never in." Zilastra smiled at Burlug. "This is terrific!"

"Terrific? He's going to bury us!"

"If he was going to, he'd have done it already." She shook her head. "But that's not it. It's the Republic out there, not another gang. Which means the plan is still on!"

Burlug stared at her. Then he got it. He turned around and joined Jodak and the other crewmembers at their work.

She climbed atop a boulder and called out, "Listen up, Riftwalkers! We are still a go. Clear your ships and head for the rendezvous point. The entrance turrets will cover you on the way out. *We're going for the biggest jackpot of all!*"

CHAPTER 40

ABOVE THE RIFTWALKER HEADQUARTERS
VALBORAAN

On a small plateau near the top of the ridge on Valboraan, Qui-Gon and Obi-Wan knelt beside their shuttle. It was parked near a lava tube their systems had mapped during recon; it connected to the network beneath.

"Natural ventilation," Qui-Gon said, attaching his rappelling line to the winch assembly behind the landing gear. "All the amenities."

Obi-Wan finished checking his own line and looked down the mountain. "I wonder why Master Windu didn't have us enter through the mouth of the cavern?"

As if in response, a sizzling erupted from the turbolaser inside the opening. Aimed at *Assurance*, it failed to strike its target—but the action sent a shudder through the cave system.

"That answers that." Qui-Gon took his comlink in hand. "Captain Baylo, you might want to avoid being targeted."

Baylo's response was abrupt. "I'll take that under advisement, Master. I never thought of trying that!"

"I mean the automated battery fire is endangering the complex."

"The one we're attacking," Baylo replied. "So we can't shoot at it, and we can't fly past it. Check and check. *Assurance* out."

"He sounds charming," Obi-Wan said.

He sounds like he's got a lot of people under his care, Qui-Gon thought. He tugged at his line. "Let's go."

The T-5 shuttle came stocked with everything a Jedi could ask for, but while the ample line could bring them up in a hurry, descending was on them. They dropped meters at a time, pushing off against the rocks as they plunged into darkness. The tube grew worryingly narrow at one point, only to open up again just before they touched bottom.

He and Obi-Wan detached their lines and activated their lightsabers. Green and blue light revealed a grotto with three outlets leading from it. The mountain shuddered, causing rains of silt in two of the three passageways.

"The easy choice is not always the right one," Qui-Gon said. "Still, there's no reason to be reckless about it." He made for the safer-looking opening.

Obi-Wan trailed him, speaking low so as not to let his voice echo. "What are we to do?"

"Search for Master Billaba, as well as the girl who sent the warning— and meet Master Windu."

The getting from here to there, Qui-Gon knew, was up to them. The shuttle's picture of the mountain was rudimentary—and clearly, the geology was changing by the minute.

They'd taken several more steps when Qui-Gon sensed something. It was familiar, but its presence here was completely out of place. He was ready to dismiss it when his natural senses told him there were voices and motion up ahead, where the corridor intersected another one.

"Be ready," Qui-Gon said, wielding his lightsaber before him. "Watch for the unexpected."

The voices became shouts—and thunder, from footfalls. Three figures ran through the corridor in front of them from one side to the other, completely oblivious of the Jedi.

Obi-Wan raised an eyebrow. "That *was* unexpected."

Qui-Gon stepped into the intersection. The light was too poor and the fleeing figures too fast for him to make out anything about them. It was only when the runners reached a dead end and returned up the corridor, arguing, that he realized his feeling was right.

He lowered his lightsaber and gestured for Obi-Wan to enter the intersection. "You're not going to believe this."

He barely did, either, as the three would-be hijackers of *Regal Voyager* hurried toward them, arguing with one another the whole way about who'd sent them in the wrong direction. In the lead was Lobber, who had several bandoliers of thermal detonators draped over his chest. Ghor, the Houk, was covered in grease and dust, like his companions. Wungo, the timid Klatooinian, was in a sweaty panic—and his eyes only grew larger when he saw the lightsabers before him, and their holders. "*It's you!*"

"And you." Baffled, Qui-Gon scratched his head with his free hand.

"Hello there," Obi-Wan said, giving a little wave. "Welcome to our cave."

Lobber snarled. "*Your* cave? This is our base!"

"And you've done wonderful things with it," Qui-Gon said. "Is someone chasing you?"

Ghor offered an explanation. "We were in the arsenal when the shaking started."

"It seemed like a place not to be," Wungo added.

Lobber stalked between the two groups and batted his chest. "What are you doing talking to these guys? They're Jedi. We're Riftwalkers!"

"Oh!" Obi-Wan looked to Qui-Gon. "Do you hear that? They've found positions."

"We didn't receive the memorandum," Qui-Gon said. "I'm pleased for you. But as you said, this is not a good place to be."

Another stone creak, and the cavern shook some more.

It was lost on Lobber. "I'm serious. They're not invincible. You know what Zil said."

"She'd better not hear you call her that," Ghor muttered. "Zil is for her friends."

"Whatever. You saw her with Depa!"

"Depa!" Obi-Wan said. "Depa Billaba?"

"Yeah, she was Zilastra's prisoner," Lobber said. "And she taught us that you Jedi are just people. Not magical at all!"

Qui-Gon's patience was infinite—but the time available for his mission was not. "Just tell us where Depa was."

Ghor was about to answer when Lobber leapt in front of the Jedi. "Stay back, both of you." He pulled a thermal detonator off his bandolier and triggered it, only to put his thumb over the safety.

"Careful," Qui-Gon said, alarmed. "Those aren't toys."

Obi-Wan nodded. "Hold on to the safety!"

Lobber sneered at them. "Don't tell me about thermal detonators. I know grenades! *Why do you think they call me The Lobber?*"

THAT WON'T WORK, either. One more pass!

Mace had wanted to enter the pirates' nest from two directions, to increase the odds of finding Depa and the girl. But after escorting Qui-Gon's shuttle to its landing site, Mace had found that his intended entrance no longer existed. Every time his fighter or *Assurance* had struck at a turret on the slopes, the resultant impact had reshaped a bit of the landscape underneath. The same geologic features that made Valboraan an attractive place to hide also made those scurryholes dangerous.

The girl who'd said her name was Kylah had continued talking, though her speech had turned into a whisper. "Hurry. I can't leave to find her. They'll get me."

Mace reassured her—even as tracing her transmission reassured him that his goal was somewhere behind the entrance the turrets were guarding. On a hunch, he executed an extremely low pass. He was skirting less than a meter above the upper slope when he noticed it.

A sinkhole. The location had been the recipient of the first barrage that *Assurance* had fired—a heavy-firepower fusillade that Baylo had called his "attention getter." It was now more than a crater: It was a possible way in.

He slowed the Delta-7, approaching the hole just like any elevator platform he'd ever landed on in a shipboard bay. Only this one had no surface on which to alight. He switched to vertical repulsors and watched the sky disappear, surrounded by rocky blackness. The fighter's sharp nose clipped protruding rocks several times, on the way down, and Mace had to rotate the vessel continuously in tighter spots.

His astromech squealed, unable to comprehend, much less navigate, the descent. With a waterfall of rocks showering down on all sides of the opening, he prepared to abort, yawing the flying arrowhead so its nose pointed up, for a fast exit. Instead, that maneuver brought the Delta-7 to the exact shape it needed to be to fit through the final stone keyhole going down.

The vessel entered a domelike chamber. Debris from the sinkhole had formed a new little mountain on the floor beneath; the starfighter's lights revealed crates, buried beneath and spread about. A storage area, or it had been.

After parking the fighter in a relatively clear spot, Mace disembarked and looked around. A shaft of light came from above, reminding him how narrow his passage had been. He thanked the Force for being with him.

Several wide corridors opened horizontally onto the chamber. The largest was big enough for the starfighter and still showed evidence of tread marks amid the dust; clearly, a way for the pirates to get their ill-gotten gains here from the landing bay.

"I'll be there soon," Mace said quietly into the comlink. He silenced it and put it away before heading down the hall.

"WHERE'D YOU GO?" asked a faint voice.

Zilastra wasn't sure she'd heard it. So much noise, so many voices were echoing through her precious mountain hideaway that it was hard to follow anything. All she knew as she knelt atop the *Randomizer*'s starboard wing was that she and Burlug had to get the intakes cleared if they wanted to escape. Jodak was right: Turbine damage could stop them before they even got to space.

"Jedi, where are you?"

Zilastra's eyes narrowed. "I definitely heard that!" She called out for Burlug to join her. "Over here! We've got a mynock."

Together they swung open a manifold cover on the fuselage, revealing Kylah, crouching in an impossibly tiny alcove. She had something clutched in her shaking hands.

"Uh-oh," Kylah said.

"'Uh-oh' is right." Zilastra and Burlug seized a limb each and dragged Kylah out of the opening.

"Let go, Luggy!" she squealed. "Leave me alone!"

"It's a good thing for you we found you, Stowaway. That compartment's not pressurized." Zilastra frowned. "You're usually smarter than that."

"She's holding something," Burlug said.

"Let's see what you've got there," Zilastra said as Burlug held her. It was the comlink that Depa had carried in the final case.

Burlug scowled. "You little thief. You plucked that from the security room! Did you get her lightsaber, too?"

Zilastra wasn't concerned about that. She was more alarmed about Depa's comlink. "She's probably been talking to the Jedi. This is how they found out!"

She thought for a moment—and decided she couldn't resist. She toggled the comlink and spoke in a high voice, mimicking Kylah's. "Master Jedi! Master Jedi, where are you?" She leered at Kylah and smiled. "Master Jedi, you're such a disappointment to me. Abandoning me in the middle of my hour of need!"

A commotion sounded from the west, in the direction of the storage areas. Shouts, at first, followed by blaster shots. Zilastra hurried over to the edge of the fuselage, her remaining weapon in hand. She called out, "Riftwalkers, be on the lookout for—"

Yelps interrupted her. Bodies flew through the air, thrown by some unseen power. When other Riftwalkers raised their weapons to the western entrance, the very rocks on the floor rose up, pelting them until they were senseless.

"There is no need for the comlink anymore," boomed a voice from the corridor. A determined-looking Jedi entered, purple lightsaber aglow. "I am Mace Windu. And I have come for Master Billaba!"

CHAPTER 41

RIFTWALKER HEADQUARTERS

VALBORAAN

"What a relief," Zilastra said as she walked on the *Randomizer*'s wing. "It's just another Jedi!"

"*'Just another Jedi'*?" The response came from Ventner. Mace Windu's arrival had caused a wave of Riftwalkers to stream toward the *Randomizer*'s starboard access ramp, her signals expert among them. He looked up at Zilastra, incredulous. "Mace Windu is a member of the Jedi Council!"

"Which should mean nothing to you, if the last week has taught you anything."

"I am not alone," Mace said, striding in her direction. "I'm supported by a warship from the Republic."

"Oh, right. Pell Baylo and the crew of *Incontinence*. That's even better!" Zilastra clapped her hands. "We're sure to get away now."

Several Riftwalkers, emboldened by her confident display, lined up with their weapons drawn, screening the others still boarding. Mace took a defensive stance, seemingly unconcerned by the number of blasters pointed at him. "Where is she?"

"I'm here!" Kylah shouted from behind Zilastra. Burlug held the girl by the shoulders. "I'm right here!"

"I meant Master Billaba," Mace said. "But I am here for you, too."

Zilastra grinned. "Depa is dead, Jedi. And I didn't even do it. You killed her when you hit this place."

Mace stared. "I don't believe you."

"No one should," came a voice from a far corridor. "Wrong again, Zilastra."

The pirate watched, stupefied, as Depa staggered inside. Her clothes were in dingy tatters, and where her skin was exposed, cuts and bruises were visible. She looked like she'd made her way up a hundred vertical meters on her hands and knees. Maybe she had. Zilastra's blaster, holstered for Windu's arrival, came out. "You don't know when to give up, do you?"

"No." Depa stopped. It was clearly a struggle for her to stand—but she was unbroken. "It's over."

"Not at all. I still have my trump card." Zilastra glanced back at Burlug. "Show her."

Burlug stepped forward on the wing, his mighty Feeorin hands on Kylah's collarbone. His eyes on the two Jedi, he spoke to his boss. "You sure about this, Zil?"

"I'm sure."

Kylah strained against his hold. "Luggy, we're not friends anymore!"

"Sorry, kid."

Zilastra eyed Depa, who had straggled up to a position beside Mace. The older Jedi didn't move from his stance—but he did seem taken aback by her condition. "Are you all right, Master?"

"Don't worry about me." Depa kept her focus on Zilastra. "I can't believe you're doing this again."

"It worked the first time."

"It's like I said before: You lack imagination. Let Kylah go."

"Not a chance."

Mace studied the young girl. "Kylah seems to know these people. Is she one of them?"

"Was," Kylah shouted, squirming. "Definitely *was*!"

"I'm glad," Depa said. "But it doesn't matter. I'd save you anyway."

The pirate boss looked at Depa—and back to Kylah. Somehow, in the space of a short time, the Jedi had completely supplanted Zilastra's influence. She had no idea how it had happened, but that didn't matter.

"Touching," Zilastra said. "I won't hurt her—but here's what I want. Safe passage past Baylo."

Mace rejected that immediately. "The captain doesn't answer to me."

"Like hell he doesn't. The Republic pays his bills. You're Republic."

Kylah strained again—and Burlug's grip grew stronger.

Depa, somehow still standing, had never taken her eyes off Zilastra. "If you want safe passage, leave Kylah here, with us. I'll make sure Baylo holds off."

"I don't trust him—or you," Zilastra said. "If Baylo is somehow able to beat us, he kills her, too."

She watched as Depa considered what she'd said. The pirate had seen that look across many tables over the years. She'd sold her hand as a winner. The Jedi was looking at defeat—and her next statement confirmed it.

"If we let you go, how do we know she won't be mistreated?"

The girl called out to Depa. "Don't let her take me. She'll hang me in the air, like she did you!"

"She won't. She won't dare." Depa eyed Zilastra. "She knows what I'll do to her if she does."

"And what's that?" Zilastra asked. "You're in no shape to swat a fire gnat."

"There'll be another hand." She pointed. "You'll do no harm. At your next planetfall, you let her go."

"No!" Kylah cried out. "Depa, don't let her take me!"

Zilastra looked back at the girl. "What is it, Stowaway? Are you afraid they'll forget about you?" She looked back toward Depa with a sneer. " 'The Jedi stand with you.' What a joke."

The cavern quaked, sending more rocks raining down. They clanked off the *Randomizer*'s hull. Zilastra saw that—and made a calculation. "Deal."

Depa turned to Mace. "Call Baylo. Let them go."

Mace shook his head. "You can't trust this woman."

"I know, Master. I'm asking you to trust *me*."

ELSEWHERE UNDER THE mountain, Qui-Gon shut off his light-saber. It cut down the light in the cavern by half, but he thought it necessary to calm Lobber down. Nothing else during their minutes-long standoff had worked. "Please," Qui-Gon implored, "deactivate the thermal detonator. You're endangering us all."

Obi-Wan looked nervously to Qui-Gon. He kept his lightsaber on, but had lowered it to hang at his side. "Please, Lobber, do as he says."

"'Please!' 'Please,' you heard that?" Lobber jeered at them to his companions. "*Oh, please, Master Lobber! Please, we're so afraid of you!*" He laughed and faced the Jedi. "Who's in charge now?"

Before Qui-Gon could advise him otherwise, Obi-Wan waved his hand. "You want to deactivate the thermal detonator."

Lobber looked at him. "What? Why?"

That's something I was afraid of, Qui-Gon thought. If someone believed in nonsense hard enough, an empty mind could be as hard to change as a full one.

Lobber strutted around. "Now, let me tell you how it's going to be. This place is a mess. You're gonna march us out."

"Out where?"

"To your ship."

"That may not be so easy," Qui-Gon said. "We came down on cables. They retract, but they won't carry five."

"Aw, you'll have to stay then." Lobber didn't look too disappointed over that.

"They can't carry three, either," Obi-Wan added.

Lobber frowned. He appeared to do some mental math before looking at his companions. "I guess it's time for a command decision."

Qui-Gon was going to try a different tactic when Wungo screamed, startling everyone. He grabbed Lobber by the collar and yelled into the Devaronian's face. "I've had it with you! Every time you try to take charge, something terrible happens to us. I can't take it anymore!"

"Hey, I'm the—"

"Don't say you're the brains! The Voxx Cluster is not a kind of candy! The number at the end of a droid's name is not its age!"

Ghor nodded to Qui-Gon. "Yeah, that's true. I asked one."

"You're not the brains and you're not the boss, Lobber. You're not anything. You're just *louder*!"

Gritting his teeth, Lobber raised a hand to Wungo, only for the Klatooinian to slap it away. Then Lobber raised his other hand—resulting in the same response from Wungo. Unfortunately, as Qui-Gon saw, that was the hand in which Lobber held the thermal detonator. The device flew and bounced against the cave wall, spinning away in the dark.

There wasn't time to try to find it and deactivate it; only one option remained. Qui-Gon called out, "Obi-Wan!"

His apprentice understood what had to be done. Both of them swept their hands in the direction the sphere had fallen and pushed mightily with their minds. It worked: The grenade shot along the corridor, bouncing until they could no longer hear it.

Lobber did not seem to appreciate the gesture. "*Oh, no.*"

Obi-Wan looked down the passage. "It's far away now. What?"

"That direction is the arsenal!"

Obi-Wan's eyes widened. "Another memorandum we didn't get."

"Run!" Lobber, Wungo, and Ghor took off up a corridor.

Qui-Gon grabbed at Obi-Wan before he could follow. He pointed up a different corridor. "That way!"

"THANK YOU, CAPTAIN," Depa said into Mace's comlink. "I appreciate it."

The order had been given not to attack, and Baylo, like it or not, had acquiesced. Depa stood by Mace and watched as the last of the Riftwalkers filed up the ramp. Zilastra, on the ground now, stood guard as Burlug walked past, carrying Kylah over his shoulder. She hollered the whole way up the ramp.

It ripped at Depa to see and hear, but even with Mace present, she feared it would only take Zilastra or her minion a second to carry out their threat. She'd come this far in part hoping to get Kylah out of the pirate life. Keeping her alive meant that hope still remained.

The *Randomizer*'s engines warmed up, filling the stone recess with their hum. Mace took a step forward. "I don't trust her."

"Nor do I," Depa said. "But I believe her."

"Good call," Zilastra said. "I've still got your lightsaber aboard. I'm sure it would pain you to know it had been misused—"

"Stop it. You're despicable."

"You've lost, Jedi. I keep telling you that, but you won't listen. You're all talk—but your own words will destroy you."

Mace was still poised to go. "She will turn the ship's guns on us as she leaves."

Zilastra's sneer vanished, and she scratched her chin. "Now, that *is* an interesting idea—"

A colossal blast shook the cavern. The ground beneath them swam, throwing Depa and Mace off their feet. The frigate leapt a meter off the cave floor, slamming down angrily. Cracks formed where it landed. Above, more rocks came down, banging off the hull.

Zilastra had fallen into one of the ramp supports, and clung to it. She recovered just as Mace did.

Holding on to the fallen Depa, Mace looked back. Smoke and dust poured into the rocking chamber from the west. Depa knew the look—but had to shout to be heard. "Our escape route?"

He nodded. "My fighter was back there," he yelled.

"That's a shame," Zilastra called out. "That would be the magazine going up. Our pal Tokchi mixes up some nasty stuff, don't you think? But you two don't have to wait to open a case to experience it." She turned and headed up the ramp. "Take us out—and don't stop for anything. They're finished!"

Depa got to her feet with Mace's help. The cataclysm probably meant Zilastra wouldn't bother having the *Randomizer* fire on them, if it could depart at all. But that was cold comfort. The frigate lifted off, advancing slowly as it hovered a meter off the ground. Its ramp was still down, however, and Mace looked toward it.

He glanced to Depa first. "We can save the girl—and ourselves."

"I don't think I can manage it," Depa said. "But go. Kylah should never have been in this position. I let it go too long. Save her!"

"I'll be back!" Mace began to dashed toward the ship—only to stop suddenly as a series of boulders tumbled from the darkness above. Mace dove for the ground and rolled—whereupon he used the Force to divert the rocks from landing on Depa.

Before Mace could recover, Depa heard raucous laughter. *What in the name of—?*

Lobber, Ghor, and Wungo emerged from the smoke-filled western grotto, screaming all the way. As they charged toward the Jedi, Mace withdrew his hand and readied his lightsaber, prepared for battle.

Depa waved him off. "I think they're with me."

The trio ran right between the two Jedi and kept on going, running after the departing starship. One after another, they leapt for the *Randomizer*'s ramp, grabbing hold. Lobber, the last to reach it, dangled precariously and was in danger of falling off before his companions pulled him in. The ramp snapped shut.

Mace looked at her.

She shrugged. "I just said I *thought* they were with me."

Another blast shook the complex. Behind them, a pillar of rock collapsed, smashing the nearest ships that remained and closing off access to anything beyond. The *Randomizer* lurched forward, out of their reach. Her eyes followed it until it was gone.

Mace looked in that direction, as well. "The cave entrance is a sheer drop. I don't know if *Assurance* can reach us there."

"You'll put the whole ship in jeopardy," she responded. Her body sagged. "No more. Not for me."

Telling Mace not to do anything was futile, she knew. He put his arm around her shoulder and began helping her in the direction of the exit. "The Force will find a way."

A high screeching sound came from behind them. "Don't look back," Mace advised her.

She did, anyway. "Mace. Look!"

The source of the sound emerged from the dark cloud. It was Mace's starfighter, battered and bruised—and piloted by Obi-Wan. The Delta-7 was a one-seater, but its cockpit was open, and Qui-Gon was perched on the fuselage and hanging on with one hand, while with the other he used the Force to push away falling rock.

"Your fighter?" she asked Mace.

"And our ride!"

Obi-Wan hovered to a stop just before them and deployed the landing gear. Qui-Gon released his tenuous hold and slid off the slanted surface just before the vessel touched down. He hurried to Mace's side and helped Depa stand.

Depa looked to the slanted surfaces on the fighter. "There's no way I can hang on to that," she called out. "Please, just—"

"I have a solution," Obi-Wan yelled. He hopped out of the ship and worked with Mace and Qui-Gon to help Depa into the cockpit.

Qui-Gon made sure she was secure. "You've hung on quite enough, Master. Now it's our turn."

Depa got the idea. She toggled a control and took the ship up a meter. "I can't see you down there, so I'm going on ten!" The roof collapsed over the passageway the ship had entered from, changing her mind. "I'm going on five," she corrected.

The three other Jedi disappeared beneath the Delta-7—and a generous second after her count ended, she directed the fighter forward. When it cruised past a turbolaser battery pointed outward, her breath caught momentarily. But the whole complex had lost power. There was no threat from anything but the mountain itself, which heaved. A closing jaw, reluctant to let anything escape.

Depa gunned the Delta-7 forward—and saw the sun for the first time in days. Behind her, the opening to the Riftwalkers' hideaway slammed shut, expelling a blast of smoke and dust.

Cautious not to lose those she was carrying, she cruised a safe distance across the valley. She could see *Assurance* much higher, aloft. Baylo was probably keeping an eye on the survivors, below, while trying to get a fix on the *Randomizer*'s departure vector. *That's what I'd do*, she thought. She hovered above the desert floor for several seconds—and when she saw Obi-Wan, Qui-Gon, and Mace again, she put the ship down.

The Masters dashed around the ship and its open cockpit. Obi-Wan stood apart, looking at the mess that had been made of the mountain range. "I'm not sure what shape our shuttle will be in."

"I'm more concerned about *you*," Qui-Gon said on Depa's left. "Are you all right, Master?"

Qui-Gon had asked first—but Mace asked anyway. "*Are* you, Master?"

"I had things under control," Depa said, sliding back in her seat. "But I appreciate the assist."

CHAPTER 42

ADDOA KEY

KWENN

"**D**epa is saved."

"Thank the Force," Yoda said. "And you, Master Windu."

Yoda put away the comlink. He knew his colleagues were almost certainly busy—hearing their stories could wait until another time. The person he was with didn't have much to spare.

The Jedi Master had been at the side of Lyal Lunn when he had been carried away by the medics; all the time since, he had spent with the Sullustan's father, trying to see that he not suffer due to his son's absence.

Erwen Lunn was Kwenn, through and through. His great-grandparents had watched the Grand Renewal as children. The holograms they recorded had been handed down through the family, which had continued to commemorate the events long after most others on Kwenn had decided that the past was no longer relevant to their lives.

So it was that even with his failing eyesight, Erwen had recognized Yoda when he appeared at the Lunns' small, impoverished flat on Addoa Key. Yoda had remembered the island being nicer; it had fallen on hard times. But it said something to Yoda that Erwen, who was barely mobile, was still willing to open the door to welcome an unexpected visitor. The Kwenn of the Grand Renewal was energetic, optimistic, and hospitable—and so had the elder Lunn remained, despite his and the planet's declines.

On learning that a famous figure from the past had been sent by his son, the aged Sullustan had invited the Jedi inside. The news that Yoda had ordered a medical droid to be delivered with credits that Lyal had raised delighted Erwen, who then asked the Jedi Master to wait with him for its arrival. Yoda had found it hard to refuse.

The main room was simple and homey, and Yoda admired the efforts Lyal had taken to make his father comfortable. Railings had been placed on every wall one might walk alongside. There were holes in other walls, which Yoda realized were from Lyal repositioning shelves so they would be easier to reach. Erwen offered Yoda his comfortable, well-worn chair without hesitation; Yoda had deferred, taking a different seat. Thereupon, Erwen had peppered him with questions about the past. The Jedi Master, who infrequently talked to civilians—much less journalists or would-be biographers—spoke to him without reserve.

Over the hours, it became clear that Erwen was close to dying—and had been so before Yoda arrived. Medications were stored beside his chair; there were more in the tiny bedroom, where Yoda walked him once his coughing grew too much. Their hours in the living room were, for Erwen, just that: another chance at living, one more day, having been given a reason to stay.

Once in his bed, Erwen had continued to talk—but now he spoke of his own life, not Yoda's. Of how his grandparents had built a home on Zyboh Key, positioned so Sanctuary Mount and the Unquenchable Fire were visible from the front porch. Of how Erwen's late wife, when offered a chance to move the family to the Core worlds when her corporation relocated, had quit her job, taking work that was harder—but on Kwenn, their chosen place to raise Lyal.

And most of all, Erwen had spoken of his pride in his son's accomplishments, despite his understanding that caring for his many conditions had delayed Lyal starting his own life. Lyal had made the same decision his parents had, declining opportunities to leave in order to remain on Kwenn. Erwen was delighted his son had made a friend of the Jedi Master. "He has so few friends," he'd said. "And he works so hard, trying to get people to visit here again."

When night began to fall, Erwen grew tired and spoke less, his breathing growing shallow. Yoda's voice had filled the air, then, with comforting words in soothing tones.

"Rest. Rest, you have earned." Yoda held his hand. This was it, he understood. Erwen was on the way to another sky.

"Wait!" Erwen opened his eyes.

Yoda did not startle often. This time he did. "Yes, Erwen?"

"Sit me up."

Yoda did his best to help him sit up in bed.

"There," Erwen said. "That's right." He turned his face from Yoda.

The Jedi Master stared at the old man—and his eyes widened as he realized what Erwen was looking at. The apartment was poor, to be sure, and his room minuscule, hardly more than a closet. But Lyal Lunn had selected a place where his father's small window looked out across the soiled industrial rooftops of Addoa Key. And while the sea itself was not visible, the peak of Sanctuary Mount just barely was, amid gathering clouds.

Erwen watched. And Yoda watched him.

"There . . . it is," Erwen said when the brazier atop the outpost was lit. "There it is."

"Yes, Erwen. There, it is."

"Tell Lyal . . ."

"Yes. Knows, he does."

Erwen lay back against the pillows, eyes still on the window and the light, growing brighter as darkness overtook the rest of Kwenn.

And then he left.

Yoda let out a deep breath. He released Erwen's hand.

He sensed he was not alone. "Master Gallia, you may come."

With obvious reluctance, Adi stepped in front of the bedroom door. "I didn't want to disturb you." She gestured to the living room. "The droid was delivered just as I got here. A full nursing and mobility-assist model." She looked to Erwen. "Should I activate it?"

"There is no need."

Adi bowed her head. "We were too late."

Yoda didn't agree. "Nature took its course, in its own time. Heard us, you did?"

"I'm afraid so. Again, I'm sorry. It was a private moment."

"Such is the journey that awaits us all." Yoda finally looked to Adi. "What of Lyal?"

"In bacta. He hasn't regained consciousness—"

"But he has not joined his father."

"No. He's stronger than the medics can account for."

Yoda was glad to hear that. "Other things, you have learned."

Adi nodded. They covered Erwen and walked into the darkened living room.

"We were right about the affiliations of those three attackers," she said. "Two, we knew. The knife—zolall venom, usually deadly for Sullustans. Only the Poisoned Blades on Kwenn would really know that. It also means the attack was targeted—and prepared for."

Yoda could believe that.

"The driver was a Filthy Cred—the suit gave it away. The speeder looked cheaper than they like to use, but they were probably trying to blend in. That makes four different outfits that played a role in this— four who, when last we checked, were tearing one another apart."

"Spoken to Lyal's attackers, have you?"

"No—and neither has anyone else. Their releases were arranged before they even reached the constable's station." Adi frowned. "Skulls and Vile do *not* have legal representatives, and certainly not high-priced ones. The Creds appear to have secured their freedom."

"To our colleagues, we must speak. More, they may know."

"And I agree there was something else involved. Lyal's drug connection was a member of the Creds, which makes sense—I can't see him talking to the Vile or the Skulls. The Kwenn authorities are keeping quiet about Lyal's activities, as you'd expect. But I spoke with some of the other workers at the arena. Nobody knows why he was in the neighborhood, as early as he was. He doesn't work that time of day. It's a strange place for him to be making contact with any gang members, that's for sure—I'd expect he was getting his illicit product at remote locations."

"Such as the Paths of Harmony." Yoda remembered Lyal speaking to someone there after dark. "Busy, you have been."

Adi looked toward the bedroom door. "Somehow, I sense your day was correctly spent, as well."

"Odd that we use such terms. Spend days, we do, like credits. Sometimes for things of value. Sometimes not. And sometimes we do not know." He looked to the door. "Well spent, Erwen's were."

When he looked back to her, he saw Adi looking pensive. "Master, I have to ask—"

"Yes?"

"You didn't tell him about Lyal, did you?"

"His crimes—or his stabbing?"

"Either."

"No good would it have done. There are times when the truth will not help." He glanced back at the door. "Not a good way to spend this day."

Adi did not respond.

He walked to the droid. "We should activate it now to help carry Erwen to his place of repose."

"Yes, of course."

But Adi still did not move, he noticed. He looked ahead into the darkness. "More to say, have you?"

"Be mindful, Master Yoda. A lie for the greater good is still a lie."

"I know." He looked up. "Live with it, I will."

She helped him with the droid.

CHAPTER 43

ABOARD *ASSURANCE*
ORBITING VALBORAAN

ssurance did not have a bacta tank, but it was just as well; Depa would have refused it, anyway. It wouldn't have done much against sleep deprivation and the other weapons Zilastra had used against her, and it would have felt too much like being in the stasis beam. And though she'd suffered cuts and bruises making her way up through the shattered base to reach freedom, those had served more to keep her moving than anything.

And while she did not have her lightsaber, she still had her billet on the corvette—which meant she had her Jedi robes again. It felt good leaving "Hotwire" behind, though the feeling of how much she'd left undone plagued her. She had learned a lot about Zilastra and the Rift-walkers, but they were still at large, with Kylah as their hostage. As Depa expected, Baylo had been sorely tempted to pursue the *Randomizer*—but had remained on station to collect his Jedi passengers. He was committed to duty, regardless of his opinion of those he owed his duty to.

Just as committed were Qui-Gon and Obi-Wan, who had resurrected their T-5 shuttle and brought it alongside *Assurance* in orbit over Valboraan. They had to get on their way to Kwenn, and their previous assignment for Master Koth.

"Thank you, Qui-Gon. Thank you, Obi-Wan," Depa said from the bridge of *Assurance*.

"It was our pleasure, Master," Obi-Wan replied in hologram. "Thank the Force that we decided to drop out of hyperspace where we did, allowing us to hear Kylah's call."

Qui-Gon agreed. "I know you'll find her, Master."

Depa nodded. "May the Force be with you."

The image vanished, and outside, she saw the shuttle going to hyperspace.

The celebration was impending, and while Depa intended to forgo it to find Kylah, her options were narrowing. They'd had no luck tracing the *Randomizer*'s route; its destination could be any of a dozen other Riftwalker scurryholes. That hadn't stopped Mace and Baylo from poring over everything available—including the stunning information she'd brought that Zilastra had assassinated the other gang leaders, precipitating the war they'd seen. And it was the last, most peculiar phase of it that occupied them most.

"There's still no information about why we saw the gangs disengage," Baylo said. "I guess they called a truce."

"There's more to it than that," Mace replied. "I have reports from several of my colleagues on Kwenn—Masters Yarael and Gallia the most recent—of some level of cooperation going on."

"These people? That's impossible."

"I believe my fellow Masters. They saw what they saw."

"Hmm. There's got to be something else. Signals officer, get with it!"

Depa had seen Baylo put the young man at the communications terminal through his paces. Zilastra's transmitter had been an early casualty of *Assurance*'s assault, but the ship had continued to surveil the cave base even during the firefight, looking for other potential messages besides Kylah's.

The kid had something. "Captain!"

"What is it, Veers?"

"You had me recording all transmissions. This was a low-strength holocam message—probably just internal."

The image appeared on the bridge deck before them. It was a view of Zilastra from behind—and Depa, suspended in air.

Depa recognized it. "From my imprisonment. Zilastra wanted a record of my death. I imagine it was being transmitted back to the frigate."

The young man nodded. "It ends with the quake."

"That was no quake, that was us!" Baylo said, slapping the back of the kid's chair. Then he looked at Depa. "Oh. Sorry. Guess that got rough down there."

"Don't apologize. You saved me." She watched the eerie record.

So did Mace. As the ghostly Zilastra brought something before Depa, his interest piqued. "What is she holding?"

Baylo stared. "This is a damn strange execution. She's doing card tricks!"

Depa asked for the image to be paused. "That's it," she said, pointing to the single card Zilastra had pulled from the deck. "The Idiot."

Mace raised an eyebrow. "The sabacc card?"

"Yes, she apparently reserves it for Jedi that she kills."

Mace's eyes widened.

She knew the look. "What is it, Master?"

Mace looked grave. "When the Jedi Knights discovered Xaran Raal's body, he had a sabacc card—on his person."

"On his person?"

The elder Jedi exhaled. "Stuffed in his mouth."

That was news to Depa. "That wasn't in the report you gave me. How is it you're only telling me now?"

Mace looked to Baylo and his crew—and decided to take the conversation to a more private place. He led Depa to an alcove. "I didn't tell you," he said in lower tones, "because I thought it would trouble you."

"Trouble me?"

"You seemed deflated after learning of his death. And I was concerned it would send you off on an odyssey to find his killer. That was not your responsibility. I had already dispatched other Jedi for that."

"Who came up empty." Her trademark cool slipping, Depa scowled. "Did you tell *them* about the card?"

"Of course."

Depa's head swam. "Mace, what did you think you were doing?"

Her former mentor seemed taken aback. "I had always taught you to avoid attachments—and you did an admirable job. You did it so well it impacted your choices when you became a master. You had the chance to take Xaran as a Padawan and chose to tutor him instead."

"I could help more students that way, instead of only the one. What of it?"

"I saw you two interact. I believe you made that choice because you feared what would happen if he were your Padawan. If he was lost on a mission—"

"I'd have mourned him. Just as I did in reality."

"And in reality, you took a mission that brought you out here, pursuing those who killed him." Mace raised his hands deferentially. "I know, you told us that you were only seeking to learn more about the region and its gangs—"

"I admit it. I did care. I won't deny that it motivated me—in part."

"And that is the part I feared." Mace stared at her. "Depa, your ascension to the Jedi Council is one of the proudest moments of my career. I would not see you lose effectiveness by falling prey to feelings you once handled easily."

She stared at him—and then looked back at the frozen image of her and Zilastra together. Depa's composure was shaken. She spoke sharply to him. "I haven't been your Padawan for a long time. I am a member of the Jedi Council—and I keep my own counsel when it comes to what I care about. My decision making was *not* compromised."

"And what of the girl?"

"The girl?"

"Kylah Lohmata," Mace said. "You aren't going to the celebration on Kwenn, because you expect to continue searching for her."

"Of course. I promised to save her. *We* promised to save her."

Mace nodded. "I tried to—"

"And I'm the whole reason she's in danger at all. She *begged* us not to let her be taken away. I owe her. Even if I didn't already owe her my life, *I owe her*."

"I know." He clasped his hands. "And we're doing everything we can to find her. But that's not our only responsibility. Kwenn is important to the whole region. The larger picture—"

"The larger picture called for you to bombard the Riftwalker base, not come in looking for me. But you did."

Seeing her eyes, he went silent.

Depa clasped her hands together. "Mace, we do counsel against connections—to ensure Jedi will not do harm to preserve them. But if we truly think that allowing even one innocent to suffer to stop another harm is the will of the Force—then perhaps we do not understand it at all."

Her words hung in the air between them.

Back in the middle of the bridge, Baylo was still checking out reports—and not believing what he'd heard from Mace. "Cooperation among gangs? That's ridiculous."

"What could possibly bring them together?" Lieutenant Nellis asked.

"Nothing." Baylo chortled. "But can you imagine? You want to talk about a real idiot's array, there it is."

There it is. Depa's eyes opened wide.

She left Mace's side and strode toward the hologram. "Cadet, enhance that image."

Veers did so, and she walked around it. It was the moment when Zilastra had fanned the cards before her. But this time, she could see the cards in the pirate's hand from behind. She got up closer.

"It's a trick deck. All Idiots!" She counted. "The one for me. And then in her hand." Depa counted the cards. *"Eleven!"*

"Eleven?" Mace appeared beside her.

Depa thought back to her first aborted execution—and the message that Zilastra got. "Mace, when was the celebration on Kwenn announced?"

"Yaddle took care of that." He cited the date and time. "It was on a broadcast. It was picked up everywhere."

"Everywhere." Depa turned to him and Baylo, as confident as she'd ever been. "Zilastra is the one bringing all the gangs together. And the prize is *us!*"

PART THREE
THE COUNCIL RULES

CHAPTER 44

ABOARD THE *RANDOMIZER*
APPROACHING KWENN

"The council will come to order!"

Zilastra didn't know if anyone on the Jedi Council actually said those words to open its meetings. Before Yaddle's broadcast, she doubted many listeners had ever thought about the Jedi having conferences at all. But Zilastra had playacted through a lot of holographic meetings with the other bosses to open the bribes-that-weren't, and it was important to communicate that this was a summit of a different kind.

It was certainly larger. In Tokchi's absence, Ventner had hastily reconfigured her gaming parlor aboard the *Randomizer* into a replica of the conference chamber on Valboraan. In addition to the four would-be gang leaders she'd contacted before that base's destruction, she'd added several rivals within their organizations to the slate of holographic attendees, bringing her total audience to eleven. That, likewise, wasn't an intentional copy of the Jedi Council. It was just how the pieces had shattered when she destroyed the system they'd all known.

"I object to *her* being here," declared Bazallo, the Trandoshan who'd claimed the leadership of the Vile. He was referring, Zilastra knew, to another declared heir to power: Nanna Frouj, the elderly—and notoriously vicious—Chagrian female who had laid claim to a chunk of the gang. "She has no place at this meeting!"

"For my part, I appreciate you inviting my rival," Frouj responded. "I intend to dine on Bazallo's organs one day. It is good to see he is keeping them fresh."

Seated in the chair she usually used at her gaming table, Zilastra rolled her eyes. "I know you're all still arguing with one another over who's in charge. That's why I expanded the circle. We'll sort out the rest later. What we're doing is big enough that everyone gets a piece."

"How big a piece? Or is that something else we'll 'sort out later'?" Linn, the Twi'lek from the Filthy Creds, had been Zilastra's biggest skeptic. "And how big a piece are *you* taking?"

"I've told you, you've got to look past this stuff. Think bigger."

"I think this is madness."

"Are we going to have a problem?" Zilastra raised her voice. "You're all fragmented. I'm not. But what I broke I can put back together. With or without you."

Every meetup had involved putting down the restive voices. But they had all, ultimately, listened, and followed her directives. It was good that nobody knew that she'd gotten pummeled by the Jedi and the Republic on Valboraan, but then none of her rivals were aware the Riftwalkers had a base there to begin with. To protect *that* information, she'd left bodies all across the system for years. And while her haunt's defenses were ultimately no match for Mace Windu and *Assurance,* word still hadn't gotten out. That boded well. Windu and Depa were probably dead.

And there would be more Jedi corpses to follow. So many more.

"Stay focused, people. I've shown you the holovids of the other Jedi I've slain. That was just a warm-up." Zilastra held up a datapad. "My aide's just sent you another update. Everyone's got to be in position when the Jedi convene at the arena on Kwenn. Both down there—and in space."

That drew chatter from both rivals for Staved Skulls leadership. Neither's name had the panache of the late Eviscerator's, but they matched him for menacing growls.

"You hit the Jedi that hard, they're going to come back," declared Menace Machine.

Bloodbath agreed. "They'll hit us all harder than you can ever imagine."

"With what?" Zilastra snorted. "All the Republic fields out here are disjointed outfits like Pell Baylo's. Untrained, low morale, no resources—and the ships barely talk to one another. The whole reason any of us have been able to do what we've done over the last few years is because the Senate already thinks the Ootmian route isn't worth protecting."

"Yeah, but what about the Jedi?"

"What about them? One big, decapitating stroke leaves them thrashing around—"

"They'll want revenge!"

"The Jedi don't do revenge. They're very precious about it. And remember: They work for the Senate. They can't do anything without permission. And they certainly can't declare war on another state."

Her listeners buzzed with conversation, as they had every time she'd mentioned it. The old pirate's dream: *a territory of their own,* completely free from interference by the Republic, the Jedi, or anyone else. A place where the outfits protected one another—because they knew it made them stronger.

Zilastra recapped the steps. "As soon as we take Kwenn—and clear it of the Jedi—we declare independence from the Republic. Kwenn and Keldooine and Ord Jannak and every other planet we're already set up on. And that's when the dealing begins."

"Dealing?" Linn asked.

"I brought all of you together. I can bring together another table, with a place for the Trade Federation, the Mining Guild—even some of the corporations. Anyone who wants to continue doing business in this part of the Slice. We'll be able to promise safe passage for anyone who buys into what we're trying to do."

"Nonsense," Linn replied. "Do you know these Trade Federation guys? They'll want guarantees. Solid ones. They don't trust pirates."

"We can show them what we've already done. All five gangs agreed not to hit any ships from Regal Voyager—and we kept to that, for months. Anyone who looks at the record will know that's true." *At-*

tempted hijackings by fools notwithstanding, she thought. She carried on. "They'll know we can be good to businesses if we want to be."

"But that whole scheme was a lie," interjected one of the new Poisoned Blades bosses. "There never was any deal with Regal Voyager—it was all a setup to kill our bosses." He paused. "Not that I don't appreciate it—or admire it. But it was a sham."

"They don't need to know that. Keeping it secret serves our purposes."

"Ours, too," Linn said. "The truth makes us look foolish. But what about the Hutts?"

"The Hutts will go along because they respect strength—and because they'll think they're gaining a friendly state next door, between them and the Republic. Cleared of Jedi—because it had the *power* to purge them!"

It was tiresome having to go over it every time anyone new joined the summit—but Zilastra knew it was also the last time. She went over what she expected to happen in the next several hours.

"You heard the funny little green woman, same as I did. They're going to assemble in the Gala Key Arena—and one of them is going to say *The Jedi stand with you.* When one of them does, that's the signal to go."

Menace Machine asked, "What if we don't hear it?"

"You'll know. Believe me, you'll know."

She went over the assorted backup plans. It seemed like everyone understood.

"Keep your heads in the game," she urged. "We'll conquer—then we'll divide, the next time we meet. Lovely Kwenn resort islands for everyone. And then we'll make sure we *keep* them."

Bazallo had a final question. "What are we going to call this territory?"

She put up her hands. "I told you—we'll decide that later."

She meant it—but she thought the Free State of Zilastra had a nice ring to it.

"Everyone to their places," she declared. "I'll meet you on the ground!"

A STORM IS coming. Looking down from an observation room on Kwenn's space station, Depa could see the clouds churning in the western ocean, many kilometers from the Windward Chain. But her concern was more on a different threat as she turned to face her colleagues.

"Zilastra of the Riftwalkers has struck a deal with the four major pirate bands in the Slice," Depa said. "I expect them to attack Kwenn, using their members that are already on the planet—and others they transport in. More specifically, they will strike *us,* during the bicentennial celebration."

Depa was accustomed to attending Council meetings where the other eleven masters appeared in hologram, but she couldn't remember a time when everyone, herself included, had called in from outside the Jedi Temple. She and Mace were together, *Assurance* having put in at the Kwenn Space Station, but everyone else was many kilometers below.

She certainly had their full attention. "How do you know this plan?" Yoda asked.

Depa hesitated before answering. "I do not, for certain. I know that she hates Jedi enough to murder them. When she had the chance to kill me, she stayed her hand only because she learned of the gathering of the entire Jedi Council."

Mace stood next to her. "The corvette *Assurance* has observed multiple sudden cease-fires between rival bands—groups that had been at each other's throats hours before. The timing follows shortly after Master Yaddle's announcement; we suspect there may have been communications from the Riftwalker nest on Valboraan."

The shimmering Piell looked perplexed. "The Riftwalkers are the newest to the game, right? Why would the others follow them?"

"Because Zilastra decapitated the leaderships of all her rival groups in one stroke," Depa said. "Maybe they fear she could do it again. Or maybe they just want to see her do it to us."

Corroboration came from the holographic Ki-Adi-Mundi, whose devotion to the investigation was evident in his spiky-headed disguise.

"There is a cease-fire, for sure—and operations are being planned. Many in the thrall of these criminal outfits on Kwenn are being called upon."

"Word in our livery pool is that many of them have illegal airspeeders in storage," Plo Koon said over his clasped hands. "Those beat hovercraft any day."

"Depends on who's driving," Saesee Tiin muttered.

It was too much for some. "We must cancel the celebration," Adi said. "Too many people would be exposed to danger."

Yaddle agreed. "We can then meet our opponents in a less complicated setting."

Several masters voiced strenuous objections. Oppo clearly couldn't abide the idea. His whole serpentine length writhed. "Canceling the celebration now would damage the Order irreparably in the minds of the citizenry."

Piell piped in. "We can't very well claim to stand with the people of Kwenn when we're fleein' our own festival!"

"But fewer people would be harmed," Yaddle said.

"We have an out if we want one," Adi said. She consulted her datapad. "As I noted, a storm is building to the west that will impact the day of the event. It is not expected to be dangerous, but we could use it as cause for postponement."

Ki-Adi-Mundi put up his hands. "My friends, this option is ephemeral. I have been in their midst. The adherents to the various gangs on the islands *will* rise up, no matter what."

"We're not the only ones they're coming for," Yarael said. "From what we've seen, they're looking at civil authority, too. If we're not around, they're defenseless."

Plo concurred. "The local constabulary would be quickly overwhelmed."

Mace spoke. "What if nature is our ally?" He gestured toward Adi. "The rains fall. Those on public grounds would find shelter, correct?"

"Yes," she said.

"And quite secure shelter, at that," Ki-Adi-Mundi added. "There is a supplier who would cooperate with us. But there would be demands when it comes to setup—and local transportation."

"Transportation, we've got," Saesee interjected. "In abundance."

"A frontal assault is likely not the only danger," Eeth said. "The Poisoned Blades are involved—and were also subject to this call. There may be further ploys against us, yet to be determined."

Yoda agreed. "And already in action, one plan is. As Adi knows."

Depa looked to her. "Master Gallia?"

Adi told them what she knew. "An arena manager was attacked by gangs operating in concert. He remains unconscious, in critical condition, and ultimately may not survive. The constables believe they demanded something of him—and when he did not provide it, they tried to kill him."

Mace raised an eyebrow. "And what do *you* believe?"

She looked to Yoda before speaking. "We believe he would have done anything for anyone to help his father."

"He provided something to the villains—and was silenced," Yoda said.

Depa concentrated. "Which gangs were in on this?"

"All but the Riftwalkers," Adi replied. Her glowing eyes widened. "We did see a worker exit the arena, just before the murder."

Yoda nodded. "An Ithorian."

Depa's mouth dropped open. "Did he have a shiny golden translator collar?"

Adi did a double take. "How did you know?"

"That's Tokchi, Zilastra's bomb maker!"

Even those who had not yet spoken much broke their silence at that.

"That's the end of it," Yaddle said. "We cannot bring innocents into danger."

"Bombs in the arena!" Oppo shook his head. "I thought our electronic sweep found nothing of the sort."

"Wait," Depa said. "Did you see Tokchi go inside?"

"No," Yoda replied. "Only his departure. Emerged alone, he did."

Depa touched her chin—and brightened. "Master Windu, I think I know what Zilastra has in mind."

Mace clenched his fist. "Then we will confront it, head-on."

"No, this is going to require finesse." She tilted her head. "*You* will confront them, here in space—with the help of Master Qui-Gon and his apprentice—and Captain Baylo, if he's still talking to us." She looked to the others. "For everyone else, this will require all of us, working together—on Kwenn. We must present the appearance that nothing has changed, while we work to minimize the danger to civilians. And Master Ki-Adi-Mundi—I regret that you may have to remain in disguise a little longer."

He bowed his spiked head. "I live to serve."

Yaddle smiled at Depa. "You're joining us here, aren't you?"

"Soon." Depa thought for several moments. "Yes, I know what we have to do." Then she had another thought, even more important: "Master Yaddle, we need to discuss what everyone plans to say at the event."

"Certainly," Yaddle said. "Do we need to change something?"

"You can't tell the people the Jedi stand with them!"

CHAPTER 45

BRAZATTA KEY

KWENN

Nice planet, Zilastra thought as she stepped off the shuttle. *Good one to start my collection with.*

She'd arrived incognito like this on Kwenn several times before, surveying the local Riftwalker branch and sizing up the planet. It had never been ripe for the taking. The gangs all had footholds on various islands, to be sure; slowly, they were corrupting the places the constabulary still policed. But archipelagoes were like galaxies—little bits of land with lots of in-between that nobody could control. That had kept Capital Key and several of its nearer islands relatively safe. That, and the sight of the accursed Jedi outpost and its nightly beacon.

There was no traveling to Kwenn aboard the *Randomizer* this time; *Assurance* had seen the vessel's escape from Valboraan, and surely had alerted the space station and the few local sentry ships. She and her advance team had instead arrived quietly in nondescript shuttles on Brazatta Key, where the spaceport officials were paid to ask few questions. There, they made their way through the breezy evening air to the staging area for the coming assault.

She saw it docked at the harbor: the *Pelagic.* She knew the barge well, and knew not to gamble there; the Filthy Creds had secretly controlled the casino for years. It was the only legal action to be found on Kwenn, but not a fun place to visit. The interior was cheap and tawdry. Canto Bight, a much better venue, at least put some money back into the place.

But the present alliance had made it an asset. Kwenn locals had applauded the casino management when it declared that the barge would be closed during the celebration. Yet it was no benevolent gesture. Once the gamers were gone, the *Pelagic* had collected a variety of gang members for delivery to Gala Key, while Zilastra and her new allies commanded events from the control cabin.

Tokchi was hard at work here, she saw, working alongside members of the other bands. Monitors that usually showed feeds from the casino decks were being tied into surveillance imagers from Gala Key and the other islands. Zilastra would be able to see everything during the next day's celebration. This was where she needed to be. The *Randomizer* was still off in space, being piloted by Jodak; it had its part to play, as well. But Kwenn was where her targets were.

"Good to see you, boss," Tokchi said, words coming from the Ithorian's translator collar.

She patted his shoulder. "Looks good so far."

He gestured to an area in the center of the room. "That'll have the hologram from the arena, once the broadcast begins."

Zilastra nodded. While this setup would make it possible to observe events from anywhere, she'd decided the *Pelagic* would dock at Gala Key, just in case something went awry.

Her eyes lingered on the space at the center of the room. The members of the Jedi Council were probably at the arena now, rehearsing whatever they intended to do. In the morning, she'd see them—and see them destroyed. She'd visit their mass grave—in person. It was just a shame there wouldn't be any remains for her to tag with her calling cards.

It was, Zilastra thought, a masterstroke of planning; the irony was just an added bonus. The final Regal Voyager case that Kylah had delivered to her on Keldooine days earlier had only been for show. Zilastra had needed one to hold when she spoke with the other pirate chiefs for the last time. The case had, of course, turned out to be where Depa hid her belongings. The comlink, which the annoying runt Kylah had used to bring down doom on the Riftwalkers' base on Valboraan; and her lightsaber, which Zilastra had kept for herself.

Depa's execution hadn't gone off as planned, but Zilastra had kept the spare case, which had proven itself as an excellent delivery system for Tokchi's high-explosive cocktail. The replacement gang leaders knew its effectiveness for sure; some of them had only barely survived destruction themselves. They knew, as well, that the contents of the cases could not be detected.

So the case had made for a handy opening play—and one that promised to take out not just the Jedi, but the civilians most devoted to the old order. The deaths of thousands had not weighed at all on her new allies. The right people would die.

After her first meeting with the other bands' new leadership—but before the destruction of the Valboraan base—Zilastra had dispatched Tokchi to Kwenn. There he had met with representatives from the other gangs, who'd worked together to get him inside the arena. *With the case.*

She peered at Tokchi. "You're sure the case is in place?"

"Oh, yeah," he said. "An electronic sweep shouldn't detect it—or what's in it."

Zilastra nodded. The case's voice-activated lock system required a spoken code, but they wouldn't have been able to hide a comlink alongside it without the receiver being detected. Fortunately, one wouldn't be necessary.

"It was an easy delivery," Nanna Frouj said from the section of the control center that the Vile had claimed. "We had our hooks into some poor sap that worked for the place."

Tokchi nodded. He held up a small device. "This got me inside the arena. I did the work fast—and then they drove me away."

Zilastra was gratified. Not just for Tokchi's competence—but also because it meant that she'd been right to ally with the other gangs. While there were Riftwalkers on Kwenn, their presence was smaller. Her rivals here had the connections, the assets in place to be exploited.

But something bothered her. "What happened to the 'poor sap'?"

"We whacked him!" Bloodbath shouted from the Skulls' roost.

"What are you talking about?" Hansher, representing the Poisoned Blades, spoke up. "The assassin was ours."

"We *all* participated," Linn of the Creds said. "Just as you suggested, so nobody could back out."

Zilastra nodded. It would be just like the Blades or the Creds to hang on to their turncoat for possible use as a bargaining chip. She wasn't about to be blackmailed. "You're sure he's dead?"

Tokchi shuffled on his feet. "I left before that happened."

Zilastra looked to the others. "*Well?*"

Silence. Finally, Hansher spoke. "Our people got pinched. But nobody talked. Our attorneys bailed them out fast."

"*My* attorneys did that," Linn corrected. More bickering ensued.

Great, Zilastra thought. She'd wanted more certainty. *What else might be wrong?*

Tokchi, at least, worked for her. She glowered at him. "You're *sure* nobody saw you?"

"I'm sure, I'm sure." He glanced at a display identifying the various Jedi and changed his tune. "Well, I nearly ran into those two on the way out."

Zilastra's eyes went wide. "What? What two?"

"The little guy and the tall woman." Tokchi pointed them out.

One was Yoda—hard for anyone who ran afoul of the Jedi not to know about. Zilastra guessed at who the tall Tholothian was. "Yoda and Adi Gallia. What do you mean you 'ran into them'?"

Tokchi quivered under her questioning. "It was nothing." Then, after a pause: "They seemed nice."

Zilastra rolled her eyes. "I don't need anyone else being charmed by the Jedi!"

As if on cue, she saw Burlug enter, looking as if he'd been through a war. He'd been charged with bringing Kylah aboard. "Stowaway's in lockup."

"Are you sure she can't escape? No windows, vents, or removable floors?"

"We're going to be moving soon. She gets out, she'd better learn to swim."

Good point, Zilastra thought. She gave the command. "Cast off. Gala Key by morning!"

"THE COUNCIL WILL come to order!"

Standing in the Gala Key Arena on Kwenn, Yoda looked up from his contemplations to see Yarael climbing the ramp to the stage. "I do not recall anyone ever using that phrase."

"Well, I just did," Yarael said.

The arena was an enclosed coliseum in the style popular during the High Republic, with twenty thousand empty seats of various sizes looking down on a circular dais that sat at the exact center of the structure. The evening before the big event, preparations were taking place everywhere. And Jedi Masters who had not seen one another in person in a while were looking forward to the chance to do so—while also speaking more with the people of Kwenn.

The Council members were not, however, all present for the walkthrough. Only Eeth, Oppo, and Yoda were already in attendance. Yarael put his hands on his hips and looked around. "Where *is* everybody?"

"Preparing. It is the calm before the storm," Yoda said.

"Literally. Did you see the clouds out there?"

"Not yet. But closer to them, you are."

Yarael laughed. He clapped his hands together. "You should give Ki-Adi-Mundi humor lessons. He and Saesee could turn a party into a wake." He looked around the arena stage, which had few decorations beyond his colleagues' chairs. "Oh, wait. Have they been here already?"

Yoda glanced across the dais, where Oppo Rancisis looked up from his discussions with Seneschal Voh and the arena's staff. He shot Yarael a cool look. "I take it you do not approve of the stagecraft."

"Oh, no, no problem at all," Yarael said. "We're celebrating the Grand Renewal. A barren stage will remind people of what the world looked like before just fine."

"Much thought has gone into this," Oppo said, slithering toward him. "The Jedi do not put on airs, Master Yarael. It would be wrong to have columns and banners here. If the *people* wish to decorate, that is their affair."

Yoda nodded. "We do not seek acclaim."

Yarael smirked. "Excellent. I'll tell everyone at the parade tomorrow that we'd like to pass by without being noticed."

Oppo's eyes narrowed. "I remain concerned about those outdoors. Have we provided for them?"

"Make no mistake about that. Yarael Poof is on the job!" He clapped his hand on his chest.

"Masters Plo and Tiin are, as well," Yoda said.

"Sure, if you want to get technical."

Yoda was well aware of the preparations. As the night progressed, more steps were to be taken. He thought his colleagues had done admirable work.

One colleague that he hadn't yet encountered on Kwenn entered just then: Even Piell, followed by a dozen or more children.

"It's too soon for the parade," Yarael said. "Or are we starting an academy here, too?"

"These are our ushers," Piell said. "Or the ones who can stay up this evening. We'll have more tomorrow."

He introduced the oldest, a Twi'lek teen named Hadaro. The kid looked around. "Staring at this place will put everyone to sleep."

"Any ideas?"

Hadaro glanced at Piell. "We still have our art supplies in the speeders." He pointed to the round three-meter-high wall that the dais stood upon. "How about a nice mural around the base of the stage?"

"Sure," Piell said. "Why not?"

Oppo waved both sets of arms. "Master Piell, I *must* object!"

Yarael smirked. "You said it was the people's affair if they wished to decorate." He gestured to the smiling children. "They're the people."

Oppo spoke more calmly. "I meant they could decorate our route to the outpost. *Outside*," he emphasized.

"I was just there. Looks like rain." Piell nodded to the kids. "Better bring in the paint before you get wet!"

Hadaro and the kids bolted for the exit.

Yoda smiled gently. He had known many of his fellow masters for years; Oppo, Yarael, and Yaddle, for centuries. Their responsibilities were many, their burdens crushing. Yet being away from the Temple had allowed them to interact anew, expressing themselves to others as they seldom had the opportunity to. Yoda thought the journey was worth it for that alone, even if it had taken on more serious overtones.

Yoda and Eeth were discussing the schedule when the latter's comlink buzzed. He took a look at it—and did a double take.

"Trouble, Master Koth?"

"Excuse me. It's a call. From, er—" He paused and shifted uncomfortably. "From a woman I know."

The others looked at one another—and then at Eeth.

"Excuse me." He hurried offstage to a place where he could speak confidentially.

Yarael's mouth hung open as he watched him go, but Yoda made little of it. "A woman Eeth knows."

Yarael gawked. "Eeth knows a woman!"

"Said that, I just did."

"Not quite the same." Yarael started walking toward the edge of the stage in order to hear better—until a stern look from Oppo halted him in his tracks. Yarael put up his hands. "I'm just curious."

"You are many things you were not two hundred years ago," Oppo said. "Not all of them are improvements."

"Be kind, Masters." The Jedi turned to see Yaddle walking up the ramp to the stage. A purple-skinned woman walked alongside her. "May I introduce Morna, from the *Remember Kwenn* program. She's taken a brief leave to assist our production."

The Jedi greeted her. The Woostroid woman looked down, her face flushed. "Masters. Or is it Councilors?"

"By any name, we're glad you're here," Yaddle reassured her. "Our event needs to appear before many. Your skills are needed."

Yoda nodded. "Much, we can do. Not all."

Yaddle asked Morna to excuse her for a moment. She stepped over to confer quietly with Yoda.

"The young woman seems frightened."

"She can manage it," Yaddle said. "Morna works with the most trying couple I have ever met."

"And from no small experience, you speak."

"It could be a trying morning tomorrow for many." Yaddle stepped closer to confer quietly. "Master Depa has not arrived yet."

"There is time."

"We're still going to handle this her way?"

Yoda nodded. "In this matter, Master Billaba knows best. The right, she has earned. Master Windu believes in her plan."

"Then I am satisfied." She looked to Morna. "Many of us will be tested. We will be ready."

Eeth hurried back up the ramp, holding the comlink in his hand and looking about furtively. He stepped over and put his hand on Piell's shoulder. "Master, I could use . . . your advice." He looked to the other masters as he guided the Lannik to the edge of the stage. After conferring quietly for a few moments, Eeth spoke again to the others. "Please excuse us."

"Yeah," Piell said, following Eeth offstage. "It might be a while."

The remaining masters watched them exit. Yarael looked about, baffled.

"Was Eeth asking Even for advice—about a *woman*? I don't even know what I'm seeing anymore."

This time, Yoda nodded along. "A strange trip, this has been."

CHAPTER 46

ABOARD THE *PELAGIC*

KWENN

The trouble with waiting for an explosion, a demolitions expert once told Zilastra, was that sooner or later, everything sounded like one. Sonic booms, door slams, pets leaping off furniture. Everything was a detonation.

That certainly applied to the sound she heard in the control cabin of the casino barge *Pelagic* in the hour before the Jedi Council's celebration. Once again, it was only thunder, but she still found it unnerving. The clouds had opened up over Gala Key, where they were now docked. Zilastra didn't necessarily think that was a problem, but she didn't want the weather to introduce any delays. The wind was also causing the floating casino to bob on its cushion of levitation, which was doing nothing for the stomachs of all the people in the cabin.

Another flash outside the window. Burlug opened the cabin door from outside, the sky rumbling behind him. "One thing's for sure. The Jedi can't control the weather."

"They won't control anything by the time we're done," Zilastra said. "Close the door!"

She turned her gaze upon Burlug. "Did you move the stowaway?"

"Manacled to the barge's skiff, like you said, in case you have to move."

"She can't start it, can she?"

"I'm not that foolish." Burlug rubbed his elbows. "She bit me—twice. She's tired of being a bargaining chip."

Zilastra didn't really care what Kylah thought about that—or anything else. But if Depa was so soft as to do anything to protect the stowaway, that might go for all of them. She was going to keep the kid nearby, wherever she was.

As thunder sounded outside, she paid attention to the middle of the room, where the holographic feed from the arena was live. She noticed that more Jedi had appeared on the stage. Seven, by her count.

"Is that it?" Nanna Frouj asked. "There are supposed to be twelve, right?"

"Possibly minus two." Depa and Windu's absence was heartening to Zilastra; a tally provided her by Ventner suggested that the Cerean, the Kel Dor, and the Itkotchi members of the Council were also missing. The important thing, Zilastra saw, was who *was* there. Yaddle, the little green Jedi Master who'd first announced the celebration—and who had, in so doing, caused Zilastra to interrupt Depa's execution in favor of a shot at a greater score.

Bloodbath joined the other leaders staring down at the hologram. "How is this supposed to go again?"

"For the hundredth time, if they stick to what Yaddle promised—and what's in the official program—they'll open the event by saying, *The Jedi stand with you.* That's the code that opens the case Tokchi planted under the stage."

The leader of the Filthy Creds stared at the platform, the base of which was surrounded by painted murals. She winced. "That's some of the worst art I've ever seen."

"It won't be there for long." Nanna Frouj grinned. "And goodbye, Council!"

"That's everyone else's signal, too," Zilastra said. "On the ground—and in space. We all act as one."

"Don't worry. We're on it," Hansher said, visibly impressed by Zilastra. "Some of the ideas you came up with—you're pure Poisoned Blade material."

"Just remember, I made this happen. This is only the start!"

The event was starting, too. The first speaker stepped to the center of the circle. "*I am Yaddle.*"

The crowd applauded heartily. From all reports, Yaddle had become a local celebrity in the wake of her appearance on the *Remember Kwenn* broadcast—not least for keeping cohosts Reez and Grom waiting an hour while she reportedly counseled someone offstage.

"We are not all in attendance yet," Yaddle said. "But we have a quorum and can start the program."

Hoots from the audience.

"Before we begin, I'd like everyone to spare thoughts for the Lunn family, lifelong residents of Kwenn. Lyal Lunn, the victim of a horrible crime—and his father, Erwen, recently passed away. In the short time we knew them, we saw a family that truly believes in what this planet stands for."

Yaddle got her moment of silence.

"People like the Lunns are the heart of Kwenn," Yaddle concluded, to applause. "And we thank Lyal—and everyone else, for helping to make this event happen."

"Lyal certainly helped make things happen for us," Zilastra said. Her reaction to the sob story drew hoots from the pirates in the cabin with her, but she found the display to be a relief. Had the Jedi not mentioned the arena worker's fate, that would have been suspect, though she noted Yaddle hadn't said whether he was dead or not. It didn't matter. *Let the fools make him into a hero.*

One thing was testing her patience: the impatience of her fellow listeners. "What happens if we don't get them all?" Linn asked.

"If the bomb takes seven of them out, we can do the rest," Zilastra said. She could tell the others were getting edgy. It would be good to get this part over with, so they could move on to the killing.

"Thank you for your kind reception." The holographic Yaddle clasped her hands together. "First, however, an announcement."

"An announcement?" Bloodbath shook his fist at the image. "Get on with it!"

"As you may have seen, a storm system has developed over Capital Key and the associated island chains. The event will proceed, but for your safety, we'd like to ask those of you outside the facility to remain in the safety tents that Aptorr Industries has so graciously provided."

Groans came from the audience. Zilastra looked to Burlug. "Tents?"

He nodded. "Didn't you see all the camping shelters? They had trucks out all night, giving them out and setting them up all over the place."

Zilastra had seen the festival grounds but thought little of the structures, other than to admire their sturdiness. "Did you say they were *giving* them out?"

"Free advertising, I guess."

"Make sure to stay sealed in tight," Yaddle said, "especially if you have little ones to protect from the wind and rain. I'm assured that the Aptorr shelters come equipped with holoprojectors so you won't miss a moment."

One of her rivals' underlings came in from outside, dripping wet. "It's the damnedest thing. Everyone's off the plaza."

"So much for vendor sales." Burlug chortled.

It was a strange happenstance, Zilastra thought, but it wouldn't change anything. She focused on the image. "Here she goes again."

"At this point," Yaddle said, "I'd like to turn to my great and good friend Master Oppo Rancisis for some words. As you know, the Grand Renewal was his initiative. Welcome, Master!"

Zilastra put her head in her hands. *Another one. Get on with it!*

"Get a load of this one," Burlug said, watching the Thisspiasian slither to center stage. "You'd think for something like this, the guy could do something about his hair."

"They think it makes them look smart."

"Smart for not wasting his credits on barbers. From the look of it he's saved up quite a pile by now."

She shushed him as Oppo began to speak.

"Two centuries ago, I joined the people of Kwenn in reshaping this world into something that would be more than habitable. An example of what could be done when the Republic, industry, and the people came together in the spirit of . . ."

Zilastra wanted to drive her forehead into a wall. *I swear, I'm going to run out there and open the damn case in person!*

"'The Jedi stand with you,'" Bloodbath parroted. "Tell me again why we couldn't set off the bomb by remote control?"

"They'd have found the receiver—or the explosives—in their security sweeps, you dolt." She glared at the Staved Skull. "The case just has to hear the words in order. That's it!"

And this may be it, she thought, as Oppo Rancisis came to the end of his deathless salutation. "To open today's ceremonies, I turn to my good colleague who was also here two hundred years ago. Master Yoda!"

Burlug stared. "Another one." He looked between the images of Yaddle and Yoda. "He's not the right one, is he?"

He is not, Zilastra thought. But she was all ears now as Yoda reached center stage.

"Greetings," the green one said in a voice that Zilastra found peculiar. He looked up to the crowd. "*With you, the Jedi stand!*"

An eruption of sound from the image—and quaking. But it soon became clear that was from applause in the arena. The Jedi Council stood.

"You said it wrong!" Zilastra said, losing her cool before the others for the first time. "He said it wrong!"

The clamor in the image as the seven Jedi raised their hands and ignited their lightsabers was nothing compared with the uproar it created in the *Pelagic*'s control center.

Tokchi shook his head. "The passwords have to be in order."

Zilastra shouted. "Somebody say it right, dammit!"

Her rivals were bombarded by questions from their aides. "Was that it?" Linn asked. "I've got people who heard the audio. Do they go now?"

"No, they don't go. Not yet." The attack without the blast still posed a strong chance of success, but Zilastra wasn't giving up on it yet. "Tell your people to hold."

Nanna Frouj snorted. "You've never run the Vile before. They're hopped up on who-knows-what and ready to kill. They're not going to wait because of bad grammar!"

Commotion ensued. There was only one thing to do, Zilastra realized, if she wanted to have a hope of keeping the combined gangs together. It was time for an act of leadership. "I'll fix this. Nobody do anything. *I've got this!*"

CHAPTER 47

GALA KEY ARENA

KWENN

"My name is Master Yarael Poof. I, too, was present two hundred years ago during the Grand Renewal. And it was a sight, let me tell you—"

Zilastra crawled in darkness, wishing she could cover her ears. *I would have to be here while that fool is talking!*

In the minutes before she left the *Pelagic*, nobody on stage had said anything close to the key phrase, *The Jedi stand with you.* There was a chance they might yet do so—in which case, being under the stage was a deadly place to be. But a big Ithorian lumbering about below the dais might well be detected—and while Kylah was the queen of hiding spaces, the kid could no longer be trusted.

She had to make sure, and she had to do it herself. Before she left the *Pelagic*, Zilastra had obtained the key to the arena's maintenance area from Tokchi—along with information about where to find the case.

"—and on behalf of the tall and the small, let me say the Paths of Harmony were a brilliant idea that should be replicated in every store and spaceport—"

Yarael's voice came from above her, still blathering on about the miracle of the Grand Renewal. The thought of throttling so long a neck as the Quermian's had some novelty to it, but she would shut him up soon enough. They'd known the Regal Voyager case would be proof against electronic detection, but any such sweeps would be done by now. All she had to do was deposit an activated comlink near the case, its channel open to the outside—and set it up for public address. She could trigger it from anywhere.

She reached an area where she could stand. The case should be ahead, beneath the stage, dead center. *Pun very much inten—*

"Hello, Zilastra."

Zilastra froze. The voice had come from the middle of the room, and was just audible over the droning Quermian from above. But there was no doubting who it belonged to.

"Yes, it's me," Depa said, as if to confirm it. "And I expect I know what you're here to do." The voice moved, as if the speaker was pacing in the darkness. "I'm not surprised, really. A good card player like you wouldn't hesitate to reuse a gambit if you were facing people who'd never seen it before. Well, I've seen it—and I'm still in the game."

Zilastra's mind raced. No, she hadn't been assured of Depa's death on Valboraan, and her plan didn't require it in order to work. But she'd left the woman a shadow of her former self. *How can she possibly be here?*

It didn't matter. Zilastra stood rock-still and silent as Yarael above regaled the people with more memories of Kwenn's past—going on about the actors who used to live on Kwenn, and what restaurants they liked. She slowly clipped the comlink back on her belt.

"I know it all now," Depa said. "It was learning of Yaddle's announcement that caused you to stay your hand against me. She told you where the Council was going to be and when—and even the words they would say. I know you heard that. You repeated them to me. You'd told me we'd be destroyed by our own words. But then you didn't hear those words a few minutes ago, did you? Not in the right order, anyway. So now you're here."

Above, Yarael had finally reached his conclusion. Depa sounded as if she was about to do the same.

"I'd better let you get going," Depa said. "You'll want to get to a safe distance and say the magic words."

Zilastra heard a sharp sound ahead of her, as if Depa was rapping with something on the underside of the stage. In response, the Jedi Masters above shouted in words amplified throughout the arena: "*The Jedi stand with you!*"

No! In a panic, Zilastra stumbled forward, dropping her unactivated light. She heard it clatter to the floor—and that was all. No explosion.

Across the darkness, Depa responded to the sound by activating a lightsaber. It glowed purple before her.

Eyes wide, all the pirate could say was, "That's new."

"Master Windu loaned me his. He wishes he could be here."

Zilastra had a blaster in her left hand already. "Where's the case?"

Depa took a step toward her. "I found it, earlier, with the help of a broadcast engineer that Yaddle knows. We didn't dare open it, of course, but it was moved someplace safe. We'll dispose of it later when—"

"I hate players who talk too much." Zilastra started moving, circling the edge of the darkened space. "*Assurance* brought you here?"

"They're not my taxi service."

"And you're not a speeder truck driver."

"Were you in the market for one?"

"No. I've got my own driver." Zilastra used her left hand to trigger her comlink. "Burlug!"

A response came from the device. "Yeah, boss?"

"Listen in. If you don't hear me for more than thirty seconds on this channel, kill the stowaway."

A beat. "Will do."

"Threatening Kylah a *third* time?" Depa shook her head. "I told you, I've seen this ploy."

"It still works. You want to hear her scream?"

Depa frowned. "No."

"Predictable. And strange. Jedi don't usually care about anyone—certainly not those you deem unworthy of your Order."

"I told you, I'm sorry about how that transpired. The Jedi doing the recruiting, she should have—"

"*He.* And sorry isn't good enough."

"Fine. We're ending this. You know where you are—and you know who's above. You can't escape. It's over."

"You *are* an idiot!" Zilastra laughed. "It's already started. The code phrase wasn't simply going to trigger the explosion. Your foolish friends up there have given the signal to start the attack!"

"Then it's a good thing that *our* attack is already under way."

"*Your* attack—?"

Depa's eyes glistened in the glow of the lightsaber. "We've been doing more than festival planning. Give up now."

"Never!" Zilastra backed up. "If I see you leave this arena before I'm gone—"

"Harm Kylah—and you know what'll happen."

The traded threats were followed by silence beneath the stage. Above it, Yaddle began talking. Zilastra turned and scrambled toward the exit.

It's not over. But it will be.

CHAPTER 48

GALA KEY ARENA

KWENN

"Remain calm, everyone," Yaddle said from the stage. "Please, remain calm!"

Yaddle had been delighted to see her friend Depa earlier that morning, before the audience had been allowed inside the arena—but there had been little time for conversation. It had taken them a few tries to find a way for Depa to signal Yaddle from beneath the stage. The simplest method, rapping against the underside of the floor, had worked fine.

Depa had been through a lot during her imprisonment, and there was no telling what she'd be able to do in case an enemy did come to check on the case. But she'd suggested that with seven members of the Jedi Council just meters away, someone would get the cue. Yaddle had, stepping forward to interrupt another of Oppo's historical reminiscences with the slogan. Their enemies were likely to attack whether or not they were signaled—or if the arena were destroyed. By the Jedi shouting the code phrase, the signal went out to those within the arena and without: *The defense of Kwenn had begun.*

"Now, younglings!" Piell gave a hand signal to the ushers for the event, who stood by each entrance. They acted as instructed, sealing and locking each door.

"Remain seated, you must," Yoda called out to the crowd. "Arrived, the storm has!"

Yaddle spoke to the viewers outside the arena. "Wherever you're watching from, please stay there. We'll let you know when the situation is safe!"

The Jedi had not lied about the weather: There was a storm over the island chain. But it served the Council's defense plans. It kept many viewers safely inside their homes—while those on the outdoor grounds had all received protection, courtesy of Ki-Adi-Mundi and his new friends. Aptorr had bragged that his shelters could withstand not just storms, but blaster bolts. The Jedi wanted to avoid putting that to the test—and had taken steps.

"Deploy, we must," Yoda said. Several Jedi Masters made for ramps leading off the stage and through the crowd. Eeth and Piell went for one exit, while Yoda and Adi headed for another. Oppo slithered after Yarael toward a third.

Yaddle beckoned for Morna's attention. The engineer, who'd been overseeing the sound and holographic systems from a spot just offstage, had a bewildered look—and not just from the sudden events. "You want *me* onstage?"

"Yes, Morna. Please!"

Clearly aware of all the eyes on her, the purple-skinned woman hurried to Yaddle's side and knelt by her. Morna gave the signal to her team to mute the onstage audio pickup. "What is it, Master?"

"I must help my colleagues. I need you to keep these people here—and calm."

"Calm?" Morna's black eyes went wide, and Yaddle could notice her shaking. "Everything about this is terrifying!"

"For these people, too." Yaddle put her hand on Morna's wrist. "But you know where fear leads—and you know where courage leads. *Pick your path.*"

Morna stared, frozen, at Yaddle. She looked to the crowd and opened her mouth wide—only to close it.

"I know what I'll do," she said.

She stood and gave the signal to restart the sound system. "You're on."

Yaddle, who had struggled with how much to tell the crowd both in the arena and at home, came to a decision. She took Morna's hand and walked out to the center of the stage.

"I will speak frankly to you all," Yaddle told the audience. "There are those who are trying to take advantage of the storm—and this event—to take control of this planet. But that will not happen. We have made preparations. We will keep you safe." She lifted Morna's hand. "Morna will stay here, continuing to broadcast. Should anything unexpected happen in this arena, we'll see it. And we'll be here."

She turned to Morna. The Woostroid woman straightened—and found her voice. "Kwenn is strong. We will be fine." She released Yaddle's hand and called a holocam operator over. "The masters were sharing stories of Kwenn before we were interrupted. We can do that ourselves." She approached the oldest person she could find in the front row. "I'm sure you have stories."

"I do," the elderly citizen said. "I do."

WHILE THE RIFTWALKERS may have been the craftiest gang working the Ootmian route, Eeth Koth knew that the Poisoned Blades had been working their deceits a lot longer. They had schemes upon schemes on the shelf, waiting to be pulled whenever the opportunity for gain arose. From small-time thefts to audacious power grabs, the Blades operated from a catalog of chicanery on world after world.

On Kwenn, the Blades had limited themselves to crimes that could be perpetrated while hiding in plain sight, taking advantage of a transient tourist population while the planet's authorities focused on keeping the nastier gangs at bay. But practically overnight, the pirate alliance had motivated the gang on Kwenn to raid its mayhem file, activating multiple scams within the tapestry of the newfound cooperation with their former rivals.

A plan to sicken the forces aboard the Kwenn Space Station became possible thanks to a break-in by the Staved Skulls at a catering supplier in their territory on Kwenn. The Vile staged a prison uprising at the planetary justice center, distracting the authorities while a Poisoned Blade member installed a timed-release paralytic gas device of Rift-walker manufacture in the police barracks. It was the same stuff Zilastra had intended for Depa.

And the Filthy Creds had lent one of their shell company holdings to the most repugnant scheme of all, turning one of the most innocent of things into something deadly.

All of these plans, Eeth had learned about the night before in his surprise call from Inisa, the woman he'd met at the bar. She had spoken quickly, for fear of being overheard—but it became clear the Blades had traded operational security for speed, allowing news of their plans to disseminate through the organization's gossip network. Eeth thought her words had the ring of truth. When he asked why she had revealed what she knew, she suddenly disconnected.

Eeth had been concerned for Inisa's safety, and still was. But her warnings had to be heeded first. Mace had quietly dealt with the space station matter that morning, and Yarael had foiled the attack on the police without leaving the Blades any the wiser. But one matter, Eeth left to himself and to Piell. When Piell had heard about what the Creds and Blades had done, he insisted on being involved.

The two ran from the arena and toward the plaza. The sky had darkened further during their time inside, and a wet wind was blowing just shy of gale force. All around, the shelters that Ki-Adi-Mundi had obtained from Aptorr's factory stood strong—and every one was sealed.

That meant the only people in the tempest were vendors. And not just any vendors. Most had followed their customers' leads by getting out of the open. But all around, hovercarts belonging to the Tasty Comet Frozen Confection Company were still on the grounds, despite the wind. And they all seemed to be doing the same thing: fighting to open their freezer cases.

Eeth and Piell approached one of them. Unkempt looking—except for his white uniform—a thick-maned Gotal pounded at the lock on his cart.

A frantic voice came from his comlink. "The word's been given!"

"I heard, I heard! I can't get this damn case open!" The Gotal looked around across the plaza. "Nobody can!"

Eeth stepped up. "Two Tasty Comets, please." He looked to his friend. "Did you have a flavor in mind, Master Piell?"

"Surprise us," Piell said. "And this is on me, Master Koth."

"Very generous, Master Piell." Eeth looked to the struggling vendor. "Is there a problem?"

The Gotal shouted, "*Get lost!*"

"That's no way to talk to customers."

The vendor cast aside his comlink and pounded at the lock on the cart's cabinet. "I can't open it, okay? Now get out of here!"

Piell looked to Eeth. "Sounds like a problem, Master Koth."

"No problem, Master Piell." In a swift motion, Eeth drew his lightsaber from within his robes and ignited it. He brought it down on the locking mechanism, destroying it. The lid sprang open.

"You're Jedi!" The Gotal vendor reached hurriedly inside the cart. "There's nothing in here! Where are they?"

"No treats?" Eeth asked.

Piell smirked. "If you're looking for the blasters and grenades, you ain't gonna find 'em."

The Gotal poked his head out, flummoxed. "What?"

"We struck the Tasty Comet warehouse last night just after you loaded up," Eeth said. "It took considerable time to undo your preparations."

"My students would've gone to that factory in a heartbeat," Piell added. "But what we removed is bad for their health."

The would-be vendor reached inside his uniform and drew a blaster pistol. He held it on the Jedi as he backed away from the cart. Seeing a sealed tent behind him, he moved toward it. "You two stay back!"

The Jedi Masters made no attempt to stop him as he unsealed the tent.

"There's nobody in here!"

"That's a shock," Piell said. "You want to check another tent? Be our guest."

The Gotal did and found the same thing: nothing. "Where is everybody?"

"Watching the show—but not from here," Eeth answered. "The Kwikhaul vehicles that brought the tents in last night carried people back out to the viewing centers on other islands."

Piell nodded. "Our colleagues Plo and Saesee were behind that. People were told it was in case the weather got too bad for them to return. Others we just let into the arena itself." He gestured outward. "But there's nobody directly outside but you people."

Eeth gestured to the cart. "It's just as well—you don't have anything to sell them anyway."

The Gotal growled and raised his weapon. Eeth and Piell gestured together, hurling him with the Force and knocking him senseless.

The vendor's hat fell off, revealing his Gotal horns—and something else. "Staved Skull," Eeth said. "They *are* all working together!"

"And we have their attention," Piell said. Across the plaza, at least a dozen other vendors had seen their altercation. One after another, they gave up on their stuck cabinets and drew their personal weapons.

Piell activated his lightsaber. "Let's keep them away from the arena."

"Right," Eeth said, starting to advance.

Piell laughed as they charged toward the incoming blasterfire.

"What's funny?" Eeth asked.

"My medical droid back on Coruscant would love this. We're declaring war on dessert!"

CHAPTER 49

ABOARD *ASSURANCE*

ORBITING KWENN

"There they are!"

The ships emerged from hyperspace one after another, so many that Mace Windu was startled none of them collided with one another. That was a real danger, since they had, according to *Assurance*'s observations, arrived from many different directions.

"Good guess, Windu," Baylo said as he looked out from his bridge. "Right on schedule."

There was no hiding the accumulation of multiple starships in a region as busily traveled as the Ootmian route; Mace and *Assurance* had received reports that vessels from multiple factions were gathering just a few minutes' hyperjump away from Kwenn. Some had jumped in early, having interpreted Yoda's version of the "go" phrase as the actual one; *Assurance* had stayed back then, hiding behind Kwenn's moon. The version of the phrase shouted by the seven Jedi had triggered the moves of everyone else.

"Twenty-five—no, thirty. No—" Lieutenant Nellis, fully healed and back at his station, lifted his hands from his console. "The system's lost count, Captain."

Mace saw many ships that *Assurance* had typed for its tactical archives as connected to the Poisoned Blades, the Staved Skulls, the Vile, and the Filthy Creds. But there were other vessels that hadn't been encountered before.

The captain looked perplexed. "What's the holdup? They're not attacking."

"Some may have been expecting the destruction of the arena," Mace said. "But believe me, they will attack anyway. Master Billaba was sure of it."

Young Veers piped up. "Captain, we just got a response from the Republic."

"What is it?"

"They appreciate having been alerted to our situation and have complete confidence in our abilities to deal with it."

Silence on the bridge—and then nervous, infectious laughter. Baylo pushed his hat backward on his head. "After inspiring words like that, how can we lose?"

"Stay focused," Mace said. He pointed. "Some are going for the space station."

"Interdict," Baylo ordered.

Assurance yawed, making for the gargantuan space haven—a marriage of a great space city atop a docking cage large enough to accommodate all but the biggest capital ships. A prize for sure, and Mace and Depa had expected an assault on it. But while its armaments were strong, as yet they hadn't been activated against the invaders. Meanwhile, the guns of the vanguard of the pirate flotilla were alive, wildly firing past *Assurance* at the station's colossal communications relay.

"Maybe we should lean out the window and tell the pirates the Republic's policy on distress calls," Baylo said.

"Disabling the relay helps their ground assault," Mace said. "Many of Kwenn's official communications route through there."

Importantly, most of the station's large population had already decamped for the planet and the celebration. Even the Vile were unlikely to destroy a facility with such large landing bays and a fully stocked depot. "Our opponents' greed is working to our favor," Mace said. "They're pulling their punches."

He checked the intruders' distance to the station. "It's time. The maneuver, Captain."

"Here goes nothing," Baylo said. "Hard to starboard. Get us out of the firing line!"

Assurance peeled off, appearing to abandon the station. But as the first wave of pirates came into range, turbolaser batteries that had been inactive woke and began blazing away.

"Direct hit!" shouted Nellis as pirate vessels began erupting into flame. "Another. *Another!*"

Baylo clenched his fist. "They walked right into it!"

"Station reports readiness to repel boarders," Veers called out. "The intel you provided them was correct, Master Windu. The food shipment was tampered with—but you warned them in time."

"They should try ours." Baylo stared forward into the zoo of spacecraft filling the forward port. "Stage two?"

"Affirmative," Mace responded.

"Very well. Find us a lane—and locate the frigate. Find the *Randomizer!*"

Several seconds later, Mace saw it—and noted the size differential between the frigate and their own corvette, half its length. The Riftwalkers' vehicle looked little worse for wear from its escape from Valboraan, but appearances could be deceiving.

Nellis called out, "Should we engage, Captain?"

Baylo looked to Mace, who lifted his hand. "Hold," the Jedi Master said.

He waited—until he saw two small pods rocketing through the confusion from the space station toward the frigate. In the cacophony of craft, the tiny vessels traversed most of the distance between the two without prompting a response.

"They didn't fire on them," Nellis said.

"You're damn right." Baylo smiled in wonderment at Mace. "*You* were right!"

The Jedi Master was satisfied, as well—because those vehicles contained two very important agents, Qui-Gon Jinn and Obi-Wan Kenobi. But before the pilots of the pods could do their jobs, they had to make it the rest of the way without being noticed. He watched as the *Randomizer* rolled, leading the mass of the expeditionary force away from the station and toward Kwenn. "Harass the *Randomizer* on the way down, Captain. Delay it, no more."

"She's *Pelta*-class, regardless of the age," Baylo said. "We might be able to spit at her." He looked to Mace. "I hope you're right about this."

Veers called out, "Should I broadcast a message telling the pirates to depart, Captain?"

Baylo chortled. "Sure, kid, that'll help." He looked at Mace and pointed a thumb to the youth. "I'm telling you. Your next chancellor."

Mace was already running. "I'm heading for my fighter. May the Force be with you all!"

DOWN ON KWENN, Kylah Lohmata gritted her teeth—again. She'd been filled with rage every waking minute since leaving Valboraan. Zilastra's second betrayal was bad enough, but Burlug, her other presumed protector in the Riftwalkers, had decided his loyalty lay with the boss. And the two of them had frequently left Kylah under the watch of someone she didn't like at all, the murderous droid IK-111.

They'd brought her with them to Kwenn like another piece of luggage—and they'd just as unceremoniously loaded her onto the *Pelagic*'s skiff for the trip to the arena. Kylah had sat exposed to the elements, her hands manacled and mouth gagged, under the watch of IK-111 while Burlug had listened for word from Zilastra.

It had been thirty seconds since Zilastra had spoken over comms.

Kylah shouted, but no words came out, and she wasn't speaking anything specific anyway. It was a yelp of betrayal, a call for help. A call for Depa, whose voice she'd just heard, who was clearly alive.

Forty seconds.

Burlug turned toward her. "This is bad, kid. I'm sorry." He rose—

And Kylah's eyes went wide. She yelled into the gag. Burlug got the idea—and looked behind him. Zilastra ran from the maintenance access door onto the skiff.

"Go, go!" The pirate leader hopped into the back as Burlug took position behind the controls again. A lurch, and the skiff pivoted and shot ahead.

"I take it there's no big boom," Burlug said.

"Forget that," Zilastra said. "There's a battle going on. Let's see how it's going." She turned and faced Kylah. "We're moving. Nobody can hear you yell now."

Kylah tried to say Depa's name, over and over again.

Zilastra barely understood the muffled word—but apparently cared enough to wonder about it. She removed the gag. "What about Depa?"

Kylah gasped for breath. "I told you . . . she was alive."

"With what's coming for this island? Not for long."

"—ALERTING ALL OFFICIAL channels! The insurrectionists have taken to the air!"

Elsewhere on Kwenn, Saesee responded. "This is Jedi Master Tiin. I didn't catch all of that."

"Master, glad to hear from you. This is Kwenn Traffic Patrol. The Vile are leading an assault heading toward the Middle Chain. And they're breaking the law—they're using airspeeders to get there! Beware!"

Saesee was mildly amused that in the middle of an invasion, the constabulary was worried about a traffic violation. But he wasn't too concerned about facing airspeeders. He switched off the transceiver and looked forward through the rain-spattered cockpit viewport of the starfighter. *Not too concerned at all.*

Kwikhaul owner Fraxa had told him her prized ARC-8 starfighter had seen a lot of use during the High Republic, accounting for the shabby shape she'd found it in when she salvaged it. Her restoration work on it over the years had been cosmetic, and most of the eight-winged fighter's real problems were beyond the technicians she'd dragooned from her livery business to solve. Saesee had resolved them in his few off hours on the planet, on the condition that he got to take the antique on a test flight.

Some test flight, he thought. Racing across the waters from Zyboh Key, he saw the contacts he'd been warned about far ahead. Criminal invaders from the northern islands were charging southeast, bypassing the bridges as they headed for the Middle Chain, the string of more peaceful isles from Gala to Langdam. Ahead of him, Saesee saw one storm-battered airspeeder after another, moving from his left to his right—as far as his eyes could see.

He toggled the transceiver again. "Coastal Watch, this is Jedi Master Saesee Tiin."

A different voice answered. "Do you require assistance, Master?"

"I'm calling to report downed aircraft in the water. Alert recovery units."

"Recovery?" The operator was surprised. "We're a bit busy, Master. When did the craft go down?"

"Starting in about twenty seconds—with another every ten."

"What? How many craft are we talking about?"

"Hard to tell. Let me get back to you. I'd say in about five minutes . . ."

CHAPTER 50

ORBITING KWENN

The life of a Jedi Padawan was unlike that of a student from any other discipline. Trainees in few walks of life ventured into combat as part of their educations. And while some other trades involved student travel, Obi-Wan doubted that many learners approached a planet by way of landing on top of another starship—which itself was cruising in the stratosphere.

Yet that was exactly how he and Qui-Gon were approaching Kwenn.

"Careful, Obi-Wan!" called his master through his headset. "Correct your alignment."

"Correcting!" Obi-Wan nudged the controls in the tiny workpod. He was finding that the tiniest of deviations could send the pod spiraling to one side or the other. He and Qui-Gon had only had an hour's training on the maintenance vessels—and were lucky to have gotten even that much.

After leaving the company of *Assurance* over Valboraan, their shuttle had barely emerged from hyperspace over Kwenn when word came from the people they'd just left. Masters Billaba and Windu had divined a new danger and had ordered them not to land. Qui-Gon and his

Padawan made for the Kwenn Space Station instead, where they were told to wait for further orders. When those instructions finally came, they were accompanied by Council-level authorization to exchange their shuttle for two of the station's maintenance pods.

Mace and Depa had correctly guessed that the cloud of pirate ships would stop first at the station to knock out its emergency beacon. That had given Qui-Gon and his student the chance to launch themselves in the pods toward one of the capital ships in the pirate alliance. The *Randomizer* had been named the top target, and while the two of them had missed seeing it on Valboraan, *Assurance* had sent over plenty of identification files for their study.

Obi-Wan just wished there'd been more time to train on the workpods, which had never been designed for anything he and Qui-Gon were asking them to do. They did not normally travel long distances, nor were they designed for pursuit. And shielding was nonexistent. *Assurance* had at least taken off some heat by shadowing the *Randomizer;* none of the other vessels, most run by the Riftwalkers' former rivals, seemed willing to get close.

The pods certainly were not intended to enter atmospheres, as he and Qui-Gon found when they caught up with the frigate. Enclosed in a passenger chamber not much larger than a storage locker, Obi-Wan struggled with the controls. "We won't get more than one try!"

"You know what Master Yoda says about trying," Qui-Gon responded. "The frigate's wings are in motion. Go now!"

As on many of the *Pelta*-class frigates, the *Randomizer's* rear stabilizers swiveled out for aerial travel, creating a sizable flat surface on either side of the conn tower. Following the lead of Qui-Gon out of the corner of his left eye, Obi-Wan brought his pod in to hover just above and behind the *Randomizer*.

During their earlier planning, Qui-Gon had advised that they needed to touch down simultaneously or the frigate would buck, possibly throwing off or striking the other pod—and doubtlessly alerting whoever was piloting the *Randomizer*. But grappling onto starships was the one thing the pods were actually designed for. So after Qui-Gon gave a countdown, Obi-Wan was able to bring his vessel in for a magnetic—if violent—landing. "Contact!"

"Watch your altitude," Qui-Gon said. "You know when to go!"

Obi-Wan checked the altimeter they'd added to the pods, something a vehicle designed only for space had no use for. Neither did a pod require much protection against reentry—but there, the *Randomizer*'s wings and shields had come in handy. After a turbid ride through worrisome flames, Obi-Wan saw skies again. And when he saw the right number on the altimeter, he blew the hatch.

The *Randomizer*'s pilot leveled off, cruising across Kwenn's night side at an elevation where Obi-Wan no longer needed his breathing apparatus. What he needed instead was a way to stay on the frigate despite the ship's extreme speed. He found it in a pair of grapples that allowed him to climb out of the pod and hug the hull.

His traverse was not long, but it was perilous—and it could end, along with his life, at any second if the *Randomizer* suddenly returned to orbit. Instead, it reached a midair staging area over an atoll. As the vessel circled, Obi-Wan made his way to the starboard docking port. With one hand hanging on a grapple, he used the other to strike the locking mechanism with his lightsaber. A death-defying leap, and he was in.

After he cycled an emergency door, the noise from outside finally died down. Exhausted, Obi-Wan leaned against the bulkhead, waiting until he could hear his own breathing again.

Then he heard something else, more unbelievable to him than any of the exploits he'd just performed. He reached for his comlink, thinking about sending a warning.

Then he changed his mind. *If Qui-Gon hears this,* Obi-Wan thought, *he might just get back off the ship. I know I'd certainly like to!*

"HERE COMES MORE rain," Burlug shouted.

"Don't worry about it," Zilastra said. Standing aboard the *Pelagic*'s skiff as it cruised across the plaza outside Gala Key Arena, she remained confident, despite the unexpected setbacks.

Zilastra regretted that her bomb was out of play, but it had only been one part of her plan. Her allies were approaching Capital Key—and they already were on the festival grounds, battling two of the Jedi who'd emerged from the arena. More forces were approaching the entrances, and while she was surprised she wasn't seeing more blasterfire, she knew the numbers favored the pirates. If she couldn't wipe out the Jedi Council all at once, she'd settle for killing them one by one.

And it would only get better. At that moment, the poisoned defense forces aboard the Kwenn Space Station would be surrendering—and, with any luck, dying. The planetary police would be literally paralyzed. More invaders would be arriving across the bridges and the water, and from space. It was only a matter of time, and of maintaining focus. The fact she'd received no updates about anything spoke not of failure, but how busy everyone was. Zilastra had missed nothing in the planning. Her entire life had led to this score. Success was assured.

The skies let go once and for all, pounding her with tropical rain. She reveled in it. A Nautolan's kind of weather, it added to the misery, to the confusion—and both worked in her favor.

"You're crazy," shouted a drenched Kylah.

"I love it," Zilastra said. Kwenn would be cleansed of Jedi, this day. And a whole lot more.

"HMPH."

Saesee Tiin had long been skeptical of the design philosophy behind the ARC starfighter line. For years, some engineers had been in love with the daft notion that there was no number of wings that was too many for a snubfighter; its worst expression had been a twelve-winged metal lotus blossom from a manufacturer that was deservedly long gone. In more recent times, makers had reined in their more fanciful instincts. Saesee thought the new ARC models showed much promise.

Fraxa's vintage ARC-8 had called out to be tried if only for the perverse novelty. A set of wings that separated—and then separated again—did provide Saesee with a much wider weapons spray. He saw it repeatedly as he fired at the hapless airspeeders caught in his path. The ARC-8 offered a full circle of laserfire with a diameter equal to its wingspan; just pointing the fighter anywhere near an enemy usually resulted in a hit.

The design had also made the relic a screeching terror to pilot, as the gale blowing on the ocean repeatedly treated Saesee's fighter like a windmill. Over and over again since he'd reached the end of the Middle Chain and turned back southwest, he'd had to force the control yoke to center with such force that it nearly snapped off in his hands. That there was a consequence to his firing went without saying. For the fourth time, his intended glancing shot against an airspeeder operated by the Vile provided a more solid hit.

"Sorry!" Saesee called out as his aerial target broke apart under its occupants, sending pirates tumbling headlong through the air and into the ocean. He expected they'd survive. The pirates had responded to his attacks by negating their advantage: flying closer to the sea and nearer to the shorelines. That would save them.

Saesee had the upper hand, but Plo Koon had prevailed upon him the need for mercy. "Many of these people were part of Kwenn's civil society once," he'd intoned. "They can be again."

If that were the case, Saesee thought he saw the makings of a future Good Citizens' Society meeting up ahead. A landing, on Gala Key, where an earlier wave of invaders was gathering for a ground advance— likely against his fellow Jedi.

A rainy gust blowing over the island hit the ARC-8 full-force, causing the ship to tumble and the yoke to slip from his hand. "Okay, that's enough," Saesee said, grabbing control again and bringing the ship down toward the shore.

He cruised over the heads of the insurgents on the beach and landed the fighter on the first terrace above. Assured the high ground, he exited the fighter, activated his lightsaber, and tromped through pelting rain to where the steps led down to the advancing mob.

"*Jedi!*" screamed one of the Vile.

"Yes." Saesee pointed behind himself with his free hand. "The fighter is borrowed. Nobody scratches it!"

CHAPTER 51

ABOARD THE *RANDOMIZER*
OVER KWENN

Standing in the accessway aboard the *Randomizer*, Obi-Wan stood patiently as the voices got louder, resigned to what he was about to encounter.

"—quit thinking small, Ghor. I told you, if we're there first, it'll be a huge deal."

"For who? You?"

"Will you stop with the—"

Obi-Wan stood motionless as Lobber, Ghor, and Wungo stepped around the corner. He waved. "Hello—"

"*Gah!*"

Startled by Obi-Wan, Lobber dropped what he was carrying. The Jedi caught it with the Force. He was relieved to see it was a datapad, and not an explosive.

However, Obi-Wan soon realized that everything else the trio had on probably *was* an explosive. All three wore vests layered over with satchels and pouches, with grenade-holding bandoliers over those. The trio wore helmets, each sourced from what appeared to be ancient salvage from three different armies. "You're all dressed up," Obi-Wan said.

"Quit following us!" Lobber yelled.

"I'm not following you."

"Neither am I," said Qui-Gon, causing Wungo to shriek. Having entered through the air lock on the opposite side of the ship, the Jedi appeared right behind him. "Quiet," Qui-Gon said. "You don't want to cause a disturbance during an invasion."

Wungo leaned against the bulkhead and grabbed his chest near his heart. Or tried to—the explosive packs were in the way. "I can't take it anymore."

Obi-Wan wasn't sure he could, either—but he remembered that Depa had said the three had boarded the *Randomizer* at the last minute. "I didn't think you'd still be with the ship."

"And why not?" Lobber asked. He snatched his datapad from Obi-Wan's hands. "We're very important people. We're going in with the first wave!"

Qui-Gon nodded. "I suspect you're referring to the invasion force I saw queueing up in the hold as I passed by."

"That's right. We're in the—whaddya call it?"

"Guard van," Ghor offered.

Obi-Wan blinked. "You mean *vanguard*?"

"Whatever," Lobber said. "Zilastra was real impressed by our escaping the base on Valboraan. So we got promoted!"

That made no sense to Obi-Wan. "Nothing was said about how the arsenal exploded?"

Qui-Gon waved him off. "Never mind about that."

Wungo pointed at Lobber. "I'm not taking orders from him, ever again. But I will from Zilastra. She's scary."

"Is she aboard?" asked Obi-Wan.

"I don't know."

"I saw her troops." Qui-Gon pointed his thumb forward. "They were all facing the other direction. Are you sure you're in the lead?"

"We will be," Lobber said. "That's why we came back here. They tried to stick us in the back, but we're going out our own air lock. We'll accomplish our mission and be aboard before anyone else!"

Obi-Wan looked forward nervously. Qui-Gon often gave his attention to the most pathetic of life-forms, but this was ridiculous. "We have a mission, Master. Do we really have time for this?"

"Yes, we actually might," Qui-Gon replied. He faced Lobber. "What's your objective?"

Lobber patted his satchels. "Demolitions!"

"I gathered that."

"They're going to drop us on Capital Key," Ghor said. "We're supposed to go into the main government building, set our charges, and go."

"The *main* government building?" Qui-Gon asked. "Kwenn Hall?"

"No, not that one."

"May I?" The Jedi Master reached for Lobber's datapad.

"Hey, that's classified!" The Devaronian jerked the device away—only to lose it again. Obi-Wan caught it.

He read it and showed it to Qui-Gon. "The Education Ministry. More specifically, the office of the deputy minister for academic loan reconsolidation."

Qui-Gon nodded. "That *is* important."

"Yeah!" Lobber said. Then he looked squarely at Qui-Gon. "Isn't it?"

"I don't think you're mission-critical."

Ghor, Wungo, and Lobber looked at him—and to one another with confusion.

Qui-Gon made it plain. "Zilastra is trying to kill you."

"In a way in which your success or failure won't matter," Obi-Wan said.

Lobber snatched away the datapad. "That's ridiculous."

"Oh, you'll cause some damage. Chaos, certainly," Qui-Gon said. "And she'll probably get a good laugh."

"Nonsense! We've met Zil. Have you?"

"No, but I know the type." The Jedi Master tugged on Wungo's vest. "Did they tell you how to set these charges?"

"Of course they did," Lobber said. He pointed to a bulging pocket on his pants. "We've got the detonators right here!"

Qui-Gon nodded. "Did you intend to activate them already?"

Wungo's jaw dropped. "What?"

Qui-Gon turned one of Wungo's satchels around. "These appear timed. And running already."

Ghor stared—and then looked at his. "They were like this when they gave them to us!"

Obi-Wan covered his face with his hand.

Lobber, Ghor, and Wungo took turns looking at the packs they were wearing. "Don't tamper with them," Qui-Gon said. "I'm sure we can help."

The ship lurched. Obi-Wan called Qui-Gon to the side of the corridor.

"Master," he whispered, "we have a mission. We can't let this ship land." Obi-Wan gestured ahead. "We have to get going!"

"Our friends are in danger."

Obi-Wan gawked. "Our *friends*?"

"You're not seeing it, Obi-Wan." Qui-Gon looked at the quarreling threesome. "These fellows have not been repeatedly placed in our path by happenstance. And you and I did not let them go every time not to harvest an opportunity now."

An opportunity. Obi-Wan looked at the hapless onetime hijackers.

And on that thought, he had another. Apparently, at the same time that Qui-Gon did.

They both stepped forward.

Wungo's eyes were wide with panic. "You said you'd get these things off us!"

"We can," Qui-Gon said. "But we have something in mind, first."

Lobber looked at him with suspicion. "What?"

"When we met, you wanted to get into the business of acquiring starships—without the purchase price. But you hadn't settled on whom you'd be acquiring them for."

"Yeah?"

Obi-Wan got to provide the next part, even though he couldn't believe what he was about to say. "The Jedi Order would like to go into business with you . . ."

SOMETHING'S WRONG.

The situation on Gala Key wasn't any clearer than the weather, Zilastra thought as Burlug navigated the skiff across the festival grounds. Many of the invaders had fled in defeat, but still more were arriving every minute, charging toward an arena that still stood.

Yet that was not the only unpleasant surprise. The Tasty Comet vendor carts were around, but many had been abandoned, with no weapons drawn from them. And a lot of vehicles were in the area bringing civilians out—and defenders in. The constable's forces were present in greater numbers than she'd suspected they could raise. And many of the shelters on the grounds outside the arena appeared to have never been occupied to begin with.

She hadn't seen where Depa had wound up yet, but she'd spied two more Jedi in action on the grounds outside the arena. Adi Gallia and the tall Quermian, who'd identified himself on stage as Yarael Poof. The Jedi were surrounded but fighting back fiercely.

"Bring us around," Zilastra ordered as she saw a pedestrian overpass up ahead. Going back for a good strafing run could be just the thing to overwhelm the Jedi.

"Just a second," Burlug said, adjusting the skiff's heading. "I have to—*yiiiiii!*" The big Feeorin yelped in surprise as Zilastra saw the two little green Masters from the stage—Yoda and Yaddle—leap down toward them from a pedestrian bridge.

As they hit the front of the vehicle, Burlug swerved. Zilastra fired her blasters forward, only for the Jedi to hop in unison. This time, they landed on the railings on either side of the deck amidships. Trapped between them, IK-111 trained both blasters and fired point-blank. Seemingly from thin air, both Jedi produced lightsabers, and they parried bolt after bolt with their green blades, faster than Zilastra could see. Several sizzled past her, forcing her to duck. A shot singed Burlug's shoulder, while Kylah huddled behind her seat.

The droid's barrage lasted a couple of seconds before Yoda and Yaddle each loosed a hand from their lightsabers—and pulled. Before Zilastra's eyes, the blasters in IK-111's hands stopped firing, as if tugged by an unseen force. The droid struggled against releasing them—and watched, astonished, as his arms ripped free from their sockets.

Zilastra started firing her blasters in his place, then—until Burlug shouted. For a second, she thought he'd been hit by a deflected shot, and glanced toward him. That was when she saw the bridge. Another pedestrian crossing leading to the arena, it barred their path—and there was no avoiding it. She hit the deck an instant before the top of the skiff slammed against the bottom of the structure.

When she opened her eyes, the skiff was still moving—but the railings were gone and so was everything above IK's torso. The assassin droid's legs writhed and stomped about dizzily. The two Jedi were nowhere to be seen.

She ran to the rear of the craft searching. Yoda and Yaddle had leapt to safety and were already engaging more of her allies on the ground near the arena.

Burlug looked back at her, as rattled as she'd ever seen him. "*What the hell was that?*"

"The tide turning!" Kylah said.

"Quiet." Zilastra moved forward. "I'm checking with the command center. Something's not right!"

THE GALACTIC REPUBLIC had no army, and Plo Koon was no general. But he had the feeling that if the Defense of Kwenn were ever described by historians as a military engagement, he would be considered the leader of the mobile cavalry. He certainly had organized it.

The odd oroko rescue notwithstanding, he and Saesee had spent their whole sojourn on the planet assisting the management and staff of Kwikhaul. They had helped the livery firm come to an amicable resolution with its drivers, and had worked to modernize and diversify the capabilities of its repulsorcraft fleet. And while Saesee hadn't exactly told Fraxa, the owner, that he intended to take her prized starfighter into battle, Plo had been frank with everyone at the firm when he met with them the night before.

Celebration Day would not be about taking fares. It would be about making rescues.

Remarkably, more than 90 percent of the drivers had agreed to assist—beginning with remaining on the compound overnight to make preparations. This also helped keep the knowledge of Plo's plans secure. Secure until the Jedi in the arena shouted the five fateful words, which every Kwikhaul driver heard in their vehicles. Taxis that had every reason to be in the area, collecting fares; taxis that were well positioned to perform other services when it became a battle zone.

"Three people on the knoll behind the statue promenade," SK-89 reported from her station before the monitor in the open hovertruck.

"Unit Four-Six to the promenade to collect civilians," Plo said into his comlink. Standing in the back of the vehicle, he kept his balance as Teeler, the veteran driver who'd agreed to chauffeur him, circled the festival grounds. "Exit south from the promenade, Four-Six. Insurgents approaching from the west!"

Every so often, a landspeeder driven by pirates or their local allies vied with the speeder truck, trying to take it out. When evasive maneuvers didn't work, Plo defended it from blasterfire with his lightsaber. And when the shots came too close, he was usually near enough to leap to the other vehicle, taking the battle to them.

And then it was back to managing a force that was on the move, doing many things at once. He'd dispatched rides for Piell and Eeth, both on their way to hot spots; Yarael and Oppo had just called for another. The first one of all had gone out to Depa, who'd emerged from the arena in search of Zilastra.

He took Depa's latest call directly. "Have you seen them?" she asked.

For all Plo knew, his colleagues had already engaged Zilastra—but it wasn't like everyone had time to use their comlinks. Still, his network was broad. "My people are still watching for the skiff," he said to her over his device. "I'm patching you into a separate channel, just for those reports."

"Thank you, Master."

"Good hunting."

Plo steadied himself and looked back across the plaza. Eeth and Piell were still at it, he could see—now joined by Yaddle and Yoda. More people were running from them now than running toward them.

And there was one more member of the Council he was curious about.

"Saesee Tiin has reported in," the droid reported, as if on cue. "He has landed. He has been fighting a large number of miscreants on the northern shore."

Plo nodded. "Ask him if he needs us to fight alongside him."

SK-89 sent the message—and reported back, several seconds later. "I do not understand the Master's response."

"What?"

"He asked if we could send him some more people to fight *against*." The droid looked back. "Did I interpret that wrong?"

"No, you have him exactly right," Plo said. "Tell him Plo Koon says to be merciful."

CHAPTER 52

ABOARD THE *PELAGIC*

KWENN

"Your lordship!"

Ki-Adi-Mundi looked out from inside the maintenance cabinet. "Yes?"

The young human with the tool belt looked unnerved to see Ki-Adi-Mundi with his head-spikes—but also puzzled. "I'm—*uh*—the maintenance engineer for this section of the *Pelagic*. Something I can help you find?"

The Jedi Master gave him the best hostile stare he could manage. "I'm making sure this vessel won't fail us!"

The maintenance worker shrank beneath his withering gaze. He dared a response. "The barge has passed all its inspections. I mean—*uh*—the ones the Creds didn't pay to skip."

The glare persisted—and was accompanied by a hand gesture. "*You are wanted above decks.*"

"*I'm wanted above decks.*" The worker backed away and departed quickly.

In his time posing as a Staved Skull member, Ki-Adi-Mundi had learned that the head-spikes were indeed just a personal expression. The number was neither a rank nor a sign of murders committed or any other abhorrent statistic. But members of the gangs the Skulls had just allied with did not know that, and neither did the regular staff aboard the *Pelagic*. To them, the excesses of Yarael's makeup artist friend had made him into a figure of some import.

And ever since the members of the other gangs began arriving at Gutson's Pub, Ki-Adi-Mundi had been as likely to encounter a pirate who wasn't a Staved Skull as someone who was. That fact meant that his masquerade needed to continue, even if it meant missing the official start of the events at the arena.

In that time, he'd been able to convince a variety of people that he belonged, to the point that he had learned the *Pelagic*'s intended role in the uprising. The Filthy Creds had accepted him aboard with minimal Jedi legerdemain required, and it had further become apparent that the split in Skull leadership meant that even members of that faction weren't familiar with their own people.

He had since channeled much information to Plo Koon and his other colleagues—but the time for collection was past. Ki-Adi-Mundi had spent the recent minutes belowdecks, searching for the means to thwart the *Pelagic*'s communications with the pirates' minions.

He found the trunk communications line off an aft galley that wasn't in use. He'd knelt to begin his work when someone else interrupted.

It wasn't the maintenance worker. "*Hello, sweetie!*"

Ki-Adi-Mundi winced before welcoming the thought that Varralis was reconciled with her husband and highly unlikely to be aboard *Pelagic*. But what was behind him was so much worse. He emerged to see an elderly Chagrian woman decked out in gundark leather that had been stained jet black. She had done the same for her teeth, he saw. He rose and cleared his throat. "Were you addressing me?"

"Polite for a Skull. I'm Nanna Frouj." She pinched his cheek. "I run the Vile."

He thought to make a negative comment reflecting that he understood the rivalry between their two ostensible gangs, but all that came out was, "What do you want?"

"The war's going long," she said, releasing him. "I can't get anyone to make me a Flaming Tentacle!"

It took Ki-Adi-Mundi a second to process her statement. "Is that a refreshment?"

"This is a cruise ship, ain't it? A Pod Chaser, a Mandalorian Sling, anything." She wiped the sweat from her brow. "I've been stuck with the swill I brought aboard!"

The Jedi determined that she must not have disliked it too much, given how inebriated she appeared.

"The Creds never let the Vile aboard this thing—they say we're bad for business." She spat on the deck. "I mean, I know this ain't the *Halcyon*, but there's gotta be something." She looked at the open access panel—and scowled. "What've you got hidden down there?"

"Nothing. I am—er—looking for refreshment, the same as you."

"Typical Creds treatment. You even look important!" She reached up to touch one of his spikes. "That's a lot of metal. The Skulls certainly got their skulls' worth with you. You want to join forces?"

Repulsed, Ki-Adi-Mundi quickly disengaged. Then he spotted the silver door across the galley. "Yes! That's the freezer."

"Ooh, make me a Mygeeto Icebomb!" Nanna said. "Years since I've had one."

Ki-Ad-Mundi cycled the door of the walk-in refrigeration unit and was greeted with a blast of cold air. After so long belowdecks, he welcomed the change of temperature. The same was not true, however, for the adhesive holding the spikes Nanna had touched on his head. They began to fall off, one by one.

He looked down at them—and then at her. She cackled, gruesome belly laughs that unnerved him. "Looks like you just got demoted!"

She stopped laughing and produced a black blade from her sleeve. She lunged at him. He grabbed her wrists and tried to push her back, astonished at the strength she was showing. They struggled on their feet for several seconds, until he turned her around and shoved her. Nanna fell backward into the freezer, squealing. The sound stopped when he used the Force to shut the door.

He sealed it and hurried back to the conduit. He had worked a few moments when his comlink beeped. It was Yarael. "Still meeting interesting new people?"

"In a manner of speaking." He glanced back at the freezer. "The *Pelagic* is indeed the nerve center for this assault."

"Excellent! We're heading your way."

"There is no need for speed. I have just deactivated its communications. They may flee, but I doubt I will be able to do anything about that. I expect my actions will bring me attention before I can reach the engines."

"Don't worry. Oppo's got something in mind."

"Tell Master Rancisis I look forward to it."

He ended the call and began plucking the remaining spikes from his cranium. If retribution was coming, he would meet it as himself.

THE STORM OVER the Gem Cities had reached its crescendo, but the one aboard the skiff was just beginning. Kylah thought Zilastra was about to burst. Her former role model had driven Burlug to distraction, ordering him to drive the skiff one place, and then another, to check on her invasion.

Nothing was going as planned. The *Randomizer* hadn't landed its troops yet on Capital Key. Jodak was still keeping the frigate circling over the western ocean, waiting for the storm system over the islands to dissipate. It had turned out that a vessel dedicated to space piracy was not the best choice when it came to delivering assault troops.

Furthermore, reports had more than half the assault vehicles from the Windward Chain down in the water. Those that had landed had apparently run into "Jedi opposition." That was the entire message. Zilastra didn't know whether it was one or a hundred.

As near as Kylah could tell, the number didn't make any difference. Singular or plural, wherever the Jedi were active, the pirates were in disarray. Not losing—not yet—but the voices Zilastra was hearing were getting more frantic.

Until they stopped.

"Where's the message confirming the takeover of the space station? I should have gotten it by now."

"Maybe there's interference," Kylah said, trying to be as unhelpful as possible.

"It should have been over in a walk. And now the *Pelagic* isn't re-sponding."

"This is their skiff," Burlug said. "Have you tried the onboard?"

"Of course I tried the onboard!" Zilastra pounded on the device built into the console. "We're not getting anything!"

"Interference," Kylah said. "It's a killer."

Zilastra got in her face and yelled. "I will throw you over the side!"

"No, you won't." Kylah glared back. "Depa wouldn't like it. She and her friends are tearing your plan apart." She smirked. "She'll get to you. Be patient."

Zilastra let out a primal yell. She raised her hand to strike the girl, and Kylah flinched. But the pirate stopped short, and drew her hand back.

"I'm still going to win." Zilastra returned to her monitoring.

Kylah gritted her teeth. *Depa, wherever you are—don't stop looking!*

ON THE GROUNDS outside the arena, Adi Gallia deflected one blaster bolt after another. She leapt again and again, involving the benches, fountains, and statuary plinths of the plaza in her acrobatics. And she called upon the Force to aid her, shoving her opponents away or to the ground.

Her life had not been entirely without action. Most recently, she'd taken up arms against Lyal Lunn's attackers. But this was different. A reminder of earlier times on other worlds, when being a Jedi had meant more than meditation and bureaucracy. Places where lives rode on what she did in the next instant—and she could actually see the results.

And yet, as half a dozen enemies gave up their attack on her and turned to flee, her higher responsibilities spoke to her. And she knew she had to speak to her colleagues.

She saw Yoda and Yaddle across the grounds, the pair having just gotten a similar respite. "Masters, a word!"

Her elders approached her. "Yes, Master Gallia?" Yaddle asked.

"We have to think about tomorrow."

Yoda looked at Yaddle, and then to Adi. "Strange time for prognosti-cation, this is."

"I know," Adi said. "And we came here *not* to wrestle with the future. But we must." She pointed to the many injured pirates about. "We have to give the members of these bands a way out. Their attack is broken. Innocent people are going to leave the arena, these tents, their homes sooner or later. If we force the insurgents into last stands, they're going to find the islands strewn with bodies. We are defenders—that is all."

Yaddle nodded. "Agreed. We're clearing the battle zones, not scouring them. We can assist Kwenn's law enforcement officials once peace is restored."

"I'll inform the authorities," Adi said as she reached for her comlink. *And I'll let the chancellor or the Senate find out from someone else!*

CHAPTER 53

ALONGSIDE THE *PELAGIC*

KWENN

Oppo Rancisis had found the effort his colleagues had put into their visit to Kwenn profoundly gratifying. He knew they had not done it all for him, but he'd come to associate the world with himself to such a degree that it felt like it. It wasn't just the spirited defense they were putting up now—but also the little things that had led up to it, like Plo Koon and Saesee's work with the livery company.

One of their projects that had come to fruition was the conversion of a touring vehicle so that it would operate on land and on water equally well. Beyond being amphibious, it had the benefit of being light and relatively fast, while its open deck allowed his body to stretch out to its entire length comfortably.

Less comfortable was Yarael, who was hunched over the controls like an adult operating a child's toy vehicle. He was also soaked from the rain. Over the noise of the engine racing across the surf, he called out, "Tell me again why we told the driver to get out?"

"The Kwikhaul drivers have risked themselves enough. You know the danger we are entering!"

"Actually, I don't!"

There had been no time for Oppo to brief Yarael fully on his plan, and he doubted his colleague would have believed him anyway. "Master Ki-Adi-Mundi reports the command center is well defended. I would not risk others on a frontal assault."

Yarael pointed to the sky. "What about Master Windu? He's got a warship!"

"That is very busy. And a turbolaser strike on a civilian craft—even one with the passengers it carries—is something I cannot countenance. And if you have not forgotten—"

"Ki-Adi-Mundi is still aboard."

"If you know, why do you complain, old friend?"

"It's the will of the Force." Yarael held up his comlink. "Are you still with us, Master?"

"You might say I have moved from offense to defense," Ki-Adi-Mundi replied over the comlink. "My actions aboard the *Pelagic* have caused great confusion. Some of the leaders are accosting one another. And all are searching for me."

"Where are you now?"

"As long as they do not look for anyone lying on top of the sails flying above the ship, they will not find me. I simply need my dearest friends not to direct a warship to fire on me."

Yarael's smile crumpled. "You heard that, huh?"

"Whatever you plan to do, be ready. The engines are starting. They may have decided it is safer away from the coast."

Oppo tried his best to screen out distractions. His head hung over the side of the touring vessel, staring down at the water below. The ship was not touching the surface, but its noise likely was, and its shadow was certainly visible from below.

He saw another shadow, beneath. "Stop!"

The vessel slowed until it hovered in place.

"This is it."

Plo conveyed the news. "The *Pelagic* is pulling out. Making a break for open water!"

"Their mistake," Oppo said. He took a deep breath and removed his cloak. Then he dived overboard, his body snaking over the side as he went.

Gala Key separated their location from Malbaira, where the oroko nodule deposits had been looted. But that was not their home, as he had discovered days earlier. Gala Sound was the pod's territory—and while Oppo saw several oroko beneath the water, the being he sought came to greet him.

Kooroo-coo. I said I would visit again.

His words were thoughts, passing like tendrils through the Force—and as he pushed his hair from his face, the great creature swam beside him. Oppo gripped the oroko closely and concentrated. He realized he would have to communicate something complicated. Kooroo-coo understood that the Jedi Master was a separate, sentient being, but characterizing the sail barge as a vessel for other creatures was another intellectual jump.

A jump. That was the start. The oroko needed air, and knew that Oppo did, as well. Kooroo-coo broke the water, he and much of his bulk—his tagalong included—remained in air for several seconds, such was his might. The creature went back down. After two such jumps, Oppo nudged him to a position where he could see the sail barge advancing across the sound.

Hello, my friend.

A woot from the creature signified something like acknowledgment.

That not-flesh has been stealing your nodules!

A series of whoops—and the oroko took off, racing toward the *Pelagic*. And not just Kooroo-coo: Oppo realized several of the beasts were flanking them, following the lead of their proctor.

Less than a hundred meters from the hurtling casino, Oppo anticipated another dive and took the deepest breath he could. Kooroo-coo plunged down far, carrying his rider with him. Just as abruptly, the oroko rolled—and found the great shadow crossing above. The creature shot upward toward it, a missile of scales fired from the ocean.

The oroko broke the surface and pierced the *Pelagic*'s levitation cushion in one act. Its carapace slammed hard into the keel of the vessel with a colossal bang. Its companions impacted next, even as Oppo, clinging for dear life, rode Kooroo-coo back down.

Yes! Strike the non-flesh thief. Bar it from your waters!

After two more strikes, Oppo paused his suggestions long enough for the oroko to emerge in the vessel's wake. But Kooroo-coo's companions continued their efforts. Battered from beneath, the *Pelagic* left its cushion and flipped over, landing on its side in the water. Oppo watched as Ki-Adi-Mundi flew from the top sail into the waves.

"Quickly," Oppo said rather than thought. He and the oroko reached his colleague moments ahead of Yarael's arrival with the touring craft.

Oppo had once seen an oroko in its death throes. The *Pelagic* was going through the same motions. The repulsorlift generators groaned as they continued trying to operate, but all they did was cause the vessel to spin in place. After a minute of motion, Oppo saw occupants struggling to get out. They looked sickened.

Above, the last of the rain stopped, though the waterlogged Jedi barely noticed. He patted the side of the creature. "Thank you, Kooroo-coo. Earlier, we failed to protect what you valued—and yet you helped me save what I valued. Yours is truly the bigger soul."

He did not think the oroko would understand. But something in the Force told him otherwise.

FROM A PARKING spot on a promontory near the sea, Zilastra watched the fate of the *Pelagic* through her macrobinoculars. She found her mind wandering, perversely, to a visit to it years earlier. That was the time she'd learned that the Creds weren't running a square house—that in addition to the egregious rake they took from every game, they also had shill players who worked directly for them. It had angered her. Not for the offense against the game; the house deserved whatever it could get away with. It was more that the powers that be had decided she would be a loser before she turned a card.

Just like the Jedi.

She'd thought of overturning the table, then—killing everyone. Now, as she looked down from the skiff, she imagined that all the gaming tables in the casino had been overturned. Cards, credits, chips everywhere. They'd scammed their last marks.

And everyone was a loser. Five gangs were now united. All in the water, swimming away or clinging to the carcass of the would-be command center, all willing to take whatever rescue they could get from whoever was willing to offer it. That included a number of civilians, who had come out from hiding to offer assistance. It was the kind of spirit she'd needed to eliminate in order to turn Kwenn into the capital of the Free State of Zilastra.

But somehow, the people endured. They had hope.

She put down the macrobinoculars and sat down in the seat beside Burlug, defeated.

"You want to go?" he asked, the motor idling. "The *Randomizer* can probably make it in now."

Kylah was, for a change, silent. Zilastra thought over her options.

She looked off to the side. Through the haze, the clouds broke apart. Capital Key and Sanctuary Mount came into view.

She stood and snapped her fingers. "We can still get our win. Get me to the Jedi outpost!"

CHAPTER 54

ABOARD THE *RANDOMIZER*

OVER KWENN

"Finally, I can see something down there," ranted the pilot of the *Randomizer*, "and now Zil wants me to make a side trip first. This whole operation is a mess!"

"I quite agree." Advancing across the bridge of the frigate, Qui-Gon Jinn approached the hulking pilot, who was nearly too big for the enormous chair he was sitting in. "Are you Jodak?"

The pilot stopped entering coordinates and turned. Taller than Trandoshans or Saurins, Yinchorri had smooth, leathery snouts; the pilot's stuck out from beneath his mask like it was poking out of a shell. "I'm Jodak," he snapped. "Who's asking?"

"A faceless soldier to the cause," Qui-Gon said, patting his chest armor plate. He and Obi-Wan had both changed into gear they'd found so as to fit in with the passengers awaiting deployment on Capital Key. "My fellow travelers have elected me to represent their interests to you."

Jodak gawked at him—and looked around at the other Riftwalkers running consoles. "He says he's elected. Get this guy!"

Chuckles came from them. Qui-Gon forged ahead. "They'd like to lodge a complaint. We seem to have been circling for a very long time, under cramped conditions."

Jodak stood, looming over Qui-Gon. "I meant it. Get this guy *off my bridge!*"

Qui-Gon held up his hand, forestalling movement by Jodak or his crew. "There's a safety issue you should know about."

"Yeah?"

"As I said, you've been circling a long time—"

"That's for *your* safety, fool. Turns out that rockfall on Valboraan smashed our avionics package. With the storm's downdrafts, this thing could have landed with a thud. You want to do that with a hold full of people carrying bombs?"

"Well, that's part of the problem, as you'll see." He turned around and gestured. Lobber, Ghor, and Wungo entered, followed by Obi-Wan.

Jodak wasn't having it. "Oh, no. Get them off my bridge!"

Lobber was offended. "We're Riftwalkers, ain't we?"

"Zilastra warned me about you. Get back down with the others. The storm's ending. The landings will start soon!"

"I don't think there's time for that," Obi-Wan said. He spun Wungo around and indicated one of the explosive packs he was wearing. "As you can see, a timer has been set here—for one hour after your assault was to begin."

"All the packs have them," Ghor added, twirling around to show how many charges he was carrying.

Jodak's copilot looked at them with alarm. "Is it like that for all the troops aboard?"

The pilot glared. "No. It was just to make sure these buffoons bought it. She figured they'd wander around lost, looking for their target for at least that long. She was tired of them surviving."

"A kind and generous employer," Qui-Gon said. "I should say we've expended a good part of that hour circling."

"The storm's clearing. The landings will happen in time, even with the side trip Zil asked for."

"Except now that my friends are aware of the situation, they find that they don't want to continue in your employment."

"They *what?*"

"We quit," Lobber said. "I throw bombs. I ain't one!"

Jodak grew cross. "That's enough!"

Enormous green hands reached for Qui-Gon. The Jedi Master quickly drew and activated his lightsaber.

"A Jedi!"

"Two," Obi-Wan said, activating his. "I mean, two as far as you're concerned."

Jodak took a step back and looked over the bomb-laden trio. "You're not gonna tell me that these three are Jedi, too?"

Qui-Gon and Obi-Wan looked at each other, speechless. The others were not.

"Yeah," Lobber said. "Jedi!"

"I like that," Ghor piped in.

"*Master Wungo*," said the third with reverence.

Qui-Gon waved them off. "No, I don't think we can get away with that." He faced Jodak. "My student and I came here with a warning, but also to negotiate on these fellows' behalf."

"Negotiate?" Jodak snarled. "I've got a war to get back to!"

"I don't think I'd do that. Because as soon as Lobber and his friends realized the timers on the charges were active, they began shedding some of them." He added matter-of-factly: "*All over the ship.*"

"All over?"

Lobber nodded. "I didn't want all these things on me." He showed the satchels he was wearing. "I started with twice this many!"

Jodak's copilot panicked. "Bombs—with timers—all over the ship?"

"Relax," Jodak said. "We can turn them off."

Qui-Gon paced the bridge. "You certainly could turn them off—if you knew where they all were."

Jodak turned to Lobber. "You'd better tell us."

"I quit, remember?" Lobber crossed his arms. "Besides—I forget things."

"He does," Ghor said.

Wungo nodded. "Never calls his mother on her name day. Really, just a terrible person."

Jodak pointed toward the aft door. "I've got a hold full of people, ready to attack. They'll help search—and they'll take care of you, Jedi or not!"

"They might," Qui-Gon said. "But something's gone wrong with the doors to that sector of the ship."

Obi-Wan nodded. "Fused shut."

Jodak gawked at him. "Fused shut?"

"Yes. We suspect vandalism."

Qui-Gon nodded. "Very bad among pirates, I understand."

Jodak seethed for a moment—then his arms hung low beside him. "What do you want?"

Qui-Gon had the answer. "It's not a problem. We still remember where all the charges were—and my partner and I can deactivate them. But it will require concentration. We really can't be disturbed."

Ghor volunteered, "There's a cargo hold that's empty."

"Excellent. Jodak, you and the rest of the bridge crew are welcome to wait there—for your own safety—while we take care of this trifling matter."

The other members of the crew stood, compliant but incredulous before Qui-Gon.

"You're Jedi," Jodak said. "And you're helping *them* hijack this ship?"

The Jedi Master looked around. "From what I've been able to see, this vessel once belonged to someone else. I highly doubt you obtained it fairly. I think it's best that Lobber and his friends take control until all this is sorted out."

Lobber barged forward and pushed past the pilot. "Out of the way, loser!" He looked back to Qui-Gon. "Can we call the ship *The Lobber*?"

"I didn't agree to that," Ghor said.

"If that's the name," Wungo added, "I'm quitting—*again!*"

Obi-Wan smiled. "One negotiation at a time, friends."

DEPA HAD NOT arrived on Kwenn with everyone else, but she'd certainly gotten the tour.

She'd been accosted by attackers seconds after emerging from the arena—and whether Zilastra had planned it as a tactic to prevent her from giving chase or not, it had worked out that way. Freeing herself from that fracas, she'd availed herself of the landspeeder that Plo Koon had provided to search all across Gala Key, following leads that had come from his network. She'd always been too late.

On several occasions, she'd caught the trail only to have to leave it to save innocents from harm. On other occasions, she'd been forced to stop to defend herself. Others had more luck than she had; Yoda and Yaddle reported encountering a skiff and briefly battling someone who met Zilastra's description. They hadn't been able to pursue her, but they had confirmed that the pirate yet lived—and that she had a captive who did, as well.

But with the fight on Gala Key ending along with the storm, civilians were starting to peek out from their homes—and the few shelters that hadn't been evacuated overnight. And while the danger to the populace was not past, Depa felt the time to find Kylah was running out.

More of her colleagues were on the plaza outside the arena when she drove up. "Still nothing?" she asked Plo Koon.

He shook his head in sadness. "So many have needed rescue, relocation. It is possible some have seen the skiff who have not had time to report it."

"If they're even still in it."

One thing was certain, however: The skiff would not be returning to the *Pelagic*. Oppo, Yarael, and Ki-Adi-Mundi were still there, fishing would-be world conquerors out of the water; so many intent on owning this oceanic world had never learned how to swim.

Watching Adi Gallia working with the local constables, Depa looked down. Responsibility crashed in. There were still battles across the islands to fight, and they'd had scant reports from the confrontations in space. As much as she felt Zilastra posed a danger—to Kylah and everyone else—she was obliged to join her colleagues in putting the planet to rights.

"Ship coming in!" Yaddle called out.

Depa heard the shrieking engines as it approached—and recognized the battered starfighter as the one she'd flown on Valboraan. "It's Master Windu!"

The Jedi cleared people from a section of the plaza, creating a landing zone. Mace parked the ship and emerged.

Yoda greeted him first. "We could not reach you."

Mace gestured to score marks on his vehicle. "My relays are damaged—and the large one aboard the Kwenn Space Station is out. But the siege of it is broken, thanks to *Assurance,* which has fought admirably."

"I'm certain you did as well," Yaddle said.

Mace laid eyes on Depa. "How did it go?"

She explained that the plan to destroy the arena had been thwarted—but that Zilastra had escaped with Kylah. "We haven't been able to find the skiff."

"My fighter may have recorded traffic across a wider range during my descent," he said. "That, at least, is working."

She gave him back his lightsaber and took him up on the offer. She climbed into the cockpit. While Mace conferred with Adi and the others about the situation planetwide, she took a look at the last few minutes of data recorded by the Delta-7.

"What's this?" She refined the view. It appeared that over on Capital Key, an aerial contact was making its way slowly up the side of Sanctuary Mount. She called down to see if any of Plo's contacts had a visual on it.

He returned with comlink in hand soon after. "A driver reports a repulsorlift skiff struggling to make its way up the mountain."

Yaddle described the vehicle she and Yoda had encountered. "It's not a proper airspeeder—it would ascend only with great difficulty."

Depa realized something. "You moved the case—the one with the bomb—to the outpost. Is it still there?"

Adi nodded. "We haven't had time to move it. An attack was imminent. That was the farthest away from anything we could think of."

Depa understood. And she understood something else—and felt sick. "I told Zilastra we took it someplace safe. She could have easily guessed where."

"I'm calling the seneschal," Eeth said.

Whatever Zilastra intended, Depa knew someone needed to get to the outpost quickly. "Did you say Master Tiin was on Capital Key?"

"On the shore," Plo said. "The antique he was flying has declined to participate further." He pointed to the Delta-7. "You are sitting in the fastest conveyance available."

Depa's eyes widened.

Mace saw her expression. "Go."

"It's your fighter."

"You're already inside. You know Zilastra—and what she may do."

Feeling equal parts worried and thankful, Depa settled in and started the engines. She looked out to her former teacher. "You're sure?"

Mace handed his lightsaber back to her. "*Help one person.*"

CHAPTER 55

SANCTUARY MOUNT

KWENN

Zilastra had cursed everything about the Jedi countless times in her life. But never as many times in such swift succession as during the ride up Sanctuary Mount.

The Jedi two hundred years earlier had crafted a beautiful structure, but one devoid of practical means of ascent. There was no distinction between the artificial island's summit and the stonework outpost above it; no dividing line where one ended and the other began, and certainly no landing spot for an airspeeder or vehicle. The only way up or down was a narrow paved path winding all the way down to a plateau, beneath which the populated area of Capital Key began. The only way the skiff could make that trail was if Burlug carried it on his back.

None of her minions with more appropriate vehicles had answered her; most of her options had been lost in the carnage of the crossing earlier, and the survivors were either on the run or ignoring her. So they had ascended Sanctuary Mount sideways, tricking the skiff's repulsor-lift systems into thinking the vehicle was trying to hover laterally over an embankment—if one that was a kilometer high, and for ten minutes.

The generators on the left screamed from the strain, and there had been several momentary lapses when the whole skiff nearly fell.

"Finally!" Burlug yelled as the skiff reached the minor stretch of flatness that was the landing between the outpost's doorway and the path down the mountain. The skiff resisted being in the spot, a ledge too narrow for it to light upon. He could only hover there, jamming the right side against the outpost's outer wall. "If you're going, go!"

Zilastra climbed over the front railing and jumped onto the nose of the skiff. Sliding down, she slammed into the double doors, which opened against her weight. She tumbled down inside, lighting on the floor.

An old Bimm came down the ramp leading upstairs as she was trying to get up. "You mustn't come in here!"

She kicked him in the gut, causing him to double over in pain. When he did, she punched him in the head. Bleeding, he fell to the floor. Zilastra stepped forward and knelt over him, one leg over each side of the fallen Bimm. She pointed a blaster in his face. "Jedi?"

In pain and terror, her victim shook his head. "I'm . . . the caretaker."

"Take care, caretaker. If you're lying, you die." She looked around. "How many others are here?"

"Just . . . just me."

She rose and entered the main room. All around, crannies holding reference materials had been hewn into the columns. The contents stopped a couple of meters up, but the shelving spaces continued above.

She reentered the atrium and resumed her position over the Bimm. "What's your name?" she asked.

"Seneschal . . . Voh."

"Where is it?"

"Where is what?" He looked about wildly. "There are no weapons here. Only knowledge."

"Oh, there's a weapon here. The case."

"What?"

"The case. The Regal Voyager case." She pressed her knee on his neck. "Depa said the Jedi took it somewhere safe. Was it here?"

The Bimm coughed. "It was."

She pressed her knee.

"It . . . it is."

"Where?" She lessened her pressure.

"I moved it. Upstairs."

"What, to the top? With the big light?"

He shook his head, tears of pain and fright streaming from his eyes. "They told me . . . it was a dangerous thing. That they were only leaving it here . . . until it could be taken offworld. To be dealt with."

That rang true to her. The Jedi had certainly been busy.

"I was afraid . . . to have it near my library. So I took it to the attic. The crawl space . . . just beneath the level with the brazier."

"You're tiny. You carried it the whole way?"

"I have . . . a cart."

She looked up at the ramp and nodded. "Voh, there's a skiff hovering outside. You're going to crawl under it to the path—and head down the mountain. If I don't find what I'm looking for—"

"I . . . I understand. Please, just let me go."

She did, and he scrambled away, doing just as she'd said.

She looked outside to the skiff, where Burlug scowled. "Did a rodent just run underneath me?"

"More or less. Let him go. What I want is upstairs." She studied the skiff. She had already made an important call, but given how many people had failed her, she wanted options. "Will that thing hold out?"

He fussed with the controls. "We're lucky we got it to go this far. It needs to shed some weight."

"I have some suggestions," Kylah said.

"Start tearing off the railings—and throwing out the seats." She looked at Kylah. "We *won't* be taking any passengers."

"OUTPOST AHEAD," DEPA said. It was by rote rather than to anyone; the Delta-7's communicator wasn't working, as Mace had said. And she had found quite a few other faults in her short flight. Mace and *Assurance* had indeed been in the thick of it.

She saw the skiff, bobbing madly as it tried to hover in place just outside the doors of the outpost. Burlug stood in it. When he saw the advancing fighter, he began firing his blaster at her, all the while keeping his other hand on the control yoke. Unable to tell whether Kylah was on the floor inside it, Depa decided not to engage. She soared around the building, making a tight climbing arc.

There was no landing on the roof of the outpost; the weight of the fighter stood a good chance of collapsing the top of the lighthouse. But it could hover over it. She set the vessel on automatic and hoped that that, at least, was working. She opened the cockpit and threw out the emergency tether before clambering out. It wasn't likely to keep the ship hovering exactly in place in another storm, but it was something she could climb back up if needed.

Ignoring the wind and the height, she lit gingerly upon the roof of the outpost. She found the access panel in a few moments and climbed down through it. The massive cauldron stood before her: a durasteel disk within a ring, it burned a gas low in pollutants. The room was filled with fuel tanks, some large, some small.

She heard motion behind them. "Seneschal?"

"It's me," Kylah said. "Look out!"

Depa had no sooner seen the girl sitting on the floor, manacled to the large gas canisters, than the first blaster bolt struck. She had Mace's lightsaber out and activated in a heartbeat, but it was more than a glancing shot, and she staggered as she spun. Standing in the doorway leading down, Zilastra fired again at her with both blasters, mindless of any danger posed by the fuel tanks behind Depa. One shot singed the Jedi's leg; the other, her arm.

Depa winced—and threw all her energy into pushing, through the Force. Zilastra's back slammed into the wall behind her. The Jedi spun, directing the lightsaber against the chain connecting Kylah to the fuel tanks.

"It's okay," Depa said, staggered. "The shots . . . missed the fuel. They all . . . hit me."

In the entryway, Zilastra scrambled to right herself. "You're too late, Jedi!"

"Fire again . . . and you'll blow us all up!"

"Oh, you'll blow up." She gestured into the room with one of her blasters. "I kept Kylah alive for you, figuring you'd come. But we're not playing the hostage game anymore. You'll see when—"

"Shut up!" Kylah yelled. She hurled one of the expended canisters in Zilastra's direction. It clanged against the stone doorway, missing her—but it put any further conversation out of the pirate's mind. She disappeared, running down the ramp.

Depa moved to follow, but her injuries slowed her down. Kylah reached the doorway first.

"I think she's leaving," Depa said. "Did you see a small old person?"

"The Bimm? He left already."

"Then everything's all right. I found you."

"It's not all right. She found the case."

Depa struggled to focus beyond the pain. "She has the case now?"

"No. Come see!"

ZILASTRA HIT THE bottom of the ramp inside the outpost at a full run—before realizing she had to stop immediately. The nose of the skiff was directly outside the doors, hanging in midair while Burlug, still aboard, continued to rip metal from the craft.

He pulled up a durasteel plate and chucked it over the side. It plummeted down the mountain. "Hope you weren't looking for a place to sit!"

"I got what we want." She flashed her comlink—the one she hadn't left in the tower. "Hurry—the Jedi's upstairs!"

"What—*Depa*?"

"Yeah." She crawled over the prow and onto the skiff, which was barely more than a platform with a steering mechanism by now. "The stowaway's with her."

Burlug nodded as he moved to the controls. "Is she getting her out?"

Zilastra looked for a way to secure herself onto the diminished skiff. There wasn't any.

"Zil, I asked you a question. Is the Jedi going to get the kid out?"

"We're here to kill Jedi, Luggy!"

"The Jedi, not Kylah. I mean, I've done the strong-arm thing when you wanted to use her for leverage—or bait." Burlug looked up at the outpost. "But I figured you two would make up. She's just a kid."

She shouted at him. "What kind of business do you think we're in?"

He put up his hand. "All right. You're the boss."

"You're damn right." She checked the time. "I told the *Randomizer* to be here just about now."

Burlug looked to the sky. "I've been watching. I haven't seen—"

"Wait!" She spied the ship on the western horizon. "Perfect! Jodak's on the way!"

"He may not be able to land in the rain, but he can find the biggest mountain on the planet."

Zilastra laughed. "It'll all work out. They think they've won right now. But in a couple of minutes, everyone will see what I've done. And when our troops hit the ground, they'll see the Riftwalkers don't need anyone else's help to take this planet!"

CHAPTER 56

SANCTUARY MOUNT

KWENN

Depa needed Kylah's help both to exit the outpost's beacon room and to walk just several meters down the ramp. But that was as far as they needed to go to find what Kylah wanted to show her: an aperture barely a meter high on the inside wall of the spiraling tower.

"There it is," Kylah said.

Depa had seen it before. The seneschal called it "his attic"—a maintenance crawl space beneath the cauldron level where the pipes that fueled it could be serviced. Even the Bimm would have to double over to enter the area, she saw—and no one of taller stature could enter at all.

She held up her lightsaber to the opening. She could see the glint, well inside. "The case is in there."

"That's not all. When she was bringing me upstairs, Zilastra turned on a comlink and threw it in there, really far." Kylah's eyes were wide. "She's gonna—"

"I know. Same game, same gambit."

Kylah ducked and climbed into the space. "I can get it!"

Depa grasped at her. "No, don't!"

The girl looked back at her. "I can do this. I do small spaces in the dark all the time!" She dipped her head underneath a pipe. "We just need to get out the case—or find the comlink!"

They were both too far in, Depa saw. Zilastra wouldn't waste time—and she was probably on her way out of the building. "Come back, Kylah!"

"Zilastra said this building is your home. You have to save it!"

"We have to save ourselves. You saved me. I have to save *you*."

"I stole the case once. I can do it again!"

"No more!" Depa reached out with the Force and grabbed for Kylah. She dragged the girl toward her.

"I can do it!"

"No more," Depa said, grabbing her legs and hauling her out. "*This stops.*"

She held Kylah for a second. The girl had tears in her eyes. "We have to get out of here." Kylah looked up. "You came in something?"

"I don't think I can get back up there," Depa said, holding her midsection. "I don't think I can get you—"

She paused. There was something else in the attic space, just on the inside of the aperture. *The library cart!*

She fished inside and pulled it out. It must have been how the seneschal got the case up here. "You saw the path down the mountain, right?"

"It's a big spiral," Kylah said. "Like this ramp times a hundred."

Depa examined the ancient conveyance. The seneschal preferred it, she knew, because it could make the twisting turn by using the pull-handle on the way up and pushing it on the way down.

Depa used her lightsaber to cut the upper shelf off the cart, turning it into a wagon. She straddled the cart and sat down in it. "Here!"

Kylah got the idea. "Are you serious?"

"Deadly."

The girl sat in front of her.

"Take the handle. You're going to have to steer," Depa said. "I'll keep us off the walls as best I can."

"But what if the skiff's outside?"

"Then don't forget to duck!"

AS HAPPY AS Zilastra was to see the *Randomizer* approach, she couldn't understand why Jodak wasn't answering her calls. The ship approached the mountain as if flown by a droid following a programmed course.

The frigate came to a hovering stop in midair, two hundred meters west of the outpost—and at least twenty meters above their heads.

"You think he's drunk again?" Burlug asked. "Do they not see us?"

"Jodak! Descend and approach. We're right in front of the door!"

No answer.

Burlug covered his face. "I think what happened on Valboraan broke his brain. He's afraid to come near land of any kind."

"Jodak—or whoever's up there—I'm telling you for the last time!" She shook as she gripped the comlink. "Get that starboard air lock open and descend to us!"

Still nothing.

When movement came, it was from Burlug. He stood. "Long as we're waiting, I'm going for the kid."

Her head snapped toward him. "No!"

"I can do this." He clambered onto the prow, his heavy bulk causing the skiff to buffet in the air. "I'll go in, get her out. We're gone."

"You'll be gone! The Jedi's still alive in there!"

"So's the stowaway!" Burlug started to turn toward the doorway of the outpost, only for Zilastra to take his place behind the controls. She revved the engines, causing the skiff to bounce violently. Burlug lost his balance—and wound up hanging from the front of the skiff.

"What are you trying to do?" he shouted.

"Hang on!" Confident that he had a hold, she goosed the controls, causing the skiff to jerk away from the mountainside. No longer over the land, its repulsorlift generators strained—but she expected they'd be good enough for what she needed.

As Burlug tried to climb onto the prow, she guided the skiff upward and toward where the *Randomizer* was waiting. Windswept, the Feeorin cried out, "The motors are wrecked, Zil! You can't—"

She smiled as she gripped the yoke. "The hatch is opening! It's opening!"

The skiff wobbled in air just a few meters from the *Randomizer*. She could get Burlug aboard, and then herself. And there were already people in the air lock, waiting to help them—

No.

"Welcome to our ship," called out Lobber.

"Thanks for applying," shouted Ghor.

"I'm afraid," Wungo yelled. "I'm afraid we're full up!"

They stepped back inside and the air lock slammed shut.

Zilastra screamed in rage, her powerful hands crushing the control yoke and snapping it to pieces. Suddenly uncontrolled, the vehicle yawed, throwing her onto her side—and doing something else. Burlug yelled as he was slung into the blue.

"Luggy!"

The Feeorin had already fallen hundreds of meters when she caught sight of him, plummeting. The last she saw of him was when he struck the mountainside.

"No, no, no!" Zilastra looked back at the *Randomizer*, which was quickly ascending even as the skiff continued its spin. There was nothing she could do—save the one thing she had come to do.

She found her comlink, called the one she'd abandoned, and yelled, *"The Jedi stand with you!"*

The outpost exploded, the upper levels tearing themselves apart in a blinding flash. The shock wave took the skiff—and Zilastra's world went from white to black.

"EVASIVE ACTION!"

On the *Randomizer*'s bridge, Qui-Gon quickly put the frigate into motion even as Obi-Wan raised the ship's shields. The blast was a possible outcome, he'd known; on informing Mace of their takeover of the ship, he'd warned them that Depa had gone to the outpost, looking for an explosive. Since Jodak's last course was taking the *Randomizer* to the same place, they'd gone along for the ride.

But it had taken more time than they'd expected to bypass Jodak's authorizations. Enough that before the *Randomizer* could approach the tower and the still-hovering starfighter, the outpost had blown itself apart, consuming the Delta-7 in the blast.

But as the rest of the stone edifice crumbled into cloud, Qui-Gon wasn't ready to give up.

"We're shaken, but undamaged," Obi-Wan said.

"Then hold on to something. We're going in!"

DEPA HAD ALWAYS suspected there was a point in the life cycle for most species at which a raucous, thrilling experience stopped being enjoyable and became a thing to be feared, instead. She'd also noted that Jedi training had the effect of delaying that changeover, sometimes indefinitely.

She couldn't remember there ever being a time in her life in which she would have enjoyed the prospect of rolling with another person in a wagon down a ramp that spiraled down a tall building, out the door, and then down an even longer spiral down a mountain. And yet Kylah had hooted the whole way, long after her voice was no longer audible. Even after the flash from the explosion made seeing their way momentarily impossible—and after the dual shock waves, through the air and the mountain itself, caused their wagon to momentarily leap from the path.

Not seeing tomorrow—or the next second—was the youngling's secret power, as Yoda had once told her. But he had put it another way.

Depa's mind had been on keeping them flying off into infinity—and hoping that the wheels would not disintegrate. Yet as she held on to Kylah, she knew that the ride had to end, due to either the avalanche of debris falling down Sanctuary Mount or a turn below they would never make.

Or dizziness. *Was that a spaceship?*

She said "hold on" for what must have been the twentieth time when everything happened at once. At a sharp bend, the craftwork of the ancient cart finally gave way. It flew apart beneath the pair, sending first Kylah flying—and then Depa.

The Jedi Master felt as though she would never hit the ground.

And then she realized she hadn't.

Plo Koon, Mace, and Yoda stood inside a landspeeder, their hands raised. Together, they brought her down.

Wobblier than she'd ever felt, Depa looked around breathlessly. "Kylah! Where's Kylah?"

Yoda pointed up.

She looked to see the *Randomizer* hovering over the hillside, not far from where the rockfall had terminated. Qui-Gon and Obi-Wan stood in the open air lock. The Jedi Master's arm was outstretched, and he slowly brought Kylah to the ground.

"Thank you both," Depa said.

"It's none of my doing," Obi-Wan said of his master. "Catching children is *his* specialty."

Mace cupped his hands and called out to Qui-Gon. "You still have hostile forces aboard. Should we intervene?"

"Thank you," Qui-Gon said, "but we saw a nice deserted island on the way in. I was thinking we'd let them out there. They *are* expecting a landing."

"Heavily armed, they are," Yoda said. "And many are rivals."

"Then they may take the day to learn to respect one another," Plo said. "The Force will have its way. Just as it brought the seneschal back to us. He is receiving care now."

Depa needed her own medical attention, but she stopped first to embrace Kylah. Then she had another thought, and looked up at Qui-Gon and Obi-Wan. "Wait. With you two there, who's operating the ship?"

Qui-Gon and Obi-Wan looked at each other for a moment. Then the master spoke quickly. "Er—that would take time to explain."

"Oh, no," Obi-Wan said, disappearing into the ship.

"Oh, yes," Qui-Gon said. He closed the hatch behind him.

CHAPTER 57

CAPITAL KEY

KWENN

Zilastra had shown Jedi no mercy. And yet it was the mercy of a Jedi that had saved Zilastra.

Depa had not been that Jedi.

Earlier in the very long day, Saesee Tiin had alerted Kwenn's sea rescuers that many would-be pirates would be going down with their ships—or, rather, their airspeeders—as they approached their targets. And while the terrorized responders had not been able to act at that moment, they had acted, showing decency to those who would show them none.

Including to one pirate who crashed into the sea hours after the battle started, having been caught between a half-functioning skiff and a colossal explosion. The *Pelagic*'s skiff had gone down in waters many kilometers from where the parent vessel had, but before its demise it had returned to functioning just long enough to cushion the landing of the unconscious person aboard. The mastermind of the insurrection, whose artificial hands were locked in a death-grip on the broken stalk of the control yoke.

With the sun sinking over the Windward Chain, the paramedic

droids on the beach withdrew. Depa stepped over and snapped two sets of electrocuffs on Zilastra, getting both her wrists and forearms. There was no telling what she might do to free herself.

Yet the Nautolan, beaten and battered, offered no resistance at all. Perhaps it was from her ordeal, Depa thought. But more likely, it was from the company.

All twelve members of the Council had arrived on the beach, surrounding the prisoner. It was no intentional show of strength nor an attempt to intimidate. Depa thought they were simply curious, wanting to understand what could make someone act as she had.

Depa had to admit she wasn't that interested.

"It's over, Zilastra. The alliance is broken." Depa peered at her. "*You're* broken."

Sitting up on the beach, Zilastra coughed. "Go ahead. Kill me. I've been killing you."

Oppo stared at her. "*Why* have you been killing Jedi?"

"You took my friends from me. And you left me. Left me in a hell-hole."

Depa explained. "Her only friends were recruited by the Jedi, leaving her alone."

"When was this?" Adi Gallia asked.

"Nearly thirty years ago," Zilastra said, a snarl in her voice. "A Jedi came to visit our hovel called an orphanage. Talked to the droid and took away my friends. And didn't care whether I lived or died!"

Mace scowled. "Thirty years. Who did this?"

She looked over at him. "He forgot me—but I'll never forget the name. *Sifo-Dyas!*"

Yaddle put her hand over her mouth. Some of the other Jedi suppressed gasps.

"What, you know him?" Zilastra asked.

"Master Sifo-Dyas was a powerful Jedi," Yaddle said. "Powerful, yes. Great at many things—including prognostication."

Mace nodded. "He was exceptionally focused on the future of the Order. Sometimes to the exclusion of his other duties."

"It impacted his recruiting," Eeth said. "He would learn of children he suspected had Jedi skills—and he would urgently try to bring them into the fold."

"*Too* urgently," Piell added. "He was always in a big damn hurry. Like the Republic would end if he didn't swell the ranks."

"Well, he was in and out in a day," Zilastra said. "I've known starship dealers that weren't as high-pressure!"

Yarael shook his head. "Sifo-Dyas should have taken time to learn more about your situation. Our Council has rules about these things."

"Jedi never separate families lightly," Oppo said, "or any people who depend on one another. When possible, we call on other services to help those who remain, so things are not made worse."

Zilastra sputtered. "*Services?* There were no services where we lived!"

"And that is sometimes the case," Plo Koon said. "Sifo-Dyas should have taken that into account. We would have. He often did not."

Ki-Adi-Mundi frowned. "Indeed, sometimes those he brought to us were not even viable candidates."

Zilastra looked as if she couldn't believe what she was hearing. "Wait. Are you saying my friends might not have even become Jedi?"

"We'd have to consult the records," Saesee said. "But I know this. There are procedures. He wasn't following them. We asked that he no longer recruit."

Yoda looked somber. "In the end, he left the Council."

Zilastra exploded. "*He was on the Council?*"

"Was," Adi emphasized. "As we said. We have rules."

Zilastra shook her head. "That doesn't make it better. None of this makes it better. That makes it worse!"

For the first time since they'd met, Depa looked on her with pity. "It shouldn't have happened that way. And for that, we are sorry. But it wasn't worth everything else you've done. To Xaran Raal—and what you tried to do to Kylah and to Kwenn. Other people are not the canvas on which you can paint your grief."

Zilastra stared at her.

Then she looked to the side. "Beautiful sunset."

"You must learn, if more you would see." Yoda nodded to the constables, who led Zilastra away. The Jedi watched her until she was out of sight.

PEOPLE ON KWENN, Depa thought, had probably forgotten about a lot of things that day, given the tumult. But there was one big thing the Jedi could not neglect: the twenty thousand people they'd left behind earlier in the arena, not to mention those who had sheltered in other places.

By that point, many on Kwenn had seen the heroics of the Jedi. The pirates had been routed, and all offworld forces had fled. Local would-be menaces had gone into hiding, or simply home. But people had also seen the destruction of the outpost. This night, for the first time in centuries, the Unquenchable Flame would not light the sky.

Yaddle, who had been the spokesbeing all along, determined to address it—and the day's events—back in Gala Key Arena, after everyone in the audience had been fed. The Jedi found that Morna had indeed kept everyone calm and in place, interviewing people from the eldest citizens of Kwenn all the way down to Piell's kids. Panic had been prevented in the facility and planetwide, allowing the Jedi, the constables, and the responders to do their work.

The meeting had already been convened earlier; now, with all twelve present, they took their seats, facing one another in a circle, while a newly resilient Morna and her crew broadcast the event to the world.

And then—all at once—the Jedi rose. In one move, they used the Force to lift their chairs and turn them to face the audience. The crowd roared with approval.

"This is how we always intended this meeting to run," Yaddle said. "This meeting—it is our meeting, with you. We understand there is pain on Kwenn, and in the surrounding places. We understand there is fear for the future. And we understand that—while the Jedi outpost may not always have been occupied, its presence signified a bond to you."

Oppo spoke. "The bond is not broken, though the building is. We understand that now, more than ever. And so we will *not* be rebuilding the outpost."

Gasps came from the crowd.

"We will not rebuild it, because it was only stone, with Jedi you could not see. In the future, we will make sure you can see the Jedi. They will be here more often. They will walk among you. And we will share one another's courage."

Mace nodded. "*Every Jedi is an outpost.* And that is our commitment."

"But you need not miss the light," Adi said. "Instead of the processional we sought to lead to the outpost today, we will clear the top of Sanctuary Mount and install a new brazier. And you, the people, will light it every night." She smiled. "A parade every day, if you want it."

Depa, who had been through so much, barely felt she could add anything. But seeing Kylah just offstage, marveling at the ceremony, she found the words.

"I left my home in this region when I was very young. But I found my people—and there, my home. If you find your people, you're never alone. And you will never be lost."

"With you all, the Force will be," Yoda said. And then, giving a little smile to Depa, he added, "*The Jedi stand with you.*"

PART FOUR
THE JOYFUL RETURN

CHAPTER 58

CAPITAL KEY

KWENN

It was the Council's last day on Kwenn, and Zilastra's first day as a ward of the state. Any state. That it was not *her* state went without saying.

Since being processed into the Republic Judiciary Regional Detention Center on Kwenn, she'd found out a lot about what had happened. She understood, at last, that the *Randomizer* had been taken by Jedi who'd systematically isolated and then expelled her crew and passengers. As much as she hated the thought of her flagship in Jedi hands, it was some small relief to know that her crew had not been bested by Lobber and his friends alone.

She knew nothing of the ship's fate after that, other than that the authorities had found her sabacc deck aboard the *Randomizer,* and had returned it to her. They'd found Depa's lightsaber in the same place; Zilastra imagined they'd returned that, too. She didn't really care. The cards were all she wanted.

The Riftwalkers were history. The band had come to prominence overnight due to her Regal Voyager gambit; it had disintegrated just as quickly after the tactic failed to eliminate the Jedi. That was all part of the game, she knew.

Don't bet what you can't afford to lose.

She'd gotten news the night before about her toughest loss: Burlug. There were remarkably few casualties in the incident, but he was one, his body having been found on the slope beneath Sanctuary Mount. Luggy had been her minion, her confidant, her protector—and the first person who really thought she could run her own outfit. She didn't blame herself for his death, or even the Jedi. It was the ineptitude of the allied gangs that had put them in a bind, forced her to the outpost. She could hear him advising against the whole business.

The Jedi had not told her whether her childhood friends yet lived, and she had not asked. She doubted they'd have responded in any case. The Order had ample reasons to fear that Zilastra might not receive them warmly—indeed, that she might take revenge against them. That was nonsense. She'd never made any specific effort to find her friends while she was free. They were as dead to her as she likely was to them. It was the Jedi Order itself she hated.

They'd transferred her to solitary confinement, which hadn't surprised her. Part of her crime had been in associating with and organizing other criminals. She had no markers to call in, no patrons to call upon. Her life wouldn't change until the government did, on Kwenn or on Coruscant. The first might still happen. The second, she couldn't foresee ever happening.

All that was left to her were her sabacc cards—and patience games. She'd never realized how appropriate that name was before. But she could play anything. She would cope.

Zilastra sorted the cards for divination, hoping to see something good. The Queen of Air and Darkness was too much to hope for; Demise was too miserable to contemplate. All the flasks, coins, staves, and sabers were just more Idiots to her now. That didn't leave much.

She flipped up a card.

Endurance.

She could live with that. She would have to.

IT WAS THE Council's last day on Kwenn, and Adi Gallia's last day of freedom. She knew, of course, that freedom was relative. She'd helped to convey many of the ringleaders into custody, as well as several people whose crimes during the revolt were too violent to overlook. But even that act felt different from her normal bureaucratic work back on Coruscant. Here, she actually saw the people who would appear as statistics back home. Some of them, she had apprehended herself.

But to all things, an end must come. She chuckled over the thought she'd just had.

"Something funny?" Yoda asked.

"Just realizing that even my thoughts are starting to sound like you." She smiled. "Never mind."

She would be the first to leave, it had been decided—such was the workload waiting for her. Yoda had escorted her to the spaceport, and the private ship set to carry her back.

"The flight was donated by Regal Voyager," she said. "Everything was an absolute surprise to them. All they knew is that their ships had been traveling safely, and their case inventory had been raided."

"Unscathed, they were."

"I think they're hoping we'll book more Jedi on their flights now that the pirates' bargain is done. I told them the Jedi Order wasn't—" She stopped and put the palm of her hand on her forehead. "I'm already back home in my head, aren't I?"

"Mm." Yoda tugged at her cloak to stop their walk. "Master Gallia—regret, I have."

Her brow furrowed. "Not over the celebration?"

"Over you. On Kwenn, and on Coruscant. I have taken too much advantage of your skills."

She smiled. "Master Yoda, that's what they're there for."

"No. Learned them, you did, to become a Jedi Knight. A Jedi Master. Now a member of the Jedi Council. Too much, have I burdened you with."

She looked disappointed. "Master, I am equal to whatever you require."

"My requirements? Irrelevant! Mine and those of the chancellor or senators. You serve the Force." Yoda looked down and shook his head. "Old, have I become. Tired of the routines."

"And that is why you needed to be free, Master, to focus on more important things. To guide us."

"No!" He gazed up at her. "I look on you to guide us. You, and the younger masters. Oppo, Yaddle, Yarael, and I—much have we seen, and done. Your turn, it is."

Adi chuckled and raised her index finger. "You always said a Jedi does not seek adventure."

"Neither does one seek boredom." Yoda gestured with his walking stick. "Different, the world looks, to young eyes. *That* is what we need."

Behind her, the engines of the Regal Voyager yacht fired up.

Yoda spoke over the noise. "When I reach Coruscant, changes will be made. Burdens, shared differently."

She understood him. "Thank you." She turned and boarded her flight.

DURING THE TAXI ride, since watching Adi depart, Yoda thought about what he'd said. He'd meant all of it, but he also knew events often foiled his best intentions. A Jedi could spend every waking moment attempting to predict such things, and then something would still arise, making a liar of one's past self. Eight-plus centuries had taught him to expect that—but that was no reason to give up on attempting to make things better.

He might tell Padawans that trying wasn't good enough. But never trying wasn't good at all.

Yoda had one more thing he definitely intended to accomplish before leaving Kwenn, and he made it his next stop. Lyal Lunn had initially gone to the intensive care medical center on Rayley Key, and from all reports, he had rallied just as the attack on Kwenn concluded. Not only had he regained consciousness, but he was well enough to sit in a repulsorlift chair on one of the hospital's balconies, overlooking the parklands below.

"Master Yoda!" Lyal brightened as he saw his visitor arrive.

"It is good to see you again." Yoda glanced at Lyal's new companion, the medical droid that had been purchased for Erwen Lunn. "And you, as well."

Lyal attempted to rise to greet Yoda, but the droid gently placed a hand on his shoulder, reminding the man of his injuries. It was good to see the family getting some use out of the droid—if not as Lyal had planned. Yoda advanced to a position near the patient.

"They've been showing me the holos of what happened and what you did. It was amazing." Lyal lowered his voice. "And thank you so much for the droid—and visiting my father."

"A wonderful companion, he was."

Lyal took that description in and nodded. "Yeah, he was."

The Sullustan looked down from the balcony. The promontory at the end of the Paths of Harmony was on one of the lower terraces. "We're going to have a memorial service for my father over there—once I get out of here. He so loved that place." He looked out toward Sanctuary Mount. "The building's gone, but the mountain remains."

"And the sunsets."

Lyal nodded. "Of course, I probably won't get out of here for more than that. I have to pay for what I did. What nearly happened—what I nearly let happen—was horrible." He looked away from Yoda. "I swear, Master, I had no idea they planned to hurt anyone. I never—" Tears flowed, and Lyal shook his head. "No, that's not true. I was letting them hurt people already. All that's wrong on these islands—and I was making it worse. I was . . ."

Yoda spoke. "You *were* wrong, Lyal. But warned me, you did."

"But—but I didn't tell you sooner. And I didn't tell you all I could have."

"You tried. That matters."

Yoda changed the subject to the Jedi's adventures on Kwenn, to the Sullustan's recovery, and to a project that he and Yaddle had considered worthwhile, in which they both envisioned a role for Lyal.

"A way, there is, for you to remember your father—and help the people of Kwenn. If you are interested."

Lyal beamed, seeming renewed. "Whatever it is, Master Yoda—I will try."

Yoda started to say something. But he just held Lyal's hand instead.

THE MOUNTAIN BENEATH the Jedi outpost had started as a pile of debris. The peak was that again, its upper reaches covered with the remains of the structure.

It pained Oppo Rancisis to see it, but the plans they'd announced for the site were a restorative. A crew was already picking through the wreckage, preparing to clear the area for a future monument.

He had said goodbye earlier to Kooroo-coo and the oroko, whose lives he had become part of for too brief a time. He regretted now all the hours he'd spent in the outpost over the years, instead of in the sea. He hoped to change that in the future.

But there was someone who had spent even more hours in the outpost, and that reminded Oppo he had a farewell yet to deliver. He saw Seneschal Voh, bandaged from where Zilastra had injured him. The old Bimm stood plaintively by as workers continued to bring out piles of rubble.

"There is nothing to find," Voh said when he noticed Oppo beside him.

"There is something," Oppo said. "I was just informed part of the brazier was found intact in the ocean. It can be made part of the new Unquenchable Flame, reminding people of the outpost that was."

The news didn't seem to assuage Voh's sadness. "All that remains from the library is what little material Master Koth was able to recover elsewhere."

"Ah, yes—in the Lamplighter Boutique. And it was of little account, I am told."

Voh looked down. "I'm sorry your visit came to this, Master."

"I greatly enjoyed my time with the oroko. And many of my colleagues took the opportunity to get back in touch with a side of being Jedi that we do not often get to experience. This has been a grand journey."

The seneschal stared at him. "Are you serious?"

"Pardon?"

"I'm sorry, Master. But *what*?"

Oppo had no idea what Voh was upset about, and said so.

"I've spent decades caring for that building. Protecting it. Then when you all arrived, you were barely here, except to sleep. The scoundrels destroyed it—and you're not only not going to rebuild it, but you're celebrating that fact. And this you call a grand journey?"

"The brazier will remain. It will be tended to by the people—"

"Not by me. You made a point of that!" He gestured to the wreckage. "Zilastra just did for you what you were going to do anyway!"

Oppo stared at him. It was highly inappropriate for a Jedi retainer to speak to a master, much less a member of the Council, in this way. But Voh had suffered physically, and his long and devoted service had to be recognized.

"I apologize, Seneschal. We assumed you were seeking retirement. We are, of course, prepared to create a role for you here, if this is where you choose to remain."

"Doing what? Standing around while the tender of the day lights the fire?" Voh shook his head. "Having the outpost shut down would have been better."

The Bimm turned and looked off into the distance. Oppo watched him for several moments—and cursed his own farsightedness.

"In watching the future, I have failed to see what was near." Oppo put a hand on Voh's shoulder. "It is a hazard of my age, and of being on the Council. It is why we came here, in fact. It makes no difference, I am sure—but I grieve the loss of the outpost. Its fine library and the many works of the being who tended it."

Voh looked back, visibly shaken and appearing more than a little ashamed at his outburst. "It was a great place, wasn't it?"

"It was. And its legacy lives on in the careers of every Jedi who visited. Those you have served, and nourished and educated and cared for. That is something for which you can be proud. The Jedi salute you."

CHAPTER 59

ESSAFA KEY

KWENN

School was in session on Essafa Key. Even Piell had seen several of his works come to fruition in short order, and he expected the Council's feats on Kwenn, and the attention they had brought to the planet, were the reason.

The Mercantile Guild had come through with funding for the school system, while Rendili Hyperworks had restarted its lunch program. Piell still wasn't comfortable with the way education worked on the planet, but it wasn't his place to rethink how a planetary society had organized things. He just wanted to make sure the kids were all right.

It turned out they were all inside when he walked across the quad. That was well. All but one Twi'lek student, who ran across the yard, before him.

"Master Piell!" Hadaro stopped in front of him.

"Running from someone?"

The kid nodded in the direction of the building. "I'm late."

"Late is good," Piell said. "Late means you're going."

"Yeah, why not?" The teen shrugged. "We had a deal. And you've shown us all that some of the other ways to make a living on this planet don't work out so well."

Piell shook his hand. "I'm just glad you all kept everyone inside the arena during the battle. I'm sure it was tempting to peek outside."

"Oh, no. We were all watching on our datapads."

Piell looked at him—and laughed, long and loud. "The smart way to see a fight." He slapped the kid on the back. "Get inside before I remember I'm the truant officer."

"THAT'S GOT IT. Give it a try."

Seated inside the ARC-8 starfighter, Plo Koon responded to Saesee's request by pressing the activator. The engine started. "You've done it again, Master."

Outside, Saesee closed the panel on the hull. "That's fine. Shut it down and get out before Fraxa sees we've left fingerprints on the thing."

Plo did as instructed. He didn't think the owner of Kwikhaul would object, as Saesee had brought her precious antique back in one piece. And they had saved her business to boot.

Saesee gave one last look at the fighter and growled. "Too many wings."

The two walked from the hangar onto the corporate grounds. The place was abuzz with activity. Repairs were being made to repulsorcraft damaged in the fracas—and assignments were going out to employees, both organic and metallic.

Plo liked what he saw. "We can take satisfaction in this. Our work with the livery company allowed us to assist many—and they repaid us with their efforts to protect this planet. A worthwhile visit in every way."

"I suppose."

Plo turned to look at Saesee. "What is wrong now?"

"I have to get home and finish upgrading the surface vehicle pool—and figure out what's wrong with the software on the spaceships. Qui-Gon said he had to drop his shuttle out of hyperspace near Valboraan for a mechanical check."

"Yes, that was how he heard Kylah Lohmata's call."

"Hmm. Still, a check like that shouldn't have been necessary."

"It was good fortune, yet you quarrel with it," Plo said. "Never mind. I suppose you have a theory."

"At least five."

"And the Republic will fall if you do not explore every one of them in a week's time."

Saesee glowered at him. "Yes, the Republic will fall."

"You've had one of Sifo-Dyas's dread visions?"

"No. I just know. I have to get home and get to work."

Plo's sigh could be heard through his respirator. "I had hoped to see a different Saesee Tiin on this trip."

"I'm sure there's someone else by that name on this planet. Maybe you didn't look hard enough."

"Amusing." Plo studied him. "You *were* skeptical of this initiative."

"We are not mere Jedi Knights anymore. We have larger responsibilities."

"You say that, and it is true. But . . ."

Plo didn't finish the sentence.

Saesee glared at him. "Trouble with your regulator?"

"No."

"Then spit it out. 'But' what?"

"But as a member of the Council, you have managed to devote yourself to duties that allow you to practice the skills you used as a Jedi Padawan, as a Jedi Knight, as a Jedi Master. Flight. Mechanics. Fighter operation."

"What of it?" Saesee shrugged. "I know what I'm doing. You don't forget how to load a torpedo—or fire one—just because you advance."

"Of course not. And by that token, neither do you forget how to interact with the people, to help them directly. Saesee the Padawan knew."

Saesee snorted. "I was a *frustrating* Padawan. I never listened, never took to the public part of things." He crossed his arms. "*I* never would have advanced me."

"And yet that happened—again and again and again." Plo stepped before him. "We are not Yoda and Yaddle, able to speak in comforting tones. People fear my appearance. You, they simply fear."

Saesee raised an eyebrow. "Is there a point?"

"The point is that people sometimes need comforting tones—but then other times they need something else. To hear the truth directly, from someone who does not cushion the blow. To hear from someone who assumes that all living beings should strive for competence—and who expects people to learn from their mistakes. When that is what they need, Saesee Tiin must be ready." He paused. "It would be a terrible shame if he was always unavailable, in the conference chamber, garage, or hangar."

Saesee stared at him for several moments. Then he muttered, "Competence is not enough."

Plo took a step back—and laughed. "As much a motto for you as *May the Force be with you* is for the Jedi. Heartfelt and truly told." He clapped a surprised Saesee on the shoulder. "I embrace it. It will be *my* mantra, too."

"Hmph."

Plo strode away. Rows of workers cheered him as he walked by. He waved to them. "Farewell, Kwikhaul crew. And always remember: *Competence is not enough!*"

EETH KOTH HAD found that taking his leave of Kwenn was harder than he'd thought. He'd had to leave the work in the Lamplighter Boutique unfinished; even Yaddle and Piell's late assistance had only made a partial dent in the shop owner's accumulations of a lifetime. But it was clear that what they'd found there was of minimal interest. There was no sense committing even a Padawan's time to the place.

Pogee Shrag had not wanted to see him depart, and she'd insisted he take one of her favorite boolahs with him. When he pointed out that he already had three hanging from his sleeves, she'd accused him of being greedy, and had taken them all back. At least the woman didn't play favorites. She loved every one of the animals. He hoped for her sake that when they destroyed her home, she would escape without injury.

Opting for a commercial flight, Eeth sat at the spaceport bar musing over the incidents of the visit. He wasn't expecting company—and certainly not Inisa. She was dressed in conservative traveling garb, and it took him a second to recognize her. But she certainly recognized him.

"I see you're leaving," she said, setting her bag down next to the seat beside him.

"I see you are, as well."

"I see *you* everywhere."

He didn't know how to respond to that—until she gestured to the holovid running behind the bar, depicting the combat outside the arena. He bowed his head. "I suppose I have gotten a sudden notoriety."

"Notoriety, I like." She sat beside him and said his name like she was trying it on for size. "*Master Eeth Koth.* You didn't tell me you were on the Jedi Council."

"It's where my calling led." He looked to her bag. "Where are you going?"

"I'm going to take the next flight and see where it leads. I thought I'd fly Regal Voyager. Nobody seems to mess with their transports." She gestured to her bag. "I was going to get one of their security cases, but for some reason they've impounded them all."

Eeth decided against explaining. "What will you do?"

"Something else. I don't know. I haven't thought of it. But the Blades aren't in business anymore, and I'm doubting that whoever follows them will be any better." She looked at him. "Where are *you* going?"

"Home. Coruscant."

"To a big Jedi Temple."

"It is that. With the destruction of the outpost, many reports must be filed. The Jedi Order has a great interest in keeping track of things."

"That sounds like a lot of work."

Eeth couldn't disagree. "It is."

"You need a vacation."

"I have just had one."

Inisa smirked. "This is what you call a vacation?"

"Some of it." Eeth looked around. "I am thinking of making a change, myself."

"Oh?"

"I will step aside from keeping the outpost closure records. It was an important duty. But it is time to give someone else a chance."

"I'm glad. I can tell when someone's had enough with part of their life."

Eeth studied her. "Is that why you called me to warn me? You'd had enough?"

"I didn't want to see anyone get hurt."

He nodded—only to realize after a moment that he didn't accept the answer.

She watched his eyes. "What?"

"I'm sorry, but you knew what the Poisoned Blades were. You had to know they hurt people often."

She looked away. "Yeah, I knew."

"So—"

"So I didn't want to see you get hurt, okay?" She faced him. "What, do people not get to care what happens to individual Jedi?"

Eeth was taken aback.

"What?" she asked. "A difficult question?"

"No," he said, brow furrowing. "But when you put it that way, I've never thought about it. I suppose people *can* care about what happens to individual Jedi."

"But you don't get to care back."

"Oh, we certainly care," Eeth said. "But in the context of caring for all life."

"All life." She smirked. "So, like trees? Fungus? Attorneys?"

"Sort of."

"That's flattering. I guess I'm included, then. But you don't get more specific."

He shook his head. "It's kind of in the by-laws."

The announcement for her flight came. She stood. "I'll tell you what, Master. I'll care what happens to you. And if you're making the rounds, checking on the welfare of the wildlife and the ferns, I'll be happy to tell you how I'm doing."

She shared some data with his communications device. Eeth stared. "You're giving me *your* contact information?"

"Just for your official records." She finished and took her bag. "Safe flight, Eeth."

"And you, Inisa."

He watched her go. Then he headed for his boarding bay.

CHAPTER 60

CAPITAL KEY

KWENN

No sooner had Yaddle stepped through the door into the broadcast offices than Morna guided her out. "Hurry!"

"What's wrong, dear?"

"I wouldn't let Reezingrom know you're here." The Woostroid woman peeked back into the office. "They'll try to book you tonight and every night for the next twenty years."

"I take it they have opinions on what transpired during the celebration."

"And how. But it's too big. They're still sorting out who's going to approve of what and who's going to disapprove."

"I am certain it would make for excellent viewing." Yaddle remembered how the two-headed hosts had treated their producer. "You're not still afraid of Reez and Grom, are you?"

Morna laughed. "Oh, no. I wasn't ever really afraid, I don't think. I just have to not let them trample all over me."

"But you just rushed us outside."

"That was for your sake. Master. You haven't built up an immunity."

Yaddle looked up at the young woman. Morna had been through a lot, but she stood straighter, her eyes off the floor. "We can't thank you enough for your help. Both with the production, and in speaking to those who were there. Are you feeling any differently, dear?"

"You mean *better*?"

"I said what I meant."

Morna thought about it. "I appreciate what the Council did—and I know how much you risked for all of us. But you're going to leave, and Reez and Grom are going to continue bickering, and the Hutts will still be out there. And maybe things we don't even know about."

Yaddle nodded. "That is the way with life, Morna. I see glimpses of the future sometimes, and when that happens it can make me lose heart. My colleagues and I worry that we are not doing enough to make the future more secure. But I think the first step in all of that has to be making the *present* more secure. Tomorrow's suffering—it doesn't exist, not yet. Today's suffering does."

Morna looked up. "I just know this: What I did this week mattered. I need to make sure I feel that way about next week, too. Every week."

"That is the challenge we all face, my child." Yaddle smiled. "I know you will succeed." She looked up. "And what is next for you?"

"Oh, I wanted to tell you that. I'm so happy Master Yoda introduced me to Lyal Lunn—and that you told me where to find Erwen Lunn's collection of holos. His family has imagery of Kwenn's history that *no one* has—not even the planetary archives!" She gushed. "What an amazing person Erwen must have been—and what a story their family has."

"It is Kwenn's story. And the people of this world should see it."

"They will. Lyal has agreed to help me go through them all while he's recuperating. I'm going to produce my own show. To help people like Lyal's father—and those amazing kids Master Piell worked with, and so many others—tell their stories."

"I understand even Lyal is a story. Once he's healed, the authorities plan to let him work with the medical droid to help people like his father—those needing care but unable to receive it."

"What a great idea!" Morna excitedly made a note on a datapad. "Was that your idea—or Master Yoda's?"

"It was Lyal's idea, and a very good one. Make sure you let people know. The Jedi receive too much credit as it is."

Morna nodded. "So many stories to be shared. I'm going to have a lot to do."

Yaddle smiled. "All these stories, of all these people of Kwenn. Will you be asking the questions—before the holocams?"

Morna nodded. "I'm not afraid. I won't be alone—I'll be with them."

KI-ADI-MUNDI WAS MEDITATING when Yarael found him.

It was considered bad form in the Jedi Temple to interrupt anyone who was meditating, particularly a member of the Jedi Council. As far as Yarael knew, it might have been rude, too, for a civilian to interrupt another meditating civilian. He didn't know any to ask. But he couldn't imagine the sanction applied to people who were trying to meditate while sitting on the ground in the middle of a festival on gorgeous Langdam Key.

"Get up, Master!"

Ki-Adi-Mundi did not open his eyes. "Is there a need for me?"

"You're in the way," Yarael said.

The Cerean opened one eye. "It is a street festival. I am on the street."

"Get up, already. All the restaurants have reopened," Yarael said. "It's a jubilee—everyone eats."

Ki-Adi-Mundi reluctantly rose. "I am not hungry."

"How is that possible? All our food blew up. What little Piell didn't give away, that is."

"I do not want for anything. I have the Force."

"I don't shine rocks for a living," Yarael retorted. "I have the Force, too. But I also eat."

Ki-Adi-Mundi pointed off to the right. "I had an ice mound several days ago, not a hundred meters from here."

"An ice mound."

"Correct."

"That must have been some ice mound." Yarael put his hand over his face. "That's it, then. You took one walk in a harbor town and decided you were done having fun." He looked around at the hubbub. "We only have a few hours. Why did you even want to come back over here?"

"Because where others are happy, I can be at peace. But then I can be at peace anywhere. And now I am finished." Ki-Adi-Mundi started walking. "It will be good to get back to the Jedi Temple—and our duties."

"Our duties?"

"Yes."

Yarael hurried to catch up with him. "I fear you missed the lesson of this journey," he said. "We've spent too much time focusing on big things—and not enough on the small ones. Your interaction with Aptorr and his wife led to their generosity—and their product helped protect thousands of people."

"I fear *you* missed the lesson of this journey," Ki-Adi-Mundi responded. "If we had been more cognizant of the Ootmian route, we might well have predicted the pirate uprising. We could have taken steps before it happened."

Yarael stopped him. "What is 'being cognizant' besides getting out and talking with people?"

"There are other ways to learn. The data analytics that the chancellor's team uses. The feedback from the Republic and its institutions. Kwenn's senator. And, yes, firsthand interaction—"

"See?"

"—but as performed by Jedi Masters, Knights, and Padawans in the field." Ki-Adi-Mundi touched his tall forehead. "Our position, our abilities place us beyond that level. We see much—and look into the future, and see more."

Yarael chuckled. "I can guarantee you even Sifo-Dyas wouldn't have seen a grandmother whose fondness for unauthorized surgeries led her to join the Vile—and then join a revolution."

"You might be surprised. Much of this matter remains troubling to me—and has inspired further concern. I was meditating on it just now."

"Just now. In the street." Yarael groaned. "You just won't take a happy ending."

"Is it, though?" Ki-Adi-Mundi looked at him. "Think about the cases. The Regal Voyager cases that caused such destruction."

"What of them?"

"They looked innocent—yet behind a cloak that nothing could penetrate, they held something terrible. What if there was another threat like that, but one that put the whole galaxy at risk? Something we Jedi saw as routine. That we looked past, every day?"

"It would take an awful lot of luggage to collapse the Republic."

Ki-Adi-Mundi stared at him—and brightened. "You are right, of course. The systems and safeguards we have in place are the product of centuries of experience. I, of all people, should know better than to surrender to alarmism."

"I've told you never to meditate on an empty stomach." Yarael guided him toward a food vendor. "These days if I try to sleep more than four hours, my mind gets to imagining all sorts of nonsense. Just part of getting older."

"You should ask Master Yoda for advice."

"Oh, no." Yarael waved him off. "Never again. He asked me to stop telling him my dreams a hundred years ago." He shrugged. "To be honest, I had gotten annoying."

Ki-Adi-Mundi smiled. "That, my friend, I could never envision."

THE FLORIST SHOP was one of several on Langdam Key, and to Seneschal Voh's knowledge, it was no better or worse than any of the others. What made it worth the trip—and had made it worth all his other visits—was the room behind the sliding door in the gift annex.

He stepped into the darkened room. After he closed the door behind him, he heard the voice. "Welcome, Seneschal."

"Senator Palpatine," Voh said, looking into the light of the hologram. "I hadn't even pressed the control to message you."

"I had a feeling you would come. Please make yourself comfortable."

Voh pulled up his usual chair. It was not appropriate for the Jedi's retainers to have contact with senators; it was barely acceptable for individual Jedi Knights to. But he and Palpatine had met years ago on the latter's senatorial tour of Kwenn, and Voh had enjoyed their talks. It was Palpatine who'd suggested they continue them privately.

"Senator, I've been honored by your willingness to speak to me over the years. I am of little importance—"

"Nonsense. You have experience from many years in a vital role."

"That's kind of you to say. I consider you a friend."

"*But?*"

"But I feel . . . betrayed."

"Betrayed. Tell me more."

"You promised the Senate would always be committed to the Oot-mian route, so the Jedi would never have a reason to close the outpost. That was our deal. I bring records and material from the collection here, and your agent comes to the florist shop later to select what you want."

"That was our deal. But I note that you have strayed from it."

"What?" Voh nearly bolted out of his chair. "No! How do you mean?"

"Our arrangement was that you give my assistant whatever materials I choose from the batches you bring here—and that you destroy the ones that I don't want."

"So?"

"So you have not been destroying them. The leftovers wound up in a store. You sold them."

Caught, Voh clasped his hands together. "I couldn't bring myself to destroy them. They're historical documents, after all—from Sanctuary Mount. You wouldn't let me reshelve them—"

"Because it would have exposed that only the most important texts, with the most forbidden ideas, were the ones missing. And that is not something the Jedi could have ascribed to the incompetence of an old caretaker—or random thievery." Palpatine's demeanor changed, and his voice grew sharper. "They would have seen another hand at work. Mine."

"You're worried about nothing. So Master Koth found some of the chaff at the Lamplighter. There wasn't enough for him to assume the rest went to one person. This way, the works still exist—and nobody knows what you did."

The seneschal didn't know whether that had cut any ice with Palpatine. The senator was mercurial; his interests, peculiar. But he thought those could still be appealed to.

"It's all neither here nor there," Voh said. "The outpost is gone. But Master Rancisis feels guilty. I think I can parlay that into a new position at another Jedi outpost." He smiled. "With another library, of course."

"Hmm." The holographic senator leaned back. "I think not."

"What?"

"You are old. Too old, to be of much further service to the Jedi—or me. And besides, my interests have changed."

"What do you mean?"

"The pieces are almost in place for the grand game. The Republic, the Trade Federation, the rest—all are poised to play their roles. It serves me to have the Jedi Order constantly moving around, following the whims of commerce and the Senate. Shuffling forces and dividing their attention. The outpost closures along the Ootmian route are a part of that."

"And the unhappiness that causes on planets like Kwenn?"

"Is its own reward." Palpatine kept talking, ignoring him. "I admire the ruthlessness with which Zilastra carried out her scheme, but I doubted she would succeed. It is just as well."

"What are you talking about?"

"She is of interest, of course. Anyone who so despises Jedi is. I will keep her in mind."

Voh thought he was hearing nonsense from the senator. Delusions. But he couldn't help but respond. He shifted about nervously. "Why . . . are you telling me this?"

"I was not telling you. I was telling *him*."

Voh turned around, expecting to see the owner of the building. Instead, his body lifted off the chair, propelled by an unseen force into midair. His body spun around, revealing the red tattooed Zabrak behind him.

The seneschal had never seen him before, but he was pretty sure it was not the florist.

EPILOGUE

ABOARD *ASSURANCE*

ORBITING KWENN

"N o, no, no!" Captain Baylo growled. "Get back to the signals desk, before you wrap us around the space station!"

Back aboard *Assurance*, Mace watched as the young cadet slunk back to his usual console. "Another training day?"

"They're all training days," the captain said. "But the helm's not for everyone." He glanced back at the kid. "I shouldn't expect someone named Veers to fly straight!"

Mace shot the young man a look of understanding. *Everyone starts somewhere.*

It was right for the Jedi Master to stop in orbit to meet with Baylo; he'd never seen the captain on the ground and could only imagine how out of place he might look there. Space was his natural habitat.

Assurance had, in all respects, succeeded in its assignment, far beyond the imaginings of those who'd suggested the mission. What had begun as a chance for politicians to give lip service to the idea that they were fighting piracy had resulted, against all odds, in the complete collapse of every major criminal organization in this section of the Slice. It was past anyone's expectations, especially the captain's.

And the Republic had noticed.

"Chokoll Indemnity and the Hydian Way will have to wait," Baylo said as they walked the bridge. "It's hard to believe, but our contract with the Judicial Forces has been reupped."

"Was that unexpected?"

"It's damn near unprecedented. It means someone who hired us actually gave us credit for making an impact." He eyed Mace. "I suspect you had something to do with that."

Mace put up his hands. "I reported to the Republic, just as you did. No pressure was applied."

That wasn't entirely true, Mace knew, but he also knew Baylo didn't like being in debt to anyone, least of all a Jedi.

He was glad to see that he and Baylo had come to an equilibrium of sorts. Mace sat at the pinnacle of an organization of immense power; Baylo was a leader in a field where power had never been allowed to consolidate. Their temperaments were similar in some ways, different in others. Yet they both had the same sense of responsibility to their jobs, and were both consummate professionals with long records.

Baylo shrugged. "It's not me you should be doing something for, anyway. It's the crew." He gestured to the bridge. "And not just my crew. Every crew that's out here, poking the nests, seeing if anything crawls out. They deserve better than to lose their jobs because the old man didn't get a letter of marque. They need something permanent—and so do I."

Mace heard something in that—and had a thought. "I may have something permanent for you."

"I'm not sure what. Without a worthy adversary, the powers that be are always going to consider a navy a needless luxury."

"And I still do not support the idea of a military force for the Republic, naval or otherwise," Mace said. "But there may be a way to create something else. The various pirate interdiction outfits we now have would benefit from an educational component, correct?"

Baylo stopped walking. He stared. "Are you talking about a *service academy*?"

"Or a training vessel." Mace looked on the bridge approvingly. "With a permanent commissioning from the Republic, you could start one here, teaching others to do the sort of work you've been doing for years."

Baylo looked at him, speechless for a change.

"I think you could find sponsorship for such a program. What would you say to that?"

The captain looked around—and snorted with disdain. "I say no cadet should ever have to serve aboard a ship named to please an insurance corporation."

"Call it whatever you want. You're in charge—*Commandant.*"

Baylo straightened. Then he cracked a wry smile. "You're all right, Windu. I mean, for a Jedi."

"AND WHAT'S THAT? And *that?*"

Depa struggled to answer each one of Kylah's questions before another one hit her. From the *Assurance*'s bridge to its landing bays to its arsenal, Kylah had used her tour of the corvette to make a complete inventory, saying what was the same as on the *Randomizer* and what was different. It was easy to remember the girl had spent most of her life crawling in and around starships.

The most important discovery, however, awaited around the corner.

"Crew at attention! Jedi in the quarters!"

The teenager who'd called out stood beside the doorway. Her uniform was just like the other cadets' aboard *Assurance*—and the same went for those worn by the other occupants in the barracks behind her. They all stood at attention beside their berths: people of many different species, some Kylah's age, some older.

"At ease!" The order came not from Depa, but from Baylo, who approached from behind. He stopped and looked at Depa. "Is this the one?"

"Kylah Lohmata," Depa said. "Several years' service on—well, more ships than I can remember her telling me about."

Kylah stared up at the captain, spellbound. Depa and the girl had both seen Baylo when they came aboard with Mace, but the captain, as was his way, had completely ignored her. Not now.

Baylo looked Kylah up and down. "Service with whom? Spit it out!"

"Riftwalkers, sir. The *Randomizer*—and other ships."

"Riftwalkers." His jaw clenched. "They gave us quite a run. You ready to join a real outfit?"

Kylah's eyes goggled. She looked at Depa.

"We hadn't gotten to discussing it," Depa said.

"Well, read her in or kick her off. I don't want pirates scaring the cadets." Baylo tromped off down the corridor.

Depa and Kylah watched him go—then looked in the crew quarters, where the whole shift was looking at Kylah in wonderment. Baylo had spoken in front of them on purpose, Depa realized.

Kylah pulled Depa back out into the corridor. "Is this the idea you were telling me about?" the girl whispered.

Depa nodded. "I don't want you in an orphanage—and such as they were, the Riftwalkers were your family." She gestured to the barracks doorway. "I've lived on this ship for a time. These are good people, Kylah. Many your age. The postings on a ship like this are hard to get—expensive. And not only did Baylo offer you one—he just made your reputation with everyone here."

Kylah looked at the door just as the shift departed for the mess hall. Every cadet that filtered past the girl gave her a sideways, curious glance.

When they had departed, she looked urgently to Depa. "I want it. But I don't want to leave you."

"I have my role. You know that. And I can only take trained Jedi as students."

"That's not fair."

Zilastra certainly thought so, Depa thought. "The Jedi and ships like this work together all the time. There's a chance we'll see each other. I have many friends outside the Order. If things don't work out, Baylo will bring you back to Coruscant and we'll find something else."

"And if they do work out?"

"The sky's the limit—*Cadet Lohmata.*"

Kylah stared up at her in amazement—and then the tears started. The two embraced.

Then the girl wiped the tears from her eyes. "I'm going to check out the food," she said. "Can't have them see me crying!"

Depa dried her own eyes as Kylah dashed up the corridor to her new world.

The Jedi wasn't surprised to realize she was being watched. "You saw?"

"Our shuttle has arrived." Mace stepped forward. "I didn't want to intrude."

"You didn't. Thank you for helping to set this up."

"Baylo listened to us both." He looked down the corridor. "I think you helped your one person."

"I hope we helped more than that." Depa straightened—and let out a deep breath. "You know, I've been thinking about taking a Padawan learner again."

"While on the Council?" Mace appeared to give it some thought. "It's uncommon, for certain. There's seldom time."

"And we're seldom active enough to teach them much," Depa said. "But it might finally be time. Maybe not this year—but soon."

"Then it will happen." Mace nodded. "The Force will look kindly on whomever you choose."

QUI-GON DID NOT intend to be in the last Jedi party to leave Kwenn, but that was how it had worked out. With no outpost to do closure detail on, Master Koth had instead instructed him and Obi-Wan to get the *Randomizer* shipshape to head for Coruscant, where it turned out its true owners were located. Qui-Gon awaited only Master Yoda— who had gone to say goodbye to the seneschal—and the completion of his review of the ship.

"It looks good," Qui-Gon said to Lobber. "Not a single thermal detonator lying around."

"The big problem was fixing all the doors you guys fused shut," Lobber replied. He reached for the lightsaber on Qui-Gon's belt. "Can I have one of those?"

Qui-Gon swiveled away quickly. "Absolutely not." He looked down a side corridor. "Ah, Obi-Wan. How did it go?"

"Astonishingly, very well." Obi-Wan led Ghor and Wungo out of the maintenance hold. "The time they spent aboard this ship seems to have paid off. Things appear to be functioning—and the conduits are remarkably clean and scrubbed."

"That was a Zilastra thing," Ghor said.

Wungo wiped the sweat from his brow. "Don't remind me."

Lobber faced Qui-Gon. "That's it, Jedi Man. We got your ship for you—and even cleaned it up. What'll you give us for it?"

"That's what I wanted to discuss. Come along."

He and Obi-Wan led them down the ramp to the spaceport landing pad. There he faced the three.

"I made an error when we met," he said. "My student and I were concerned with the passengers you threatened, and we make no apologies for protecting them. But there were so many of them, we did not take sufficient time to look into *your* situations—what drove you to hijack the ship."

Obi-Wan took it from there. "Of course, it's possible you are committed to this career—irredeemably corrupt—in which case sooner or later, we'll come up against one another. If that's something you're looking forward to, we'll see you then."

"But it doesn't have to be that way." Qui-Gon gestured up to the ship. "You can do what you know, starting right here and now."

Lobber looked confused. "What, steal it again?"

"A contract has been offered by Galactic City Recovery on Coruscant. They do repossessions of starships—and return stolen vessels to their proper owners, for a fee. This ship, it turns out, was once the *Resilient*."

Obi-Wan grinned. "Of all things, a pirate chaser."

"They're willing to cut you in—and provide further work—if you return this ship to Coruscant now."

Ghor's eyes widened. "You're giving us a job!"

"Not I. But we can make it happen."

"Let's go!" Wungo said. His companions followed him up the ramp, nearly bowling Obi-Wan over.

Obi-Wan cupped his hands together and yelled up to the ship. "Don't leave without us!"

"Shh." Qui-Gon spoke confidentially. "I have the starter codes."

"That's a relief."

From across the landing pad, they saw Yoda approaching. Confident the frigate wouldn't be going anywhere, they met him halfway. Yoda didn't look all too happy.

"Left already, the seneschal has. In his name, a ticket to Corellia was bought."

"I suppose he's taking his retirement elsewhere." Qui-Gon looked around at the wide sweep of the world visible from the terrace the landing pad was on. "A shame he left. Kwenn is a pleasant place."

"I only wish we had gotten to see it," Obi-Wan joked.

Yoda joined them in looking out at Kwenn. "Glad I am that you came to me on Coruscant, Master Qui-Gon."

Qui-Gon nodded. "I would not have pressured the Council as hard as I did had I not thought you would be receptive."

Obi-Wan looked at them in surprise. "Wait. You two spoke of this before?"

"Over the years, on several occasions," Qui-Gon said. "But yes, before I met with Master Windu in the Jedi Temple, I finally encountered Master Yoda. We agreed that some form of retreat was necessary. Kwenn came up as a choice only after I left—but it was an appropriate one."

Obi-Wan looked stunned. "The way people around the Temple were talking, you issued a defiant challenge."

"I've told you about that building and gossip," Qui-Gon said. "I'm not insubordinate. I'm unorthodox. The insubordinate are ignored. The unorthodox are heard—grudgingly."

He faced Yoda. "So the retreat. It worked?"

"A lightness has returned," Yoda said. "The first smiles in decades, for some."

Qui-Gon looked keenly at him. "They are joyful. But are they *mindful*?"

"Flowed through us, the living Force did. Not days only for ourselves, were these. For others, they were."

"And so the days became yours as well," Obi-Wan said.

"You're getting it." Qui-Gon smiled.

They turned away from the view. After a few moments, Obi-Wan broke the silence. "Masters, there's just—"

He didn't finish the sentence. Qui-Gon and Yoda looked at him, and then each other. Yoda remarked on it first. "Confused, your student is."

"I'm afraid it's a perpetual condition," Obi-Wan said.

Qui-Gon opened his palms. "Speak."

Obi-Wan forged ahead. "Did Master Billaba act correctly in repeatedly choosing the girl over defeating Zilastra? I mean, it worked out all right. But it seems to go against what I've been taught."

"A difficult question," Yoda said. "One stage of many, life is. Cling to it, we must not."

"Our own lives—or those of others," Obi-Wan added. "No attachments—that's the first thing we learn!"

"Of course," Qui-Gon said. "Those are the Jedi rules and the Council rules. But I allow that the Force may have a more nuanced opinion."

Obi-Wan snickered. "The Force sounds like a certain master of my acquaintance."

"Laugh if you want, but the ways of the living Force are mysterious. When you help one person now, you create the potential for them to do many good works in the future."

"But—"

Qui-Gon put his hand on his Padawan's wrist. "Attachments are not the problem. *Indifference is.*" He turned and called out as he walked toward the ship. "Save a friend, Obi-Wan, and the friend may save you."

ACKNOWLEDGMENTS

Exactly ten years elapsed between the writing of my previous full-length *Star Wars* novel, *A New Dawn,* and *The Living Force*—but I could not have written this book ten years ago.

It was during the intervening decade that I recognized the connecting thread between my previous *Star Wars* works—the *Knights of the Old Republic* comics, as well as the Random House novels *Kenobi, Knight Errant, A New Dawn,* and even *Lost Tribe of the Sith*—was that they all depicted Jedi Knights who were cut off and on their own, much like the prototypical loner, Luke Skywalker. Along the way, the Jedi Order itself came in for a lot of scrutiny in those works—and not a little criticism.

But clearly there was a diversity of thought within the Order, and Qui-Gon Jinn was the greatest symbol of it. So when my editor Tom Hoeler—who had helped me keep my passport to the Galaxy Far, Far Away current with shorter works while I explored another universe's frontiers—asked me to consider a novel depicting the Jedi Council before *The Phantom Menace,* I knew what story I had to tell. Qui-Gon's challenge gave me the chance to give voice to a lot of characters, some of whom hadn't spoken much before, about what being a Jedi meant not just to them—but to everyone they served.

My thanks go to Tom for helping me wrangle the colossal cast, and also to the Random House Worlds team including Elizabeth Schaefer, Keith Clayton, and everyone else behind the scenes. Appreciation as always goes to the staff at Lucasfilm, including Jennifer Heddle, Creative Director Michael Siglain, and the whole Lucasfilm Story Group.

Thanks as ever go to my proofreaders Meredith Miller and Brent Frankenhoff, and also to my support team members Katie Dunn, James Mishler, and Ann Rosenstein, who helped me balance writing with a busy event schedule.

And my thanks to you, dear readers, for your support—and patience—over all these years. May the Force be with you!

ABOUT THE AUTHOR

JOHN JACKSON MILLER is the *New York Times* bestselling author of the Scribe Award–winning *Star Wars: Kenobi*, as well as *Star Wars: A New Dawn, Star Wars: Lost Tribe of the Sith, Star Wars: Knight Errant,* and the *Star Wars Legends: The Old Republic* graphic novel collections from Marvel. He has written novels and comics for other franchises including *Star Trek, Battlestar Galactica,* Halo, *Iron Man,* Mass Effect, *Planet of the Apes,* and *The Simpsons.* A comics-industry historian, he lives in Wisconsin with his family, assorted wildlife, and far too many comic books.

ABOUT THE TYPE

This book was set in Minion, a 1990 Adobe Originals typeface by Robert Slimbach (b. 1956). Minion is inspired by classical, old-style typefaces of the late Renaissance, a period of elegant, beautiful, and highly readable type designs. Created primarily for text setting, Minion combines the aesthetic and functional qualities that make text type highly readable with the versatility of digital technology.